I0654155

A Bad Crossing

The Autobiography of Calista Antoine

Book Two

Mark Bondurant

This is a work of fiction. Names, characters, places, and incidents either are the product of the author's imagination or are used fictitiously. To be frank, they`re part of a different universe. Any resemblance to actual persons, living or dead, business establishments, events, or locales is entirely coincidental.

A Bad Crossing
The Autobiography of Calista Antoine

Copyright © 2016, 2018 Mark Bondurant, All Rights Reserved
http://www.markbondurant.com
Edited by Sara George
Cover and Illustrations by Mark Bondurant

Published by Bongo Books
http://www.bongo.net
Publisher`s Cataloging-in-Publication (Provided by Bongo Books)
Bondurant, Mark.
A Bad Crossing / by Mark Bondurant. –
2nd ed. p. ; 16x23cm.

ISBN: 1-940995-07-8
ISBN-13: 978-1-940995-07-6

1. Teenage girls. 2. France. 3. Merchant ships. 4. Zeppelins. 5. Steampunk fiction. 6. Science Fiction. 7. Alternative histories (Fiction), American. I. Title.

No part of this book may be reproduced, scanned, or distributed in any printed or electronic form without permission. Please do not participate in or encourage piracy of copyrighted materials in violation of the author's rights. Purchase only authorized editions.

If you purchased this book without a cover, you should be aware that this book is stolen property. It was reported as "unsold and destroyed" to the publisher, and neither the author nor the publisher has received any payment for this "stripped book."

DEDICATION

I dedicate this book, my fourth, to my writers group, good people too numerous to list, who have put up with years of listening to Calista

CONTENTS

Author's Foreword

I have been blessed again to continue the work of chronicling the life of Duchess Calista Maera Antoine of Tervuren in this second volume, *A Bad Crossing*. We are here, both you and I, to witness its culmination. The first book, *Red Jacket*, covered the British takeover of Portugal's African colonies and the British failure in the Congo. In this volume, *A Bad Crossing*, we see her emerge on the world stage. It primarily covers the Dewar affair, the British efforts to obtain both the patents and process for the creation of the explosive cordite, a revolutionary propellant for artillery – her first moment in the spotlight.

From the painful process of Red Jacket's creation to the acrimony of its publication, there have been both public and private doubts as to whether there would ever be a second book. Considering the forces arrayed against us, those doubts might have been justified. But outside influence aside, perhaps the greatest obstacle to its publication was the Duchess herself. Her recounting of the events of the first book covering her arrival and the incidents in and around the Congo were very difficult for her and, to be frank, I began to doubt that we would continue once the book was finished. We started in joy, but in working through her memories of those times we brought back her nightmares and dark depressions. It was only her love for the Duke and her son that kept her there, working through the endless rewrites. The prospect of starting again, especially through another dark passage in her life; a time when everything she knew and loved hung in jeopardy, was daunting and her reluctance to relive it understandable.

We had to consider the difficulties we encountered in the publication of the first book as well. Once it was written, thanks to pressure from the monarchy, both Belgian and British, we had to fight to get it published. My publisher, De Boeck, was bought and I was banned by every publisher in Belgium and England. My agent abandoned me for fear of his career.

For myself, my house was broken into and ransacked. It was mere luck that kept them from stealing anything but older versions of the manuscript, my having taken the latest with me to work on at the club. One can write about a house being ransacked. It can even seem romantic or adventurous, but it is entirely a different thing to experience it. I suppose I should be grateful that they didn't set it all alight to destroy and evidence. A small mercy.

Finding an outside publisher for the first book was a very tedious and disappointing business. There were many who would not touch it, despite my reputation, for fear alienating the monarchy and the attending loss of future business. We had to settle on L. *Hachette et Compagnie* in Paris, a producer of dictionaries! I do not mean to deride them. We have been, and will ever be, nothing less than deeply grateful for their support. It was the nature of their bread and butter product that left them outside the normal flow of the publishing business. I remember their board as they reviewed the manuscript thinking the whole thing funny and a chance to put a finger in the eye of the English. I suppose our enemies had overlooked them in their efforts to block us. Little did Hachette understand the weight of the responsibility that they had shouldered, nor could they have anticipated the book's success. The profits thankfully more than offset the subsequent petty damages and indignities inflicted on their business by the monarchy throughout our work on the second book. Their stubborn, brave perseverance in standing by it, then agreeing to print the second volume has been nothing less than Promethean! Only the French and their lack of fear of authority could have accomplished this. *Vive le France.*

Nor has my career suffered from being banned. I have become a star in working class reading rooms all over Europe. My articles are in great demand in unstamped publications such as *Sozialdemokrat*, *Iskra*, and *Liberty*. For a rather mild mannered man who merely wishes to be clear about the truth, the role of radical is strange, but there is so much in the world that demands clarity and so many that wish to deny it.

However, we must be clear that outside demands and new fame have not swayed me from my goal. Even while the future of this book was in doubt, my research did not cease. In the time since Red Jacket's publication, I have been able to travel to some of the places she described to see them for myself. I found the dock in Portugal. The bullet holes in wood and wall are there, the memories of witnesses still fresh despite government insistence that the event was pure fiction. I travelled to Cadiz in Spain and found the tree in the Plaza de Candelaria and memories of Cuerdas, though no sign of Robert Heath himself. Let me assure you, Marita's is still there as is Zackery Kastner; still selling instruments. He remembered the girl who cried clearly. I travelled to Madrid in hopes of reviewing airship transit records, but these, I'm afraid, are closed to me. They need to be reviewed. I entreat those with access to release them for the sake of justice.

As I write this now in October 1905, we have the second volume moving to publication! I would like to thank our readers' patience. It has taken a two years to write this. As previously stated, this volume covers the Dewar Affair, an especially unpleasant event for all. Its importance in cementing British resolve against the Duchess cannot be overstated. Her reluctance to discuss it is entirely understandable. It took six months of coaxing to convince her to continue. The Baroness Valois, whom we met in the first book as Aleta, was of inestimable aid here in helping to put together the pieces. Her emotional support was vital, the Baroness herself having travelled to Tourven from Paris.

The emotional pain the Duchess suffered in recounting her time in the Congo, the rekindling of her nightmares loomed large. Even remembering Red Jacket herself, her family's ship, which she finally reclaimed, brought pain. The times of it as a family home were forever out of reach in the past. It seemed to paint her life with melancholy. But our work's purpose was achieved. Her cause has gained support in England. There are many who question the Foreign Office's accounting of the events and their efforts since. History is on our side. But her reluctance in the beginning to continue with the second volume cannot again be overstated. It finally took a trick on the part of the Duke to gain access. She turned down all attempts at appointments, even cancelling those made by her husband. She went so far as to turn me away at the door! My repeated journeys to their various estates became very taxing. I know nothing of their discussions of the subject in private, but the Duke's frustration and growing impatience were evident in our correspondence.

In the end, we ambushed her. I know no better word for it. Our first meeting, as I will recount shortly, was rude and abrupt. The Duke himself led me down dark-carpeted halls to their library, angrily silencing the servants, forbidding any effort at warning her.

As we approached, I could hear her playing her violin.

We stopped in the corridor. I didn't know why. The door was in front of us. In the dim glow of the electric lights I could see him grimace.

"This isn't good."

"What is it?" I asked. And then I listened.

It took a moment to sort out what I was hearing, the polyphonics, two, three notes at a time. Sometimes more. The frantic mad swirling and dashing against the strings. It was familiar. The first time I had actually heard her play. She is very private. The epithet, "The Recluse Duchess" is not without warrant. As I listened I remembered hearing a similar work performed in Berlin. And then recognition. She was attempting a Paganini Caprice! I'm told they have been known to drive musicians to suicide. I can count on my fingers the masters who have successfully conquered them. And yet here she was, sliding dangerously close to heaven.

The Duke shook his head.

"She's in a bad mood."

I looked at him in disbelief.

She stopped, apparently dissatisfied, and then picked it up again. We stood there for a moment, entranced. Then the Duke shook himself.

"Come. It's now or never." He opened the door quietly and entered.

She had lower her violin by the time I followed, but I was there in time to see her smile for the Duke melt. She took a step back, her violin, Francesca, loose in her hand. I could see their second child large in the womb, her dark copper locks spilling loose down her back.

She said "No," barely audible, and then again more clearly.

"No!"

"We must," he said.

"Let it die." Anger, her green eyes lit.

"We must finish it."

"They won't listen."

"Then the truth for its own sake."

"Lucien, we've had this argument so many times. I'm so tired." It came out a cry. I was embarrassed to be the cause of this, to hurt her.

"Talk to him. For our children's sake." And then he hissed, "They must let go of us!"

She had been edging back, I think toward the garden doors, but instead fell back into a chair, its wings hiding her in shadow. She seemed to sink into herself, turning pale, thin, and invisible. Almost a ghost.

"I saw things."

"I know."

"I'll never sleep again." A tear drifted down her cheek.

"I know."

"I can't."

"We must."

Then the Duke and I stood and waited while she began to cry, sobbing from the dark depths of the chair.

A Bad Crossing

The Autobiography
Of Calista Antoine

As told to the Mark Bondurant during
the summer of 1904

Chapter 1 – Bad Memories

The wave rose from the starboard dense and gray, thick with debris, filled with black stick figures. It passed over us, a wall of water. With all our sheets out we had no time to come about and over we went, the deck listing, then tipping, everything falling. I'm dragged under the dark gray water, screaming. The water itself screamed with me, like rusted metal, filling with long white teeth, and then. And then they were on me. The stick figures. Black faces and hands pulling at me, and pulling, until I drew my pistol and fired, their heads exploding one by one. The blood and fire, everywhere. Wagons turned over, buring, the dead and dying littering the ground. I can't breathe, and there's a great pounding, and hands grabbing me.

"Cali!"

I'm kicking and fighting, my pistol melting in my hand as I try to grip it.

"Cali, wake up damn it!"

I think they were trying to shake me without getting kicked. Then I realized where I was, in my cabin. It was dark except for the dim rectangle of my cabin door and the lamp light from the stair. I could see Pa and Ma. They were standing in my door, trying to hold my legs. I was lying on my back sobbing, tangled in my covers. That was my first bad dream.

"Cali, are you awake now?" Pa asked. But I couldn't answer. Not yet. Just great heaving sobs.

"Cali, please answer," said Ma.

"It's the night terrors," said Willie. I couldn't see him, he was behind Ma and Pa. I must have woken the whole ship. He slept in the bow. Willie lost his wife and kids in a flood. He had to know.

"I'm awake," I croaked. How long had I been crying? "Oh Ma," I said. "Pa." I twisted about to the bottom of my bed so they could reach me, their arms warm and sweet.

It was the fall of 1892 and we were two days out of Las Palmas in the Canaries. All the passengers we ferried out of the Congo were gone, off to the aerodrome or looking for other passage to Europe, and we were just Red again, and there was no reason I should have felt that way. We escaped from the Congo, we got away. Better than got away. We had our cargo and money. We won, even though they lost. They all lost everything, even their lives. The Belgians, the British, and even the Congolese. What would they call it now, the German Congo?

I could feel the water moving past the hull, the surge of the waves, and the blessed creaking of the mast in her step, and I knew that I was home, and my Ma and Pa were there. And Knockers. She's meowed below my door. I could see the whole crew and even Mme. Verbeeck's ghost standing on the ladder. She looked worried. How loud was I?

"Pass her up," I said, hanging out the door, reaching down toward Knockers. Crow picked her up carefully and put her down on my mattress. "Oh Knockers," I said, turning to hold her close. She purred. "I'm okay. Everyone, please go to bed." Sleep is precious on a ship.

And then I realized something. "Who's on watch?" It starts as a whisper and ends in a growl. Nobody was on deck! Léon, he was new crew, let's out a cough and turns and runs. Tristan and Léon stayed on after Las Palmas in the Canaries. They had no money and nowhere to go, and we needed the hands.

"Sorry Cali," said Tinker, and he turned and headed for the wheel too, which got a general chuckle from the rest. I love Tinker, but the watch is more important than me. If something happened to the ship, we'd all be dead. Ma and Pa gave me a last hug and went to their cabin. They all left, saying goodnight, until there was just Knockers and me. She seemed to want to curl up at my feet, which was just damn brave of her. The lamp light shining in from my cabin door was comforting. I left it open. It helped.

My watch came up at 6:00 AM, which as a certified third mate is my right. I was out of bed at 5:45. We had gray skies that promised rain, the air was warm and wet, storm for sure, way late in the season. So I dragged my wet weather gear with me up on deck, all of it thick stiff dark green waxed japura cotton. Tinker was at the wheel. I passed Léon and didn't recognize him. The new faces were confusing and I found that, for a moment, I was shaking. I had to stop to breathe. But it passed, and I told him to get Tristan out of his hammock. I saw Tinker give me a worried glance as I took the wheel.

The deck was surging under me and the wind was at my back. I stood in the worn spots, staring forward at the binnacle, checking her heading. She tossed, stretched out before me. 154 feet, riding low, the rising sea breaking over her bow, all blue in the morning light. I could feel the pull of the wind whistling in her rigging, her sails taut. I inspected them with a critical eye. We'd have to pull in the gaffs before she hits, I thought, but it could wait for breakfast. I loved that wet cold wind, washing away the world. Mme. Verbeeck was standing watch with me, the deckhouse visible through her gray form. She stood in the blue light in the ball gown she never got to wear, staring into the waves. I knew she was there to watch over me.

And there, coming up the companion way, was Ma. She brought coffee! "Thanks Ma," I said, as I carefully took the hot mug, the wind making little wavelets in its top. Heaven. Tristan was late on deck, but I would leave that to Pa.

We were heading straight toward Florida, and the Confederate States of America. We really had no choice. It's the way the wind and currents flow. We were aiming to do what we always do, run past as fast as we could and hope they didn't notice, which made the coming storm a boon. We'd ride it all the way north hidden from their navy in its wind and waves.

It was the fall of 1892, the fourth and nastiest year so far in the war between the north and south. We in the north, and I expect the south as well, had been bled white by the carnage. The land and sea crawled with great machines that reaped lives like crops, blighting everything around them. This stupid, and I mean that in the most literal sense, war was looking to be the death of everyone. It had certainly tried time and again to kill us. So far we were still here sailing the sea, but so many of our fellows had sunk into the depths, the bottom of the Atlantic was a garden of ships and bodies of seamen and their families.

A rogue gust blew my hair in my eyes. It's coming soon, I thought. I didn't think Tristan had ever seen a storm, at least a real one. I yelled to him.

"Tristan!"

He'd been on the bow. He knew he was late. He had to make his way back.

"Get your wet weather gear," I yelled over the wind and surf. "Then stay close."

"Aye Cali," he yelled back. He could feel it too, though he didn't know it. It's a nervous thing.

"Oh, and take this mug back to Ma."

Last spring Red took a shell passing Florida just like we were aiming to do now. We can all thank everything thankable, and I mean everything, that her hull was too soft to detonate it. But even dumb iron can take out a mast and go right through our decks and out the porthole in my cabin. And now, thanks to the nature of the trade winds we were heading back there again, past the Bahamas and then Florida, on our way north towards home, to Boston.

I figured we'd had to have been making a phenomenal 12, maybe 13 knots, running all out with the wind that blessed storm brought. Maybe, I thought, I'd ask Ian to toss out the chip to get a reading just to know.

The plan was to turn north before we made sight of the coast, even though the islands were all neutral, hoping not to be spotted and pursued. The storm would make that harder. It could blow us almost anywhere, even onto a shoreline. Without the sun or stars, we had no way of knowing where we were.

It'll be a shame when we take in the gaffs, I thought, wishing one of the regular crew had been on deck so I could ride the bow, but we were listing enough. The peaks were practically breaking over the port gunnels on main deck. I bet we had pumping to do. If not already, we'd certainly have it that night.

We were loaded with rubber, African hides, ivory, and sundries, all worth more than their weight in gold. The best cargo we'd ever brought home. What's more, our purses were full coming in. Considering what we'd been through, this was only fair. We were chained to the docks in Boma, Congo, for five weeks, living on weeds and bush meat while some Prince tried to use my family as blackmail to get under my skirts. Crazy, huh? I even had to play Bach as if I cared. And it all ended in a war. We had to fight our way through the streets.

Then there was the coup d'état in Portugal, and the riot in Le Harve. I was thinking then that I would be floored, absolutely floored if we lived through the war.

Ed came up to take the helm so I could get breakfast. The rain had started and I didn't have my rain gear on yet, me still in my sloppes, so I was a little wet. No reason to track water through the hold. I crossed the deck to the forward deckhouse. Down in the galley it was warm, like I'd forgotten what warm was. My fingers tingled.

Red's galley is beautiful. Ed had been carving the beams for years, seaweed, mermaids, whales, gradually covering everything. Ma plunked down a plate on the table in front of me and another mug of coffee. We had fresh bread, olive oil, eggs, and *romesco*, bought at my insistence after Aleta introduced it to me. I bought two big jars of it from a restaurant. There are good things in this world, and romesco is definitely one of them.

"Hello," Aleta said, literally climbing in through the hold. We had no walkways below decks this trip. We were loaded to the gunnels. The best kind of thing for a merchantman.

"Morning," I replied. "Storm coming. You feel up to it?"

5

"I should ask you," she said, trying to smile. "Are you okay."

I had to think about it. "No. I'm not."

"You sure made a ruckus last night."

"I guess I did," I replied quietly.

"Want to talk about it?"

"I don't know what good it would do. It was just things that happened being mean all over again." Then I looked at her, "Maybe you could tell them to stop."

"Stop," she said.

I laughed. "I don't think they'll listen to that."

"I don't know about that," Aleta said, smiling for real. "If they're listening, then they've got to be using your ears."

"That makes sense," I said. Then I laughed. "So leave me alone!" and Aleta laughed too.

I was trying to eat my breakfast fast, but still enjoy it. Oh, I do love romesco.

"We're going to need all awake soon to bring in the gaffs," I said. I was kind of trying to warn her to look for her weather gear.

"It's a storm isn't it," she said, looking grave.

"Don't worry, it's the best kind."

She frowned. "How long do you think it will last?"

"Days. A week?"

"That might be too long. I need your help."

"What?" I asked, a touch worried.

"I want to try on my dress."

That drew a big smile out of me.

They made ball dresses for us in Boma. I had to throw mine away. Really, it would have been ruined in the battle and would have made me a big target. But Aleta couldn't go to the ball because she was still recovering from dengue fever. She'd stuffed hers into her cabin unworn, which was too bad because they were something incredible. All I had left of mine were the silk gloves that went all the way up my arms past my elbows! And my pearls too, of course.

"That will be fun!" I said. "You can wear my pearls too."

"I don't think that would be a good idea," she replied. "I'd be worried they'd end up over the side."

"What good are they if they don't get worn?"

"True."

She didn't put up much resistance.

6

"I hope it's aiming to hit Florida," I said, referring to the storm.

"It would serve them right for shooting at us," Aleta said.

"Or maybe Carolina. Those banks don't get enough water."

So we were winching the gaffs down, thinking about the jibs as well. Well, not me. I was at the wheel, when a great gray shape loomed out of the rain off the port. She was big and I could see the outlines of her turrets through the mist. We lurched over her wake, coming up on her astern, the churn of her propellers white against her dark gray.

"Hard a starboard ho!" I yelled over the wind, spinning the wheel. We drove back toward the gray mist, trying to put distance in between us. I had no time to give warning, no time to identify them. On deck, everyone was scrambling to reset the sails.

"All hands on deck!" I called.

Wally was reaching for the bell, but I yelled, "Belay that." We needed to wake the crew, but not the enemy. He nodded that he understood and ran for the hatch.

Then another shape loomed up in the rain to our starboard. We were in the middle of a fleet! It was coming right at us. The gaping barrels of her guns loomed over us. We cut across her bow with only a hundred feet to spare. From somewhere, the damp air carried the sound of a bell ringing on her deck, loud and sharp, but no shots fired. They were running like ants up there, her blue sailor boys heading for their combat stations. They were ours, but that wouldn't stop them from sinking us first and looking second in this weather. At least they were as surprised as we were.

This is why you never leave the wheel unattended.

As the mist closed in around us, I watched them fade. We crossed the wake of another, but couldn't see her. Then I turned thirty degrees to the port. We stayed on that heading, north northwest, for an hour, just to put distance between us. We were clear. Then it was across the wind and back east again. I figured maybe ten miles away, gradually widening if they held course. But then we had that storm coming and once that hit, who could tell?

It was after lunch that Willie came and sat on the pile of rubber sacks across from me. I was below mending rope by lamp light. It's always chafing and we're always mending it. He picked up a piece of tarred yarn and starts worrying its frets, which come apart in his hand.

"Where's the twine?" he asks.

"Down on your left," I replied.

He grunted and stepped down to reach it and almost loses his pipe. Don't worry, it wasn't lit. Not near all that rubber. Once he got the ball, he cut off a couple of feet with his knife and set himself to winding.

"That dream you had," he said.

"Been having," I replied. "There have been more."

"That's the way they go."

"Do you still have them?" I asked.

"Sometimes," he sighed.

"It's been what, twenty years?"

"Something like that."

"Do they get easier?"

"Mostly."

"Sometimes worse?"

He frowned a bit at the rope's end, fret finished, then started working his way back down the line, looking for wear. "Best if you don't hide from it," he said, not lifting his eyes.

"I'm not hiding."

"Maybe," he replied. Then he looked up. "There are things you'd have to be loopy not to hide from."

"I'm not hiding."

"Don't shy away from thinking about it. Thinking about it on your own helps. When you choose to. Not it."

"That makes sense," I said. "I suppose I have to."

"You will, one way or the other. Think about it, that is."

"So, it's a wound that needs air."

"That's about it."

Willie was right, and I've tried. And, over the years, I've laid it all open. I've sat with some of the best doctors and talked about it. I can remember everything. But the wound is still there, still demanding more air.

That evening I was at loose ends, below deck wondering when we were going to start pumping. It's a crazy feeling to be below decks in a storm. All that water, all that rain is coming down around you, shaking and grinding everything, and yet there you are, dry in clean lamp light. I rocked with the decks for a moment, reveling in it.

I was a little worried. Aleta was up on deck, standing her watch. This was her first real storm. She was the only new crew up there and I wanted to follow her up, but she had to see it on her own. My Ma and Pa sent me up during storms when I was much younger, although it must have given them sleepless nights. I could be brave too.

That storm, and it was a righteous, big, beautiful one, was begging for music, so I climbed up to my cabin for my violin, sliding open the door. My cabin was right above the rope locker. It's about two and half feet high and about six feet long, although some of that was taken up by my sea chest. A palace on a ship. I had my own porthole and a door that slid closed. Inside, I had all my things, like a little nest.

My violin, my new violin that I got in Cadiz, was in its case next to the bulkhead. My old violin of twelve years was kept on top of it, but it wasn't there. I mean the case was, but the lid was open and the violin gone. Alarmed, I felt around and found it tangled in my covers. It got caught in my thrashing about. When I lifted it, I realized her neck was broken, hanging by its strings. It's foolish but this brought tears. I had been crying a lot lately. Her worn wood looked dull next to the new exposed bright-broken ends. I sat there on the deck under my cabin door holding her. I grew up with this violin. I didn't have many things, but the things I kept were very dear to me.

I was alone. Everyone else was on deck or forward. Then somehow I was up through the hatch, the wind wailing and crashing around me, sheets of rain stung my skin and tore at my night dress. I was drenched in an instant.

"Cali!" someone called, but I ignored them.

I was walking barefoot, the best on unsure decks, if you can stand it. The surf washed around my legs as waves broke over the deck. The din of the storm reminded me of something else for a moment, but there were no fires, no bullets. I almost stopped, my legs weakened. But this wasn't it and I was off again, up the ladder, onto the stern, near the bulwark holding on to the lines. Waves crashed and churned around us.

"Cali, what are you doing?" It was Pa in his big japara coat, meaning to pull me back from the railing. Even he was soaked despite the waxing. But I shook him off and reached up, flinging her out into the gale. She was gone from my hands the instant I let go, vanished. Snatched by the storm. I was left there alone, gripping the ropes.

Did I do that?

"Cali, get below," Pa was yelling at me.

"Aye, Pa," I replied.

I turned and made my way back below, gripping the handholds on the aft deck cabin. Back down below in flickering lamp light, the hatch closed, the steps wet, me drenched making puddles that raced back and forth on that rare piece of dry deck as it tipped.

She was gone, buried with no ceremony, twelve of my seventeen years, given as an offering to a storm. I couldn't remember not having her.

My new violin greeted me, the incense of wood and rosin rose as I opened the case. She was beautiful and I loved her too. I didn't care about rosin or tuning. I just played, rolling with the waves, I didn't care what. Mme. Verbeeck was a dim outline in a dark corner, watching me. She looked worried. After a few minutes Crow stepped into the lamp light and sat on the ladder. I suppose Pa had sent him back to watch me. He didn't say a word. He sat and listened as I played.

The storm decided it liked the Carolinas and hit somewhere below Cape Fear. Bad luck for them and good luck for us. We were free and clear all the way north. No coastal patrol boats for us! Just sweet sailing in blue water and cloud-marked sky. I swapped watches with Ian so I could have the afternoon free with Aleta. We told everyone what we were doing and to stay out of the bow.

When we pulled out the dress, I could see that it was wrinkled and had lost some of its starch. But really, who cares? This wasn't a ball. It was fun!

Our biggest problem was her hair. We had plenty of fresh water. We'd just had a storm and the cistern was full. Ma heated some up so she could have a proper bath that morning, but after we washed her hair, what did we do with it then? All we had to work with was some combs and the hair piece that came with the dress. The pins they used on mine were lost in the dirt back in the Congo. They were only bent wire, but we didn't even have that. What we had was string. The trick would be to tie it so it wouldn't show.

Ma and I sat Aleta in the kitchen on a stool and fretted over her hair, trying this and that. Trying to get her it to stay up. The thing is, her hair is so long and straight. It's nearly black too, so cornstarch wasn't going to do it. We tried. It turned to a crusty white that came off in flakes. We finally hoisted it up with braids and string under a bun held in place with my and Ma's combs, cutting the ends off the string at the knot and tucking them inside. There was no place for the hair piece, which was sad because it had pretty little silver-silk flowers, but it looked strange wherever we stuck it in. I'm sure Omama, the dressmaker who designed our dresses, had a plan, but it was lost on us.

First, before the corset, we had bloomers, garters, socks, and a chemise. Our corsets were something of a frontier compromise. They didn't have proper boning available so they ribbed them with what they had, which was steel. It made our corsets somewhat less forgiving than normal ones. Frankly, I wasn't sorry at all to dump mine, but you needed it to fit in the dress. She made noise when Ma and I pulled on it, which was kind of funny. Eventually even she had to laugh. I had my foot on her rump to get leverage. I waited until she breathed out to pull too. Fair is fair.

It was then that we realized that it was a mistake to have done her hair before putting on the dress, which had to go over her head. We managed it, but it was a near thing. Underskirts first, a loose stiff weave that fluffed out like foam, then a thin bustle. Over her head it went, one arm in, then the other. You can't bend in a corset and we had to work to get her second arm in. Last it was all the buttons up the back.

We couldn't paint her nails. We had only two colors of ship paint, white and black. I don't know why they painted mine anyway. I had gloves and shoes. No one was going to see my bare toes. The shoes were crème colored with "low" heels that laced up your calves. They were narrow and I think hurt her as much they had hurt me. Then the gloves. They are very tight and slow going to get on and off.

Lastly, and with great ceremony, my pearls! She didn't need

rouge. She was blushing enough as we put them on, then my pearl watch bracelet. I had wound and set it first.

She was simply beautiful. The dress swirled around her as she moved. I bet mine had done that too. I thought of the flamenco dancer in Las Palmas and liked the idea that I might have looked even a little bit like her.

The crew were all waiting up top. She emerged, rising from the deeps into the sun, carefully stepping up the ladder as we held her dress for her. The white of her dress made everything around her seem dull. There was no sound except the sea, the rigging, and the men's indrawn breath. Tinker was the first to leap up and bow, followed by the others. She looked absolutely royal.

We were sailing around Cape Cod, heading past Monomoy, watching the whales. For the new crew, this was a first. Even the old hands were out on deck. I was leaning on the railing with Ma. We had a beautiful day, perfect sailing weather, a rare event around the Cape. Whales and calves out there frolicking, showing their fins and dorsals, rolling through the water big as ships. I was glad there weren't any whalers about, but then I worried why they weren't. Had they been lost to the war or perhaps moved to safer waters?

After the encounter in the rain, we'd seen no war vessels, just sails, and damn few of them too, all the way down the coast. We were in the home stretch, Boston just ahead. We made the lighthouse on Brewster Island that night, then the channel, and Lovell Island, and finally President Roads.

I couldn't sit still. I was still having problems sleeping. I was up at four in the morning and then again at seven, playing my violin. Aleta kept watching me, worried all the time. Maybe Ma and Pa too. We all have to sleep, but sometimes it's a hard thing to do.

The cutter with the inspectors pulled alongside at 11:00 AM, which was pretty quick. With war losses and risk, traffic was as thin in harbor as it was along the coast. The inspectors shook their heads as they crawled over our cargo. We made way for them as best we could, but the hold was very full. There was talk of putting off inspection until we docked and could unload. But mostly I think it was what we brought. Everyone was dumbfounded. We were the first American ship to haul in a load of rubber to the east coast in four years. Most trickled in by train from California, the final leavings after having passed through half a dozen middlemen and nationalities.

And then there were the pelts. There were no tariffs or rules on African pelts in America in 1892. No one knew what to do with them other than their being entirely a sensation. During the war, people looked to anything for relief, and zebra and elephant were nothing but myths from another world. Once we docked, we had newspaper men trying to get our story. They walked up the gangway with no leave. One took an actual photograph of the pelts, still on their pallets as they sat on the dock. I had deck watch then and they ignored me and tried to walk on board. Who would stop for a 17 year old girl, and a small one at that? I had to push one off the gangway before they would listen, which, to my shame, was funny. Luckily he could float. It was ebb tide though and the water was filthy.

Once we were unloaded, the warehousers and auction houses took over. I'm told bidding for our pelts was very vigorous, as it was with our rubber too. That tree bark was picked up by the government. Apparently it's used in medicine. And our ivory, as expected, was accepted with a shrug. The war hadn't done prices for non-war related luxuries like ivory any good. People either couldn't afford it or had no time to use it.

But I wasn't there for any of that. I was back in my school uniform, back at the Carrigan School for Young Women in Boston, which is where I stay most of the year. What? Did you think I was completely raised at sea? I've had a thorough and responsible education. Mind you they had to search around a bit for a uniform that fit me. One I could wear until my new ones arrived from the seamstress.

I was now one of three 17 year olds. Not many girls make it to 17 and still stay in school. Most are working on marriage by then. My school had just one 18 year old, and she wasn't happy about it.

Chapter 2 – Goodbye

Mrs. Pettett was still there even though it felt like I'd been away for years and years. Really, it had only been an extended summer. She was waiting in the echoing front hall to look me over, the cool stone a relief from the fall heat. I stood there with my violin case and my sea chest. I was wearing my boater and best dress by the way, but not my comb. My hat still had its old blue ribbon which, considering all the places we'd been, was amazing. I left most of my things back in my cabin. My wool watchcoat, my sweater, my knit hat, all would not go well with my school uniform. Neither would my duck pants, gray thick-knit socks, and patched, stained, cotton shirts and cowgirl dresses – all hard worn – do either.

When I was little, someone would come to help me with my chest, but I was a big girl now so I had to lug it up the steps from the carriage myself. Honestly, it doesn't weigh that much. I really don't have much in the way of possessions. Just underthings, sundries, and a couple of night dresses. Most of my things, like my precious *Standards of Training, Certification, and Watchkeeping,* and my shells had been destroyed with my cabin when the shell went through it. The only book I still had was my copy of *Dracula,* which I figured was going to make me very popular at school.

Ma and Pa had learned long ago to say goodbye outside. Parents were considered an uncomfortable distraction and were not encouraged to wander the halls. We hugged and cried. They were going back to the Caribbean to do another sugar run and it might be the last time I saw them. And there was no Mackie to drive the carriage. He died of dengue fever. We had Ian this time, which was something more to cry over. So saying goodbye took a while.

Inside, Mrs. Pettett looked me over with a critical eye as always and tisked.

"Just your violin and that old chest again. I suppose you're wearing your only dress, too. We were wondering if you would make it back."

You might think that was meant to be mean, reading it here, but she said it with a little smile. The smile was something I hadn't noticed before and to me it felt a bit odd. I wasn't sure what to make of it.

"Let's at least find you a bed."

I bobbed my head and said, "Yes ma'am." I am, as always, at least outside the bounds of the Congo, a lady of etiquette and grace.

She led me at a brisk pace down the hall to the dorms, to my bed for the next year, not far from my previous one. Next to it was a dresser I would hardly use, and a shelf and a desk. The room held five other girls, all of whom were off at class. I knew from experience that that bed would be pitching that night. It can take weeks to get over being at sea, to get your land legs back.

We had workmen there in the room as well, poking holes in the walls and running pipes. The wood floor was a mess of broken plaster. The school was getting electricity and I had to step over rolls of wire as we made our way in. No more doing work by lamplight this winter. Eying the wire with interest, bright copper wound in black sticky cloth, I wondered what it would be like.

"We'll send for you when the seamstress arrives," she said. "Here is your schedule." She set a handwritten slip of paper on my desk.

We used to have a tailor, but they're too useful in wartime. All of them had gone to war. Now we had a war widow, Mrs. Bennett. Mrs. Pettett had written my schedule on a sheet of notepaper, leaving it on my desk.

"Don't be late," she said as she left.

Picking up the paper, I saw that I would be just in time for French. I pushed my chest under my bed and headed for class.

I said *bonjour* to Mrs. Claveloux.

I completely stood out, not just being the only girl not in uniform but now being substantially older. I was the eighth girl in the class, taking the next to the last seat. It wasn't the worst, but it was almost the worst. It was off to the side in the dark, away from the windows. Someone had let the ink dry in the well too. I would have to clean it, but since I had yet to be given my school box, I had no pen anyway.

"*Bonjour Calista*," she said.

"*Bonjour Mme. Claveloux*," I replied.

"*Avez-vous passé un bel été?*"

Did I have a nice summer?

"*Il a été mouvementé*," I replied. It was eventful.

This seemed to set her back. I'd spent the last three months speaking practically nothing but French. My ten years of study had stood me well. But she seemed surprised.

"We went to France, Portugal, Spain, and the Congo," I added, in French of course.

"Did you use your French?"

"Yes, quite a bit."

She nodded and moved on to the next student. Really, the day's lesson seemed silly. I said as little as I could and spent most of the hour daydreaming about Lucien. Would I ever see him again?

I swear, when I think about him I get scared and what's weird is that I enjoy it! But then I start to worry that thinking about him will somehow use him up, that he'll disappear, which is crazy. But then again, maybe he was gone already. It was just a kiss. My one and only. I went around and around, jumping from fear to joy to worry to fear again. He was a world away on the other side of an ocean. I thought, maybe, I would try to write him a letter. Just to thank him for saving us, of course.

A Bad Crossing

Next was music class and I swear that Mrs. Hartnoll actually gave me a momentary smile when I walked in. My teachers were all doing it that year. All the girls in the class seemed so young and all their lessons so basic. It was hard to sit and listen. When she finally got to me I was sitting waiting for the class to end. Everyone was making a racket except me. Her hand reached around from behind and placed some music on my stand. It was a violin piece by somebody named Saint-Saëns. The paper looked new. She must have just bought it.

"I didn't think you were coming back," she said.

"For just a bit," I replied. "I didn't think I would either."

"You have a new violin." She was standing there in her prim dark blue dress, looking down at my case. "May I see it?"

I said nothing, but leaned down to pick up and open the case. She lifted her carefully, running her hand across her wood. I could tell she could sense it too. There is something more than just the scent of wood and varnish. She gave me a strange look.

"This will do." Then she continued levelly. "I heard you went to France." She had pulled up a chair next to me.

I nodded my head.

"Did you get to hear any performances?" she asked.

I shook my head slightly no. "But I got to play in Spain, in the street, in a club and in a restaurant."

I don't think she liked that. She seemed troubled, but said nothing. She just opened the music. "Work from here. Let's see how far you can get tonight." She handed me back my violin and walked on.

I'd never noticed it before, but she seemed smaller and grayer. She looked tired. Had she always looked like that?

Thumbing through the piece, I realized it was full of thirty second notes! I might saw my violin in two! But there was nothing for it but to roll my eyes and sigh.

After class, out in the yard, Dae, my apparently now ex-friend, didn't believe a single word of my story. She stopped me at the elephant stampede and said, "Enough." She wouldn't let me continue. Apparently I'd become a teller of tall tales. Perhaps I should join the circus. Certainly no Dracula for her.

My first night went well. The nightmares didn't start until the second. I suppose I suppose it was a matter of my getting settled in. I was twisting and thrashing in my bed and the girls in my room were in a panic. Apparently, I had made some noise. Poor Lorraine was back in the corner, scared. I was loud enough to have woken girls from nearby rooms. They were looking in the door.

"Calista!"

My hands were out trying to protect my face.

"Calista, wake up!"

I could see a face looking down at me, and a candle I thought, but I couldn't figure it out. It's hard for me after I have these dreams to remember where I am.

"Calista?"

I was blinking at her, still not recognizing her. But she was Mrs. Miller of course, our dormitory mother. I was still crying and in no state to talk.

"Calista?" she asked again, still trying to hold me down even though I had finally settled.

I nodded yes.

"You poor dear. Just like my Bill. You'd think you'd been in the war." Then she turned to the others. "It's over. Go to bed."

They left one by one. Poor Lorraine climbed over the foot of her bed rather than come closer. She was only seven and I am truly sorry I put such a fright in her.

"I'm sorry," I said weakly.

"Don't you worry dear," cooed Mrs. Miller. "You couldn't help it. There's no helping these things."

"May I have some water?" I asked.

"Yes, of course." She got up and went to my dresser. My cup and pitcher were there, next to my basin. We even have chamber pots under our beds, just in case you're too scared of the dark to make it to the head. "You drink this and when you're ready, we'll try to sleep again."

It takes me forever to go back to sleep after a bad dream. I couldn't keep her up with me.

"I'm okay now," I said.

"Are you sure?" she asked. I don't think she believed me.

"Really. I'll be fine."

"Well, we'll see." She was tugging my covers back in to place.

A Bad Crossing

"I'll keep an ear open for you."

She got up and shooed everyone back to bed with me laying there awake in the dark for I don't know how long. I must have gone back to sleep eventually because morning came. Mrs. Miller had knocked on our doorway, going from room to room. They do that every morning. For once, I didn't want to open my eyes. To be honest, I was embarrassed.

Nobody said anything though I know they wanted to. Nothing at all! We had porridge, eggs, and toast. Meat was in short supply because of the war. Eggs were more common. They couldn't be easily stored or shipped to the front. Since we docked in Las Palmas, we'd been eating pretty well, so the loss didn't mean much to me. I've been told that the poor were lucky to even get eggs. I dreamed though of the glorious oranges and melon we had in Spain while I ate.

There was whispering of course. Soon the whole school would know about my noisy dreams, then everyone from here to the docks. What was I going to do? What was I going to do tonight? Would they come again?

Naturally, they did. That very night. Twice. Why should being at school make any difference? Dracula or not, spooky screaming tall tales Cali was never going to have any friends again. I was called in to the office at lunch. It wasn't Mrs. Pettett the schoolmaster, it was Mrs. Keckland, the owner of the school!

She was old and gray and her office was all wood and carpet. It was going to be hard getting electricity in there without breaking something. I'd only ever seen her in the halls, and then only once or twice a year. I have been told on good authority that she was the daughter of the founder Mr. E. J. Carrigan.

"Is this she, Janet?"

"Yes ma'am," Mrs. Pettett said, giving her head a little bow.

"Come in, take a seat." She waved at the one in front of her.

I wanted the one near the window, but sat where I was told.

"Your family was in the newspaper?"

"Yes. I think so," I replied.

"You were in the Congo wasn't it?"

"Yes, ma'am."

"There was a war there."

19

"Yes, ma'am."

"Louise was right," she said to Mrs. Pettett. Then she looked at me. "It seems you brought something back with you."

I couldn't think of anything to say. I wasn't quite sure what she meant.

"I believe it to be the soldier's terror. Traumatic hysteria." She looked down and tapped an open book on her desk. "I've been trying to read about it, but these books are out of date. Mostly sheer nonsense." She pushed it back to make her point.

"Fear not," she continued, with a little smile. "We aren't going to send you away, although we might try to find you some help. More common than a cold these days, what with the war. We'll have to find you someplace to sleep. Can't have you keeping everyone awake."

This was a lot to swallow at once. It hadn't even occurred to me that they might send me away and now I was staying.

"I am right in assuming that your time in the Congo was unpleasant?"

"Yes ma'am," I replied. Really, it was almost a squeak. I wanted to try again, just to correct her impression of me, but I thought it might make it sound even worse.

"You haven't been having any hallucinations? Think you're in places you aren't? Seeing things that aren't really there?"

I paused for a moment, thinking of the ghosts of M. Allard and Mme. Verbeeck, but they're real. "No ma'am."

"Frightened or confused in situations that remind you of the Congo?"

I blushed, which was enough of an answer for her.

"Yes, well," she paused, looking again at her book. "Apparently, in most cases, eventually, this can go away on its own. It can take years though. Mrs. Pettett has told me about a therapy, the talking cure, which can be helpful. Perhaps we can see about that. It might help that you're so young." Then she turned to Mrs. Pettett. "Janet, any ideas where we can put her?"

"I was thinking the caretaker's room."

"In the basement?"

In the basement.

"It would be quiet."

"Yes. It would. It will have to be cleaned." Then she looked at me. "It's a frightful mess down there right now."

In the basement. I knew it.

"Yes ma'am."

They weren't kidding. It was a mess down there. That's where the furnaces and coal for our heating were and the narrow stairway, and the floor, were sooty. It was dark too. No gaslight down there. The only outside light came from little windows up near the ceiling and there were none in my room. It would be candles and lanterns, even in the daytime.

We hadn't had a building caretaker in years, not since our old one died. He died in the bed I was supposed to sleep in! At least I got a new mattress. Since his death, his room had been used for storage.

I didn't have to do it all on my own at least. Mrs. Milliken and our coal man Leroy helped. Some of it went upstairs and some was plunked down in a pile in the hallway with an old blanket thrown over it.

My room was big, perhaps eight by ten feet. Plenty of room for a bed and desk. My sea chest went right under my bed. They gave me matches, candles, and a lantern, so I could study, and a big round steel alarm clock that ticked loudly. It was a palace!

I would have to go upstairs through the kitchen to get to the head which would certainly require a candle and matches. I took a bucket from downstairs and cleaned it so I could use it to carry water. A bucket is so much easier to carry than a pitcher when you're holding a candle and trying to open a door.

I went to sleep in fear that the caretaker's ghost would show up. He didn't, so I suppose Mme. Verbeeck kept him away or maybe he was nice enough to be a gentleman. Perhaps it was the new place, but I didn't have any bad dreams that night.

Every morning, the alarm would ring so loud in the quiet that I would leap out of bed before I could think, grabbing the ringer to stop it. Then I would practically faint, standing on the cold concrete with my bare feet. I dressed alone, hearing the echoing voice of Leroy singing to himself as he worked. He started early shoveling coal to heat the building. Then I climbed the narrow, creaky stairs in the dim light from Leroy's lamp, saying hello as I climbed. Up in the kitchen it was warm and full of the smells of breakfast. Sadly, they didn't let us have coffee, just tea, but I could get my cup in the kitchen before anyone else! And, unlike the dining room, everyone in the kitchen said hello and smiled.

"There she is," they would say. "Would you like your tea, dear?"

The kitchen women were nice. But it lasted only four nights. It was Wednesday, and the other girls had finally started talking to me. It was my ears. Lydia wanted to see my pierced ears. I still had my gold loops. Then Carol and Rachel were next.

Then it was my room! They wanted to see my room. I wasn't sure they were allowed down there so we crept past the kitchen. It was after dinner and the kitchen ladies were doing dishes, so it was noisy. Leroy was gone too, the furnace and boiler winding down for the day.

It was pitch black down there in the evenings after Leroy was gone, with only the dim-orange glow around the furnace door for light. He wouldn't leave a lamp lit with all the coal about, but I had a box of candles by the door. I lit one and then others for everybody and then down the narrow wooden stairs we creaked. I swear they acted like we were investigating a tomb! They wanted to see everything, but you can't go far down there because the coal dust gets on everything. We went as far as we could though. Then we huddled into my room. It's just a bed, my sea chest, and a table and chair, but everyone was impressed despite the endless clanking tick of my clock. I think it was that the caretaker had died in it. Maybe being Creepy Cali was going to be okay.

The end came when the lawyer found me, let's be honest, asleep in English. "Calista?" they called from the classroom door, as if calling gently would interrupt the classroom less.

"Yes ma'am," I replied.

"Please come to the office."

They lead me down the hall. I was pretty sure I wasn't in trouble. I'd only been back a week, but that didn't mean this wasn't trouble. And there it was, waiting for me in the school office in the form of a short, rotund man sweating in the autumn heat in an ill-fitting wool suit. Behind him workmen were banging on the wall, knocking holes in the plaster for the new pipes.

"Miss Carmichael?" he asked, as if they would bring him an imposter.

"Yes," I said. Get on with it.

"You have not been easy to find." He looked at me over his

spectacles. I stared back at him. "I represent the estate of one Countess Emmaline Sophie Verbeeck of Belgium."

Now I was giving him the eye, "Yes?"

"There is a matter of a bequest and some paperwork associated with it."

"Bequest?" I asked, now completely confused.

"Yes. She apparently set up an endowment to the Royal Conservatory for Music in Brussels. It's contingent on you and another young woman, Aleta? You wouldn't happen to know where I can find her and perhaps her full name?" I nodded yes and then no. "It's contingent on your attending the institution. You are to be sponsored by," he paused and looked at a paper. "A Duke of Tervuren."

"Oh, Lucien," I said. Mind you the women in the office were gaping.

"It covers your room and board, certain expenses, and a monthly stipend."

"Oh," it was almost a whisper.

All I could think was *I'm going to get to see Lucien again!* By the way, he wasn't wrong about the paperwork and they wanted me there at "my earliest possible convenience." The last thing I got from him was a zeppelin ticket! I was leaving in ten days on the SML Bremen. SML stands for *Seiner Majestät Luftschiff*; his majesty's airship!

So that was goodbye, probably forever, to the Carrigan School for Young Women. Perhaps to Boston itself, a city I had lived in half my life but had never really seen.

The next day I hauled my sea chest and violin alone down the hallway to the entrance hall, wearing the dress I had arrived in. We're civilized. We'd washed it! I left my loaner dress on the bed. I had only met the seamstress the day before and my regular school clothes wouldn't start arriving for a week.

Mrs. Pettett was, as always, waiting to see me off. Then Mrs. Hartnoll came walking quickly in, out of breath. I could see tears in her eyes and she was having trouble speaking. I was stunned. She gave me a hug and thrust another piece of music into my hands. It was a symphony by someone named Beriox.

"I knew you would do it," she said.

"Go to music school?" I grunted as she hugged me.

"Make something of yourself," she said, looking at me. "You can be so much more than just someone's wife. Please, promise me that you won't stop playing. Not for anyone."

"I won't," I said, very confused.

Then she mumbled something I couldn't understand and turned away, walking quickly up the corridor, dabbing her eyes.

I stood there stunned. I had no idea what to do. My teachers had always been something other, distant taskmasters, something to be listened to or avoided. The thought of a teacher crying was almost frightening.

"She said you were always her greatest student," Mrs. Pettett said.

"I am?" I asked.

"Well," she said, with a little smile. "You're not a bad one at least."

"Oh."

She didn't pinch my cheeks as usual, settling instead on straightening my hair and resettling the blousing on my sleeves.

Outside Ma, Pa, and Ian, thankfully not out to sea, were waiting with a rented pier office wagon. No steam carriages for us. We're certainly not rich. There were, of course, lots of hugs, even though I'd only been gone a week. Then we clopped-clopped down Hannover Street from Beacon Hill toward the waterfront, dodging steam carriages and trollies chugging by, leaving their trails of smoke and puffs of steam, ice and milk wagons, and people who don't seem to care if they got run down. Luckily our Boston streets are much wider than European ones. Many of the streets are dirt as well which isn't so bad as long as it isn't raining. The cobbled ones make everything rattle, although, on the plus side, they don't rut.

Since steam carriages began to fill the road, people had lost all respect for horses. People walked right in front of us, expecting us to stop in time. One man even popped our horse on the nose, dodging its teeth as it tried to bite. He had a mischievous smile and gave me a wink, which made me laugh.

We passed the waterfront warehouses and trade shops, then the harbor itself, a forest of masts and funnels. A steam ship whistled, echoing away in the cool fall breeze. The smell of the harbor, tar, salt, sewage, old fish, and cooking food, all told me I was back home.

Chapter 3 – The End of Everything

Wait. I *have* to tell you. Did you know that Aleta's real name is *Rosemary*?! I was rolling, laughing on the decks, literally, and she was throwing things at me, some of which hurt. Her name was required for the paperwork. She'd been trying to hide it, but as Crow says, I can sneak better than any Indian. I saw it when I peeked over her shoulder. But, I'm ahead of myself . . . bah ha ha ha . . . Excuse me. Really, honestly, we should start at the beginning.

Red was there at the docks, about to set sail when the lawyer showed up, which was lucky. It could have been months before Red came back and Aleta might not have even been on board by then. Jamaica can be pretty fun and she might have decided to stay and I would never get to see her again.

Red had just come back from the shipyard and she had a lot of fresh paint and new wood. We'd taken a lot of bullet damage from the fight at the Boma docks. Far more than we could reasonably patch. She was water tight, but still a mess. The deck cabins and port railings had to be torn down and replaced. You could see the filler on the masts, which are greased but unpainted, and new white patches in her sails.

Losing the deck cabins made unloading the cargo a lot easier, although it was weird seeing her stripped down to the deck. We'd packed so much in there that there wasn't room to move anything. We couldn't even use the forklift. It was wedged in and buried under everything else. We got everything out by hiring a line of steves to move all the sacks of rubber, passing them hand over hand up to the dock. Pulling things apart meant a lot of dock sorting, with the inspectors standing around impatiently waiting to see what we had. Customs put a guard on the docks that night too, just to make sure we didn't try to sneak anything out – which they charged us for, by the way. But our cargo was the least of our problems.

As I sat there in the wagon, clop clopping down to the docks toward Red, I felt cold wash of dread. I realized that I might have made a mistake. I didn't have to accept the school offer. I could have finished the term down in the basement. All I had thought about was Lucien. It had been months. He may have already forgotten about me. I may have traded Red and my family for music school on the other side of the world. Worse, for a man who might not even remember me! I was about to tell Ma and Pa to turn around when I thought about Mrs. Hartnoll. It would break her heart. But then what about breaking *my* heart? Which made me think about Lucien again. I was going around and around like this and I think they noticed I turned quiet, but they said nothing as we drove. I think they knew. I think they felt it too.

There were changes happening everywhere, and I mean all over the world, even to our beloved Red, and since I was an owner and I was going to be leaving soon, and please believe me that this is a very difficult subject, Pa felt he had to get the ball rolling. I'm not joking around! Really! All our stock holders were in Boston, and this would be perhaps the last time we'd all be together at the same time. He called us together that afternoon to consider the possibility of *selling Red*. He already had Mackie's heirs and Grandpa onboard.

Crow, when he heard it, just said "No," and got up and walked away. But Pa had to continue. It's just that it was a very hard, very bitter pill.

It had been getting harder and harder to turn a profit with Red, and it wasn't just the war. It was our cargo capacity versus our overhead. Profit margins on shipped goods had been going down because more goods were moving in bigger ships. There was less buying and selling, more packet shipping, commission shipping contingent on predictable shipping times. And, because we relied on wind and current, our shipping routes were less flexible and we never knew when we would arrive. She was still profitable, but the end was in sight. Pa was talking about selling Red and buying a steamship, maybe two. The war would be ending soon, everyone knew it, and Pa was thinking that with the loss of military contracts, the dockyards were going to be desperate. He was thinking that it might be a good time to look for bargains.

But how could we let go of Red? I'd spent my whole life on her. I was born on her, in Ma and Pa's cabin! We were all sitting down in the hold with the afternoon sun shining down from the open hatches, when I realized that I'd curled up, and so I tried to relax. This was a hard, hard, bitter pill! But Pa was right, we had to make a living somehow. He wasn't asking for a vote yet. He only wanted us to consider it. New ships are expensive. It would certainly mean borrowing, which entailed extra risk.

I was crying a lot in those days. It was all the endings. They kept coming until I didn't know what to do. I didn't even know I had a bank account until our last trip. I'd never even been in our bank in Boston, but Pa and I were there that day. Apparently not only was I a stockholder, but I'd been receiving dividends for pretty much my whole life, which were sitting in our bank. I was in my one nice dress, my boater, and my hair was tied back with my new blue ribbon. I got it off of a flag. There had been a parade, which we missed, and someone had left it on the ground. The flag was useless but the ribbon wasn't, so I pulled it off and used it to tie back my hair. Pa helped tie it! He could see to make the bow straight. So my hair matched my hat. It looked quite fetching.

We were in the worst part of humid fall which made being inside a big stone bank feel like heaven, but only for a moment. Once we were in its enclosing darkness, a dread crept over me. We were there to transfer my money to a bank in Belgium. It was necessary. I wouldn't have access to it if it was sitting in Boston when I needed it. The inside of the bank was one big room, lit by shafts of light from iron barred skylights. I stared across an expanse of desks filled by old men scribbling in ledgers. In the back I could see long barred counters, behind which sat tellers.

We were greeted warmly by a peg legged man in a suit. "Captain Carmichael," he said. They know my Pa. The bank man was probably smiling because we had made some large deposits lately.

"We've come to discuss my daughter's account," Pa replied.

"Then you must be Miss Carmichael!" the man said with a smile. He had a thin little mustache. Weird. I was more than just about sure that I disliked him and I was certain that he wouldn't be smiling when he found out we were here to make a withdrawal.

"Yes sir," I replied.

He'd turned to lead us to his desk when Pa added, "We're here to make a withdrawal." Yup, there was a twitch. Maybe he'd get a crick in his neck when he found out how much.

"Please sit down." He waved to the chairs in front of his desk. "Will this be from Miss Carmichael's account?"

"Yes," I said.

"I'll just get your balance." And off he went.

"Pa," I said. "I don't want to do this."

"Cali, you're going to need money."

"I don't want to leave."

"This is the opportunity of a lifetime."

"I don't want to leave you and Ma. I don't want to leave Red."

"Cali." Then Pa stopped to take a breath. "Red can't last forever."

"That prince told me that too."

"Did he? Maybe he wasn't quite the idiot he seemed."

Then the bank officer came back with a piece of paper. "Here we are," he said with a cheery tone. "Your balance is very healthy."

I looked at the paper and it said $32,612.32. A breathtaking sum. I could buy a house and live in it, frugally, for the rest of my life. I showed it to Pa and he nodded.

"That's about what I calculate. I suggest you take at least $10,000," I heard the bank man stifle a squeak! "$20,000 would be wiser. You'll be gone a long time and you may need airfare or medical expenses. You'll need to be able to survive until we can find you, which could take many months."

I could feel myself curling up. "Please." There were more of my stupid tears.

"This is only a different school. The contingencies and concerns are no different. Split the difference, $15,000? Money doesn't go as far there as it does here. That should get you through any emergency and back home, and leave you some to have a little fun as well."

I told him twelve and he nodded. I was sobbing as I signed the papers. I think the bank man was too as he watched the money leave. It was going to the *Banque Nationale de Belgique*. Pa and I both knew that it was not just a different school.

When we got back, the lawyer was there with Aleta. I remembered that her going was contingent with my going. She couldn't go without me! I couldn't deny her this. I stopped and watched her work at the pages. She had to wade through all the same paperwork as I did. Really, I only wanted to give her a hug, but that's when I saw her name. Rosemary Rucker.

Chapter 4 – Farewell to Boston

We anchored Red out in the bay, near Governor's Island. It was much cheaper than the docks, and we were done with cargo. Pa was fixing to do the sugar run down to Jamaica again one last dangerous time. The hold was full of shovels, iron fittings, and other manufactured goods, but they were lingering in harbor for us. Aleta and I had tickets to Brussels on a Lufthansa zeppelin, paid for by Mme. Verbeeck. I hadn't seen her ghost since we made shore. I hoped it meant she was satisfied.

If we were going to do it, travel to Brussels, then we'd need clothes. Aleta still had her dress from the Congo. Her cabin was far more crowded than mine, but a ball gown is not a travelling dress. I still only had the single dress I bought at the start of summer. I had to give the school uniform back. So it was off to Eagleston's department store. Ma, Aleta, and me, piled into the yawl, rowing for shore. We took turns at the oars.

Up beyond the docks, we caught a steam trolley. It was late morning, and it wasn't crowded, so we got the pick of the best seats. In the humid fall, it's furthest from the boilers. We gave the white conductor our nickels and bounced along. He stood in the front, ringing his bell for no good reason, and the Negro coal man stood in the back shoveling away at the boiler, standing alone against the heat. I could hear him singing and humming. I put my hand on Aleta's and looked at her. I could see her nod just a little. She was listening too. The rhythms were simple and strange, they bounced with the clack of the wheels. In the quiet moments I could hear him singing about whatever came his way, the traffic, who got on, who got off, people, stores, all in time to the wheels and his shovel. His music was his only shield from the heat and the world.

We had to get off at Eagleston's. Ma was buying dresses for both of us, even though Aleta insisted she would not accept them. Her pay so far, at her rating, wasn't enough even for one outfit and we both had to have things to wear. We couldn't show up in our sloppes in Brussels. Travel dresses are apparently different from day dresses, night dresses, work dresses, evening dresses, and formal dresses, although frankly, in most cases, it was difficult for me to see the difference. Our travel dresses had to have coats, gloves, and hats, all tailored and form fitting, without the puffy shoulders. I suppose that was so we could better wear our coats. Mine were pale green and peach prints. Aleta picked a dark green and pale blue. And I was going to get a real purse! But what was I supposed to do with it? Apparently they're consolation for none of the dresses having pockets. You have to hold them in your hand. And yes, I got a corset. It was called a travel corset, as if that makes any difference!

It was, at least, not as insane as the one I had at the ball. But Aleta still had fun cinching me in just the same. It's a strange feeling walking around, not being able to bend. At least I could breathe. Thankfully, travel dresses don't have bustles or crinolines. Maybe that's what made them different. I'd be able to sit at least, and our new boots were fairly sensible, the heels a bit more than an inch. With at least eight inches of clearance on the hem, it meant we would be able to walk. And, of course, a trunk for each of us to put it all in. They were special air travel trunks, which to me seemed to be merely another word for flimsy. They wouldn't last a year onboard ship.

At the door, on the way out, we practically ran into a young woman coming in. Actually she walked through us, nose in the air, as if we were furniture. She was very pretty. Her dress was crisp, skin perfect, hair immaculate, which is difficult in the fall in Boston where things tended to wilt. Her expression was anything but pretty. The doorman opened the door in our faces to let her through. Outside, we could see a steam carriage waiting, a nice one too. By her stance and countenance, it was clear that she disapproved of both the store and her being in it, and had no intention of exchanging pleasantries with the likes of us. She walked down the center aisle and stopped, waiting to be served. She was going to have a bit of a wait, I thought. They don't do that here. But then the store manager came running out to greet her, stumbling, trying to adjust his clothes as he ran. When she spoke, she sounded English.

"Damn nobs," Aleta muttered as we stood outside.

"Or worse," I added.

"Their children," we said in unison, breaking out in laughter.

Ma snorted. She's Ulster Presbyterian. She hates nobility even more than papists.

But luckily we were done with our shopping and she was, thankfully, not in our way, so it was back out into the sunshine and humidity.

"Where'd *she* come from," I wondered.

"It has to be the aerodrome or a steamship," Aleta replied.

"I hope we don't have to look at her the whole trip."

"Maybe she's headed west," Aleta replied hopefully, as she adjusted her bags. We had a lot of them, even though much of what we bought was going to be delivered to the dock office. The dresses, for instance, had to be altered.

"Hmmm," I mumbled. I really hoped so, but I suspected we would be seeing her again.

Of course, we had to stop for Chinese food, which was something new for Aleta. She stared at the geometric woodwork and painted paper panels, her eyes wandering around the room looking at the walls with their black lacquer art. And then again, when he arrived at our table, Mr. Wong himself. He'd gained weight over the years, but still dressed in Chinese clothes, just for work I'm sure. As I've grown, I've watched his mustache and chin beard grow longer and longer. At that time they were closing in on his belt.

Chinese writing is crazy. You wouldn't know it was writing just to look at it. It's mostly squares with crisscrossed lines. I asked Mr. Wong about it years ago. He could read everything in there. Some of it was people's names, but most of it was poetry, which is very important to Chinese people. Most of it though, even when translated, still made no sense. For instance,

Toward evening there was thunder and lightning. Why was the lady sad? The high lord did not reveal his majesty. What was he seeking?

Which, as I said, makes no sense. But when I asked Mr. Wong what it meant, he laughed and said, "Not until you are older." I will miss Mr. Wong, I thought.

On the way to the trolley we encountered four street musicians. A lot of freed negroes had been streaming north but could find no work when they arrived in Boston, so they'd wander the streets begging, or, in this case, performing. These were singing acapella, which was pretty common. Those that had been here longer sometimes fashioned instruments out of things they could find, buckets, barrels, pieces of wood, and string and rope, eventually, even acquiring real instruments. But these four were just singing, still practically dressed in rags. Winter would be hard if they couldn't get shoes and coats, I thought.

We stopped. We had to; the sidewalk was blocked. They'd chosen a spot behind a street cart selling yams and potatoes. With all the traffic in the street there was no going around.

"Do we need potatoes?" I asked Ma. Food was dear during the war.

"Not at those prices," she replied, looking for a way around.

I like to listen to street performers, but Ma doesn't. She generally doesn't have much patience for street people. Which was strange since she let me do it in Spain. But in this case we had little choice.

They finished, then picked up another song. A chant called "Blind Tom." The shifts in tonality in the chorus were crazy complicated. I was fingering the changes in my palm when I looked down and saw Aleta's fingers moving unconsciously as well. I had gotten some money at the bank. My own money! So I gave them a quarter before Ma dragged us around and on down the sidewalk. They would all eat that night.

Even though a lot of our new gear would be delivered, the yawl was so full that it was hard to row. We sponged out the bottom until it was dry, then passed the bags down the ladder. It was ebb tide, but the breeze was off shore, wanting to blow us out rather than across, so it wasn't much help. It took us until late afternoon to get back.

Melancholy. I read poems and stories about it, but to experience it . . . I was so sure that I'd never see Red again. I would write, but of course they wouldn't see the letters until they got back from Jamaica, and it would take least a month for them to get there. I knew I wasn't alone either, as I sometimes saw tears in the eyes of the old crew. I knew that Pa knew, if only by the way he was constantly hugging me, that this wasn't just a new school. I was leaving.

I would practice my violin, standing aft below decks in the dim light, that melancholy draining away into the air, until Aleta would join me. She would follow for a bit, drifting with me, then she would start pushing and pushing until I pushed back, until we were dodging around and around, and the sun shone again, playing just like two kids. Two kids, for a little while longer.

The night before we left, Ma made my favorite ham. She soaks it all day in molasses then fries it, but unlike my homecoming dinners, this was a goodbye dinner, and it was a quiet one. I held on to each moment, trying to pin them down, but they rolled by, unstoppable. The food gone, the table cleared, dishes cleaned and put away. I watched everyone's faces, afraid I wouldn't remember them. That night I fought sleep, the light from the moon shining in through my porthole. Probably the last time I'd sleep in my cabin. When it finally took me, I thankfully had no dreams.

In the morning I pulled all my things out to stuff them in my travel trunk, even my dirty clothes. I was leaving my sea chest behind. Weight is important when it comes to air travel. Saying goodbye to my old sea chest, scratched and worn as it was, brought tears. Some of those dents had stories. I'd had it my whole life. It wasn't going away, I told myself. Grandpa would keep it. I'd see it again. But it didn't make it easy.

We were taking the longboat, leaving the ship in the hands of the new crew. That was a first for us. Tinker, Willie, Ed, Crow, Ian, Ma, and Pa, piled in with Aleta and me and we rowed for the docks in East Boston. The tide was still coming in so the water wasn't bad and the rowing not hard. I looked back at Red until the morning fog swallowed her, me not rowing. I was just sitting there, another first, in my corset and fancy dress, new trunk at my back.

We tied the boat and made the long slimy climb up the gray docks, then hauled the trunks up with a rope. Climbing was hard in my new shoes. I could barely bend my ankles. Up and down the docks I could see ships loading, both sailing ships and steamships, and we walked amidst the bustle and clutter of the docks, nodding to captains and crew who stared back at me like I was some sort of kelpie walking the land. I suppose it was my new clothes or that it was the whole crew walking together. There would be rumors flying. I saw so many faces I grew up with. I wanted to stop and talk, but we walked on in silence, each one of us lost in his own thoughts.

Pa had requested a carriage from the harbor office and when it clopped up, both it and the horse were old and careworn. The carriage turned out to be a bit small for all of us, but we piled in anyway. I was sitting on Ma and Pa's lap. Aleta was sitting on the floor with her legs hanging over the running board, kicking at the street as it went by. Ian and Tinker had to hop out to push to get it started.

The Boston aerodrome was just north of East Boston and we could see the airships tethered over it before we left the docks. The sun was burning through the morning fog, leaving silver sky and white light. The aerodrome grass, grazed short, sparkled with dew. Many airships were on the ground, but many more were moored above in an eclectic mix, most of them gray, but many painted in bright colors with American and European advertisements. And they were all sporting flags of one sort or another. We were still at war, and any doubt of allegiance could mean death.

The flat grated road continued across a wide field dotted with grazing cattle and concrete mooring points. I was sitting with my arms around Ma. She had started crying again. Our zeppelin stood out amongst the others. Her silver and blue fins, clean polished aluminum, and varnished wood lines left no doubt that we would be flying with the best. Our crossing would take three days. Red sometimes takes four weeks.

We pulled up at the terminal building. Lufthansa has its own terminal buildings, and this was one Aleta, a former Lufthansa employee, hadn't been to. It was low and wide and all window, its sides a latticework of crisscrossed window panes. Carriages and steamers were parked all around it and inside I could see people moving about. This was also going to be Aleta's first time flying as pampered passenger instead of an overworked crew member and her stare was, for once, unreadable. Two men in slate blue met us as we stopped, taking our horses and trunks.

"Aerodromes all look the same," Aleta grumped. Sound familiar? I say the same thing about ports. And again, in the terminal; "Lufthansa lobbies too." She headed straight for the cookies. They had cookies, and coffee too! And we were going to fly!

So it was cookies and coffee. Ma had tea. We were an hour early, but you never know what kind of delays you'll encounter so it's generally better to be early than late. The terminal was light and airy. Unlike in the Canaries, this one had padded armchairs, tables, and bookshelves full of books. There was a sign in five languages that read, "Take a book." I smiled when the bookshelf failed to produce anything like Dracula. Many of them were in languages other than English and French. I picked an old yellowback called *Kidnapped*. It was the only one that sounded like an adventure. There were lots of newspapers as well, many from Europe, all days old. So I was sitting there munching. Maybe it was the coffee and sugar, but I had an idea.

"Pa?" I asked.

"Yes?"

"Get someone to take a picture of her for me."

"That's a great idea," he replied, smiling.

"I want one too," Ma said. "We should have done it sooner and more. Oh, all those days in Jamaica, we were always thinking about work."

"You'll be back there soon," I said.

"Yes, but they won't have our little Cali in it," and she picked up crying again.

"It'd be great to have one of me naked on the beach," I said.

"Naked?" asked Aleta.

"She was four," Crow said, his voice sounding a little hoarse.

Passengers were wandering slowly in, and carriages were lining up outside waiting to take friends and relatives back, when who should walk in but Herr Schuster. Maximilian Schuster, the Krupp field representative for Africa, and a German spy. Max is thin, a bit on the short side, with a pale round face and wide thin lips. Not a handsome man, but nice, and he saved my life. It was Max who gave me the warning about the German invasion. He saved my whole family and Red herself as well. He glanced around the room as he entered. Max spends a lot of time watching. When he saw me, I think there was a moment of confusion, then genuine pleasure.

"Miss. Carmichael! I'm so glad to see you alive," he said, as he walked toward us. "And you have your violin case. I hope we will get to hear you play. I'm afraid I had to leave before the end of your last performance."

"You sure did," I replied, smiling back. "Ma, Pa, this is Herr. Schuster . . ."

"Please, call me Max," he said, and actually clicked his heels and bowed a little.

"I met him at the ball." I wasn't sure how much to say. Max is, after all, a spy.

Pa shook his hand and gave a little bow back. "It's a pleasure," he said. "A friend of our daughter's is a friend of ours."

"We were all very impressed by her," he replied.

I noticed a girl about my age, accompanied by a balding gentleman come through the door. It was strange, but her hair was dark brown while his was bright blond, almost green! Weird. Max took no notice, which was also strange. Max notices everything. Following was a dark haired man of eminently draftable age, carrying their bags. Apparently he didn't want to give them to the men outside. His eyes, like Max's, tended to dart around the room.

Maybe they were why Max was on the flight. Spy stuff!

Aleta was scowling at the clock. "They're running late. Where's the liftoff toast?" But she was cut off by the clatter of a cart from a side door and a woman in a slate blue uniform with yellow trim. Sitting on the cart were those tall narrow bubbling wine glasses and the bubbling wine itself packed in two pots full of chopped ice.

"Ah yes. Here we are," Max said, clearly a flying veteran and in the spirit of the occasion.

"Will the passengers please gather round," the woman called, followed by a loud pop. The lad behind her was filling glasses and I was hugging everyone. "Will the passengers please gather round," she said again. There were maybe thirty of us. "I would like to welcome you to our Boston to Berlin flight on the *Luftshiff Bremen*. We will be stopping in London and Brussels. Your baggage is already in your cabins. I would like to remind you that this is your last chance to smoke. No smoking will be permitted on the flight." Several people were already availing themselves. "Everyone, please take a glass." Then to a lady whispering next to her she replied, "Yes ma'am, even if you don't drink. You can still toast. It's our tradition."

The glass was cold.

The hostess raised her glass, as did we all, "To the works of man, and the heavens above!" and we carefully touch our glasses together. "May you all experience the perfect flight," and we all repeated it. I was quite beginning to enjoy this wine. I took a few sips and then went back to the others.

"Ma, you should try this. It's that bubbling wine. We had it in the Congo."

"Champagne," said a tall thin man, a passenger. He had another one of those horrible thin mustaches. They must be in fashion somewhere, I thought.

"Pardon?" I said.

"It called Champagne. They make it in France," he replied. He had a weird accent.

"Well, it's lovely. What do you think Ma?"

"It's very nice. Want to try it John?"

"I've had it before. You should drink it. It's difficult to get outside of Europe."

"Hey Pa, maybe we could try shipping it," I suggested.

"It's fragile and temperature sensitive. Perhaps in the winter though, if it's packed carefully. That's a good idea." He looked thoughtful.

"Then you could visit."

"That's also a good idea."

Then they asked us to board and we were heading toward the door far too quickly. We traded hugs and kisses and tears, but it was time. Outside, we walked across the grazed low grass in the silver morning sunshine toward metal steps on wheels, the zeppelin arching over us.

The *Bremen* was huge! It was beyond real, silver-gray, floating above the ground. Blue fins and the word *Lufthansa* painted in gold across her round ribbed side. The impossibility of it denied its reality. I simply could not believe it existed until I touched it.

"Please be careful as you board the gondola," The attendant at the top said. She was just a girl, clearly younger than me. Aleta said they hire them small and young to save weight, and she was clearly both.

The gondola itself was long and sleek, like a giant teardrop. It was made of polished wood and aluminum, bigger than a house, glinting in the low morning sun. The vast gas envelope hung over us like some kind of cathedral roof. Aleta stared as we entered. She almost seemed uncomfortable. I think she never thought she would be on that end of things.

The floor was moving a bit as we stepped inside out of the sun and breeze. Its rhythm was different from Red. The sway was slower. We were led through a dining room with big windows, and down a central hallway to our cabin by another young girl. Our room was not quite six feet wide with only a small chair, two narrow fold down bunk beds, and a little fold down desk. When you think about where I grew up, to me it seemed luxurious. Especially for a ship.

Our trunks were sitting side by side on the floor beneath where the bottom bunk would fold down. They had been brought up for us. They just fit when we folded the bed down. I suppose that's why they're called travel trucks. I set my violin case down next to them. The upper bunk came with a ladder that folded down with the beds. They had hooks too that hinged out of the wall so you could hang things and clip up nets to hold loose stuff. The bed, the chair, the desk, everything seemed so fragile and thin. Our door clicked shut with spare precision. The desk was down and on it were two chocolate bars, two little booklets labeled "*Flughandbuch,*" a pad of paper, a pen, and two little red roses. Hand written on the pad of paper was the word, "*Welkommen.*" Aleta said the chocolates were 2.35 Belgian ounces each, including wrapper, and the roses not over 2.50 English ounces, since those were the depots this flight crossed.

We had a window, which unfortunately looked away from the terminal. If my family was waving, I couldn't see them.

"We need to go to the lounge," Aleta, the woman of experience said. "We can explore later."

We made our way down the narrow hall to the lounge where we found windows facing the terminal. I could see Ma and Pa, I hoped they could see me.

"This won't do," Aleta said. "It's too bright out there. They won't see us. Come on." She pulled me by the sleeve back down the corridor, past our cabin. "They'll all be up cranking the engines so now's our chance." She opened a door marked "*Speicherzimmer*" and pulled me inside. It was a very narrow room, lined with shelves filled with bedding and gear, ending with a metal ladder. Up she went, pushing open a hatch in the ceiling. "Come on or we'll miss them." Bright daylight rained down from above.

Climbing out on the gondola roof, surrounded by a forest of cables, the zeppelin's silver envelope above us stretched away in each direction as far as I could see. Crawling over to the edge, we could see the terminal, and there, I could see Ma and Pa! We waved and they saw us and waved back! I swear Tinker was bent over laughing. I also saw that snooty woman from the store. Apparently she had missed the flight, which was fine by me.

The zeppelin's engines were shuddering to life one by one, each settling into its own particular drone, the deck unsteady under us. We were free of the ground.

"We better get down now. They'll be back along here any minute," Aleta said.

"Aye aye."

Scrambling down the hatch and ladder, Aleta popped her head out the corridor door, glancing both ways.

"All clear," she said.

Our dresses were a little dusty and we brushed ourselves off as best we could, laughing like only the naughty can, when an elderly couple walked by us, which wasn't easy in a narrow zeppelin corridor. The man looked confused, but his wife had a little smile. Perhaps she was remembering when she was young.

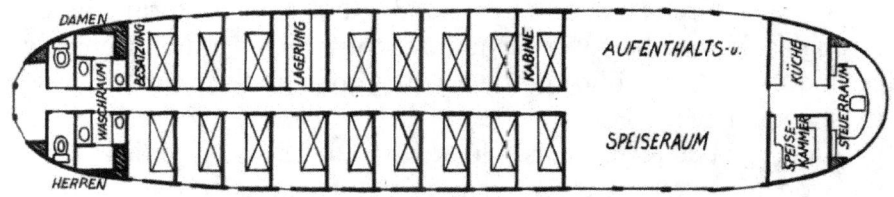

Chapter 5 – The First Day

We were back in the lounge, the windows crowded. We found room at the ones facing away from the terminal. The shoreline was already way below us as we passed over Apple Island.

"*Alle Passagiere bitte berichten zur Esszimmer. Les passagers sont priés de se présenter au salon.* All passengers please report to the lounge." A thin crewwoman, girl really, since she was perhaps fourteen, in a crisp powder blue uniform was walking down the cabin corridor and into the lounge, calling in high piping German, French, and English. "Please feel free to sit. We have seats for all."

Someone was knocking on cabin doors. "The Captain would like to greet you."

Aleta and I plunked down on one of the little couches. There was just room for two. Everything was so beautiful, and entirely unshiplike. The lacy patterns in the carpet, the scrollwork in the thin wood furniture, the stamped roses in the tin ceiling, the rapidly shifting sunlight as we turned! You can't see me smile because I wasn't. It was all too amazing!

"I wonder if I'll know him." Aleta whispered.

"Know who?" I replied, but she didn't hear.

The lounge had become quite crowded, with the passenger voices overcoming the drone of the engines. We had one empty seat, I suppose for that awful woman. A pale looking man was sitting on the edge of the couch across from us with his wife, clutching a paper bag. He didn't look well. She was rubbing his shoulders. And the deck was hardly moving at all! We had passengers like him on the trip home from the Congo. They are a test of patience.

A short, thin man with a beard and a dark blue uniform entered through a door in the bow side of the room, which was unfortunately behind us. He was followed by a young man and woman. I had to twist about to see.

Aleta gripped my arm and I looked at her. She was smiling. Then the woman following the Captain's eyes lit up as she saw us and nodded in our direction with a little smile.

"It's Helga!" Aleta whispered.

The Captain addressed us in German, translated by the two very young flight attendants into French and English, which was weird. Hearing French and English at the same time was confusing.

"Good morning ladies and gentlemen. I'm Captain Mathy and I want to welcome you aboard Lufthansa Flight TZ 113. We'll be stopping in London and Brussels before our final destination, Berlin. We expect to reach London in approximately three days, depending on wind, which should be fairly steady according to ship reports and seasonal average. Please take this time to get settled. We will be closing the lounge at 11:45 for fifteen minutes to set it up for lunch."

"We understand that some of you may not have experienced electric light. Be assured that it is completely harmless, however we request that you restrain yourself from turning the lamps on or off unnecessarily, as this causes the bulbs to burn out prematurely. If you need help with their operation, do not be afraid to call a steward or stewardess."

"Lunch will begin at 12:00. Notice the clock on the wall above me. It will be adjusted at midnight as we cross time zones. The sign below shows the amount of adjustment. Use it to set your watches before bed. Thank you," he said, ending with a slight tip of the head. Then they retired again to the crew compartment.

"Time zones!" I laughed. "Two every day!"

"Yes. People always miss breakfast because of them," she replied. "And there's always someone who doesn't believe they exist," she added with a sigh.

"So who is Helga?" I asked.

"She was crew with me, but she's an officer now, an engineer. She works on the engines." She looked wistful.

"If you had stuck around, would you be one too?"

"No. I grew. Size and weight are very important. I'm too big now to fit into some of the crawlways and I weigh too much. Helga was always small and it's best if you can keep yourself under a hundred and five pounds."

"I don't even know how much I weigh," I said, frowning.

"You're small, but still too big."

We moved to one of the windows facing away from the shore. Those windows were crowded with people. With everyone on one side, I wondered if it made the floor tip like a boat. I suspected we were too big for it to show, but air doesn't pull at you as much as water does. Beneath us, the ocean rolled by, smooth and pale blue in the morning's silver haze. I saw a few passing sails and a steamship or two. It was fun seeing them from above, their white decks and sails laid open like a deck plan. On the horizon we could see clouds too, and we were climbing to meet them, which was definitely something I was looking forward to. When you see clouds from the ground, they look like huge castles and mountains. I had always wanted to fly up and sit among them, and here I was!

They brought out tea and crackers, set out on thin aluminum plates on the buffet table. They didn't have saucers. Instead we held paper napkins under the delicate, white, porcelain flat bottomed cups, each with the yellow Lufthansa bird on them. The napkin paper was thin and spongy. Not like writing paper at all. I wanted to keep one of the tea cups, but really, they wouldn't last a minute onboard Red. How did they manage to wash them without them breaking?

Max vanished back into his cabin after the announcements. When the time for lunch came, they shooed us all out. They could have left me there at the window. I wouldn't have been any trouble. I could have sat in that window all day, but instead they pushed us all back into the corridor. Many people stayed to watch them change the furniture, but the corridor was too narrow and clogged with other watchers, the back windows too. Aleta could see but I couldn't, the curse of being short.

Our airship had women's and men's restrooms. I used the *Toilette Damen*, but I had to wait in line. Like everything, it was very small. It didn't flush well either. Not enough water, and I had to go to the next room to wash in the *Washraum Damen*. This we could not use alone. We had two brass and polished wood sinks and a little stall you could use to dribble water on yourself, all dimly lit with electric light. I supposed it was for washing. Aleta explained that they tried to balance water usage with air temperature and gas loss. Depending on altitude, air temperature, and gas loss, the water pressure would improve.

Explorations over, it was time for lunch. They put tables in between the sofas and chairs, and opened wings on the buffet table. We had premade sandwiches, cut in triangles, and tea. Some of them were great. Who thought of putting carrots in sandwiches? It was good! A couple beat us to our couch and the window seats were taken, so we sat at a two person table against the forward bulkhead. I saw Max and he nodded and smiled back at us as he walked past. Afterwards they gave us more tea and cookies.

I saw that girl again as well, across the room at a table with the older man with the blond hair, who had to be her father. The dark haired man sat nearby, his eyes still darting about. She nodded when she saw me looking, so I smiled and nodded back. She looked sullen and bored. Max was sitting with that man with the pencil mustache. They seemed to know each other, yet they didn't seem to be enjoying their conversation.

"These were made before we boarded," Aleta said, catching my attention. "Tomorrow, they'll be cooking for us. We'll be smelling it all over the ship." I could see several passengers were seasick, or I guess in this case it would be airsick. One had to leave the room. Three days would be a long time to go without being able to hold down food. Longer if they were continuing on past London. The smell of cooking would make it worse.

"People will be sick," I said.

"I had to clean up a lot of that." She rolled her eyes.

"But now you're a passenger."

"It's really strange," she smiled. "You know, I've never sat at the tables."

"Not even when you were setting them up?"

"There wasn't time. But I still miss being crew."

I thought of Red. I would miss her, but I tried to be brave and smile.

"So what do people do on these trips?" I asked.

"To pass the time?"

Having never been on a trip anywhere where I didn't have to pump or stand watches, it seemed an obvious question. "Yes."

"Play cards, read, collect signatures, talk, stare at the ground . . ."

"Collect signatures?" I interrupted.

"Definitely. The passenger handbooks have blank pages. You get passengers and crew, when you can catch them, to write messages and sign them. It's a souvenir of the trip. It helps you meet people too so . . . so you can play cards with them, and talk."

"Oh."

Aleta drifted for a second, then perked up. "I should warn you! We might be asked to play. I'm sure they saw our instrument cases. Do you want to, if they ask?"

"Sure. I suppose."

"It will be fun."

After lunch, we played old maid with an elderly couple, Mr. and Mrs. Dreyer. He had a line of four enameled pins on his lapel, little zeppelins. They were crossing pins. Apparently, Lufthansa gives you one each time you cross the Atlantic. The Dreyers were retired and liked to vacation in Europe. They owned a lot of dairy farms and milk processing plants. When they heard we were musicians, as Aleta had predicted, they politely asked if we could play some evening. We replied we would if they wanted us to. Everyone brought what entertainment they could to the lounge as there was very little provided. I got my first signature, Mrs. Dreyer drawing a pair of dancing cows in my book!

Helga dropped by after lunch. Aleta and I were sitting at a small table, watching the clouds go by, playing cards with a deck we found left out. Clouds are, by the way, even more incredible from above than they are from below. Your dreaming is not wasted. They're everything you can think of and more.

"*Rose, ich wusste es war sie,*" she said, as she pulled up a chair beside us.

Aleta beamed. "Helga, I missed you too." And they hugged.

"Helga, this is Cali," she said, introducing us.

"Hello Cali. It is very nice to meet you."

I loved her German accent. It made me want one too.

"You are travelling together?" Helga asked.

"We are," Aleta said. "We're going to Brussels, to school."

"To the Royal Conservatory for Music," I added.

Aleta rolled her eyes, but Helga seemed impressed.

"*Ooo, ser schön,*" she said. She took Aleta's hand. "I was so worried for you when you left. Nothing but a bag and your flute."

"I don't have much more now," Aleta replied.

"But we have now the whole crossing. That is something. You must the places tell me you have been. This evening I have rest time."

"You have to go?" I asked.

"Yes, we have a problem engine. Something blocking *der Krümmer* I think. *Vermutlich Karbon.* I told them to inspect it, but they did not. The schedule. They are all running a little rough." She sighed and shook her head. "The work never stops," she said, her voice trailing away melodramatically. "I must change clothes." Then she laughed. "I will drop by when I am done," she said, and we said goodbye. She got up briskly and headed toward the corridor, but not before she signed several books in passing.

"Where's she going?" I asked.

"To the crew compartment."

"Can we see it?" I was curious.

"No, someone would see us and it's always occupied. They sleep in three shifts. Besides, it's three bunks and a lot of dirty clothes."

"The men and women together?"

"I'm afraid so. Honestly, when you finally make it to your bunk at the end of your shift, you're too tired to care."

"Sounds like a ship," I said.

"It is," she replied flatly, as if that should be obvious.

Then we were joined by that girl I told you about. She plunked herself down and said, "Deal me in." She had a Scottish accent, which is at least as interesting as a German one.

There was that young dark haired man sitting near a window with a cup of tea, watching us. He followed her in.

"Don't mind him," she said. She had seen me staring. "He's here to watch Da and me."

"Da?" Aleta asked. "Oh, my name is Aleta."

"Cali," I added.

"Vic."

"Vic?" I asked.

"Don't call me Victoria, or Vicky, or I'll deck you," she firmly replied. "My Da's a research chemist. They're always watching him. What is this? Old Maid?"

Aleta tossed down her hand. "Let's redeal," she said.

"Not enough for whist," Vic mumbled, looking around.

"Whist?" I asked.

"Then again, maybe not," Vic said with a frown. "Do you know pharaoh?"

"Vic," Aleta replied. "All our money is in the safe."

"That's no fun," Vic said, smiling to herself. "We could play for credit."

"Perhaps," Aleta said.

"Hell?" Vic suggested. "That isn't gambling."

Aleta looked confused, so I said, "You must have a lot of time on your hands."

Vic flopped back in her chair with a groan. "Oh! You have no idea. All I do is sit in the back of lecture halls or get pestered by tutors."

"We work on a sailing ship, a schooner," I said.

"That sounds like fun," she said, warming a bit, sitting up.

"It is," I said.

"You're sailors?" Vic asked.

"My family owns a ship," I replied.

"I thought you were musicians."

"You can be both," Aleta answered.

"You're sailors and you don't gamble?"

"I'm afraid so," Aleta said. "No tattoos either."

"I suppose I should learn," I said, thinking about Mme. Verbeeck and that game in the Congo.

"Poker then," Vic said, with a shark-like smile. "Only, we need chips." She started looking about.

We ended up cutting up sheets of notepad paper with borrowed scissors, and I did not win. Vic had to give me all my chips back twice. She constantly stopped to explain how I should have played my hand differently. The idea of odds was both intriguing and mind numbing. I thought wistfully about math and wished I could ask Mrs. Johnson about it. But then again, she probably would have been aghast at the idea of her young women gambling.

Vic's ma was dead and she and her da lived in Cambridge, which is about fifty miles north of London. She went with her father to work at Magdalene Hall most days, where she had to sit in a library or out on the lawn with her tutor. Her da worked a lot so she often stayed at the university late and was free to wander. Wander down into the dining hall where there was almost always cards and chess. She was the unofficial mascot of the all-male school.

A girl crewmember finally dropped by our table to ask about our performing later, and we said yes. Helga did not come back that afternoon as she had promised.

That evening Max sat with us at dinner. Our fourth, apparently another friend of Max's, was a French woman named Emma Calvé, who spoke English. She had a beautiful dress, split front with embroidered crème ruffles and little pink silk roses at the sleeves and collar. She was a singer, coming from a job in New York. She was going to school in Paris, taking lessons, just like us!

"I heard that you two will be performing tonight," she said.

"I can vouch that Cali is very good," Max said. "This will be the first time I've gotten to hear Aleta, but I look forward to it." He smiled at Aleta.

"I caught dengue fever," Aleta said.

"I had to perform alone," I added.

"Oh my." Emma looked surprised, then said to Aleta, "And you're alive."

"I hope so. We have to perform," she answered, which got a laugh.

"It was scary."

"I don't remember much of it," Aleta added.

"Your parents are sending you to school?" Max asked me, changing the subject.

"No. Do you remember Mme. Verbeeck?"

"The friend of the Duke of Tervuren?"

"Yes. She's sending us."

"But she died."

"It was in her will."

"Very nice of her. A surprise, as she knew you for so little time."

"Max!" Mme. Calvé exclaimed.

"I can't think of a polite way to pose the question," Max replied, shrugging.

"Then you shouldn't."

"Very true. I apologize," Max replied, bobbing his head toward us. "May I ask, which school?"

"The Royal Conservatory for Music in Brussels."

"In Belgium. Interesting."

"Mme. Verbeeck was Belgian." I don't know why I felt defensive.

"Naturally," Max said, a little lost in thought. "That explains all."

Mme. Calvé gave Max a little frown. "It will be France's loss," she said.

"And Germany's as well," Max added.

That evening we performed. Everyone came out to hear, even Helga, and we had a good time. Some people even dressed formally! Helga came in after we had started and stood in the back. She looked happy, that was until a crewman came in and talked to her. She nodded her head and they left quickly. I signed nineteen books, two from crew! They waited as I signed each one!

Chapter 6 – The Second Day

At breakfast the captain announced that our arrival in London would be delayed due to engine problems. Passengers asked him when we would arrive, but he said he couldn't be sure. It depended on the weather, but that we wouldn't be more than ten or twelve hours late. Our three day flight was now four and there was no sign of Helga.

Eggs, scrambled, fresh bread, kippers, coffee, tea, and . . . orange juice! This was perhaps the third time in my life that I'd had it. I asked for olive oil for my bread and got it too.

Mme. Calvé joined us at our table, and naturally we talked about the delay.

"These things happen," she said, shrugging it away. "I was once caught in a storm."

"Those can be very frightening," Aleta said. She would know.

"Oh yes. There was lightning! It delayed us too. A whole day."

"So you've made the crossing before?" I asked.

"This is my sixth."

"So many," I said.

"They're so much better than boats." Then she leaned forward. "I need to ask you two something."

"What?" Aleta leaned forward and whispered back.

"They want me to sing tonight," she said. "But I've no accompaniment."

Aleta looked at me and I looked back.

"Sure," I said.

"Yes. It will be lovely," Aleta added.

Mme. Calvé had some work she needed to attend to and wanted to think about which songs she would like to do, so we agreed to practice after lunch.

After breakfast, over at the card table we were playing Old Maid again. Vic took one look and left in disgust. She had a book from the aerodrome bookshelf, *The Moonstone*, which she said was readable. Mr. Dreyer, the experienced flyer, told everyone as he drew from my hand that he and Mrs. Dreyer experienced engine trouble before and that it was nothing to worry about, but it meant they had less time in London. Mrs. Dreyer was disappointed. She had been hoping for a stopover.

"Engines are finicky things," he said, as he put down a pair. "We use them on our farms, but with all the expense and trouble, you have to wonder if they're worth it."

"You know they are, dear," Mrs. Dreyer said. "We can never go back to the way we used to do things."

"What? Slaves?" Mr. Dreyer said. "Well, yes. I suppose so," he mumbled.

I liked the Dreyers quite a bit less after that.

Gunfire! They were coming down the hill, great screaming gray boulders, tusks glinting like steel bayonets in the sunlight. I raised my rifle and shot, cocked and shot again, shooting until it was empty. But they kept coming and coming! Then the hands, stick thin, grabbing at me and pulling while I fought.

"Stop it. Cali! Wake up!"

It was light.

"Cali, wake up!"

I had been trying to run, but the covers were wound around me and I was tangled, which was good. Zeppelin walls were so thin I might have kicked a hole in one. I let my arms drop to the bed. There was Aleta, trying to hold me down.

"Wake up," she said.

I had stopped struggling, but I was crying.

"Oh, Cali," she said.

It took me a moment to realize it was Aleta. It can be like that after my dreams. I was awake, but why hadn't the gunfire stopped? I looked around, confused.

"What is that?" I managed to get out, still crying.

"It's one of the motors," Aleta said. She sounded distressed. "I think they're trying to start it. I should have woken you."

There was a knocking on the door. "Miss, miss, is everything alright?"

"We're fine," Aleta called back.

"Can we bring you anything?" the man's voice asked.

"No. We're fine," Aleta said.

"Oh God, everyone heard me," I moaned.

"Probably," she sighed. "Don't worry. We dealt with this sort of thing all the time." She looked toward the window. "That motor doesn't sound good, though."

We sat for a moment while I calmed down. I pulled a handkerchief out from under my pillow.

"Do you think they could use help?" I asked.

"They're always shorthanded, but they would never ask, let alone allow a passenger to help, especially up top."

"Even ex-crew?"

"Even ex-crew," she said.

I took a shaking breath. "I'm going to take a bath." I'd fallen asleep reading despite the coffee at breakfast.

"Are you going to be all right?"

I managed to smile and nod as I wiped my tears. I was a mess, my dress damp with sweat. It was definitely time to brave the washroom. Ma had bought me a *nightrobe*. They're halfway between a coat and a nightdress. I hadn't worn mine since we tried them on in the store and this was the time it was meant for. Pushing off the tangle of covers, I rolled out of the bed. Feet on the deck, first rubbing my eyes, then pulling out my trunk. There it was, still folded from the store. I doubted I'd get it back in so neatly.

Padding down the echoing corridor in my slippers, another first and kind of useless too. Perhaps if it got cold, I thought. I opened the *Badezimmer Frauen* door and found inside two ladies occupying the sinks, but the shower empty. Doffing my robe, bodice, and bloomers, I climbed into the little stall.

"Warn her about the water," one of them said, in French.

"Careful," the other lady called from outside. "The water is cold."

"It's okay," I called back in French. "We bathe in cold water all the time. It'll feel good." I thought we were supposed to have had warm water.

"She speaks French. How nice," the first woman said.

The water was cold. "Not well, I'm afraid," I replied.

"Nonsense, and with an American accent. How interesting," the second lady said. "Americans never speak French, at least not that I've heard before."

"They do in Canada," I replied.

"They do? Well then, they never visit."

I had the worst time getting my hair clean under that dribble of water. The washroom was empty when I finished. Odd, until I realized I was going to miss lunch. I am though, in addition to being a woman of poise and wit, a quick dresser.

We had sausage, sauerkraut, potatoes, leftover morning bread, tea, and beer. I tried the beer, but didn't like it. Aleta had saved me a seat. That tall thin man with the awful thin moustache was sitting across from us.

He opened the conversation.

"You two are very good musicians," he said. "Last night was lovely."

Was that a French accent, I thought? Aleta and I mumbled our thanks.

"Are you professionals?" he continued.

"We're going to music school in Brussels," I replied, in French.

"Really? Which one?" he replied in French too, but with that weird accent.

"Excuse me," I continued in English, because Aleta was frowning. "But you're not French?"

"No," he replied. "I'm Canadian."

I smiled. "There are two women here you need to meet."

"Yes, well," he said with odd reluctance. "Perhaps later."

"We're going to the Royal Conservatory," Aleta added. I think she felt left out.

"Oh, you are!" said the lady who sat down next to him. In American English, by the way. "Well, I'm not surprised."

"Thank you," I replied. "Are you on vacation?"

"We are," she replied with a smile. "We're going to England for a month. My husband, Mr. Jefferies, has a business there. I'm sorry, but I don't know your names."

"Cali. Calista Carmichael."

"Aleta," she added. "It's a pleasure."

"And yours?" I asked.

"Amanda Jefferies," she replied.

"And I don't believe we've been introduced," I said, to the pencil mustached man.

"Oh, that's true. I'm so sorry. Jules Comeau. I'm a salesman. But I feel like I've heard of you. You played in the Canaries and the Congo before the revolution."

I was floored speechless!

"Why would you have heard that?" Aleta replied, coming to my defense. She was frowning.

"It was in the papers, at least the London ones. They claim this Carmichael woman was some sort of seductress spy. Quite scandalous. Seduced a Belgian prince. Led a revolution."

He must have seen the look of confusion in my eyes.

"But I can see you obviously aren't her," he continued. I thought he looked a bit confused as well. "I can't see how you could possibly be her."

"That's nonsense," Aleta said. "Do you have one of these papers?"

"No. I was reading it back at the terminal."

We had flown into a rain storm while we were talking, the raindrops tapping the windows. I noticed the windows suddenly go gray as we flew into cloud, the water drops leaving streaks down them. People were oohing and awing at the view, but all I could see was gray.

We had to perform that night, so we were in Mme. Calvé's cabin. Her roommate, Frau Abbink, had left to give us room. Frau Abbink is a rich widower who likes to travel. She had a big trunk, almost as tall as me which took up the place where the desk folded down.

"She keeps half the world in there," Mme. Calvé said. "Apparently she rarely goes home."

We were sitting on Mme. Calvé's trunk and Frau Abbink's bed, the lower bunk.

"She paid extra for its weight," Aleta said.

"Oh she does," Mme. Calvé replied. "She even has a first aid kit. If you have a headache or need something bandaged, come to our cabin." Then she smiled and looked at the trunk. "If we crash, I'm looking forward to using it as a boat."

Trust me when I tell you that although I gave it serious thought later, it wouldn't work.

Mme. Calvé is an opera singer. She sang in several operas in both France and Belgium, which posed a problem for us. She had a folder of music, just like me, but they were operas. They all required at least a piano, if not a full orchestra. We had only a violin and a flute and no time to study new works. How could we reduce *Foust* to flute and violin in an afternoon? We didn't know any of them and she certainly didn't know any sea shanties, but she had grown up poor in Spain and had studied in the town square on summer evenings as a child. When she talked about it her accent changed and her eyes grew distant. As we worked, humming tunes, we realized that we knew many of the same songs. They had different names and she only knew them in Spanish.

She sang and we hummed along, eyes closed, our fingers twitching, and I forgot all about the newspaper, thinking instead of Cadiz, oranges, and warm summer breezes.

The storm meant that the crew were all inside and therefore able to pay more attention to the passengers, and sign a lot of books. They set up the tables early so they could plug in the table lamps to augment the dim outside light and many people came out to curl up near the windows. Even some of the airsick ones. They sat with their blankets, leaning their heads against the bulkheads, at least when they could, and looked out the gray streaked windows. That was until the smell of dinner began to drift about. Then they vanished. We asked about Helga, but they said she was asleep.

That evening we had wine, thin sliced ham, two soups, fruits, warm breads, cheese, and pretty little cakes that someone called petit fours, and, of course, coffee. We sat across from two elderly men, one of which was making eyes at me. At least I think he was making eyes at me. It could have been a tick. It's hard to tell with old men. At least he only ticked when he was looking at me. It was hard not to laugh. He wanted to know all about me so I suppose I had a fan. His name was Mr. Harmon.

The other was M. Marmontel, who said he was a music teacher in Paris. The good thing for me about M. Marmontel was that he didn't speak English, which left Mr. Eyes out of our conversation. Sadly, Aleta had to take up the slack with him.

"Pardon, but I must ask. Are you self-taught?" M. Marmontel asked. I had to translate.

Aleta blinked, then answered hesitantly, "Yes."

"Amazing."

She broke out in a smile.

"I can play it backwards too. Just not every note," she said, at which he smiled.

"Can you sight read?"

This is where Aleta lost her smile. "No."

Then he lost his. "You should see to that."

"Yes."

Like we've had any time to work on that!

M. Marmontel liked my music as well, although he was of the opinion that I lacked discipline and training. I replied that my teacher would agree. He had friends I might like to meet if ever I found the atmosphere in Belgium too stuffy and he even gave us his card, my first. M. Marmontel had been in New York to visit friends and his U.S. publisher. He writes music! I sadly told him that I had none of his music in my folder, but he didn't mind. He mostly writes for the piano.

A Bad Crossing

We had an hour after dinner before we were to perform so I sat in the common room and cracked open Kidnapped, but it was kind of depressing. It's hard to sit around and read about bad things that happen to somebody in a story over and over again. You know it will get better, eventually, but it makes for tough going.

Then, thankfully, we popped out of the storm and just like that the sky lit up with a big silver moon. I jumped up and went to the window. We had left a wall of clouds and were crossing a vast white canyon. Down and forward there was a round silver ring visible arcing from the side of our shadow in the clouds. And through gaps in the silver white clouds, I could see dark patches of ocean below. It looked rough. The clouds were beyond beautiful, their shadows black, showing their every bump and curve. It had been wise of me to jump up when I did. The windows became a bit crowded moments later.

Vic stood next to me, watching too, and said she wanted to try again to teach me poker. Aleta is pretty good at it and I think I could be. It's really about thinking about what's left and what's possible, balancing it against what you want. That and lying. Lying a lot! Then laughing about it afterwards, even if you lose. Which I do a lot. Lose that is. It's odd, but I think Max was watching while I was playing. I think several people were. More than just Mr. Letch.

Helga was there that evening when we performed, in the back leaning against the wall. She was smiling and Aleta beamed. It was uncomfortable at first, but when we relaxed it was like playing in the town square. Calves' accent thickened, and became looser. She even danced a bit as she sang. Our music rolled around her like the skirts of a flamenco dancer. She seemed genuinely happy as was our audience. M. Marmontel was there, watching with a certain intensity, which made me nervous. I tried not to look at him.

Afterwards I actually signed more books! Helga sat with us. I listened to her and Aleta's stories until I was simply too tired to keep my eyes open, despite the coffee.

Chapter 7 – The Third Day

After breakfast I was leaning over the sink, trying to get clean with that dribble of water, feeling depressed and worried. I really needed to find one of these newspapers. The only papers I'd seen onboard were old. But that isn't the important part of the story. Well it's important, but not yet. It's what happened next. It was one of those, *"wouldn't you know it?"* things. My face was covered in soap and I was trying to splash it off when the explosions started.

There was a distant, deep, sharp, report, and the cabin swayed and all I could do was fumble around for a towel!

But, I'm not just any woman, the kind who panics in the face of crisis. I finished with proper grace. When I tried to push the door open, I found it blocked by a man standing in the hallway. He grunted and pushed forward against the crowd as I pushed out and past him. It was Mr. Dreyer, by the way. I regret I didn't push him harder – keeping slaves!

Outside, the corridor was full of people all talking in their various languages and no crewmen in sight. Looking about, I noticed that the back windows with the best view were free. That's how confused people were. I elbowed my way over and grabbed a spot before they all realized what they were missing and rushed the windows.

The envelope of the zeppelin stretched away behind us, the engines lined up along each side. The second port engine was a ball of fire. Then, as I watched, the one on the starboard side, right next to us started burning as well. Then the first one exploded! The pane of glass on my right cracked and something hit the wall behind me, but most of the shrapnel hit the lounge. I heard glass shattering and people yelling and panicking from down the corridor.

Looking around the edge of the window frame, I could see flames jetting out the engine sides. All its coverings had come off. Then smoke and flames starting coming out of the engine on the port side next to us as well. It wasn't more than 40 feet away! We were right next to it! I yelled, "Everybody down!" and ducked just as it exploded, as if ducking and the cabin walls were any protection! New morning sunshine streamed in the holes that riddled the walls and ceiling of the gondola all around me. A hot piece of metal, a ricochet, had fallen on my dress and started to burn it. I had to shake it off. People were screaming and falling, and the floor was rocking, the gondola frame creaking. I could hear the roar of the flames over the wind whistling through the shattered windows.

As I stood, pieces of broken glass from the window above me fell from my hair and dress. I stood and bent, shaking my hair to get rid of as much as I could. In a daze I made my way toward the cockpit, but before I could go far, I saw an elderly woman on the floor bleeding badly. It was Mrs. Kappel! I remembered her from dinner. No one was helping her. It was her side. A kidney I thought. Not good.

"Is there a doctor here?" I yelled, just as the third engine exploded.

Something hit the man standing above me and spun him around, shoving him down into the sprawl of bodies. Aleta bounded past me from our cabin, on her way toward the cockpit. Everyone had been knocked down by the blast, many were yelling, some were bleeding. I yelled again, but I doubt anyone could have heard me.

I knelt down by Mrs. Kappel. Her hand gripped my arm while I tried to press her wound, but couldn't get it to stop bleeding. It was soaking her dress. She kept bleeding between my fingers! I couldn't hold it back. Then her husband was there, lifting her head. He was calling to her, but she wasn't listening. Someone gently pushed me aside and I was sitting there on the floor, in the glass, my hands bloody. I swear I heard gunfire and saw flames, but only for a moment. I blinked it away.

"Miss Carmichael," said a woman's voice. She had a Southern accent.

I looked up at her. She was kneeling next to me. It took a moment to figure out who she was.

"Are you still with us?" she said. I remembered her. Older, maybe thirty. Straight brownish golden hair. She often sat in the corner with her needlepoint.

"I'm okay," I said, although my voice may have sounded a little shrill.

Vic came up behind her. "Cali, you need to wash your hands," Vic said. She frowned at them with obvious distaste and perhaps a little fear.

"That might be a good idea," the woman added with a slight smile. She was wearing a plain but prim dress with low heels, clutching her sewing bag to her chest.

I looked myself over. I was a mess. Blood had gotten everywhere.

"Yes. I will," I said. But getting up was hard. My legs were stiff. The corridor was no longer strewn with bodies, many people having moved to the chairs while they gathered their wits. The breeze was cool. It felt good as I stood and made my way to the sinks, which were very busy. I washed my hands and dress standing in the shower. The blood took a little scrubbing. I supposed some time had passed. Then I headed forward again, toward the cockpit, the air now cold, doubly so in my wet dress.

The lounge was a shambles; most of the windows broken. People were hurt, sitting in the seats in various stages of shock. The floor was covered in blood and glass. At least the breakfast gear had been stowed and most of the tables taken down. A few people were crouched at the windows despite all the wounded and the broken glass to watch the flames and smoke. But amongst it all, there was an elderly man and woman helping the hurt. He was working on a tall thin gentleman with a nasty shoulder wound, maybe even a lung judging by the location, a bad place to get hit. Trust me. You don't want air to get loose inside you. But the man was still in shock. I don't think he knew he was wounded. The older man helping him was trying to get him to sit down.

They must be doctors, I thought. At least I hoped they were. The sign above the cockpit door said, "EINGANG IST VERBOTEN," which, I think, is pretty clear even if you don't know German, but I could hear Aleta inside so I went in.

On the left was a kitchen and on the right, a pantry. Straight ahead was the cockpit. All their windows but one undamaged, and it was only cracked. They faced away from the engines. Under the windows were panels with dials, levers, and lights, many of which were red. On the sides, desks were strewn with charts and open books. In front was a control seat and a couple of chairs. Sitting in one of the control seats, holding a tiller that poked through the floor, was the captain. Standing next to him arguing in German was Aleta. She looked up as I came in.

"Cali, you shouldn't be here," she snapped.

"Neither should you," I replied.

"Something's gone wrong and I can help. I could, except for these pig-headed German rules."

The captain growled something in German, tied off the tiller, stood, and yelled at us to leave, finger pointing at the door. He was quite clear, even without my knowing German. As we were leaving, Aleta furious, we ran into several others who were coming forward to see the Captain. We tried to shoo them back, but they were having none of it and barged right past us.

Outside, we availed ourselves of now empty seats, sweeping the glass off before we sat. Mine was stained with blood, but then so was my dress. I sighed and sat, then looked at Aleta questioningly.

"The captain told me it was a blowout," she replied.

"A blowout?"

"They do that occasionally," she said, with a matter-of-fact wave of her hand. "They run at the very limit of what steel can stand. If it will make you feel better, you can think of it as having popped. But these were the biggest blowouts I've ever heard of. And one engine is a blowout. Three is something else."

"Are we going to crash?" I asked.

"No, we still have three engines," she replied.

"Two," I said.

Aleta frowned. "Two. That's right. One's broken."

"Is that important?"

"It depends on the wind," she said. "It will be hard to hold course."

"What if we lose them too?"

"If we have warning, then we can generate more gas, but normally we have to keep moving forward to stay up."

"So we would crash."

"Yes," she said.

Then we heard a yelp and exclamations from the corridor. A blond haired crewman ran through the lounge toward the cockpit door in blue overalls. He had more than burn and grease stains on his uniform. There was blood. He had been hurt, but was still working! And since the door was unlocked and open, several passengers decided to barge in after.

I realized I was cold. I suppose I was finally shaking off the shock. The wind was blowing through the broken windows and my dress was damp. I must have tried to wash out some of the blood stains, but at the time I couldn't remember. I hid my hands down under me in the seat. They'd been shaking.

It was strange but the lounge seemed like it was lit with an otherworldly light. Someone was calling from the corridor that they needed help. An elderly woman got up and walked toward the voice. Mrs. Kappel, who'd been sitting in a chair, got up too to follow but I was pretty sure she was a ghost.

The breeze blew around us, slowly flipping the pages of a book left in the seat across from us. We could hear yelling in the cockpit but in the lounge people were just standing or sitting. It was quiet. Only an elderly woman crying quietly to herself in the corner.

"We need to do something to help. I wonder if they have some coffee," I said. Warm coffee would nice. Maybe a coat would be a good idea too.

"Maybe he might let us make some," Aleta said. "He might." She looked worried. "It might keep people calm."

"We should ask."

"Let's see if that fool of a captain will let us."

So it was back through the *verboten* doorway into a storm of yelling. The crewman was physically pushing passengers out. Quite a feat for so small a frame. He was pushing us too as Aleta rattled back at them in rapid German. The door had had just been shut in our face when it popped opened again. The crewman waved us back in.

"You are the musicians?" The crewman translated for the captain.

We nodded.

"You may make coffee," he said. "Calm them if you can. Play something after maybe. The ship is unsteady and I have to concentrate. They must stay out."

Then the crewman was arguing with him in German.

"*Dann nehmen Sie Ihre!*" He nodded toward Aleta.

"It's about time," Aleta said, with exasperation.

"*Jawohl.*" The crewman looked relieved. He turned to us. Pointing at me, interrupting Aleta's translation, he said to me in English, "You, make coffee." Then he turned to Aleta. "Follow me. We have to hurry."

"*Jawohl,*" Aleta said, and they ran off just like that, leaving Cali standing there clueless. At least it wasn't cold in the cockpit, and it was quiet.

I looked at the captain. "Sir? Do you speak English?" I asked, carefully.

"*Nein.*"

"*Parlez-vous français?*"

"Some," he replied in French.

"Where do you keep the coffee?" I asked in French

I found cookies, coffee, and tea in the pantry, and a big urn in the kitchen. The cookies were neat! They came in all sorts of colors and shapes and the stove had gas fire to heat things which made everything crazy easy. You just turned on the valve and lit it with a match. The urns clamped down on top of the burners so they couldn't tip. The matches, by the way, were very strange. They were made of paper and it was a trick to get them to strike. Once lit though, you could make the burner fire bigger and smaller by turning the valve. Ma would love this, I thought. So much better than coal. And it helped so much to be doing something, especially out of the cold. When people came in, I told them to wait outside and that we'd be having coffee and tea momentarily.

They locked their crockery down just like we did. Really, it was all like our galley on Red, only a whole lot better. All steel. I eyed the ovens with envy. They had bread rising, but they hadn't had time to punch them down and knead for the second rising. Easy!

I brought the first cup to the captain. He actually smiled. Then I couldn't haul it out fast enough for the passengers. I plunked the urn down on the buffet table along with plates of cookies and kept it coming.

I asked the captain what was planned for lunch. He tried to tell me, but it wasn't anything I recognized and he didn't know the French or English, so I improvised. I found vegetables and canned meat in the pantry. I tossed them in a pot with seasonings and made our old emergency standby -- stew and fresh bread. By the time the smell was getting around the ship, I had help, those two French ladies from the washroom.

"*Bonjour*," one said, sticking her head in the door. "I thought it was you in here," she said to me. "Do you need help?"

"Oh, yes please," I replied.

They tisked over my creation, but helped serve it anyway.

There was another explosion somewhere, not as bad, just as I was hauling out the stew pot. The deck tipped and swayed for a moment, but I rode with it, and landed the stew successfully on the table. Mrs. Kappel's body was gone. There was just a big puddle of dried blood on the floor. I had been so confused that I forgot that she died. The whole floor was a mess. Something needed to be done about that. The sharp smell of blood fought with the smell of the food.

But now I was worried about Aleta. I left the cooking for the French ladies. Grabbing a big piece of bread, I headed for the storeroom with the ladder. Vic intercepted me, grabbing my arm.

"Where are you going?" she asked. She had wisely gotten her coat.

"I have to check on Aleta," I said. "That last explosion. She might be hurt."

"She's out there?" She looked incredulous.

"She's ex-zeppelin crew and they needed help. Come on."

I barged by her, she following me through the storeroom to the ladder.

"You're out of your mind and you're going to get in trouble," she said.

"Probably," I replied. "But I'm just going to look."

The hatch was already open to the wind. It was blowing at my back as I looked down the length of the airship. My hair blew loose. My tortoise shell comb Ma had bought me in Cadiz was gone, blown away! Above me the envelope stretched away into the blue like a huge roof. It was too big to be believed. The engines nearby were blackened and dead, trailing smoke. The cloth covering on the underside of the envelope had burned and torn too, the wind pulling bigger tears in it, exposing more pipes and superstructure as I watched. Inside, I could see the gas cells, their strangely thin skins rippling in the wind.

In between, up in the belly of the envelope was a piece of machinery connected to a block of vertical metal tubes, like rows of sausages. Fire was streaming out it, blowing back along the tubes. Up above was Aleta, right above the fire, dangling below some hatch in a harness, frantically pulling on a wrench, swaying back and forth with each pull. Hanging upside down next to her was the blond crewman passing her tools.

Then I saw the bodies. Two of them, dangling in their harnesses out in empty space above me, below one of the blackened engines. One of them moved!

"What do you see?" Vic called from down in the store room.

I saw a ladder going up, anchored dead center of the gondola.

"Someone's hurt!" I called back. Then I dashed up through the hatch.

Vic yelped, "Are you crazy?"

I danced across the top of the gondola in the cold wind to the ladder, my day skirt blowing around me. Vic stuck her head up through the hatch.

"Come on!" I called, hand on the ladder. I could see a cloud passing down the length of the ship as we flew through it. We were turning into the wind, the big flaps on the stern were bent.

Vic's eyes were wide as she took in the scene. She shook her head no.

I sighed, then climbed. The cloud hit half way up, surrounding me in fog. My stupid shoes were no good here. Everything was damp. Bare feet are always best on unsafe decks, so I stopped at the top to pull them and my socks off, leaving them on the catwalk. Then I was running down the catwalk, which was made of woven wire mesh, by the way. It was really very clever and probably saved a lot of weight. I could see the sea below my feet through breaks in the cloud, the skin of the airship having been burned away or peeled back. It would have been pretty if it weren't for the cold and fright.

The catwalk was up inside what was left of the envelope, up where the wind wasn't so bad. At least my skirt mostly stayed down, probably because it was still damp. Do I really need to say anything about the foolishness of skirts?

Ahead was the glow of the fire from the burning tube things, lighting the fog. I turned right toward the burnt engine. The catwalk ended in a ladder that sloped down to an engine platform. Most of engine's covering was gone. The ones left reminded me of bug shells. One of them creaked and groaned as it pulled away, flipping past while I was climbing down, tumbling down over and over, falling toward the ocean. The engine rested on a small piece of deck, its big square block sitting in the center making popping noises. It was hot and I couldn't touch it and there was little else other than the ladder and some steel ribbing to hold on to. I had only the empty edges of the platform itself.

The crewmen had been dangling below, so I looked for their ropes, but they didn't use rope, cleats, or belaying pins either. They used metal cable attached with spring clips. How do you hold on to metal cable? Not with your hands. They'd clipped onto anchor places, loops of welded metal. Looking down over the edge, I could see the crewmen swinging in the wind and nothing else but the deeps far below. I yelled, but it was no use. I could see no movement. Only burn and blood. Looking about I found a hand winch bolted to the deck at the base of the engine and the bent remains of a locker.

Inside the locker were all sorts of tools, rubber handles melted, but nothing I could see a use for. The winch, though, made sense. I slipped the ratchet and pulled out cable, drawing it over toward the first crewman, thinking I was going to clip it onto the crewman's clip.

The deck lurched. Looking up, I got a great view of that big flaming tube-machine piece breaking loose from the ship and falling like a fireball arching down toward the white capped sea. Something had popped on one of the sausage things, sending out a jet of flame sideways, making it spin like a pinwheel spiraling downward. Above, Aleta and the crewman were dangling limp in their harnesses. Panic. But she moved and punched the crewman, who took the wrench from her, and they began to work their way back up inside, hand over hand. Relief.

I found a pulley piece in the locker and a place to clip it on the rib above so the winch would be able to pull straight, but how did you make damn thing go? I think it was electric. Was there any power?

"Cali! What are you doing up here?" It was Aleta.

"What do you think?" I called back, as she climbed down the ladder.

"You are in so much trouble. You'll be lucky if they don't dump you in London. And you're doing that all wrong. *Dietrich, die Winde machen.*"

"*Jawohl,*" he smiled and saluted.

Both the crewmen, one a crewwoman actually, were still alive. Once we had them laying on the catwalk above, another crewwoman bounded up to help, which was a godsend because getting them down the central ladder and to the gondola's side hatch was a trick. We used a stretcher basket thing to winch them down.

Later, we all looked and looked, but found no sign of Helga. Aleta figured she had been working on one of the engines and had gotten blown off. Back below Aleta and I sat in the lounge, she still in her dirty, blue, too-small overalls, looking sad, and me in my bloody stained day dress. Vic made an appearance, but kept her distance. Then that crewman friend of Aleta's, Dietrich, returned from the cockpit and tapped Alete's shoulder.

"*Kommst du. Wir sind nicht fertig.*"

She groaned and followed him back to the ladder, but I think she was secretly happy to be crew again.

So there I was, alone in the lounge. The stew was gone. I had missed it along with the coffee and the cookies. My dress was ruined, so I headed to the washroom to see what could be done, but there was that rotund graying man who had been helping people in the lounge in there scrubbing his arms. He had his coat off and collar unbuttoned.

"I'm sorry my dear, but there's no soap in the men's washroom and no time to hunt for it," he said in French. He had long gray sideburns and a long nose.

"You're the doctor," I said.

"A doctor in a bit of a hurry," he replied.

"Do you need help?" I can't help it. It was the way I was raised.

"You're a nurse?"

"I have experience. I mean, if you have no nurse, I've helped stitch wounds," I said. Seriously, I have. "Far too many."

He finished washing and held his hands out in the air. "That was you screaming this morning?" he said.

"Yes sir." Now I was embarrassed.

"Then I expect you've had too much experience. You'll need to unbutton those sleeves and wash. I'm sorry, but I couldn't find any aprons. Just dirty overalls." Then he gave me the eye. "Miss Carmichael?"

"Cali please."

"Dr. Péan. You may call me Émile when no one is listening." He had a nice smile.

I began to scrub, damn that dribble of water, while he continued.

"We're boiling thread and towels in the kitchen. Their aid kit is out of date and under stocked. We'll use the cat gut on the worst cases and we've only one small bottle of antiseptic."

"We've used rum," I said.

"Vodka is better." There was that smile again. "They're still in their clothes, so we will have to undress them. I assume you have no problem with that?"

"No sir," I replied.

"Good. Then we must hurry."

The deck lurched unexpectedly. We both looked about, but then he picked up where he left off, leading me out of the bathroom. "We'll need a sharpening stone for the scalpel and needle. Probably too much to ask for an Arkansas stone. You were working in the kitchen earlier?"

"I don't remember what they had. They may have one," I said.

"Then go look after we finish."

"Yes sir," I replied.

"Wash again when you come back," he chided. "We'll get everything clean eventually. No point in adding to it."

He asked a passenger to open the crew cabin door for us. Inside, the crewmen were where we had left them. They were children really, both of them so small.

He shook his head. "The bed arrangements are very inconvenient. We're going to need help with moving them between beds. We have very little room in here as well, and terrible light."

"We used the kitchen table on our ship."

"I'm afraid that's all too common," he replied, half to himself, as he worked. We pulled and cut apart their burnt and torn uniforms to expose wounds until Dr. Péan felt satisfied. "Everything's a mess. We'll have to cut it all off," he said, waving at their uniforms. "We must hurry. These burns need to be scrubbed out before they wake."

Then he stood up. "Right, you go get a sharpening stone and I'll start getting the rest of these clothes off, but I'm going to need better scissors, and dressing. These are terrible. Olivie should be in the kitchen getting us some warm water to wash with. Maybe she's found something."

"Olivie?"

"My wife and assistant."

As I left, I heard him call out for two strong men to help move patients.

When I got back, Olivie following with a steaming pot of water and clean wash rags, Dr. Péan had cut off the rest of their clothes. They were ruined anyway. There were too many burns and shrapnel holes. We scrubbed, dug, and stitched. Dr. Péan showed me some interesting tricks, folding back skin to help prevent scarring and different stitches to reduce skin stretching. I filed these away to show Ma. For lack of better, we put towels wet with salt water on the burns. Their bedding was wet and bloody when we finished, so Émile's wife brought in their own bedding.

Then Aleta stopped in to check on us. Émile saw her ill-fitting uniform and lit into her. He thought she was regular crew.

"Young woman. It's unconscionable that your aid kit is so poorly stocked considering the hazards of this environment!" he said, sternly, as if Aleta actually still worked for Lufthansa. And believe me. It took some negotiation for me to translate that. So many new words. When do you learn *hazards* and *unconscionable* in French class?

"Yes, I apologize," she sighed, looking weary. "They worry about weight too much, but these things are not within my control." Very diplomatic, I thought. She must have been a great crewwoman.

"Yes . . . well. We'll have to make do," he muttered.

I looked out the window, then remembered something.

"Frau Abbick!"

Aleta growled with exasperation and dashed for her cabin. She came back with an armload of boxes.

"Oh! Very good. Thank you," Dr. Péan said.

"What's going on outside?" I asked.

"We figure it had to be sabotage," Aleta said. "Too many things went wrong at once. The captain suspects the fuel must have been doped."

"Doped?" I asked.

"Yes. The engines run at their very limits. If you put anything in the fuel to make it burn quicker, they explode."

"Was that the thing that fell off the ship?"

"No, those were fuel cells, control valves, and regulators. The fuel lines have to be made of copper or the fuel corrodes them. The fuel is so flammable, it can melt them when it burns. They burn like fuses and set other things on fire if we don't shut them off. What bothers me is why sabotage only three engines." Then she stopped, her eyes went wide. "Oh, my God!" she said.

"What?" I asked, concerned. But she was already turning to run toward the cockpit.

"What is wrong with that woman?" Émile asked, half to himself. He didn't know English.

"I think we're still in trouble," I said.

We heard, then saw, Aleta and one of the remaining crew running past our door for the ladder.

"Aleta?" I called.

"Can't stop!" she yelled back. We could hear their footsteps on the storeroom ladder and the clang of the hatch. And that was it for another five minutes.

Five minutes until our last two engines stopped.

Even with only two, you could always hear them, and you could certainly not hear them when they stopped. There was nothing but the wind and the creaking of the gondola around us. Did the floor shift a bit more under my feet?

"I think we're going to crash, Émile," I said.

"Really?" He began moving to the window to look out.

I followed. It was late afternoon outside, the sky blue, spotted with clouds. Were some of them above us now? Yup. Definitely.

Émile stared down at the ocean below. Then he cleared his throat. "Well," he said. "I wish it would hurry up."

"We need to find something that can float." I began casting about.

"Not on this thing," he said with a chuckle. "Perhaps a table? They're awfully small and flimsy though."

"The mattress?" I suggested.

"Cotton on steel springs. That won't work," he muttered.

We were quiet for a couple of minutes, I think, both at a loss.

Then an engine started. I held my breath. Then the other.

"Oh thank you," I sighed.

Émile chuckled. "Too bad. It would have been an interesting end."

Emergencies done, we had a long string of smaller injuries, some still nasty, digging out glass and metal from patients all too awake. It seemed like everyone had something. And we still had our airsick. I was so tired, but when I relaxed and plunked down on the cabin stool, Émile looked down at me with that smile. "Don't get comfortable. We need to find food."

"Have we missed lunch? I've had nothing to eat since breakfast." Not even really that.

"Lunch? We've missed dinner. Let's assault the kitchen," Émile said. "After that, we must talk about attending to our patients tonight."

We walked through the dining room, Émile and me in our smudged and bloody clothes through into the galley.

"*Bonjour*," came a cheery voice, followed by an exclaimed, "Oh my!" They'd been washing dishes. The water doesn't dribble in the galley by the way.

"Look at you!" said the other, and they were on me.

"Where have you been?"

73

"Oh, your dress!" she said, inspecting it closely. "Ruined for sure."

"I've been helping the doctor," I replied. "We are very hungry. Is there any food?"

That stopped them.

"Yes there is, but there's a problem and we can't get the captain to understand."

Just then, the door opened and Dietrich came in. "I'm famished," he said. He was followed closely by Aleta, a young man, and then a young girl, the last of our crew.

"Time to celebrate!" Aleta said.

"We switched the tank order," Dietrich said to me, like that should mean something. "Jammed screwdrivers in the valves."

The girl slumped down in the corner, leaned her head against the corner mumbling something.

Aleta and Dietrich laughed.

"She says she's too old for this," Aleta said.

The captain yelled something back in German and all of them moaned.

"He wants to know who's volunteering for first watch," Dietrich explained. He answered the captain with a rattle of German.

Aleta snorted, her eyes wide with amusement. "Yes, first feed us," she said. It became a chant. "Feed us, feed us." Even Émile joined. At least I think that was what it was, because it was in German.

"Goodness!" Cirille said.

"I haven't heard such a ruckus since the last invasion," Yvonne added, luckily in French, as she headed for the pantry.

I haven't introduced you yet have I? They are Yvonne and Cirille. They wanted to see the Wild West, but, thanks to the war, it got a little too wild for them. They made it to Saint Louis though, and barely got out.

They scrambled us eggs and served it with bread, oranges, and tea. Oh, I love oranges, and egg too! It wasn't restaurant fare, but there was certainly enough, which, by the way, was what they wanted us to talk to the captain about.

"There isn't enough food," Cirille said to me while they were cooking. "The menu only goes for four days and there's hardly any extra."

"I wouldn't worry," I said. "We can trade with ships at sea along the way. We did it on our ship sometimes."

"We can't land on a ship, can we?" she replied, obviously confused.

"No, but we moor to one and pass things up and down the anchor line."

"Oh." She still looked confused, but seemed willing to trust that it wasn't going to be a problem.

We took our food into the lounge and sat on the floor in the corner, laughing. Émile took a plate of food to his wife who was doing the rounds between patients. I could see Vic. She looked a bit lonely, so I nodded her over. She thought for a second, then headed our way.

Introducing her around was how I found out that girl crewman's name was Sigrid and the boy's name was Antonio. Sigrid had straight brown-blond hair cut short and blue eyes. She was very quiet, although she did know how to laugh when there was a joke. She couldn't have been more than 14. Antonio, a whisp of a boy with curly black hair, was Italian. He talked less even than Sigrid. I think he was shy around new people, especially girls.

"So what was it that you figured out?" I asked Aleta.

"That the rear engines didn't explode because they weren't using as much fuel. There are two separate fuel cells, one for each set. We hadn't gotten to the bad fuel yet because we were down an engine."

"We had bad fuel?" Vic asked.

"Someone doped it," I said.

"Someone tried to blow us up?" Vic's eyes were wide. "I've got to go." She started to get up.

"Wait," Dietrich said. "This wasn't supposed to get out without the captain's permission."

Aleta grimaced. "I'm so sorry."

"Vic wait," I said. "You aren't panicking are you? Because there's no place to go."

"And we stopped it," Dietrich said.

I could tell that Aleta wanted to say something at that point, but held back.

Vic though didn't look panicked. She looked troubled.

"It's all right," she said. "But I have to go." And she practically hopped down the corridor.

Aleta growled, "I'm so stupid, I'm so stupid . . ."

"And in so much trouble," added Dietrich.

"*Was ist los?*" Sigrid asked, and they were off in German. As they rattled on, Sigrid started laughing at Aleta.

Dietrich, Sigrid, Antonio, and Aleta needed to discuss watch strategy with the captain. The captain had been wrestling with the controls for over 18 hours and was about to drop, and I had to discuss patient watch schedules with Émile. So we took our empty plates to the galley and then set about our work. To be frank, it had been an exhausting day for us all and I didn't envy whoever it was who drew first watch. I hoped it wasn't me.

Émile had gone to wash his hands and I found Olivie, his wife, rewrapping the bandaging on the shoulder of the tall thin man with a long moustache. I remembered him getting wounded and shivered. It missed his lung by the way. She was using torn sheet, pulling them from a loose pile on a dinner tray. More were hanging over strings she had stretched across the cabin. They had been boiled.

He looked surprised when I came in. I think, perhaps, he was hiding his embarrassment at not wearing a shirt.

"Don't worry dear," Olivie said. "She's a nurse. A good one too."

He mumbled something to her.

"And I'm too old," she replied. "What do you need Cali?"

"I need the watch schedule," I replied.

"I suppose we both do," she said, then listened. "I think Émile is with Mrs. Kappel."

I was pretty sure Mrs. Kappel was dead. They must have been trying to decide what to do with her.

"And where are you going to sleep?" I asked. We used their bedding for the wounded crewmen. I needed to change my dress too. I was very tired of the smell of blood.

"Oh goodness. Another good question," she said, trying to make the bandages hold with as few pins as possible. "I suppose we'll have to ask the captain." She tugged on the bandages until she seemed satisfied. "Don't move that arm around or it will all come loose. Go sit somewhere and rest."

"Yes, ma'am," he said. Then added after a pause, "Just like the war, isn't it?" He didn't look happy.

"I'm afraid so," she said. She lifted his shirt, thought for a second, but could see it was no use trying to get it back on, so she draped it about his shoulders. "You go sit in your cabin and rest."

"Yes, ma'am."

I held the door for him, then opened his cabin door as well. His wife was there waiting.

"Thank you," she said, then gave her husband a kiss on the cheek. She looked like she wanted to hug him, but thought better of it. I could see the glint of tears in her eyes as I left them alone.

Voices drifted down the hall from the lounge.

"We're out of whiskey, damn it."

"They took all the vodka."

I wandered down the corridor. I realized that the sun was down and the breeze had grown colder and damp as well. I swear, when I'm busy, the weather can sneak up on me. In the middle of the lounge were men, draped about the couches, four of them. Two brought blankets from their cabins and they were holding glasses. One of them, a man wearing his dinner jacket over his day clothes, had gotten up and was standing at the cockpit door, holding one of the glass bottles they used to serve liquor.

He pounded on the door.

I could hear a thin, high voice inside, but I couldn't understand what was said. It had to be Sigrid.

"No more today?" the man replied, rather loudly. "Nonsense!"

Another man, rotund with gray hair, Mr. Jefferies if I remember right, his head wobbling slightly said, "If there was ever a day for a stiff drink, it's today."

"Jimmy, go in and get some," said another.

"*Nein, bitte!*" said an elderly lady. She and another lady, Frau Abbink, had been sitting in the corner, next to a lamp. She continued in German. It was clear she was trying to placate them.

Those that could, turned their heads.

"What is that? German?" said one, thickly.

"Maybe Dutch?" said another.

"Go on Jimmy."

"Right," Jimmy said, and he turned the handle and walked

77

through the door.

I could hear Sigrid yelling at him in German.

"There's bodies all over the floor," Jimmy called from inside.

"Did you say bodies?" his friend said.

Then I heard the captain, and then Dietrich.

Dietrich, at least, could yell at him in English. "Sir, you are not allowed in here."

"We need more whisky," replied Jimmy.

I started toward the cockpit. The Péans needed bedding and Jimmy had done the waking for me.

"*Aus! Los! Jetzt!*" yelled the captain.

Dietrich was firmly escorting an unbalanced Jimmy out the door. "No more," Dietrich said in English, and gave Jimmy a little push to get him started back toward his seat. Then he looked at me. "Hi Cali," he said. "Need something?"

"The Péans need bedding. They have no place to sleep tonight."

He heaved a weary sigh, "I suppose we will have to do something about that. Be right back." I could see blankets on the floor before he closed the door. They were sleeping in the cockpit. We had taken over the crew cabin for the wounded.

When he opened the door again, he was carrying some sort of handle tool and a metal tube. "Come on," he said. "I'll need your help." He trudged barefoot toward the corridor with me following. The floors were clean now by the way. "We keep all that down in the hold," he said. I could hear Jimmy and his friend's slurred voices muttering to themselves.

Stopping at the aft end of the ship, Dietrich squatted down on the floor and stuck the tool into a little notch in the floor panel. I hadn't really looked at them before, but the floor panels all had them.

"They'll be down around here. Come on. Help me lift."

He pried the panel up and we stuck our fingers in around the edge to pull it open. It wasn't heavy so much as disinclined to let go. It was the sticky rubber seal. Down below, lit by the dim hallway light shining in little shafts through the shrapnel holes in the ceiling, was the cargo hold. Neat!

Dietrich picked up the metal tube. It had glass on the end. Suddenly, light sprang out of it! I started. Dietrich chuckled.

"They're called *taschenlampen*. Here, look," and he handed it to me.

It was heavy and warm. In the end was a light bulb and on the side a toggle. I pointed it down into the hold and the light cut through the darkness.

"This is amazing," I said, waving it around at the different shapes below. "We could really use these back on the ship."

"They're terribly expensive, so please be careful. And they don't last very long, so we should hurry."

I gave it one last jab at the darkness and handed it back. Then Dietrich hopped down.

The hold floor was four feet down and stretched most of the width and length of the gondola. They'd done a nice job of packing it, leaving narrow crawlways. Dietrich headed aft and I hopped down to follow. We were in the section that had all their ship supplies. At the end of our crawlway, behind Dietrich's silhouette, was a door.

"It's good you don't need more than two. It's all the spares we have."

I could see aluminum shelves stacked with linen and square tins mixed in amongst paperboard crates. He pulled down a big bedroll and pushed it toward me.

"Here," he said.

"Right," I replied. "What's that door?"

"The mail room. It's sealed."

"We don't lock up the mail on our ship, but then there's only us."

"They make more money with a sealed compartment," he replied. "We can carry first class mail as well as airmail."

I wondered if Pa knew about that. He had to, I thought. I began dragging the bedroll back to the hatch. At the hatch, I tipped it up and pushed it through end first. Above, I heard footsteps walking by and muttering voices. The men. I hoped they decided to go lay down.

Dietrich was pushing the next bedroll down the aisle when I saw something glint on the floor.

"What's that," I said.

"What?"

"Down on the floor, on your right."

Dietrich stopped and picked up something. "That's odd," he said.

"What?"

"Wait, I'll show you." He continued pushing, then I helped him tip the bundle up through to the deck above. With our hands free he pointed his light at the thing and we took a good look at it. It was a silver fountain pen.

"Nice," Dietrich said.

"Could one of you have lost it?" I asked.

"None of us could afford this," he said. "Maybe the captain, but he doesn't waste money like this."

"Then how did it get down here?"

"One of the passengers," he said quietly, and then to himself, "Very strange."

Then he looked up and smiled. "We'll save this for the captain. I'm really, really tired."

I groaned back, "Me too. And there's still things left to do."

We climbed back up and closed the floor panel, Dietrich giving it a good thump with his bare foot to make sure it was closed.

Mme. Péan came out of a cabin and saw the bedding.

"Oh bless you," she said. "I hadn't gotten to that yet."

We dragged the bedding to their cabin and helped unroll it.

"You might tell the captain that one of your crew, the girl, woke up."

"Anika?" he said, brightening up.

"Yes, but don't bother her. She's fallen back asleep, which is for the best." She finished arranging the mattresses, then pulled the blankets loose so they could get in. "Oh, and Émile said that you should sleep tonight, but that he'll need you in the morning."

"That isn't fair. I can take a watch tonight," I said. "You both need to sleep."

"Nonsense! What isn't fair is us both sitting down tomorrow to eat a civilized breakfast, while you watch the patients," she said with a smile.

That got a snort from Dietrich. "Back to bed for me," he said. "Good morning, night, oh . . . I lose track," he said, looking around. And he left to walk back down the corridor.

That left me at ends. Aleta was asleep. I didn't want to disturb her. No Vic in the dining room. The crew was up top or asleep. I had nothing left but the weight of the day. It came crashing down on me, suddenly. I felt like I was made of lead.

Then the floor dipped and tipped again. What was that?

I went to the back window, now a windowless hole. They had somehow popped out the frames to get rid of the glass shards. It was an empty square looking down the length of our airship blue in the twilight. I saw that two of our engines were completely gone. I could see the shapes of Antonio and Sigrid up on the catwalk, walking away from one of the missing engine platforms. I guessed we were shedding weight.

"Not more trouble." It was Max, appearing beside me. I must have been tired, because I didn't hear him.

"They're dropping the burnt engines," I replied.

"They're looking for more lift. It's better than generating more gas. I suppose it's because our airspeed is so low now."

"You know a lot about Airships." I gave him the eye.

"I work for Krupp. I could sell you one," he smiled back.

"That would be funny."

"It might be a good investment for your family."

"The competition is too fierce. The risk is too great. The profit margin is too low."

"Allard was right. You are a merchant's daughter."

"He was a good man." I thought of his ghost trying to warn me.

"He was a good agent. But now he's dead."

"Through no fault of his own."

"Luck is so important."

I looked out at our airship. "Is this luck?" I asked.

"Someone tried to kill us, but here we are."

"Then I suppose it is. Why did they do it? Try to kill us?"

"Try not to ask too many questions. I've watched you play cards." That got a bitter laugh out of me. "You're terrible. I suggest you stay out of high stakes games. You were lucky to live through the last one. Be grateful you're alive. Go to Brussels and play your violin."

I had no intention of doing anything but that.

That evening I sat in the lounge with a blanket and fell asleep. I did not dream, I slept so soundly. It took Sigrid a bit of shaking to wake me.

"Cali," she said. She was holding a plate. *"Cali. Du muss Essen."*

It took a few seconds to figure out what I was seeing. It was Sigrid, holding a plate, sausage, peas, boiled potatoes, and tea. The breeze was cold and the moon was lighting clouds silver in the darkness outside. I snuggled in my blanket as I ate. After I took back my plate I went to bed. And was almost immediately asleep.

Chapter 8 – The Fourth Day

"*Wachest du.*" Someone was shaking me.

I was on my feet, on the floor before I knew what I was doing.

"*Auch. Nein, mein Fehler*," he said.

"He wants me Cali," Aleta said from the bunk above. "Go back to sleep."

In the dark, I realized it was the captain. I moaned and flopped back down.

"*Wir müssen beeilen*," he said to Aleta.

She hopped down and pulled on her boots. She'd been sleeping in her clothes.

"*Tut mir leit*," he called as they left.

Of course, now I was awake. I lay in bed for a bit staring at the moonlight coming in the window, east southeast. I closed my eyes for what seemed like a long time with no results. Then I opened them again. Why was there moonlight coming in the window? So I climbed out of bed and opened it. Yes, our cabin still had its glass. The wind whistled past, the moon just bright enough to show whitecaps far below. It was close to the horizon, waning gibbous. Ebb tide. The cold felt great, which brought to mind the shower. It was close to dawn, 4:30 AM I guessed. We had changed tack. It must be the wind, I thought. The problem with engines is that they play with your reckoning of the air and its direction. But I needed to get sleep while I could and being clean might help.

So I was in my night robe, padding barefoot down the dark, cold, breezy, empty corridor with no sign of Mrs. Kappel's ghost, when I decided to check on our patients. I opened the cabin door and there was Émile, sprawled snoring in a chair, so I came in quietly. The towels over their burns were only damp. I squeezed more water on them with a rag and the bowl, which had been sitting on the fold down desk.

As I was leaving, Émile woke with a snort.

"*Éléonore, c'est vous?*"

His wife's name is Olivie!

"No Dr. Péan. It's Cali. I just checked the patients."

He snorted and his eyes came fully open.

"Oh yes, I'm sorry." He said, blinking and stretching his neck. "I was asleep." A flat statement, and then he rallied with a chuckle. "Oh. Éléonore is our daughter. You remind me of her when she was young."

"She isn't travelling with you?"

"No, no." He smiled. "She's married. We have grandchildren." He stood slowly and stretched some more. "I'm sorry," he said. "I'm getting old. I fell asleep."

"We had a long day."

"Yes, we certainly did." He got up slowly and turned to the bed, feeling pulses and foreheads, tisking as he went. "This one has fever," he said, looking at the crewman. "It's as I feared, infection and we have nothing to bring it down."

"There's ice in the galley," I said. "They have a machine that makes them." They did. It's like a little ice house. It was incredible! It's funny. When the cubes are half frozen, you can tip them and they get a bubble in the middle. But honestly, I wasn't playing in the kitchen. I was looking for the coffee.

"Not enough to make any difference I'm afraid," he replied. "We would need a tub and a lot of ice. But we'll use what we have, of course." Then he scowled at me. "You should be asleep. Tomorrow is going to be very difficult. People are in shock now, but tomorrow they'll start to think. Especially after the funeral."

"Mrs. Kappel."

"Yes. Mr. Kappel doesn't know it yet. Please don't talk to him about it, but we have no place to store her body. Especially not if it takes more than a week to get to land."

"A week?"

"If we lose a day without one engine, how many will we lose without four?"

"The wind's on our side."

"Let's hope it stays that way," he said. "It may be all we have. I have to wonder how much fuel we have left."

"We dropped half of it in the sea," I replied. "And shut off more out of fear of it."

It was a troubling thought, which was cut off by a low moan coming through the wall from the next room. Émile and I stared at the spot.

"No." said the man's voice. "Shoot, damn it." He shouted something unintelligible followed by a thump against the wall. Then there was a woman's voice, trying to sooth him. It sent a cold shiver through me.

"He did that last night too," Émile said. Then he looked at me. "Always remember that you aren't alone. The world is full of people who've seen too much."

I smiled and ducked my head, trying to avoid the subject. "And fuel and wind come tomorrow. Tonight I need a bath."

Émile brightened. "I could use one too," he said.

"Maybe it'll be warm," I added, as I headed to the door.

"I hope so." Then he said good night.

The shower was warm.

The next morning I got to see Aleta. She was undressing while I was dressing.

"I got to fly last night!" was the first thing she said when she saw

85

my eyes open. "A four hour shift."

"Really?" To be truthful, I'm not sure that really came out as a word. Maybe more of a groan or a moan.

"It was so fun! I've always wanted to do it. This afternoon I'll get to fly while there's still daylight."

Yes, I got up. Honestly, I'm not normally like this. The morning rays of the sun were streaming in through the window, lighting up the wall. Northeast. What were we doing? The wind must have shifted again, I thought. I hoped we weren't making for Iceland. It's so cold there.

It was certainly cold in the corridor and the breeze only made it worse. Those waiting in line for the bathroom and shower stood there bundled up. I could hear people muttering.

In the lounge, though, there was coffee!

I drank down a cup and then refilled it, before looking for the Péans. Someone had tacked a note to the door of the cockpit. We were going to have a meeting after breakfast.

"Good morning," said a voice behind me.

I turned and there behind me was Max. He checked his pocket watch.

"Another half hour until breakfast. I wonder what they will find for us to eat today."

"Yvonne and Cirille aren't that bad," I said.

"Is that their names?" He glance toward the cockpit door. "No, not bad, but maybe a little inventive. I hope they get paid for their time," he added, squinted at the note. The day's menu was written under the announcement. "I think we're having fish quiche this morning," he said, with mock incredulity.

"They have to work with what they have, at least until Pieter wakes up."

"It's good you are keeping busy."

"Perhaps," I sighed. "But not this way. We have too many hurt

"Well, it's good you're here. I could even end up being one of them," he chuckled.

"Is it that bad?"

"No. It's only that it's a long way to the other side of the Atlantic."

"Well. My patients."

"Yes."

I started toward my rounds, but met Vic coming out of her room as I passed.

"Could I sit with you at breakfast?" she asked. She looked worried.

"I can't. I have watch," I said, but added, "But I would love to if I could."

"Oh, well," she replied. She seemed different, tentative. Where was that shark-like grin? "Maybe lunch?"

"Lunch would be great. If I'm out by then. I'm not sure, but you can visit if you want. I'll mostly be sitting. I have to make sure they don't roll about, choke, or start bleeding," then adding with a roll of my eyes, thinking about our makeshift chamber pot, adding "or something. And sometimes people come in wanting help with their bandages or just to complain about them."

"Bleeding?"

"Yes," I sighed. "We're very short of pins, and bed sheeting isn't that good when it comes to tight wrapping. Then there are the airsick."

"Maybe I'll come by," she said, without conviction.

"Please. It would be nice," I replied, nodding my head. I was almost pleading. I needed company. I checked the crew cabin first. Mme. Péan was sitting in there. The crewman on the bottom bunk with the fever was twitching fitfully.

"*Helga, nein,*" he muttered, then grunted, gritting his teeth.

"You'll have to watch this one," Mme. Péan said. "He'll roll about and pop his stitches if we don't. He's already wet the bed and we haven't been able to get much water in him so I don't think you'll have trouble there." She sighed. "But please try to get him to drink. We don't want to lose him."

"Yes ma'am."

"I'll be back as soon as I can," she said.

"Take your time," I replied. "I'll be fine."

"Of course you will, dear," she added, as she closed the door.

Looking around the room brought no new information. The sun had risen above the zeppelin's envelope and no longer showed through the window. There was only blue sky outside. Looking out and down, I could see whitecaps. We hadn't regained the altitude we lost yesterday, which was troubling.

"So," I said to my unconscious patients. "We start with the most important."

I poured a quarter cup of water. Lifting the feverish crewman's head, touching the cup's lip with my finger, I began trying to dribble it into his mouth.

Aleta brought me breakfast, my fish quiche. Max was right. They were very inventive. I sat there eating, Aleta telling me something about soldering copper tubing or something, when I heard a groan from the top bunk.

"*Ist das Essen?*" the voice mumbled.

"*Na ja!*" Aleta said. "You're awake."

She put her plate down and stood to look at our patient. Something I needed a chair to do. Then they jabbered away in German, which I really will learn someday.

"She needs water," I suggested.

"*Ja, bitte,*" the girl said. So I got her a cup and Aleta helped her drink, then we gave her a bit of egg. Her name's Anika, by the way. She's Dutch. Aleta asked her if she could handle some bread and she said yes, so Aleta took off to the galley to get her a plate.

"Do you understand French?" I asked.

"A little," she replied in French.

"English?"

"A little," she said.

"Which is better?"

"French, maybe," she said in French. As I suspected, their speeches in English and French were mostly memorized.

"Then we will use French."

"Yes," she said, sounding very spent.

Aleta dashed back in with a plate.

"Can you help her?" Aleta asked, putting the plate down on the desk. "I have to go to the meeting."

"Have fun," I replied. "Please fill me in when you're done."

I broke off little pieces of bread and egg and put them in Anika's mouth. She didn't eat much and I missed the meeting. No. All your poor Cali got to do was help Anika fill the kitchen pot we were using for that purpose, which I dumped out the window. I figured that I managed to get at least a quarter cup of water into our feverish crewman that morning and maybe another quarter cup that afternoon. It was hard to tell.

M. Bonnet, our shoulder wound, attended the meeting wrapped in a blanket, which got him bleeding. Mme. Péan insisted on staying up to wrap him, despite being up most of the night. M. Laurent's hurt foot was causing him great pain, but we could do nothing to help. He needed an operation. Then there was the stream of minor injuries and we still had people seasick. I practically had to physically push Olivie out of the room so she would get some sleep. Seasick I can do on my own. In between were long stretches where I tried not to think of Lucien. A foolish thing to fill my head with, but I couldn't help myself. So I tried to think about cards instead. Vic didn't visit.

Dietrich brought me lunch, but had to run. The crew were up top trying to reroute fuel lines. The floor tipped again midmorning, so I suppose we were less another engine. I heard Mr. Koppel crying from down the hall, after lunch. But no one told me anything. No news.

It was that afternoon that we found the convoy and moored to a big merchantman. I didn't know until the floor dipped. Not the rocking of an engine dropping but a great slow downward tug. I rushed to the window. Down below were five ships. Six if you counted the one we were moored to. There had to be more out of sight on the other side. Certainly an escort as well. I could hear the air crew, including Aleta, scampering back and forth across the roof above me. The convoy were all steamers, naturally, trailing black columns of smoke in their wakes, the smoke stretching back like tails beneath us. One was an older paddle wheeler. She was showing sail.

I took a quick break to take a peek out the rear observation window, but interrupted Mr. Adams and that southern woman arguing. I would have thought nothing of it except they stopped as soon as they saw me. Weird. You'd think they were married, which I don't think they were. Perhaps it was a travel romance!

And that was your Cali's big day of glamorous zeppelin flight.

That evening I got to have dinner with Vic and her father, Dr. Dewar, along with their bodyguard Dmitri, who hovered in the background. I was wearing my last good travel dress. A simple skirt, a belt, and light jacket. Sadly, I still had no earrings besides my pearls, which were locked in the safe. Just the gold loops I got in the Congo. Dr. Dewar and Vic, who has a lovely gold locket, sat on one of the sofa seats and Dmitri and I in chairs, dead center in the lounge. I was thinking that a locket with a picture of Ma and Pa, and Red would be wonderful.

Dr. Dewar is thin, balding, with a long straight nose, and a carefully trimmed beard which, like the rest of his remaining hair, was quite blond. He looked tired. He was wearing a vest and jacket, which was far more effective than my flimsy travel coat in the cold breeze blowing in from all the missing windows.

Most had retired to their cabins. Still, we had quite a few there sitting about. Mme. Calvé was there, that Canadian man with the pencil moustache, M. Comeau, the old letch too. Max was sitting in the corner, reading. I ignored him and everyone else. There had to more spies than Max. He said it was a game. That meant there had to be players. Who here was a spy besides Max?

We lined up to be served from the galley, the evening sun lighting the back wall gold. Grab a plate and a cup, then carefully make your way back to your seat or room.

The lights on the tables worked, which were fun and we had them on even though the sun hadn't set yet. We generally only got to see them at dinner. They have a wire to carries the electricity into them that ends in round thing with two prongs on it. You poke it into a hole in the table top, which connects through the table to the floor, the electricity coming out from down there somewhere. It's really fun, like lamplight, only it's not shining in your eyes. You can see everything, with no after images. Vic seemed to take no notice of it.

Dr. Dewar opened the conversation as we sat down. "Victoria," he said, and Vic scowled, "Has told me that your family lives on a ship"

"Yes sir," I answered, while I was putting my napkin on my lap. We were eating some kind of thick soup, not quite stew, with potatoes, boiled cabbage, and bread. The soup was made with dried meat. It must have come up from the ship below. There was wine, which I declined.

"We have a schooner," I said. "For the most part, I only spend the summer on her. Most of the year I go to boarding school."

"Is that were you learned the violin?" he asked.

"Yes sir."

"Both you and your friend are very good. It must be a good school."

"Thank you."

"Well mannered, and your French is excellent," he said in French.

Which forced me to block a laugh. French with a Scottish accent.

"Thank you. I've had a lot of practice lately."

My turn now. The accent was a dead giveaway, but I needed an opening so I started with nonsense. "If you don't mind, are you from Scotland?"

"Yes we are. We moved to Cambridge when I received my professorship and joined the Royal Society, but I work for the Royal Institution now." That last bit had an odd, unhappy ring to it. "I used to teach at the University of Edinburgh." That, at least, sounded happy enough.

"Vic tells me you're a chemist." Open statements are better than questions. People can make what they want of them.

"Yes," he said, looking up for a moment at Dmitri with a frown. "I've worked mostly with gasses, the permanent gasses. I studied hydrogen, the gas that is holding us up for instance. I used to freeze them."

"Freezing gasses?" What an odd idea. "You can freeze them?"

"Oh yes," he said, warming to the subject, and really, I didn't mean that as a joke. "All sorts of things happen when you can get them cold enough."

"Like what?"

"Well," he said. "They begin to separate into their components. First the water, then carbon dioxide, then nitrogen."

I was lost. I supposed these were gasses.

"They freeze. Like ice," I said.

"Oh yes," he replied, with a boyish grin. "In layers. If you're quick, you can scrape them up before they sublimate."

Dr. Dewar was something very special. Which confirmed my new Congo honed cynical suspicions. He must have invented or stolen something.

Our conversation progressed, on and on, grill the new friend. I swear, you'd think I was going to ask for Vic's hand. Dmitri was silent through all of this, glaring at any who walked too close. Finally, Dr. Dewar asked, rather nicely, if I could play something. Vic's eyebrows were up, looking at me, her eyes saying, "Could you?"

I did this often in the Congo, playing for my dinner, and I was sorely tired of it, but I said, "Yes, of course," because I'm far too nice. Never mind that I've spent the last nine hours running the pan back and forth to the window and trying to get bandages made of bed sheet to stay on with no pins. "I need to practice anyway," I said. Which was true. Vic followed me to my cabin.

Around the corner, in the corridor, she whispered, "I'm so sorry. He's been like this the last few years with everyone I meet. I think it has something to with Dmitri and his job at Cambridge."

She was so worried that I couldn't be angry. "It's all right," I said. "I wasn't kidding. I need to practice or I'll lose my calluses."

"Calluses?"

"Yes," I replied, stopping and showing her my hands.

She stared for a second. "Oh."

"I'll make a deal with you," I said, and then resumed walking. "I'll play for your father if you keep teaching me cards."

She looked up at me, the shark grin back. "Deal!"

Aleta was up in the cockpit gleefully flying, keeping us in line with our tow, so our cabin was empty. I hadn't been in there since morning. It was dim, the sun on the other side. I turned on the light and was leaning down to pick up my case, when noticed something strange. Where we previously had stuff thrown all over the cabin, one floor panel was curiously clear of dirty clothes. I stopped and stared at it.

"What's wrong?" Vic asked.

"Nothing," I said.

She looked at the floor and frowned for a moment, trying to figure it out.

"I've got it," I said, holding my case. "Let's go," and I pulled her into the corridor.

Back in the lounge, Dr. Dewar was waiting at the table. Interestingly, the crowd had grown. They all had to be finished eating.

There was no other flat space, so I opened my case on our table, which, strangely, seemed too personal, although why I should care that they could see in my case I don't know. Heaven knows I leave it open when I'm playing for money. It was an odd feeling.

I rosined, then started to tune. Others came out from their rooms. Someone propped open the cockpit door. The setting sun edged in the starboard windows now, since we'd found a tow and were being dragged instead of pushed by our engines. We were now facing west northwest, our tail toward Norway, hanging like a child's balloon above the fleet.

The first thing that came to mind was Bach. Good with dinner. It's also one of the few pieces in my school folder that I didn't have to play for that prince. Time and again I had been "asked" to play for him in the Congo. It stained my music and now there are some pieces I simply cannot play.

I launched into the first movement's rolling notes and for a few minutes everything was gone, spies, sabotage, the blood, my ruined clothes. Even the cold breeze felt good. Orange sunlight raked across the tables. I finished the first movement and paused to breathe before the second movement. Someone started to clap, but I ignored him, and rolled into the second movement. It started as it should, but as it unfolded it slowly began to drift and I realized I had become somewhat melancholy. I put down my violin.

"I'm sorry, but this isn't working."

So I took up a shanty, but without Aleta, it seemed simple and hard. Almost embarrassing. That's when I realize that I missed her. It's no fun playing alone, especially when I was tired and perhaps a little miserable.

I tried to relax and listen. There was the ship herself, the wind, the murmur of voices. There was music. There's music everywhere, even at 5000 feet over the Atlantic Ocean. I listened and followed, the sound of the wind, adding Aleta's parts with my voice, weaving back and forth. I find this relaxing and it sounds a bit like Chopin's Nocturnes, but this was a new song. I mean I made it up on the spot. I do that sometimes, winding away with no real melody. Just shifting motifs, mixing and breaking chords into long tangled drifts that roll with my feelings. I wound away the time, drifting with the rolling breeze, almost asleep. Many came out to listen, including M. Marmontel. Mrs. Kappel was standing behind her husband, but I ignored them. She seemed to fade as I drifted.

Someone down below, though, requested we shut off the lights to not give away the convoy's position, so I stopped. I was very tired anyway. When I finally made it to bed, I slept the hard kind of sleep that comes from pure exhaustion, finally waking with a wicked need to pee. Sometimes you sleep so long and so hard, that you don't wake until the need is acute. Attempts at movement revealed arms and legs of lead, and difficulty in even moving my covers. But there is no escape from a wicked need to pee. There's only one solution. It was pitch dark. The corridor empty. I wasn't wearing my night robe. Just stumbling along in my night dress, my bare feet silent on the cold floor.

So I was sitting there in the pitch black on the cold seat when I heard the sound of something being moved in the cargo hold below me. The sound was coming up through the floor vent. I could see a glimmer of light there. But, as I said, I was tired. Tired of these people and their idiot games.

"You know," I said, somewhat loudly. "I'm entirely tired of spies. Especially spies who don't know when they should be asleep. You honestly don't think anyone with something to hide, with half a brain, would be so stupid as to leave anything useful in their trunks do you?"

Quiet.

I stood and straightened my nightgown. "You need to go back to spy school," I said, as I left.

Chapter 9 – The Fifth Day

The morning sunlight was not shining in the window as it normally did, which confused me for a moment. Then I remembered we were facing west because of the tow. Aleta was up in the bunk above, asleep. Was it the fourth day or the fifth? It was the fifth, but I had to count. We were supposed to be landing in Brussels today. What were we doing about food and fuel? Were we still moored to the freighter? How was the convoy doing?

I'd missed both the meeting and Mrs. Kappel's funeral. Émile and some of the passengers had wrapped her in sheets and sent her down the tow cable to the ship below. It was a prayer and then out the door she went, up into the zeppelin's superstructure above us and then winched down the tow cable to the deck of the ship below, at least that's what Mrs. Péan told me. I heard that they let Mr. Kappel get drunk and sat with him while he cried.

I asked her why we didn't send the wounded down and he replied

95

that they had no doctor below.

"You could go too," I said.

"Then who would tend to the rest?"

"We could all go."

"Some are going. Most are old and a little frail and to be honest, a bit frightened as well. But some are going to try."

The Dreyers made the journey, as did the Harmons. At least I wouldn't have Mr. Harmon staring at me. I couldn't go of course. Not without Aleta, and we were both needed up in the Bremen.

Putting my bare feet down on the cold floor, I hobbled over to look out the window. Believe me, wood doesn't get this cold. I had no idea what these floors were made out of, but they were next to useless. Slippery when wet, cold and drafty, and noise echoing everywhere. It will be a sad day when they start using it in ships. I asked Dietrich and he said the stuff was called "linoleum." I vowed to remember that, so I could forever avoid it.

The convoy was still down there, far below. I could see figures moving on the ship's decks. Since the engines were off and we hadn't crashed, I guessed they made more gas or perhaps dropped the last burnt engine.

That morning I got to have breakfast in the lounge. I whimpered as I poured my coffee, slurping it greedily. It had come up from below and wasn't as good, but it was still so welcome. I was standing about, looking out through our one intact window in the lounge in hopes of seeing our escort. She was down there. Her guns seemed small in relation to her size, at least compared to some of the monsters I'd seen, but she looked fast and trim - in as much as any gray iron monster can look fast and trim. I couldn't tell if she was Confederate or Union. Something else to ask Aleta.

There was a middle aged man standing next to me doing the same, looking out the window.

"She doesn't look like much does she?" he said. He was American, northern.

"Maybe, but I'm pretty sure they're glad she's down there," I replied. I know we would have been. I wished they would let sailing ships in with the convoys.

"I guess I'm glad they're down there at all," he said.

"Are they Union or Confederate?" I asked.

"The captain won't say and I suppose I don't care. Not really.

Not anymore."

I felt the same way.

"I lost my son to it," he continued. "It's a war for fools, the biggest one being me."

I looked at him closely. He looked miserable.

"I waved the flag as much as anybody in the beginning," he said.

"Why do you stare at her if she makes you sad?"

"I drew morning watch," he replied. He looked like I should know.

"Morning watch?" I asked.

"It's the deal we made with the convoy. In return for the pull and food, we're to keep watch and warn them about approaching ships."

"That seems fair."

"The captain made a list and we all had to sign up. You have a job too. You're our nurse aren't you?"

"I am," I sighed.

"And not too happy about it either," he chuckled. "We all have our jobs. At least that's fair."

There was no breakfast yet, but the tables were up so I thanked our watcher and sat down at one and watched the people coming out of their cabins to wait.

Dr. Dewar came in, for the first time without Dmitri, looking worriedly around. Then he gave me a panicked look. He was followed by M. Comeau, the man with the horrible thin mustache, who seemed very agitated, barging forward, making course straight for the cockpit door.

They had brought out the food by then and the cockpit door was, of course, blocked by the line, but most were still sitting, waiting for it to thin.

"I must see the captain," the man said, in accented English, pushing his way forward.

Cirille answered at the door. "I'm sorry, but I don't understand English," she said, in French, which was strange because M. Comeau spoke French. Then he repeated himself in poor French! He was clearly lying. They woke up Dietrich to translate English for the captain. Poor Dietrich.

"My roommate is missing," M. Comeau said. "He didn't sleep in his bed last night, I haven't seen him this morning."

Something was said from inside, then M. Comeau said, "No. I've looked everywhere. There aren't many places to hide." Then I couldn't hear more because they were inside the cockpit. "M. Tomescu, Dmitri Tomescu," Comeau replied. Dr. Dewar's eyes went wide and he turned and headed straight for me.

"I wonder where he went," I said to myself. I had a feeling he was sinking in the deeps.

"We have to talk," Dr. Dewar said, standing before me. He looked stricken.

"No. I don't know what he was. From the east," Comeau's voice continued from the cockpit. There was more talking, then, "No, I don't know him. Never said a thing. Not a pleasant fellow."

"Okay," I said.

Dr. Dewar blinked at me, but apparently understood, then said, "In my cabin."

"Sure." I understood he was upset, but why did he want to talk to me?

I got up and followed him. He stopped Vic, who was entering the dining room, when I remembered Aleta. She was missing breakfast.

"Wait," I said. "I have to do something."

I was about to open our cabin door when Sigrid walked up.

"*Wir mussen wachen sie,*" she said.

Which, is what I suppose we did. When we got to our cabin, she began nudging Aleta.

"*Wachst du!*"

Aleta groaned. "*Ich muss schlafen.*"

"You're missing breakfast," I added.

Then Dietrich came in. Dr. Dewar looked even more agitated.

"*Du wolltest wieder das Luftpersonal werden,*" Dietrich said.

More groans followed by, "*Ja, ja.*"

"Hello," I called near her ear. "Need any help?"

"Maybe you can sleep for me. I need four more hours," she moaned, but then she lifted herself up and slung her feet over the edge of the bed. "What's the emergency?"

"We have a lost passenger," Dietrich said.

"Oh wonderful," She moaned.

Sigrid grabbed Aleta's crew boots. Aleta was still wearing her overalls. It had to be at least two days since she changed! "*Heir,*" Sigrid said, as she handed them up.

Aleta hopped down and sat on my bunk as she put them on. She knew what I was thinking. "Cali, you can't go up."

"I know."

"I'd gladly trade. This isn't going to be fun. I'm not sure how useful I'll be this time. I'm not familiar with this ship and I'm too big for half the crawlways."

"I could check the hold," I suggested. "That's not dangerous and I'd get to play with the tashalampa."

"*Taschenlampe*," corrected Dietrich. Then he sighed, "Anything to speed this up so I can get back to sleep. *Frauen, auf Suche*. I'll let Cali into the hold and then join you."

"Can Vic come with me? Two is safer."

"In the hold?" Vic asked.

"It's really fun," I said.

"Yes. As long as we get it done," Dietrich added. "*Alle los!*"

He herded us all out into the hallway, then headed to the cockpit to get the hand lamp.

"Can we talk later?" I asked Dr. Dewar.

He still looked upset, but nodded yes.

Dietrich came back with three, one for Vic and me, and two for the crew to take up top. I guessed some places up there were dark, even in the day time. Aleta and Sigrid took off up the ladder leaving Dietrich to pry open the floor.

"Right," he said, squatting down next to the hole. Passengers, passing by, glanced down with interest. "If you find anything, tell the captain," he said. "I'll be back as soon as I can, but this will take a while. There's a lot of crawlways to search up there." Then he took off toward the storeroom yelling back at us, "Good luck!"

I hopped down into the hold. It was dark. I motioned to Vic to follow. She sat down on the edge and lowered herself down. It was barely four feet down to the floor! I supposed she didn't get to climb around on things much. People were stopping to look in.

"This is the best part," I said, and turned on the light.

"Oh!" she said, brightening up. "Can I hold it?"

"Sure," and I passed it to her. "Be careful. They're fragile."

She waved it around with a giggle. I could see she was going to be no use with the light. We crawled around for a bit and explored, but even without the light, it was pretty clear that there was nothing

99

there. I could see no sign of trunks having been searched by my bathroom spy either. We came to the spot under my cabin and I could see nothing. No sign of anyone entering my cabin that way. Since I had Vic alone, which is not easy to do on a zeppelin, I decided to ask her a question.

"Vic?"

"Hmm?" She was shining the light down the aisle just to see the dust floating in the air.

"What's wrong with your father's hair?"

"Oh, you noticed. It did that about three months ago. He said it was something he mixed up in the lab and now he can't get it to go away."

"You know, there are people who might like to be permanently blond," I said.

"You want to be blond?" She aimed the light at my hair. "You have nice hair."

"No. But it's a little strange."

"Sure. Da does a lot of amazing things. Don't worry though. I'm sure he's patented it. The university has a law firm that works for us. He patents everything."

"I think," I said, climbing over a loose box. "I think that sounds like a good idea."

We started moving on down the aisle. "Yes," she said. "Someday he'll figure up something that will make us rich. Then we can stop all this and go live somewhere fun."

"Where would you like to live?" I asked.

"Anywhere but London. In fact anywhere but England. Maybe the Mediterranean. Somewhere warm."

"That would be nice."

"At least somewhere where you don't find soot in the bottoms of your tea cups each morning and fog as thick as porridge."

The hold was as disappointing as I expected. That was until we came to the mailroom door. The lead seal was broken, the wire dangling loose.

The Captain came down himself with a clipboard. He wrote the time. The lack of evidence. The lack of Tomescu's body inside. The seals broken on the mail bags and boxes. I had to sit there while he filled out each section on the forms. Germans!

They never found him by the way. Not down on the ship below either. Gone, over the side in the night, I suppose. The thought of that makes me shiver. I've lived my life surrounded by the sea, and it could take any of us without a moment's notice. A broken lifeline, a rogue wave, or simply slipping and falling over the side would be all it would take. But I needed breakfast, and it was my shift. My problem was getting water into Pieter, whose fever was definitely worse. We were losing him.

I heard a knock at the door. It was Yvonne.

"I brought you lunch," she said. The day had been passing.

"Oh thank you."

"I've brought you more ice water. Go slow with the ice. It'll be an hour before that infernal machine makes more." She gave me a big very cold steel bowl.

"Thank you," I said, taking it carefully, smiling to myself. An infernal machine making ice. "I will."

"Is everything else all right in here?" she asked.

"Pieter still has his fever. I'm a little worried."

She looked at Pieter. "He'll pull through. Dr. Péan is one of the greatest doctors in France. Pieter couldn't be in better hands."

"Is he?"

"Oh yes. I read an article about him in the paper."

"Really?"

"Pieter will pull through." Then she had to go. "Bread to knead," she said.

I took the towels we had draped over him, one by one, and dipped them in the bowl, lightly wringing them, and draping them back over his head and body. He had ceased to sweat, his skin hot despite the cold breeze. I lifted his head yet again and began trying to dribble water into his mouth. If only the fever would break, I thought. But it didn't. He died that night.

But I'm getting ahead of myself again. So much happened before that.

I was relieved in the late afternoon. Olivie came in to take over. She looked over Pieter with a frown and then nervously shooed me from the room.

Standing in the hallway, at a loss, I wandered into the lounge looking for Aleta or Vic. But neither were there, so I sat down with a sigh and a cup of tea, when who should sit down next to me, but Max.

"I'm on this flight to get to Brussels," I said, tired of his probing questions.

He chuckled. "I know," he said quietly. Obviously he didn't want to be overheard. "You would have to be the most brilliant actor in history. No one could pretend to be so guileless and incompetent."

"I'm not incompetent!" I said.

This time he laughed out loud. "But you are. Brilliant, but incompetent," he continued. "And guileless."

"Who killed Dmitri?" I asked.

"I didn't," he replied. "I thought about it though. I might have."

"I think it was M. Comeau."

"That's likely."

"So you're chasing Dr. Dewar? He has something you want?"

He looked at me with a sly smile. "Yes. He's an amazing man. Any country would beg to have him. I know we will, at least now that his leash is dead. Now it's a matter of the highest bidder."

"The highest bidder." I sighed to myself, "Poor Vic,"

"Hmm?"

"I suppose she's going to have to learn a new language."

"Yes," he said thoughtfully. "That will have to be part of the bid." Then he turned and looked at me again.

"What?" I asked.

"It's nothing. It's just that everything points to you, but you are so clearly not the Belgian."

"The Belgian?" I felt a moment of fear.

"There's a Belgian agent here." He looked around. "Somewhere."

"But not me?"

"Perhaps." He paused. "Be careful. Guileless often ends badly. Remember that I warned you."

"I can't help it. Things are happening, but no one tells me anything. Would you still talk to me if I was the Belgian?" I asked.

"Of course. In our business these things are never personal. At least we try to keep them that way." Then he frowned. "Sometimes I wonder if you're toying with me."

There was another pause while I chewed on that. Then I asked, "I suppose Dmitri worked for the British?"

"Yes. But the Institution is gone now, out of the equation. Dr. Dewar is a free agent. Apparently, Cali, this affair could change the balance of power in Europe."

I wasn't sure how I should feel about that. I didn't care about Europe then. Only my family and friends, and Red of course.

"So who do you think killed Dmitri?" I asked.

"Normally I would think it was the Russian, Comeau. Actually his real name is Petrov, but it would be somewhat overt, even for him. He's so obviously guilty."

"There are others?"

"Perhaps. Please understand that not all spies are from nations. The murderer might not represent any single country."

"Really?"

"There are many power blocks." He waved his hand matter-of-factly. "Who do you think sabotaged the engines?"

"I've been so busy, I haven't given it thought." Then I looked at him, "Someone wants Professor Dewar dead?"

"Maybe the daughter to," he suggested. "Perhaps it's an issue of inheritance? There's probably a great deal of money involved. It might even be anarchists wanting to silence him. My point is that Germany or Britain might be the least of the professor's problems. We could protect him."

"Are there other British agents here?"

He sighed. "No. I left her at the docks."

"That lady."

"That would probably be her."

I thought for a second and then an odd notion came to me. "So the killer isn't the one who sabotaged the engines."

"It's unlikely they're related," he agreed. "The killer would be killing himself along with the rest of us."

"It's the patents. He's patented something valuable." But certainly blond hair wasn't worth a zeppelin full of people. "What did he invent?"

"You don't know?" Obviously, he still thought I was a spy. He took a sip from his tea. "I'm not even positive that I know. But if it's what I've heard, and trust me in this, then you're better off not knowing."

"Why?" I asked.

"It's one of those secrets that's as big as the discovery." He could see that I was confused. "If the discovery were common knowledge, then it wouldn't be as valuable."

"That makes sense."

"And if knowing makes the secret less valuable, then your death becomes profitable."

"Then I definitely don't want to know," I said with conviction

"Nobody knows, at least not for sure," he chuckled, then took another sip. "Except the Doctor himself."

"So if they're dead, then perhaps someone inherits their patents or the patents become void. What happens to patents when there are no heirs? "

"An excellent question. Which is why it would be best if he dealt with us. Germany will make a fair offer and reasonable protection. But I doubt he's patented anything really important. If he had, then his discovery would be common knowledge."

I sighed. I needed to talk to Dr. Dewar.

Our conversation turned to lighter subjects. He told me about Hawaii, where the sea is bright blue and you can see to the bottom, fifty or a hundred feet down. It sounded like the Caribbean. They apparently have fish colored like the rainbow as well and black sand beaches, just like the Canaries, and volcanoes shooting lava too, which is something I would dearly like to see up close.

Max had been very forthcoming about Dr. Dewar, which made me wonder why he was telling me so much. This was all way more than I wanted to know. I needed to talk to Dr. Dewar, but I thought I'd ask Aleta about it first. So I excused myself and headed for our cabin, but she was still out working. At a loss, I sat down on my bunk.

It was Lucien who bought me my ticket. "What has Lucien neglected to tell me?" I asked myself. Maybe I *was* the Belgian. Looking around, I realized that someone had been through our stuff again. My case was open and there was a piece of airship stationary on the floor. I felt dread as I stared down at it.

It had been folded. Someone had written, "I await your instructions," on it in a loose scrawl. Terrible handwriting. It had probably been in my case. Dr. Dewar had slipped it in the night I played for him.

"Damn you Lucien!" I spat in a whisper.

Apparently, I *was* the Belgian.

The note spoiled everything. There was no longer any doubt. I wanted to curl up in bed and hide. Then fear turned to anger. *Thank you Lucien, thank you!* I thought. What was I supposed to do? Save Vic and Dr. Dewar?

The first thing I had to do was get rid of the note. Someone had read it, but if I kept it everyone on the ship would see it eventually. I might as well put in a ladder down to the hold and sell tickets. I definitely didn't want to disappear like Dmitri. I wadded it up into a small ball and tossed it out the window. Then I searched the rest of the cabin for other unfortunate notes. Thankfully, I found none, so I flopped down on the bed, deeply depressed.

But feeling sorry for yourself is stupid. I decided to practice, after all, my case was already open. I started with scales with increasing tempo, then couplets, and then a jig, the Hornpipe, to lighten my mood. I kept it going with the Butterfly, but broke down in tears halfway through. What were you thinking Lucien? Why didn't you tell me? What went wrong? What hasn't gone wrong? I was pretty pathetic.

But crying is no better than feeling sorry for yourself. I decided to work on Vieuxtemps. It's not much to listen to, but good for technical practice. I launched into it, but it took three tries before I could find it. Once started, as always, its demands consumed everything, leaving no time for thought. Then I kept going. Bach. I'd almost gotten through Bach when there was knock at my door. I realized my cheeks were wet so I dried them. It was Mrs. Yount.

"They sent me with food for you," she said.

"I'd forgotten. Thank you."

"We all wish you would play in the lounge, not that we can't hear you as it is."

"I'm sorry. I wanted to be alone," I said. "I think it's that I'm so tired. The thought of other people watching is too much."

"Yes, of course. I'll leave you alone."

I said, "Thank you," as she pulled the door shut.

I heard her say to someone in the hallway, "She's been crying."

I had no way to respond to that. I looked at the plate. It was beans over mashed potatoes with a hunk of cheese on the side and a pale tea to drink. The tea smelled odd, but not unpleasant.

After lunch I worked on Saint-Saëns, thinking of Mrs. Hartnoll as I sawed at those thirty second notes. Finally I lay down and slept.

I had the evening watch slot, but without Pieter there wasn't that much to do, so I tried *Kidnapped* again but got nowhere. People had been swapping books at mealtimes and I would try at dinner. Sadly, Dracula was back in my cabin on Red. I would have gladly read it again.

Anika was awake for dinner time and I fed her. It was boiled salted beef, cabbage, and somewhat stale petifores, all kind of chewy. So I cut it up for her into very thin pieces and spooned them in. She could have done it herself, but we didn't want her moving around. We had moved her down to the bottom bunk to better reach her, carrying her down mattress and all. With the sweat, urine, and blood, nobody would want to sleep on Pieter's mattress. It went out the window.

At dinner I managed to swap my book. I took a break and walked around asking. I got an old yellowback called *Workers of the Sea* that had a man with a knife single handedly fighting some kind of giant hairy octopus on its cover. In English no less. It looked to be ridiculous fun! Oh the adventures we who live at sea have.

Then your Cali fell asleep on watch, book still open, to be caught by Émile.

"Now we're even," he said with a smile. Then he sent me off to bed.

I had been so worried about myself that I'd completely forgotten about Dr. Dewar.

Chapter 10 – The Sixth Day

I woke in thin moonlight, my shoes off, my violin still in its case. The floor still in place, so apparently I had no nighttime callers. Above I could see the sag of Aleta in her bed. I was cold, still in my clothes but no blanket. I got up and hit the head, then changed into my night dress. Sleep was no problem after that and the night passed to morning with no more effort from me than shutting my eyes.

Breakfast that day was oat porridge with raisins and real tea.

I could see Vic sitting with Comeau, which was worrying since he was probably a murderer. She seemed upset. I thought I'd go sit with her to make sure she was okay after I got my food.

"Cirille," I asked as she handed me my bowl of porridge. "What was that tea last night?"

"Chamomile," she replied with a smile. "Did you like it?"

"I think so," I replied uncertainly.

"I hope so," she replied. "We found some boxes of it with the regular tea. It's interesting isn't it? I wonder why we have it?"

"It helps you sleep," said a voice behind me. It was Emma.

"Does it?" replied Cirille.

We were interrupted by an elderly lady jumping about by the windows saying, "Oh, oh."

An old man put down a magazine and stood up. "*Marta, was ist jetzt los?*"

"*Rauch! Ich kann Rauch sehen.*"

"*Rauch?*" he looked surprised.

He stepped to the window and stared.

"*Rauch. Rauch!*" He exclaimed, the last coming out a yell.

The captain, who had been sitting in the cockpit, flew from his seat and rushed the cockpit door, knocking Cirille and me out of the way. He was followed by Dietrich. Everyone headed for the window including half the people waiting for their breakfast. Behind us I heard someone exclaim in French, "The floor, it is tipping. Get your cup!"

Still holding my bowl of porridge, I stared out the window. The tipping floor brought the horizon into view over the tops of everyone's heads.

Our watcher couldn't have had very good eyes. There wasn't just one column of smoke. I counted at least eight. How could she have missed them?

"*Wir mussen signal!*" the captain yelled.

I could hear whistles below as our rocking brought our convoy into view.

"I think they already know," I said to myself.

But he rushed to the cockpit.

I stared down in horror as the first shells came in. I know what they feel like. There was no way our escort was going to fend off a fleet, not that she didn't try. I could hear the thump of her guns next to the detonation of incoming shells. They blossomed below us, a mix of white and fiery yellow flowers, clawing away great handfuls of hull and superstructure.

Then the deck lurched, then lurched again.

Dietrich yelled something in German.

The floor jerked under me and I lost part of my porridge. My body felt heavy then light. The ships below rocked back into view, the tipping so bad that I could see through the window even though I had dropped to the floor. A shell had struck the paddle wheeler, wood was flying into the air, and then it was gone and I was looking at sky. Things fell and crashed and people screamed.

When we rocked back the other way and I got another eyeful of ocean, the convoy was gone, just empty ocean. We must have turned or moved. Then we entered a cloud, the outside fading white.

I was sitting pretty securely on the floor, holding on to my bowl, but some people were sliding back and forth as we tipped. I could see thin glimpses of the ocean below us through foggy breaks in the cloud, the reports of detonations and fire lighting the clouds as shells struck home. They were hard reminders of our mistake.

Our rocking gradually quieted. Behind us, the convoy swung back into view, white wakes veering in every direction, many leaving ribbons of black smoke. Two ships at least were on fire, one almost certainly in its death throes. Yellow flame sheeted up through its superstructure, bellowing from deep inside. Their crew were dying or flinging themselves to slow death in the waves.

I shuttered. I thought of the Dreyers and Harmons.

Our spotter's husband must have said something mean to his wife because she was curled up sobbing in the corner.

"Dietrich," I called.

"What?" He was wedged in the cockpit doorway, waiting like all of us for the rocking to stop.

"What happens now?"

"We drift," he replied.

"Can't we start the motors?"

"No fuel. We'll need them to land or moor again."

We were drifting east, toward Europe. Perhaps, I thought, we'd land before we starved. I looked at my bowl. It was quiet then, except for Frau Hochberg's sobbing. I tell you her name now because she died soon after. We never got the chance to meet. I had started counting the deaths.

I began to eat quickly, the deck still gently swaying under us. People looked at me, so I looked back.

"I can't help it. I'm hungry," I said. And food was going to be scarce, I thought.

They had generated extra gas to keep us up without the engines and now it took us up above ten thousand feet, back above the clouds. I kept popping my ears while I ate. Later, some people got headaches and dizziness. It didn't help that the deck rocked freely now with every change of the breeze and we started to slowly spin around and around, about once every ten or fifteen minutes. I didn't have any problems with it myself, except that the sunlight was constantly shifting from one side to the other. It was impossible for me to tell what direction we were going, which I hate, and passing through clouds leaves everything cold and damp.

I came in to check on the schedule and ran into Mrs. Péan. She was sitting there looking spent and defeated. Pieter was still laying in the bed. He looked gray, his eyes already sinking under their lids.

"It was peaceful at least," she said.

"How's Anika?" I asked.

"Oh, good. She doesn't know yet."

"No, I do," came a small voice from the top bunk.

"I'm so sorry, dear," said Mrs. Péan.

I thought she might have been crying up there, but I couldn't see.

"Will we have the funeral today?" I asked.

"Yes. Émile is talking to the captain."

"*Ich möchte gehen,*" Anika said.

"No dear. We can't move you yet. We don't have enough to stitch you up again if you pop them."

Then Mrs. Péan asked me, "Have we lost our ships?"

"Yes," I said. "It was terrible. They were hit hard."

"I heard it, and felt it," she said. "We can't be too far from England though."

"It has to be at more than 300 miles. That's the treaty limit for combat. Maybe the captain will tell us. We're going to have to have another meeting, about food if nothing else."

"Yes." She sounded tired.

This time I got to go to the meeting. We met in the lounge. We were down to twenty four passengers, eighteen attending. Mrs. Péan stayed with the patients. The Hochbergs, our spotter and her husband, were missing. Dietrich and Aleta translated.

"First, some good news," the captain said. "We'll be passing within 120 miles south west of Cornwall tomorrow. The bad news is that we'll miss it as well as England. We expect to cross the coast either in Southern France or Northern Spain. We plan to save the engines to try for a soft landing, but it will all depend on the wind. I'm afraid that we can't expect any sort of ground crew so we will need all able bodied help if we are to land safely. We'll have training for that starting tomorrow. You'll all have to help in one way or another. Of course, there's still the possibility of finding another tow, but I'm afraid we don't have the fuel to spare to hover while we negotiate. We can be thankful for the weather as well, since it's carrying us east. We expect this to hold until we make land."

"Next is the food situation. We're going to have to cut back. We hope to land in three or four days, but it might take longer. I'm afraid you will have to be forgiving with our menu. We will do the best we can with what we have left. Luckily, since we generated extra gas, we have plenty of water. We can balance buoyancy by venting gas instead of water. We're more concerned now with staying down rather than staying up."

"We have some sad news as well. One of the wounded crew, Pieter Misch, died last night of fever. We will be having his funeral after this meeting."

He gave us all a rather bleak stare. "And that's it."

I sat there feeling tired. I'd tried so hard to help Pieter. I could feel tears welling up inside, so I got up quickly and went to my cabin. Laying on the bed, staring up at the cot above, I tried to cry quietly. Aleta was gone. Zeppelin crew never seem to rest.

After about twenty minutes, there was a knock on the door.

"Cali?" It was Émile.

"Yes," I said.

"You should come. It will help."

"I will."

I sat up and put my feet on the floor. Drying my eyes with my last clean handkerchief from under my pillow. Me, with handkerchiefs! I never had one before. I just used any old rag. Now I had six.

When I came out, Émile was waiting. He helped me make my way forward. They opened the door and I could see sky, ocean, and clean sunshine outside. I could also see how much we were rocking, the seascape rising and dipping with the sway.

Pieter was wrapped in sheet along with a two foot long block of something. A piece off an engine probably. It left black oil stains soaking into the white fabric. His blue socked feet and blue pants stuck out the bottom.

Aleta and Dietrich were on each side of him, wearing leather harnesses clipped to rings in the wall. I could see tears in their eyes.

The captain read to us from the Bible in German. There were ten of us besides crew. Max and M. Marmontel were there. Most were sitting. Aleta and Dietrich pushed him along the floor and out the door. Then I turned to Émile and he put his arms around me while I sobbed into his shoulder.

So I can hear you ask. Cali! Were you wearing your corset all this time, and how could you get in it with Aleta gone being crew?

Don't be silly. My stupid corset went in my trunk as soon as I got on board. Aleta's too. But they're really simple to put on. So far I've encountered two sorts, but I suspect there are probably more, thus said Cali, the worldly woman of experience. My travel corset had hooks on the front. The one I had at the ball didn't have those. I needed help getting into that. It's not possible to get them tight enough on your own. Well, maybe someone's made a machine, but I wouldn't trust it. My travel kind wasn't hard, at least as long as you have some flexibility in your arms and shoulders.

You loosen the strings, put it on, and then do the hooks in front. You reach around back and pull out the slack from the strings, working down from top to bottom. You don't need to start exactly at the top, but you have to start as high as you can and cinch downwards. That's it. By the end the laces are long. You pull the ends around and tie them in front.

Of course, I'm no fool. I stuck to my bodices. Really, the thing itched! I tell you this because things had gotten grim and I want to warn you that they're not going to get better for a long time, and I felt I had to say something light. Not wearing my corset was about the best thing that happened that day. It's helpful when the only thing you want to do is flop down in your bed and never move again, which I was doing, staring up at the empty bunk above me. Again.

No tears though this time. I was too tired to cry.

So many terrible things happened that day. We lost the Hochbergs. They didn't turn up at lunch. When Antonio checked their room, he found it empty. Just two notes. Frau Hochberg had committed suicide, followed by Herr Hochberg when he discovered her note. They jumped from their window. So many deaths in one day.

I could hear the Jefferies arguing next door. It started with a bitter word and had grown until neither knew what they were saying. I understood. We were all at the end of our endurance.

I guess the rocking bed put me to sleep because it was lunch time. No call to stand watch on the wounded, so I supposed that I would be up that night. We had fried cheese sandwiches and tea for lunch, and it was good! So I was wrong. That was another good thing. We had two good things that day. After lunch I got to play cards again with Vic. I think she was angry with me, but she wouldn't talk about it.

"Da says I'm to stay close to you," she said, as she dealt. It was the two of us at that point. The Dreyers were gone. "You wouldn't happen to know why?"

"No, I don't. That's strange, but this whole trip is crazy." Oh Lucien, what did you want me to do? "But maybe you should. Two might have a better chance than one when we hit the ground."

"Don't say it that way," she said as she picked up her cards.

"We're young so they'll probably want to push us out early with anchor lines or something."

"I hope not." She put two chips under the cup along with the ante. "I hate heights." The wind blowing through the cabin tended to pick up our paper chips so we took to keeping them under tea cups.

"Do you know how to tie knots?" I asked.

"No."

"They use clips for everything anyway. We'll find out tomorrow. Are you okay?"

"I'm fine," she said curtly.

We played quietly for a bit, but I could tell she wanted to talk.

"Da has been going queer since Dmitri died. He's very spooky. Looking around all the time."

"You should be too, I think. Anyone who wanted Dmitri dead,

probably doesn't bear kind feelings toward your Da."

"I already thought of that. But there's nothing we can do, being stuck here and all. We try to not go anywhere alone." Dr. Dewar was sitting on the other side of the room. "So what do you have?" she asked.

We compared cards and I lost of course. Pure frustration. I dealt this time, something I could now do on my own.

"They sabotaged our fuel," she said.

"Yes," I said, putting down four cards.

"I told you not to do that," she said. "Now I know you have nothing." She drew one. "Do you think they were trying to kill us?"

I didn't know what to say, but she continued without me.

"It's hard to believe." She set her hand down and began rubbing her eyes. "I don't know what I can do about any of it."

"Neither do I. Where are you coming from?"

"California. Da had a symposium there. He delivered some papers."

"Couldn't he have mailed them?" I asked.

"No. You have to give lectures," she said, looking up at me. Her eyes were red. She looked tired. "They all listen to each other's lectures."

"California is far away, even from Boston."

"It's not bad by zeppelin, when they work. We can get there in ten days from London, if we pick our flights carefully. It's where Edison's campus is. Menlo Park. Scientists come from everywhere, Europe, Russia, Australia, India, China, even Japan."

"Who's Edison?"

She looked up at me, eyes wide. "You don't know who Thomas Edison is?"

"Should I?" I asked.

"He's a scientist industrialist. Maybe the greatest. He has a million patents."

"So maybe someone from the symposium wants you dead?"

"Why?"

I looked over at Dr. Dewar. I'm thinking, a rival. A rich rival. He was sitting in a chair alone, rereading an old newspaper. "Maybe they don't like blond hair. Maybe it's a wicked consortium of hairdressers."

That finally got a little laugh out of her. I swear though, in the current light his hair almost looked a little green.

Aleta, my long lost friend, made an appearance, coming from our cabin. She finally found time to shower and change clothes.

"Are we still learning?" she asked.

"No, we are losing," I said.

That got another smile out of Vic, which was nice.

"Do you have room for another?" she asked.

"Sure. Poker with only two is boring," Vic said.

Aleta got a cup for herself and we divided the chips up. Then I watched Vic shuffle. I really needed my own deck of cards so I could practice. We rarely played cards on Red. There was never enough of us off duty at any one time. Everyone was always on watch, asleep, or eating, so we tended to do things by ourselves when we had time to relax and cards at school, especially gambling, was not an appropriate skill for a young woman expecting to land a good marriage.

"I really need my own deck to practice," I said.

"You know, they'll give you a deck of cards don't you?" Aleta said.

"Who?" I asked.

"Lufthansa. Ask one of the crew."

"Really?"

She waved at the cockpit door with a little smile, "Try. Go ask."

So I got up and went to the cockpit door and knocked. The cockpit door opened. It was Yvonne.

"Yes?" Yvonne asked. But the deck chose that moment to take a vigorous dip and one of our elderly passengers slipped and fell hard on the deck. Frankly, I'm surprised that it hadn't happened sooner. Linoleum is slippery.

I danced over to her across the tipping deck and knelt down beside her. She was breathing, but unconscious.

"*Éléonore, êtes-vous blessée?*" her husband asked, kneeling next to me.

There was something wrong with the lay of her body. Her leg wasn't sitting right.

"*Appelez le médecin*," I said. "Call the doctor," I repeated. He sat back and looked at me in terror. I yelled to the room itself, "Call the doctor!" The floor took another dip, a tea cup rolled off the table and hit my back, breaking on the floor next to me. So much for my last clean dress. Éléonore started to slide, her head leaving a bloody streak. People were just sitting in their seats, transfixed. Her husband and I tried to hold her in place.

"Éléonore!" he called.

I looked closely at her. Her left leg was laying at an odd angle to her right with me thinking that it was perhaps her hip. I couldn't see all of her left arm either. I had no idea how to deal with a broken hip. Better if she were gun shot. But I could find out about the rest of her though. Feeling under her head I found more blood. Then I began to unlace her collar.

"What are you doing?" Her husband said, leaning forward to restrain me. Great! I thought. He can stop me from helping her, but he can't call for the doctor!

"I want to look at her neck," I said, as I continued.

He clearly was afraid and confused. Her neck looked fine, although a little strange because she was old. I'd never seen an old person's neck before. She was pale. I'd lift her legs if it weren't for the hip. Then I began to lift her dress. I had to see her hip.

He grabbed my hands. "You . . . stop, stop what you're doing. Stop it."

"I have to know if she's hurt," I said, looking up at him. He was gripping me quite hard, his eyes were wide.

"I could use some help!" I called.

Then Aleta was there, and that southern woman, trying to hold him, but he struggled.

"He's strong," the southern woman said, as she moved to get a better grip.

"No." he said. "Éléonore, wake up."

"I think her hip is broken," I said. "Please, let go." I was starting to get a little scared. But then Émile's hand carefully gripped his upper arm, the other slipping around his shoulder. He must have heard me calling. "There, there. I think you should sit down and let us attend to your wife."

Her husband looked up at Émile with an empty stare. "Yes, yes, of course," and he let go.

Oh! I thought. You'll listen to Émile, but not to me!

Émile sat the man down, leaning against the bulkhead. Then he looked back at me. "So what do we have here?" he asked.

"Her head and I think her hip," I said. "A little blood under her head, but I don't know what to do about hips," I said. I think I sounded a little bit helpless.

Émile sighed, sounding as tired as he looked, and stood and came over. He lifted the side of her skirt carefully.

"She's pale, but I didn't lift her legs." I continued. "I was afraid for her hip."

"Good," he said. He was trying to work her bloomers down. "We're going to need to cut this."

That's when I realized he was wearing a nightshirt.

"Pardon monsieur, but could I bother you for a pocket knife?" Émile asked the husband.

The man stared at him for a second, then answered, "Yes, of course," and fished his out.

Émile cut the side of her bloomers. Underneath, her skin looked bruised and it seemed to be spreading.

"Internal bleeding. We'll need a stretcher or at least something flat to carry her on," Émile said to himself.

"I'll get the stretcher," Aleta replied, and took off for the storeroom.

"You're going up top?"

"It's clamped to the roof," she replied.

"Oh. That's right."

Émile cut away her dress top, sleeve to shoulder, and was looking at her shoulder. "I think it's dislocated," he said, carefully trying to feel her bones.

The cockpit door opened and Dietrich and the captain came out, arguing.

"We could use some help!" I called.

Now people finally started to get up, I suppose to help, but the captain waved them back down as he walked over. I don't blame them for not trying to help sooner. I think everyone was in shock.

"*Was ist jetzt los?*" the captain muttered.

"Dietrich, tell him she has a broken hip and internal bleeding," I said in English.

"*Auch,*" the captain muttered.

"*Éléonore, Éléonore,*" her husband kept mumbling.

"*Auch* is correct," Émile replied. "We need to hurry. I want to try

117

to set her leg before she wakes." Émile looked at the husband. "Sir, you'll have to lead us to your cabin. The rest of you, we'll try to lift her onto the stretcher by her dress. Try to keep her arms close to her body."

We all took positions around her and lifted together, setting her on the stretcher. Then the men took her to her cabin. Setting a bone, especially a hip bone, is matter of leverage and physical strength. The work of men. Cali was not needed.

I said thank you to the woman who helped.

"Belle. My name is Belle Boyd."

"Cali," I replied. "Calista Carmichael."

"I know. I think we all know that.'

She had a slight southern accent.

"Where are you from?" I asked.

She smiled. "Montreal believe it or not. A Georgia flower in the frozen north. My daddy moved us north to escape the war."

I could sympathize with that. Which was when I notice that Vic was gone. So I thanked Belle again and went to look for her.

I knocked carefully on the Dewar's door.

"Hello, Vic? Are you alright?"

"Leave us alone!" She called from inside.

I could hear Dr. Dewar inside. "Victoria," he said. "What has gotten into you?"

She answered her father quietly, but really these walls were next to useless.

"She lied to us! She's working for the Germans."

"I already knew about that," he said. "It's been in the papers."

"You knew?" she cried.

"Of course I did. It's political bunk. Foreign Office protecting their behinds. She works for the Belgians."

"I do not!" I yelled. Then I noticed M. Comeau, who hadn't helped with Éléonore by the way, sitting in the lounge staring at me.

The door opened and Dr. Dewar was staring at me with a look of astonishment.

"What do you mean you don't?" he said.

"I don't." I repeated as quietly as I could. He stood there, seeming to be at a loss for words. So I continued, "Can we talk about this? But not out here?" The corridor was full of people who had been watching the trouble with Éléonore unfold.

His eyes darted about, then he said. "Yes, of course. Come in."

"Daaa . . ." Vic wailed behind him.

"You have to be," he said, his eyes flaring at me.

"I think I was supposed to help you, but the instructions must have gotten lost somewhere," I said. "And I don't work for the Belgians. I just have a friend or two there."

"You lost your instructions?" His eyebrows were up.

"I never received them. I think Lucien meant to tell me, but it must have gotten lost between Europe and the US."

"You're just someone's friend?" he said, raising his voice.

"Please, everyone can hear," I said. "That's how Lucien works."

"Lucien?"

"The Duke of Tervuren," I said. Really, it was almost a whine.

"The Duke of Tervuren." He relaxed a bit. "Now we're getting somewhere."

"I'm glad. Can we please do it quietly?" I realized then that this had all been set up. Someone, almost certainly Comeau, wanted to force me to reveal my hand, not that I was really playing. Honest!

"You did lie to me!" Vic hissed.

"I didn't!" I hissed back. "I have no idea who you are or what you want." But then I stopped. That actually wasn't true. "Well, not much of an idea. At least not yet."

"Then why are you always talking to that German?" she snapped.

"He's a friend!" But then I had to stop again. "He's a German spy, but he's a friend." I shook my head and thought, that didn't sound like I meant it to sound.

"Like you have friends in Belgium," she said.

"Yes, like I have friends in Belgium," I sighed. "But I'm not working for any of them."

Dr. Dewar was looking alarmed again. "Then why are you here?"

Then it was my turn to be exasperated. "I supposed to be going to music school, but I guess I am working for them too, the Belgians at least. Not that I'm getting paid."

"You're not getting paid?" he said. "You're doing this as a favor?"

"Yes," I replied, ready to be defensive again.

"You're doing this as a gentleman then." But then he sputtered, "Gentlewoman then?"

"Yes," I frowned. "I suppose I am."

"Oh, I see," he smiled. "That makes it different." Then he held out his hand to shake.

"Daaa . . ." Vic wailed again.

"Quiet," he shushed. "This is an affair of honor."

"We want to immigrate to Belgium." Dr. Dewar explained. "I can't stand what the English are doing with my work. It's bad enough what they've done to Scotland, Ireland, and Wales, but now they're trying to do it to the entire world. And don't get me started on the Royal Institution and their body guards and locked doors. I'm a bloody prisoner. They read everything I write. Every letter. They go through my notes when I'm asleep. They'd supply me with a wife if they thought I'd accept one from them."

"Anyway, I've come up with an idea. A bloody incredible idea. It's going to change everything . . ."

I had to interrupt him. "Please. Dr. Dewar, I don't want to know. It might mean my life if I knew."

"Your life?" Vic asked.

I nodded. I tried to explain it as Max had. "If my knowing makes your invention less valuable, if too many people know of it, then they might start killing people to keep it secret."

"That's awful," Vic said.

"That's the Royal Institution," Dr. Dewar added, nodding his head. "So anyway, it'll change warfare as we know it."

I rolled my eyes. He just had to talk about it!

He blinked back at me twice, then continued, "And I didn't want the English to get their hands on it. If anyone should have it, it should be a small country. A country everyone is always pushing around. So I thought a bit and came up with Belgium. It's right in the middle, in between the great powers. If Belgium was undefeatable, then everyone would have to stop walking over it to get to each other. Maybe they'd stop fighting. Like there was a wall between them."

Not likely, I thought. But I appreciated his good intentions.

"And they speak a little English at least," he added.

"Mostly French, Dutch and German," I said. "Lucien speaks

quite good English though."

"That's the Duke of Tervuren you say. I never knew his first name. Court's like that. People's titles are more important than their names. I managed to slip him a note that I wanted to meet him alone. I'll be damned if he wasn't waiting in my room. I'd like to know how he beat the guards. I couldn't go to the bathroom without someone knowing."

I knew Lucien to be a good military leader and great scrounge, but that he could sneak about as well was surprising. Oh Lucien. What did you want me to do? What can I do to help these people?

"I kept getting notes from him. They'd turn up in the oddest places. Under my pillow, in my coat pocket. He said to be prepared to leave and that a young woman with a violin would be meeting me on the flight."

"That would be me," I said. It was clear that Lucien intended for me to be here. I had hoped that somehow this was a mistake, a coincidence, but there was no avoiding the truth.

"There have to be more people involved than me though," I said.

"Exactly," Vic added. "How could you get us out of Britain? They'd come onboard in London if they wanted us off."

"Actually, that's not true," I said. "Airships and boats are the sovereign territory of their flag of registration. Technically, we're in Germany at the moment. They could force us off. There're a couple of ways authorities can board ships, claim we were smuggling or are pirates for instance. Of course, that wouldn't pass in court, but you'd be in England where they wanted you anyway."

"On the other hand, that you were kidnapped might give Germany some claim over you," I said, half to myself. "It could also be considered an act of war. Then again too, we could resist. We would be under German criminal jurisdiction, not English." I swear, I was talking to myself, just like Pa, which was more than a little weird. "If someone got hurt, we would get better than the fake trial England would give us."

"Where did you hear all that," Vic asked.

"Maritime law. Part of my seaman certification tests. I'm certified third mate. I've got a certificate and everything," I said smiling. I'm proud of my rating. It was fun being the only girl amongst all those grown men during those examinations. They all thought it was pretty funny and mussed my hair for luck, but my certification is real. It's a fact, and it's mine.

"I think we'd be safe landing in England as long as we could manage to stay onboard," I continued. "But that's not a problem as we're past England already. It's France or Spain now. I'm happy with either one. And when we land, it won't take long for Lucien to find us."

That evening, after a dinner of a few thin slices of canned ham, steamed carrots, and crackers, I was practicing in the lounge, Saint-Saëns and those damn thirty second notes, when there was a commotion from the cockpit and Sigrid burst through the door heading for the bathrooms. I stopped playing and watched. She was knocking loudly on the men's shower door, calling for the captain. Apparently, he foolishly tried to find the time to bathe.

"*Kapitän, Kapitän!*" she called.

"*Was?*" he moaned, over the sound of the water.

"*Ein Schiff. Sie bieten uns eine abschleppen!*" she replied.

I got the ship part.

Then a woman sitting next to an unbroken window said, "Oh look! It's a ship."

Everyone rushed over but me. I had to put my violin away first. She's too precious to risk having her fall on the deck. By the time I'd gotten there, we had just turned away from it. So I ran to the other side and waited. We twisted around in the air until she came into view. All I could see was her lights, but she seemed to be a warship, a cruiser. She was signaling.

I waited, collecting each letter, stringing them together in my mind, until it was clear. "Can we assist?" It was English. She was an English cruiser. She was going to want to haul us back to Britain!

I knocked on Vic's door.

"Hello?" I called.

"Cali?" It was Vic.

"I have news," I said.

I heard movement inside and then the door opened. It was Dr.

Dewar in his night robe.

"Miss Carmichael," he said. "Can't this wait for morning?"

"No, I'm afraid not. This is important."

"Aye, I can see it in your eyes," he said. "Come in and tell us."

Vic was sitting on the upper bed. She put down a book.

"There's a ship below us. A British cruiser."

Dr. Dewar frowned.

"No," Vic said.

"They're offering to give us a tow. I don't see how the captain can refuse, which means we're probably going to end up back in England."

"We can stay on the ship, right?" Vic asked.

"Yes, but she has no engines," I said. "She's not going anywhere once we land."

"We'll have to leave when the food runs out," Dr. Dewar said. He looked a bit stricken.

"I don't know what to do. Perhaps Lucien will be able to send some help. At least a lawyer."

"Well, we're not there yet," Dr. Dewar said. "Let's wait and see."

"Don't worry about us Cali," Vic said. "Da is too valuable to punish."

"I suppose so," I replied. "But they'll never let you out of their sights again."

"No," Dr. Dewar said. "No, they won't. But maybe that's better, at least for Victoria, than having people trying to kill us. No, you're the one to worry about."

"What do you mean?"

"I didn't realize who you are at first. You haven't seen the newspapers," he said. "They've been blaming you for the loss of the Congo. The German spyess most call you, but *The Daily Telegraph* has started calling you "The Rabbit" for some reason. Seduced the Belgian prince, and the Telegraph's the biggest newspaper in the world too. It's bound to stick. They're all too committed to you being their scapegoat to let you go easily. And it's too good a story for the newspapers."

I looked at Vic. "You don't believe any of that do you?"

"No. But then I don't read the newspapers. A great big load of lies and nonsense mostly. Worse than the ladies in court."

"Thanks," I said.

"Did you seduce a prince?" she asked hopefully.

"Victoria!" Dr. Dewar snapped.

I laughed. "No, but he tried to seduce me."

"No!" she said, sitting up.

"And he wasn't very good at it. He kept my family hostage!"

Dr. Dewar's eyes went wide at that. "No!" he exclaimed.

"He did. He interred our ship, which, in the Congo, is the same thing. There's no way to leave or even get food."

So I had to tell them about the Congo.

That night was my watch night and I got to sit up with Éléonore, who was awake and in great pain. It wasn't hard. She, at least, had the presence of mind to not move. That could change though if fever set in and I checked every once and awhile. She couldn't move to use the pan like poor Anika, so we cut a hole in the mattress.

Émile said she needed an operation to pin the bones, but that it simply couldn't be done here. At the very least, we didn't have anything to use as a pin, let alone anesthetic or antiseptic.

I listened to her moan and thought about us crashing. We'd never get her off unless we collided and caught on something. The cruiser was for the best, but I couldn't help wallowing in depression.

Chapter 11 – The Seventh Day

I woke with Aleta climbing down from her bunk.

"Morning," I said.

"We've got a ride!" she said, looking happy.

"A ride to England?" I asked carefully.

"Probably. She's British," she answered. She started pawing through the dirty overalls on the floor, trying to pick the cleanest.

I plunked my head back down on my pillow, a little depressed.

"You okay?" she asked.

"I'm okay."

"Don't worry. We're lighting up the engines this morning, in about an hour. Cold starts take a little time. It's lucky she's a cruiser and can keep up. Once she levels out and we're steady, we'll drop the lines and be home. We're even going to have a nice breakfast this morning. At least we will as soon as we can steady her. It'll be a party. Last of the coffee and everything."

"We still have coffee?" I asked.

"We've been saving it for the pilots," she said.

"Oh. Good idea."

"I've got to get up on top. It'll take all of us to get them started again." Then she looked at me. "Are sure you're all right?" She looked worried.

"I'm fine," and put on my best smile.

"You don't look fine."

"Really, I'm fine," I said. "Go get us back to shore. Anika needs a hospital."

"True," she said as she pulled on a boot. Then she looked at me again, a little worried. "I'll be back as soon as I can." Then she left, the door clicking shut behind her.

They're going to arrest me, was all I could think.

It was a very a depressed Cali laying there in her bed. Look if you want. I was not smiling. I was laying there thinking that Ma and Pa wouldn't find out for months and then it would be months more before they could get there to help. By then it would be long over. Nigel would have the last laugh. The Prince, who'd probably already forgotten about me, wouldn't even notice.

Thinking they would probably take away my violin got the tears going. They drifted into sobs, until I was left empty and bleak, staring up at the bunk above me. In the distance I could hear them trying to start the motors. They kicked over and kicked over until finally success. There was that thrum, growing, and then growing more, which was odd. Then the whole ship shook, and then shook again!

My eyes, sore and wet, went wide. "Aleta!"

I was up and through the door, night dress be damned.

People were yelling, laying on the floor, holding on to things, trying to look through the windows. Cries of "*Gross Gott, was ist jetzt los,*" and "*Quel est le problème cette fois?*"

Down the corridor I skipped, dodging people and doors, into the storeroom and up the ladder only to realize that I was in my slippers. But there was no time. Something had gone terribly wrong with the engines. Somehow the bad fuel had gotten in.

The deck tipped as my head popped up through the open hatch. We were crossways to the wind and it kept blowing my hair across my eyes. I caught sight of a flaming engine as it dropped away from the burnt steel lacework all by itself. The explosion had set the curling canvas alight, carving out a dent from the underside of our bow as flaming hydrogen vented from ruptured cells. The other engine next to it was a ball of fire as well.

I hopped and scrambled up the sloping roof as it tipped toward blue sea, to the central ladder and began to climb, which wasn't easy. The ladder was tipping with the airship too, going up at an angle.

In the distance, I could see a figure, dangling over the burning engine, bobbing back in forth in the heat, and the shimmer of invisible flame below the bow. Burning hydrogen. It had breached the gas cells! All I could think of was Lisa Bruce, The Mouse. Six months in the burn ward.

"Aleta," I sobbed. And I began to climb.

On the catwalk as I ran, I could feel the wind blow hot and cold as heat swept back from the bow in gusts.

"Cali!" A voice, thin with the wind drifted by. It came from behind me.

I stopped, confused, and turned. It took a moment and then I saw her. It was Vic, just top of the hatch.

"Cali, stop!"

I didn't have time for this!

"Go back," I yelled over the wind, but she didn't hear or didn't care. She was crawling across the deck to the central ladder.

I have to go, I'm so sorry, I thought. That body might be Aleta. And so I ran on across the narrow catwalk. Our ship was twisting about as it blew loose in the wind, which, as it turned out, was a godsend as it kept the flames away from the central superstructure. Below, our cruiser drifted by as we turned. And on I ran, slippers gone, bare feet on sloping woven metal and empty air, past the bay that used to hold our abandoned fuel cells, down a catwalk that led to a small platform where I found panels with gauges and cranks and wheels. I saw a figure laying on the deck. It was Dietrich. He'd been burnt! He was trying to move.

"Dietrich!" I cried, and ran and ran.

He was a mess, half his clothes burned away. I wanted to help him, but I didn't know what to do or even where to touch.

"*Schalten Sie es*," he rasped. He was trying to point.

There was a wheel, but I didn't understand.

He rallied, trying to focus.

"Turn it, damn it!" he croaked.

I drew a sobbing breath and jumped for the wheel. It was hard but I threw my shoulders into it, pushing with my legs. It slowly turned. I kept at it, turning it, pushing it around with all my strength, until I thought it would come off in my hand.

When I turned back to him, he was dead. His burnt lips were pulled back from his teeth, eyes wide open. I screamed.

It came from so deep inside.

Then somehow I was running, running forward. The air to the starboard rippled with heat, the catwalk growing warm under my bare feet. It was lighter here, the morning sun shining in under the bow. Our broken envelope sloping up to blue sky. Bits of white fluff, foam, broke loose from above and followed the flames.

Finally, I came to a point where I could go no further. The catwalk bent to the left and down, wobbling back and forth in the wind, its supports burnt away.

"Aleta!" I called.

The remaining engine had burnt itself out.

"Aleta!"

Nothing. I ran back and found a side way.

"Aleta!"

The deck lurched and I heard a rending of metal. Our last fuel cell dangled above, hanging by a bent strut which broke with a bang, drifting away down trailing foam, falling down toward the gray ocean below.

Aleta!

To the left was a ladder, so I started to climb. It led to another higher catwalk.

I ran back toward the fuel cell bay batting my way through the foam. And there, stumbling along in the dark was a figure. I ran without holding on, I didn't care.

"Aleta!" I called.

She looked up. Her beautiful hair was burnt. She was carrying a wrench, which she dropped as she stared at me, trying to focus. It hit the catwalk then twisted tumble twisted down hitting a few struts as it slid between the hydrogen cells on its way to the sea.

"Cali?" she said. She frowned, like she was trying to figure something out. "You shouldn't be here," she said finally.

And then she stumbled once, collapsing, her arm dangling down over the tipping edge of the catwalk.

I jumped forward to grab her to keep her from rolling over. We sat together on that narrow catwalk, suspended over silent space, so close to death. I saw the British ship as it swept by beneath us, visible between the gas cells. They were helpless to aid us.

The Captain found us after a long while, looking for survivors.

Aleta was a bit burnt, but mostly it was the blow to the head she took when she collided with a girder during an explosion. She had a darkening welt down the side of her forehead. The side of her face and arms were as red as a beet. Vic said later, after we got her down, that she looked like a devil. It took all of us to get her down to our cabin. She was barely conscious. We kept her clipped to the railings and ladders as we made our way back to the gondola.

We left Dietrich up there. I think even the Captain was in shock. Down in the gondola, he sat in the lounge reading a week old paper, having given up trying to steady us.

"*Ich habe es noch nicht gelesen!*" he said, when people stared.

No big breakfast after all. Just a scrambled egg, our last, a piece of toast and water. I was noticing my hunger. With the loss of our last fuel cell, we had no electricity. It was dark in the kitchen, bathrooms, and cockpit. It would be an early evening for us all.

Our airship, at this point, was completely dead. We no longer had any alternative but to crash. It was just a matter of picking the spot. The cruiser was pacing us below, but they couldn't help.

This was one of the lowest points in my life.

But think, says Cali the woman of worldly wisdom! Now you have so much to look forward to! Nowhere to go but up. Trust me. It will take time, but just wait until we get to Paris!

Aleta woke, trying to go topside, clearly still not with us. She had the bottom bunk now. I was sitting in the Dewar's cabin with the door open and heard her. They love to hear me talk about Red for some reason. I caught her in the corridor and pushed her into the head instead, and then back into our room. It wasn't hard, she was so weak and dizzy. Émile was at a complete loss. There was nothing he could do. She had a concussion and just needed rest.

After lunch, potato, a bit of cheese, and peas, which sadly Aleta couldn't eat, the Captain tapped me on the shoulder and said, "*Komm.*" We climbed up top and into the interior of the envelope. He brought a sheet from the crew cabin tied around his waist. Up on the platform where Dietrich's body lay, he opened a locker and pulled out a harness. Then he kept his eyes on me as he pulled it on. I was staring at Dietrich, tears rolling down my cheeks. He grabbed a couple of wrenches and clipped them to his harness.

"*Diesem weg,*" he said as he headed down the catwalk.

I followed him to a ladder and we climbed up into the dim interior. The foam was gone, but we weren't burning anymore so I suppose it'd done its job. We made our way over to the port bow engine. It was still attached.

"*Wir müssen sie diesen Motor gaben. Verstehen Sie?*"

I nodded, still crying. He wanted to drop the engine. We were too heavy. We had lost gas to the fire.

He clipped a line to a railing and climbed down the ladder to the engine platform. Its blackened aluminum groaned with his weight. I started to follow but he waved me back.

"*Nein. Warten Sie. Es ist nicht sicher.*"

I watched him undo the bolts on the top of the engine and pull off a big piece of metal. He had to move it in steps. I moved to help, but he waved me back, "*Nein, nein!*"

With the metal piece on the catwalk, he set to work on the support girders, undoing bolts, each one making the engine platform less steady. He undid them one by one until finally the superstructure of the ship gave up and the last bolts popped with a bang. The engine platform and the captain fell, the captain being pulled up short by his cable. He laughed, dangling over empty space. I saw the engine sail away below.

Then it was up his own cable and a clinging climb over and onto the catwalk. He just lay there for a bit, leaning against the big piece of metal.

"*Können Sie führen?*" he said, then looked at the piece of metal. It was for Dietrich. I nodded yes. "*Gut,*" he replied. "*Es ist sehr schwer.*"

We carried it, he walking backwards, back to the Dietrich's

platform and tied him to it with the bedsheet, his feet, still in their shoes, sticking out. Then we pulled and pushed, dragged him over to the edge.

"*Warden*," the captain said, and he pulled out a pocket Bible began to prey. It was the burial prayer, and I followed in English, my hand on Dietrich under the sheet:

We therefore commit his body to the deep, to be turned into corruption, looking for the resurrection of the body when the sea shall give up her dead, and the life of the world to come, through our Lord Jesus Christ; who at his coming shall change our vile body, that it may be like his glorious body, according to the mighty working whereby he is able to subdue all things unto himself.

Then we pushed him over. Below, the cruiser must have seen the body fall because they commenced to toll their bell.

I was in no mood to talk to anyone at dinner, but Max sat down across from me anyway.

I was sitting there in a blanket. We'd been passing through clouds and everything was damp. "Max, I'm tired."

He ignored me and began talking. "Cali. I'm very disappointed."

I gave him the eye. We're adrift in a dead airship in the middle of the Atlantic and all he cares about is his mission.

He frowned at me. "I'm very disappointed in myself. You had me completely fooled."

"You're crazy," I said.

"You were the Belgian all the time."

"I didn't know."

"Were you working for them in the Congo?"

"I'm not working for anyone."

"You admitted it."

"I'm just doing a favor for Lucien," I said, wincing. "At least I think I am." It sounded like a whine. I hate whining.

"You are a fool."

"Max!" I said, losing my temper, but no one seemed to notice. A lot of people had been losing their temper lately.

"This isn't a joke. You could get killed." Then he looked deeply hurt. "I might have to do it myself."

"Are we making threats?" Mme. Calvé said with a little smile as she sat down next to Max.

"A simple statement of fact," he replied.

"Max. I've never seen or heard of you killing in cold blood," she replied with a smile. "We aren't assassins."

Max looked at her levelly.

"I'm a thief, not a murderer," she replied coldly.

"If not us, then one of the others."

"Petrov's the one to watch."

"Yes. I agree."

"Petrov?" I asked, watching them both.

"Your M. Comeau dear," Mme. Calvé replied.

"He's Russian," Max added. "Cali, the problem is you."

"Don't be silly Max. She's the victim here. Her situation is completely unreasonable," Mme. Calvé said.

"Your situation is more precarious than you realize," Max continued.

"Perhaps not. We should discuss this with the doctor himself."

I let out a long growl. "Will you stop?"

They blinked at me.

"This is *friend and foe*." It's a negotiating tactic where you team up, one hostile, one sympathetic. "Max, I'm the one disappointed. You could do better."

A small smile slowly spread across Max's face. Mme. Calvé, slowly let out her breath.

"I told you Emma. You must look past her age."

I frowned at the compliment, suspicious of anything from them left lying there for free.

Mme. Calvé thought for a moment, then started again.

"As you said. She is a merchant's daughter. Cali, I want to make an offer to the doctor."

"We all should," Max said. "Cards on the table."

"They won't accept," I replied. I knew Dr. Dewar wouldn't, not from them. His mind was set on going to Belgium. But then again, I thought, I would get to know the players. I could see a little inner laugh in Max. He had seen what I had seen. "Of course, it's a long way to land," I continued, hoping to deflect their thoughts.

"And we have time," Max continued for me, but he knew.

"It seems so," I sighed.

We were so close to land. I remembered the joy of crossing the 300 mile war limit. We sailed our ship through the waters just below hardly six months ago, dancing toward the channel and France. I thought of the pure joy of sailing in clean wind, blue sky, and a friendly port ahead. But up here we had nothing but empty days to look forward to, apparently now full of hunger. And in the end, nothing but a rocky coast or dry sharp mountains.

Our conversation left the Dewars behind. I'd given my blessing to making offers. Instead Mme. Calvé wanted to talk about performing again. I told her that Aleta was hurt.

"Oh dear! Not another."

"She hit her head when the engines exploded."

"She will be concussed," Max said. "It's always miserable."

"She is. The only crew we have left now is the captain himself."

"No one to keep order," Max frowned.

Mme. Calvé suddenly looked worried. "No, there isn't."

Chapter 12 – The Eighth Day

Someone bumped me. It was Dietrich! He was standing over me. I could see his hand slowly reach out to me, stretching toward me, trying to wake me, the moment of vertigo as he made contact. And then he did it again. I fought to wake, willing my legs to move.

There was a noise. It was a struggle, a shape below in the dark. I could move. Sort of.

I rolled off the top bunk with a growl and down onto the bent form below. He swung back with his elbow to throw me off, but I had his collar and his shirt tore as I fell back with him on top. We hit with a yelp, then me yelling for my life. He tried to roll, but I held on to his back, clinging to his shirt until his buttons popped, and then to him, grabbing his shoulders, trying to get to his neck. He tried to hit me with his head, reaching back at the same time to get to my hair which was flying lose.

"Cali?" It was Dr. Péan, knocking, too polite to come directly in! He had been next door watching our patients.

I could only grunt as our attacker grabbed a handful of my hair, finally managing to yell for help again just as the doctor opened the door. He cursed and began to cast about for a weapon, of which there are even less of on an airship than things you can use for a raft, only to be pushed aside by Max running in his union suit. Max kneeled by the man on top of me, who gradually let go of my hair.

"Konstantin Pavel Petrov, give up. The move is over."

Petrov grunted, "Of course," his accent now distinctly Russian. "The stupid little minx was in the wrong bunk!" he complained offhandedly.

Aleta was still choking, trying to breath, and Dr. Péan rushed to her side. More people were looking in our door. I was trying to roll over as he got up, but wasn't making much headway.

"Her roommate was wounded," Max replied. "They must have switched beds."

Petrov snorted in disgust.

"What did I miss?" It was Mme. Calvé, rushing in.

"Petrov tried to eliminate Cali," Max said. "Did he hurt you?" Max asked, offering me a hand.

"Something poked me in the back," I said, kind of surprised at how steady my voice was.

"Let me look," Max said. "Konstantin, a light."

He had to step over the hole from the open floor panel as he searched his pockets, coming up with a lighter. Dr. Péan was gently telling Aleta to breathe slowly.

Max tisked. "I think it was that belt buckle. You're bleeding on your night dress."

"I might as well," I moaned. I was starting to hurt. "Everything else I own is covered in blood." Creepy, tall tales, now bloody Cali.

Aleta began to curse. I could see her from the light of Petrov's lighter.

"That's better," Dr. Péan said, clearly relieved.

"Oh good, she's all right," Mme. Calvé said. "We can go back to bed."

"Go back to bed!" I yelled. "He tried to kill me." I heard exclamations from the hallway.

"Do you want me to push him out the window for you?" Max asked with a little smile.

Petrov snorted again, with even more disgust.

That brought me up short. What were we going to do? Tie him to a support strut?

"Enough," Petrov said flatly and started for the door.

"Konstantin," Max said, quietly.

Petrov stopped.

"If anything happens to her or anyone else, we will make sure you don't reach shore."

He growled then pushed his way through the door.

"These Russians . . ." Mme. Calvé started.

"Always too ready to kill," Max finished.

"Yes. So lacking in subtlety," she added. "Well, goodnight," she sang, and followed Petrov.

"He could have at least put my floor panel back," I hissed.

"Yes. Typically rude," Max said. "Let me help."

And we both bent to get it, but I jerked up with a pain just as Vic came rushing in. My back at least was going to be bruised.

"What happened?" Vic asked.

"M. Comeau is a Russian agent," I said, trying to feel my back for injury. "He tried to kill me."

"I'm going to kill him!" Aleta croaked and tried to rise, but fell back.

"Stay still," Émile snapped, still probing her neck.

"I knew it!" she said. "He killed Dimitri." And then with clear unease, "Cali. Your back is bleeding."

"I know. It hurts."

But then the captain showed up in a cloud of bluster wanting an explanation, but Émile wasn't having any of it and pushed everyone out to check my back. That's why I didn't hear about what happened until after the gunshot.

Apparently I got rather deeply poked by Aleta's belt buckle, and a few other things as well. There are good reasons why you should keep your cabin picked up. Émile was going to drag me next door to clean them when we heard the shot.

Tie him to a strut was exactly what the captain intended to do. He had a pistol and handcuffs just for that purpose. But when the captain confronted Petrov, Petrov was in no mood for it and tried to bat the gun out of the captain's hand. The captain, a war veteran, shot him, leaving one more hole in the side of our airship. Petrov was no more.

We dumped him that morning. No sheet, no weight, no wake, no ceremony. His cabin was full of blood and he left a bloody scuff on the floor by the hatch. The cruiser below tolled their bell again and I felt guilty that we hadn't prayed over him. Then I was back on watch – which was fun because I got to watch Aleta trying and trying to get out of bed.

She was funny. Her head throbbed when she sat, but her neck hurt when she moved, which was okay because it distracted her from her nausea when she stood. We had nothing left to give her for the pain. The hard liquor we had was reserved for surgery. And she looked so odd with half her hair burned.

She groaned. "I'm in hell."

"Would you like my book? It's not as silly as the cover seems."

"I can't focus my eyes. Why am I always getting hurt around you?"

I looked down at the floor. "I do seem to be bad luck sometimes."

"Oh," she growled. "I'm sorry Cali. I didn't mean that."

"It's true though." Really, to be fair, I think it was the war, and my family works in a dangerous line of business. "So it turns out the airship is full of spies," I continued.

"Do you really trust this Max?"

"No. Not really," I replied. "I mean I trust him in some ways. I'm pretty sure he won't try to kill me like Petrov. But I wouldn't be surprised if he left me tied to something up above just to get me out of the way."

"Oh," she said, suddenly realizing something. "They'll threaten Vic."

"Really?"

"I think her father would be completely lost without her."

"You should be a spy."

"I hate getting knocked on the head."

"There's probably a lot of that in the spy business," I agreed. "What can I do to protect Vic?" I asked myself. "They could threaten you to get to me too."

"Don't worry about me," she said, but then continued, "Oh, maybe you should. I don't think I'd be very happy getting tortured."

"You couldn't fight back. Not now."

"No. Not unless they died laughing."

"We'll be landing in Southern France. Max would have to get Dr. Dewar across France to Germany. He isn't going to try force. Too many things could go wrong."

"You could use that against him."

"I was thinking that if he has hope of cooperation then he might defend me." Then I remembered, "Oh! You need to write a note."

"A note?"

"Yes, Jimmy has a bottle with a cork. He told me at the funeral. We're all to write notes and then toss it overboard."

Aleta moaned, "My head hurts too much to write! I'm so tired of this throbbing. I don't have anyone to write to anyway."

"Just write something. Maybe they'll print it in the papers someday."

"I don't care about the papers."

That gave me pause. I could try to refute the newspapers, but how could I fit all that on a piece of paper. We sat for a bit, me thinking about what I would write, when Aleta piped up, "I think Max will defend you just to stay close to Dr. Dewar."

"Maybe Mme. Calvé too."

"So you think there are more?"

"Max thinks so. There's an odd Southern woman I've noticed. All she does is sit and watch."

"You should talk to the captain."

"Yes," I replied, trying to think of a plan.

"All we can do now is regulate gas pressure. He has time."

I took a break from nursing and writing to go forward to talk to the captain. When I got to the kitchen I heard Yvonne exclaim, "I can't get the flame to light." Then a pause. "No, it's lit, it's just that I can't see it."

The captain, who was sitting in the cockpit reading a book, looked up.

"*Was ist jetzt los?*" He looked at the burner and his eyes went wide. "*Auch!*" and he turned off the valve. "*Der Kohlendioxid Tank leer ist,*" he signed. "*Wir können nicht kochen jetzt.*"

"What is he saying?" Yvonne asked, as if I knew German.

"*Der Ofen ist gebrochen*," he said, looking at us.

We stared back.

"*Kaput*," he said, slicing the air with his hand.

"I think the stove is broken," Yvonne said. "What are we going to do?"

"Eat cold?"

"Starve or eat dry flour," Cirille answered. "This is terrible!"

"We need to talk to him," Yvonne added. "This won't do."

"Someone here must know German and French," Cirille said. "We need a translator."

"*Wir müssen auskommen*," the captain said, not understanding at all what we were talking about.

"I need to talk to him too. I was going to bring him back to our cabin to talk to Aleta."

"She's awake?"

"Oh yes," I said. "And not happy."

"Then let's," Yvonne said.

"Yes, let's," Cirille added.

I looked at the captain and said, "Come, Aleta." Motioning for him to follow.

"*Sie wach ist?*"

"Yes."

We crowded into our cabin, along with a few passengers as well.

"I said to bring the captain, not the whole ship." She was grouchy.

"Things have gone wrong and we need translation."

"*Erzähle ihnen der Kohlendioxid Tank leer ist und wir können nicht kochen.*"

"We can't cook anymore. We're out of gas. We just have hydrogen which could explode or set us on fire. Cali, this isn't good."

"We can't eat flour," Cerille said.

"Dumplings maybe?" someone suggested.

"I suppose we can't boil bandages now," I added.

"He wants to talk to talk to us about Petrov too," Aleta said.

And we explained the spy problem and Dr. Dewar as best as we could, and all the captain could reply was, "*Auch*, and here I thought I could get some rest." Then I remembered that I was on duty and I hadn't checked our patients, but I was the only one left who knew both French and English. So I translated as best I could then made my apologies and went off the help Anika with the pot and M. Yount with his bandages, thinking all the time that these would be the last of them.

There was a meeting followed by lunch and I was called out to attend. Anyone who wanted to talk to Dr. Dewar was asked to do so. There would be no more Comeau's. We turned in our notes, Jimmy pushing the cork in as hard as he could. It was a whiskey bottle naturally. He cleaned it at least. It went out the window. It was found in Florida two years later.

Lunch was half an orange and dried meat, which was fine by me. I could eat oranges all day long. I didn't even have to cut it up for Anika. She ate it all by herself, which was nice. She was stronger. I sat with her and we tried to talk, matching our bad French, trying to ignore our hunger. Eating seemed to make it worse.

It was that afternoon that we heard the report, a large gun of some sort. We thought it was the cruiser and ran to the windows to see what bad news they had for us, but it wasn't them. It was another airship! A French navy one. The captain picked up the flasher, but put it down with *"Verdammt!"* No electricity. It was time to try the signal mirror, but we were turning and had to wait for the sun to pass an appropriate window, and then we had only a few seconds to flash. It was very difficult. They wanted to shoot us a line and wanted all hands up top to secure it. All hands meant the captain and me. The only ones left.

Off with my shoes and up the cold ladder we ran with no idea where the line would fall and no way to signal. Their first shot missed us entirely and fell low. The second ricocheted off a strut and fell beneath us again, but it gave us a general idea where they were aiming. We waited for the turn and they fired again, this time puncturing a gas cell, but made it across the catwalk. It was a little cannonball with a thin cable attached, like a throw weight. I grabbed it first and we wrestled it over to a winch, only to remember we had no electricity. We had to hand crank it fast before the turn tangled the line. There was a capstan on the side and we turned it with steel rods from a tool box, the captain barking, *"los, los, los."*

But the Bremen turned and the line went under us. Thankfully the airship gave us enough slack that it didn't tangle. I guess we no longer had anything sticking out to catch on now that the engines were gone. We waited for it to come back across. The little line led to a bigger one, then to a proper steel cable. It took us three hours, the sun now low, my hurt back aching. We left it in the winch and hoped for light wind. It wouldn't take much to pull the winch loose. It had, at least, stopped our slow spin.

Then the craziest thing happened! They sent a man across! He zoomed across along the cable on a leather harness tied to little trolley, arms out like a bird. He wore a blue jumpsuit, a leather skull cap and goggles! And when he hit our end he climbed up onto our catwalk with a cheery "*Bonjour!*" Then he looked around. Down below the British cruiser was making noise, every bell and whistle.

"This is it? Where is your crew?"

"Dead or injured," I answered.

He looked troubled for a second, but then broke out in a smile, slapped the trolley, which sent it zooming back, and then bowed. "Allow me to introduce myself, Lieutenant Brice Falcon." He saluted the captain and bent down and kissed my hand! He had big moustache and needed a shave, but cut a dashing figure in his jump suit. His rakish smile, when he looked up at me, was pure danger. It took me a moment. I couldn't talk. My face was burning.

"We can send across a tow cable, but it would be better if we could have your anchor line. We'll need our cable to land."

I didn't know what to say to that. We needed Aleta.

They sent more men over and, finally, someone who spoke German. I was leaping with joy across the catwalks barefoot, my skirts and hair flying in the wind in the setting sunlight to tell the others. Behind I heard the Frenchman exclaim, "*Mon Dieu!*" and the captain chuckle. But all I was thinking was that we were going to France and we weren't going to have to crash! Down below I whooped and yelled the news. Everyone was dancing and laughing down in the gondola, even the sick, until I noticed Mme. Calvé give Max a predatory look and Max looked back troubled. I guessed she was going to have an advantage in France.

That afternoon we had a party with Mme. Calvé and me performing and everyone dancing. The French shared some of their food with us and the ship was no longer turning since it was tethered to the French airship, which helped those still air sick. We all got to toast with the last of the whiskey, which is a lot like rum and far too much for me. I gave mine to Jimmy. I was playing and didn't need to toast. We had French airmen, four of them and they all kept looking at me, making faces to get me to laugh while I was trying to play, and trying to tease me into drinking whiskey.

Chapter 13 – The Liberté

They had us under tow that night and the deck was steady again. We'd lost gas but we were moving forward. The airmen took the tiller and gave our captain a break, but he couldn't help himself and worried around the cockpit anyway.

Breakfast was carrots, crackers, and water. Practically the last of our food, except for a wedge of cheese and some flour. But we were heading for the French carrier *Liberté* and would be off our poor hurt Bremen that afternoon. Still, hunger had taken a toll on many. They sat around like lumps and griped like it was the end of the world.

I hadn't thought of it before, but I wondered what would happen to her. She had done so well, holding together through all the violence done to her, keeping us safe. I hoped she would be repaired.

I finally got my Lufthansa deck of cards, given to me by the captain himself. They came in a little cardboard box and slid like silk in my hand. Vic and I practiced shuffling, but we used her deck which was broken in and less slippery. When the airmen saw the cards, Vic had her game. The airmen, there was Brice, of course, and André, Bernard, and Timothée, were all consummate card sharks and Vic was finally in heaven. They came and went as their duties demanded, but there was always at least one, and they all wanted me to stand behind them when they played for some reason, which was very enlightening. I could see their cards which made it fun to watch them lie and even lie about lying! I could see them watching me despite my blood stained dress, so of course, in a way, I had to lie too so as to not give away their hands. It was good practice.

Dr. Dewar at first refused to see any of our spies, now national representatives with offers to fund his future non-British lab, but I kept at him. We had to know who was there and they had to keep their hope alive so they wouldn't turn to violence to force his secret out of him. There was Max and Emma, naturally. But then there was Belle Boyd, that quiet Southern woman in the corner. She was from the South! I didn't care if Dr. Dewar wanted to go to Germany or France, but I did care about the South. Then there was Adão Henriques from the Brazilian Empire, the poor man. I thought he was American! And last was Phillip Henson from the U.S., which was difficult for me since we were supposedly on the same side and Dr. Dewar could win the war for us, and even end slavery! His pitch was the hardest to hear and he kept glancing at me while he delivered it.

Oh, and the pitches! My jaw dropped at the sums of money being offered. Houses and land for labs. Private tutors and schools for Vic. And everyone's cause was just and noble. But I kept quiet. I would go where the doctor led. As my Pa says, it was his decision to make. He and Vic. Well, except for the South maybe.

But we were heading to France and I doubted the French would willingly let him cross the border and the English would be following as soon as they found out where we were too. I figured they would probably claim he was kidnapped. And I expected the English would somehow find a way to have me arrested when we landed even though it was France. I desperately hoped Lucien would find us quickly.

All that and running back and forth with the pan for poor Anika, and carrying Aleta to the head on top of it all. It was another day of glamorous air travel for your Cali. So far, the sum total of my experience with air travel had been a mixture of hurt and fear. I told Émile that, grouched really, and he laughed. He felt that overall, it had been better than a regular trip. Once you got over the newness of being up in the air, he felt flying was rather boring.

We ate the last of our cheese and popped warm bottles of champagne that foamed all over the deck for lunch. The cooler was off for lack of electricity. It went right to my head and I was laughing. I had André's and Bernard's arms around my waist, which felt a little strange but nice too, as we waltzed around and around to invisible music. The wine was meant for the end of our trip, but I refused to admit victory. I wouldn't admit to anyone we were going to land. Things seemed to be going well in the past and failed, so I'd withhold my final cheer until my foot actually touched the deck of the ship.

But we did land. I didn't get to see her, our rescue ship, until we were practically over her and then only when wind shear pushed us sideways. They all ran up top, leaving me below, just another passenger again. The captain had squeezed my arm before he left and smiled.

"*Liebe frauline, du kanst nicht ausgehen.*" Stay inside.

Then he turned at the corridor and looked back at me sternly.

"*Nicht verlassen!*" Don't do it!

It was a challenge and he knew it. What could they do to me? Throw me off the ship at the next stop?

Once he was gone I was up the ladder and on top of the gondola. Vic called out to me, but I didn't feel like arguing.

Up top, the late afternoon sun low in the sky, shining golden across the gondola roof, glinting off the polished aluminum, I could see the tow line stretching forward to the French airship. She was smaller than us, with only four engines. They buzzed away, keeping us on station. Her skin was smooth. Not ribbed like ours. And she had two tiny gondolas on top as well as on bottom. Somehow they had gotten us a second tow line because we were lowering it from our bow downward, the end weighed with drop weights to beat the wind. I made my way over to the front of the gondola and sat down, clinging to a strut for safety.

She was there, below us. The *Liberté*. Not sleek like our cruiser, but boxy with a very complicated superstructure. I could see our British cruiser along with two other ships, a French cruiser and a smaller ship. The small one was clearly a warship, but had only two turrets. She looked brand new and I bet she was fast. It turned out later there was a third French cruiser behind us.

The line dropped with aching slowness. I let the cold wind soak into me as I sat, the sun giving little warmth. She had a flat square of raised deck on her stern with a big bull's eye painted on it and I was pretty sure they were aiming to land our drop line on it. It had to be a trick for our towing airship to keep us in line, and it took more than a few tries. But they did it and men on deck ran for it, dragging slack behind them to the big winch just forward. It took our line and our whole ship jerked and dipped nose down. I was glad to be holding on.

So I was watching them pull us down when I felt movement behind me. When I looked up, I could see it was the captain. He gave me a smile as he crouched his way forward and took a seat on the opposite side of my strut. He said nothing. We sat there, watching them reel us in, the Liberté getting bigger and bigger. I could see what looked like gondolas, five of them under big tubes, attached to the side of the ship. They were folded up airships. There was a sixth empty spot, probably meant for our rescuer. Everyone was flashing. A list of wounded. Supply requisitions. Apparently there were only two men left in our rescue ship.

Sailors waved to us from the deck and we waved back. We were almost down and the captain tapped me on the shoulder and said, "*Komm.*" It was time.

I had to pack for us both. Aleta tried to help, but she threw up her cheese and some of her carrots from breakfast and I had no patience for it after that. Men in blue jumpsuits came with a stretcher for her, clearly not pleased with the smell, but they said nothing. I stuffed our things in our trunks without folding them. I was in a hurry to leave, afraid something would go wrong. I pulled Aleta's trunk into the corridor and went back for mine. It was gone when I returned and a man took mine from me as I dragged it out. I could hear them unloading the hold below the floor panels. Everyone was moving so fast.

I had to wait at the hatch while they lowered Anika. She smiled up at me and I smiled back. I think she was crying. The captain stood next to me, clutching a stack of paper, some books, and a big leather tube almost certainly containing his charts. He looked sad for some reason.

Below, we had no steps. Just a ladder that tipped up and down as we bobbed above the unsteady deck, sometimes even lifting off the deck. I was down in a second, but some of the older people had a terrible time. They could have used a bosen's chair and a crane. Emilé and Olivie seemed to enjoy it.

I had a real deck under my feet again! Oh, and it felt good. I let out a little squeal and did a pirouette laughing, which got smiles from our Frenchmen as they worked. My fellow passengers were nothing but smiles despite their hurts. Sailors were hauling cargo out of the hold as fast as they could, tossing it to runners who stacked it forward. Our poor Bremen stretched abaft of us, her tail sometimes dipping in the sea as the wind took her where it wanted. Could she take on water? It might make it hard to get her airborne again.

Sadly they had no intention of letting her fly again. We weren't bringing her home. There would be no more tows.

The deck crew wanted to move people below decks, but I avoided them, loitering by the officers, waiting for the last. I stood with the captain and then the captain of the Liberté joined us. The last sailor out whistled and waved as he cleared the gondola. Orders where shouted and they cast her off with no ceremony, letting the winch roll free.

"No!" I cried.

The captain gripped my hand.

Her bow had barely cleared our stern when they opened fire. Her tow cable was still in the winch. They didn't even give her a fair chance to dodge. They raked her with bullets that left glowing trails, spraying from guns in bays below made of spinning barrels like the mechanical men in the Congo. The noise was deafening, like rolling drums you could feel in your teeth, lighting the deck around them in white flashes in the blue twilight. She was ripped apart, flames ballooning from half a dozen places, her sides tearing loose like burning flags flapping in the wind. The captain next to me blew his nose on his handkerchief.

We watched our poor Bremen drift, tail still in the water, fire creeping up her sides. Gas cells catching one after another. She had no way to fight it, all her foam long gone. I saw her over a wave, bellowing fire and flame, being clawed under by the waves. Then she must have collapsed because after the next wave she was just a column of black smoke in the distance that ended, drifting away into the sky. I shivered. That could have been us.

"Calista Carmichael?" The man behind the desk looked up at me with a frown and put down his pen. "The Calista Carmichael?" Then he looked down at my violin case. I hadn't let go of it. Then he looked at my bloody dress and buried his face in his hands and rubbed his eyes.

I said nothing. I could see several folded newspapers on his desk.

"If there's any trouble here, I'll have you in the brig."

"If there's trouble, I won't be the cause."

"I'll make sure of that. For now you sleep in the women's section with the rest." Then he waved me away. He didn't even ask my account like he had the others. I supposed he felt I wasn't to be trusted to give an honest deposition.

I was so angry, but he was the captain and this was his ship, second only to God and the admirals. A seaman, ordinary I think because some of them had stripes and he didn't, led me to a cabin, junior officer's quarters. It was fairly spacious, with four bunks and desks and shelves still filled with the owner's things. The nautical manuals were intriguing and they had electric lights in the bunks so I could read! Vic, Aleta, and Emma, were quartered with me, all the young women and a guard at the door. I suspect it was because I had been getting stares from passing sailors. Can you see me roll my eyes? But then, perhaps, it might have been the blood stains.

I told Vic what the ship captain said.

"That is so wrong," she spat.

"He's the captain."

"It's still wrong. I'll tell him what's right!"

"Don't. It'll make it worse. He won't believe you and we're not far from port." But what would happen when we docked, I wondered?

She growled and flopped back on her bunk.

"What are you talking about?" Aleta asked from the bottom bunk.

"You've missed so much," I moaned. She had, and I really didn't feel like going through it all, but we had to fill her in. Emma added nothing but occasional laughs, which didn't help, especially when Aleta complained about me always being in trouble.

"That is so like men!" Aleta spat. "He just left you here, expecting you to deal with murdering spies."

"I've never murdered anyone," Emma said. "I'm a thief."

"What about that Russian?"

"He was a murderer," Emma agreed.

"Da thinks so," Vic said.

"He probably intended to kidnap you Vic," Emma said.

"You think so?" Vic replied with surprise.

"The difference between the Russians and us is that we want your Da, not just his discovery."

"Oh!" I choked. "Emma, that is so heavy handed."

"Not as heavy handed as murder," she replied, clearly amused. "And southern France has wonderful weather and beautiful coastlines."

That made me angry, until I remembered where I was. Why was I arguing for Belgium? Have they defended me in the newspapers? But, then again, there was Lucien. What had happened? What went wrong? Oh please be waiting at the docks.

"You've gone quiet Cali," Emma said.

"I was thinking that I really know nothing about Southern France. My family never traded there."

"The weather is warm and things grow all year round. The sea is blue green and clear." She sighed.

We were quiet for a bit. I though Emma might have fallen asleep. I know I was tempted. But then she said, "Cali, you are too good to be in this business." she replied. She was right, of course. And Max was right about it getting me killed.

We really were quiet after that and I did sleep, we were all so relieved to be down.

The men didn't fare as well as us, being quartered with the crew, but they got to freely roam. We couldn't go anywhere unescorted. For instance, they were leading us along a corridor toward the infirmary after they fed us. Wait. Let me be frank. They were herding us, when we ran into Max coming the other way. Apparently even Max was allowed to roam free. They had to know he was a German spy, but I was the one the captain wanted to watch! You have no idea how angry that made me, even now!

"Hello," Max said, as he squeezed past.

"Max, what are you doing?" I asked.

"I just took a shower."

We hadn't gotten to shower yet. Or wash clothes.

"You don't have a guard," Aleta pointed out.

"Yes. This ship is amazing," he added with a smug smile. "Our quarters are right across the corridor," he said, nodding toward the bulkhead. "They have hot water too," he smiled.

I realized he had free access to Dr. Dewar. He and Mr. Henson. The rest of us, the ones who were alive, were women. This was not good.

"Oh, showers," someone sighed.

"When do we get showers?" Mrs. Abbink asked. "Oh bellboy!" she called to the Midshipman leading us, which stopped us dead while an argument broke out and Max slipped away. We would shower when we were scheduled to shower, and of course he didn't know.

The infirmary was nice. Clean, spacious, and well lit. Émile was there chatting with the doctor. They wanted to let us in three at a time, but Émile called out to have me let in first.

"Let me introduce you to one of the best nurses I've ever had," he said.

The doctor's eyes went wide when he saw me. "Is that so?" he said. "She certainly isn't afraid of a little blood," the doctor said, looking at my dress.

"No," Émile replied, a little uncertainly. "She isn't."

I wasn't sure what to make of that, so I settled on polite. "It's a pleasure to meet you."

He grinned eagerly, "Dr. Benoit Vipond. Émile, that American accent is certainly charming."

Émile grunted, but I wasn't sure what it meant. "Perhaps we should move on. Cali. You're not hurt are you?"

"No," I replied. "It's really amazing," I said with a smile, which got a little chuckle out of Émile and an odd stare from Dr. Vipond. "Can I see Anika?" I asked.

"I'm afraid she's asleep, and I think we should move on," he said. "I was thinking you could assist. It would, perhaps, be good experience. But with this crowd, I think it would be better if you waited outside."

The ship's doctor looked a bit hurt, but didn't disagree. I had the feeling that Dr. Péan was in charge, at least of us.

So I waited in the corridor while they brought the women in to check them. It didn't take long. Except for being dirty, none of us had any problems Émile didn't already know about. I think really, they just wanted to make a list. We didn't get to bathe until ten that night. They closed the shower and put guards on the corridors just for us. When they took our clothes to the laundry, they put guards on the clothes too. Just for our laundry! We got crew nightshirts which were too big. But it was only for two nights. We had to hike them up to walk. We also had our own bathroom, fifty feet from our door, and two guards at night. One to escort us and check that the bathroom was empty before they let us in.

Chapter 14 – At Sea Again

I heard two bells and was out of bed, morning watch, but nothing was where it was supposed to be until I realized that this wasn't Red, it was 4 AM, and I had no clothes. They were all at the laundry. The guard at our door didn't know what to do.

"Ma'am, breakfast isn't scheduled until 8:00."

"Really, I always have morning watch these days and I'm up even when I don't."

"Go to bed Cali," Emma moaned.

I felt a pillow hit my back, Aleta growling as she threw it.

I apologized to the guard, then threw the pillow back at Aleta on the way back, which got a snort out of her. She was feeling better!

They knocked on our door at seven and passed in the bags with our clothes in them, cleaned and pressed. Sadly, you could still see the blood stains, but now thankfully they were only gray stains. My dresses were ruined and I wasn't sure how I was going to get new ones. The worst was that my corset was still in the bag. Some kind sailor could have at least had the decency to steal it.

Needless to say I was dressed in ten minutes.

So I asked the guard, "Couldn't I at least go up on deck and see the sky? It's so nice to be at sea again."

"Ma'am, I can't," he stammered. He was very young, not much older than me. "There's no one to go with you."

"Then the second mate." I wasn't sure what the word for mate was, but he seemed to understand. "Let's ask."

"I can't leave my post. I'm the only guard in the corridor."

"What if I have to go to the head?"

"I'm to escort you there. Make sure it's empty, then guard it until you're through. It's down the corridor."

This was a challenge. I wasn't going to sit in my bunk and wait for breakfast when there was the whole Atlantic out there. The corridor was strangely empty considering the watch should be changing soon. Had they cleared all the cabins?

"When are you off watch?" I asked.

He frowned. "8:00."

"I want to go too," Aleta added from behind me, followed by Emma and Vic.

I groaned. I couldn't wait for the watch change, that was when breakfast started. But then, I thought, perhaps I was going about this the wrong way. I wasn't crew. I didn't have to follow orders.

"Get someone to go with us," I insisted. "Ask the deck watch." Then I added for emphasis, "Now."

He gawked and blinked for a second, then rallied. "Yes Ma'am," he stammered and ran for the end of the corridor to call for a runner.

She was a beautiful ship, despite her boxy hull and cluttered superstructure. The breeze was wonderful except it was strange to have it coming from the bow.

"She moves well," I said to our new escort, a clean shaven English-speaking first lieutenant in crisp blue. We were standing at the rail in the morning sun, staring at the ocean between the lifeboats, the sea surging by the hull beneath us. I looked up at the stacks. Black coal smoke is a poor substitute for white sails, I thought.

He gave me a ghost of a smile, "We like her ma'am. Third in her class." I felt sure he'd been told to watch me.

"I make it ten knots."

His ghost of a smile turned to a ghost of a frown. "Yes ma'am."

"Are those airships?" Vic asked looking up at the superstructure.

"Yes, ma'am," he replied, turning and looking up too. "We carry six on deck."

"How long does it take to launch one?" Emma asked, mischievously.

"I'm afraid that's classified," he replied, with a glance at me.

"Max will know," she said. "He loves that sort of thing."

She was making a joke. It's funny that a French spy should have to ask a German about her own country's ships and that she should be locked up and Max not.

"We're not going to have to fly in one are we?" Vic asked.

"No ma'am. We're docking in Brest tomorrow."

"What's going to happen to us then?" she asked.

"It's not for me to say. You're embassies have been contacted."

"How did they do that?" I asked. Poor Vic, I thought.

"Courier left last night."

"Courier?" Aleta asked, with her fading black eye, bruised forehead, and burnt hair.

"They send fast airships back and forth to shore," Emma answered. "It keeps the fleet in communication."

"Can we send mail?" Aleta continued. "Cali, we have to send a letter to your family."

"I don't have any money."

Aleta looked at the lieutenant, "All our money was in the safe."

"I'll ask the captain," he replied. "But I'm sure it won't be a problem sending out letters with tonight's currier if the need is urgent."

Breakfast was in a dining hall full of sailors. We had a table to ourselves, but it wasn't private. Everyone was staring. Still, the food was good for a warship at sea, barley porridge, apples, brown crusty bread, powdered milk, and coffee. The best parts were the racks of cutlasses on the bulkheads and their having to send a guard with us every time we wanted a refill of coffee. The guard who went with me looked so uncomfortable. He didn't know what to do with himself, finally offering to pour. He turned bright red when I thanked him, which got chuckles from the nearby tables.

Vic and her Da had a lot to talk about. Things were going to be crazy when we made dock and this time staying onboard wasn't going to help.

"Darlin, we've got to talk," Dr. Dewar said.

"Da, everyone can hear."

"They won't let us talk any other way and we're going to dock." He sounded so beaten.

"Everything's going to be fine," she replied.

"No, love. It's not."

"It will. You have to have faith."

"I'll stay, wherever you decide," I added.

"We know that, but we're heading for hell's kitchen and you're just a child. Vic and you both."

"Da. I'll be fine."

"I know Lucien will be there," I added, although to be frank, at that point I really wasn't sure.

"Aye, probably. He's an efficient one," he said.

The courier came and went last night, I thought, counting. Apparently they like to land at night because it's easier to find a brightly lit ship in the dark. It will probably make port around noon. The telegraphs will carry the story, the newspapers printing it in the late edition, so Lucien in Belgium can't possibly hear about it until tonight. My blood ran cold. He won't be there. Not for at least two days. My only consolation was that the British wouldn't be any quicker. I had to be honest with them.

"No," I said.

Dr. Dewar turned and looked at me.

"No, he won't. Nobody will. It's going to be days before anyone gets there."

"What do you mean?" Dr. Dewar asked.

"We have at least two days for the word to spread and people to get there. The courier won't arrive before lunch today."

Dr. Dewar brightened. "You're right!" Then he clapped his hands and laughed.

"We've got to run as soon as we can," I whispered.

"That might be difficult," he whispered back. "We don't have any money."

"Sir," I said, standing before the captain. "I'm going to need my money from the safe."

"Ha!" he barked. "You're up to no good. I knew it."

For once he was right. "I need new dresses."

He frowned, pursing his lips. As if staring could make the stains go away. Then he took a deep breath, still squinting.

"Well, yes. I can see that." But then he rallied. "But your embassy can take care of that."

"There's going to be reporters and they're going to want stories. There's too many stories about me already. All of them untrue," I added. "One seaman to another."

He snorted.

I understood. Why should he believe me?

"I'm a third mate in the U.S. Merchant Marine," I said. "I have the certificate in my trunk. I can't help what the British say, damn them!"

He was French, no friend of England, and a sailor too.

"You're really certified?" I'd knocked him back in his seat. He stared, utterly and completely dumbfounded.

"I've been studying for that exam, and all the others since I was four. My family's been at sea for five generations that we know. Give me a fighting chance against those reporters. Don't make me walk out there in this dress."

He sighed and looked down, pausing. "I'll see what I can do. That much of the inventory I can hurry. It's only paperwork. If worse comes to worse, I can loan you the money from the ship budget against your balance. Maybe we can find you a tailor. I know one I like to use. Works quickly and makes shipboard calls."

"And may I write my Ma and Pa?"

"Of course. We'll forward it through your embassy. It will take time though."

"They won't be back from Jamaica for at least seven weeks."

"Jamaica? With the war, that has to be a hard run."

"I sure is."

They let us out onto deck again before lunch, which was tinned ham and boiled carrots and potatoes. God bless the Navy, at least we weren't going to get beriberi. Luckily the poor Hochbergs were on a special diet due to Herr Hochberg's having not been able to keep anything down through most of the trip and their not being able to eat ham. The French Navy doesn't care if you were Jewish or not. They put food down and expect you to eat it, but they put out special effort for us when it was needed.

Mrs. Péan looked at the food and sighed. "One has to love them," she said as she looked at her plate. I think she was referring to the Navy. "It's better than the army at least."

Dr. Péan laughed.

"Better than starving," Frau Abbink added with a laugh of her own. "This has been the most interesting vacation I've ever had," her old voice cracking. Where did they manage to put her huge trunk?

I had been told on good authority that we were getting oranges for dinner! Oh, I do love oranges. Even old ones. And melon too. Emma said that they grow in Southern France all year around. To have one whenever I wanted! Oh, she was so evil!

So after lunch I was back in my cabin. Trying to write to Ma and Pa. Trying to think about how to explain without sending them across the Atlantic to look for me. They would already know the newspaper stories were nonsense, but they wouldn't know what really happened and some of it they shouldn't know. And I knew too that the captain would read it before it was sent. Almost everything I could think of to write sounded bad so I decided less was best.

Ma and Pa,

I miss you so much, and Red too. I know you know someone tried to blow up our zeppelin, but we survived. I mean I'm writing right? It was bad, but the people there were good and we worked together to make it through. Please don't believe anything the newspapers say, as if you would. We're all fine. We'll be landing in France tomorrow, Brest. Don't come. I'll be long gone. I'll write when I know where.

Love, Calista

Aleta, had been patiently watching me write, clearly wanting to talk. I put down my pencil.

"What?"

"I need to do something about my hair," she said.

It did look awful. "What do you want to do?"

"They have a barbershop onboard."

"A barbershop?" I was incredulous. A ship with a barbershop!

"That's what the lieutenant said," she replied.

"We have to find it."

"So you want to go?"

"Definitely!"

"I want to go too," Vic added, from above me in her bunk.

"I think I'll say," Emma added without being asked. "The thought of watching your hair being cut by a Navy barber, for some reason fills me with a certain horrid dread."

"I hadn't thought of that," Aleta said.

"We can go look at least. I have to take my letter to the captain anyway."

It took the usual foot stomping and whining to get an escort. When we arrived at the barber shop, there was a line down the corridor. We were coming in to port tomorrow and all the crew wanted to look nice. They only had two chairs, but they worked incredibly fast, each haircut exactly the same.

One of the barbers saw us and called, "I can cut that straight for you." He was trying to be helpful, but Aleta balked.

"No. I think I'll wait until we make port," which got a laugh out of the men in line.

The barber shrugged.

Aleta and Vic waited outside when I went in to see the captain.

I had to turn my letter over to him before I sent it. I think he actually fogged over a bit as he read it. We sent it to my Grandpa's in Boston.

That evening, our last together, we had a late dinner with the captain. It was a big crowd, too big for the captain's table, so it was in the crew's mess. The food was from his private and the officer's general store, which was generous since they have to pay for it out of pocket. They were all dressed in their best whites and were wonderful gentlemen. I didn't have to play my violin, which was nice for a change. There were spirits, which I avoided. We all laughed and best of all, I finally got my orange.

I had a nightmare. Maybe it was the coming port. It was loud and the guards were in our room with guns drawn and we had sailors and women all stirred around until they calmed me down, Aleta telling them to go away over and over again.

There is a darkness under everything in this world and there's nothing between it and you but a thin skin. God help you if you break it.

Chapter 15 – Brest

I forgot to tell you the craziest thing about the Liberté. She was so big that she had her own store. Really! Our guide showed us on the way to the barbers'. The crew could go in and buy whatever they wanted. Extra cigarettes, candy, books, new underwear, anything they needed beyond standard issue. Once I got my francs, I bought a dark blue wool knit watchcaps and gloves for Aleta and me before I left. Far more practical than my travel gloves. They served me very well that winter. There, see? Now you know I'm going to live to see winter. All this grimness will eventually go away. Just keep saying "Paris." But I've gotten ahead of myself again.

I was up early and this time our guards were ready for my request to go on deck. I had to wait for the others, which was frustrating. But not everyone was raised at sea. Some people have a hard time dressing. We buttoned and tied and primped and met our lieutenant in the corridor. He was in a good mood. The whole ship seemed to be in a good mood. We got, "Morning, ma'am's" from our guard, the guard at the top of our corridor, as well as our lieutenants, this time five! Two of them had wedding rings. Outside the morning sun was brilliant silver, the tossing waves peaked white in the cold brisk wind. I laughed at its first breath and ran to the rail.

We were near the coast and in the midst of the shipping lanes. All around us the sea was full of ships. Beautiful sails and sooty black smoke. I saw a yacht, sleek, brass shining, sliding through the water not two hundred yards off our port bow. She dove through the waves like a porpoise, her crew running to put out more sail. I laughed with delight, pointing it out to Aleta. Our lieutenant saw us and came to look.

"That would be a Rothschild," he said, putting down his binoculars, nice ones too.

"Rothschild? Are they noble?" I asked.

"No. Far more powerful. You can see their pennant on the mast."

"They're bankers," Aleta added. "A whole family."

"The richest in the world," our lieutenant added cheerfully.

"Well," I said. "She's beautiful." I was thinking I'd love to have a chance to take her out.

"Yes. Yes she is," he added with a sigh. Then after a moment, "She's in a hurry."

"It's a good day for a run."

He chuckled. "Yes, it certainly is." We stood there at the railing and watched her crew work her, pulling ahead sixteen, maybe seventeen knots towards port. We discussed their choices of sail, me getting a chance to look though his binoculars, until the call came for breakfast. It was porridge again. I'd barely finished when an able seaman appeared at our table with orders to escort me to the captain.

We met in his day room, which was lovely by the way, with carved wood paneling, a rug, and curtains. He had a table ringed with chairs, a desk, a couch, and a bar where they had coffee brewing. Every square inch that could be, was covered with boxes, papers, letters, and on his table stacks of banknotes and coin. I wasn't sure, but I thought I could see my passport in one of the stacks on his table. But what caught my eye were the sea charts up on the walls. I wanted to look, but there was no way I could get to them with so much stuff in the way, and they were waiting, Captain Duval, Captain Mathy, and an ensign to translate for Captain Mathy.

"Ah, Miss Carmichael," the captain said.

"*Guten morgan*," Captain Mathy added, tipping his head. "Looking much better. Food makes a big difference."

"I agree," added Captain Duval. "Still, we must do something about your request for clothing."

"We've been neglecting the airship logs in deference to the inventory," Captain Mathy said.

"The Sûreté will not be pleased," the captain added with a smug look.

"Normally the safe wouldn't be any trouble except its contents were tossed into bags in no order along with the mail. We made a hasty exit. So we've been sorting and inventorying it all."

"Which has turned out be quite a problem," Captain Duval sighed. "We've found a box containing a set of pearls, which I think belongs to you, along with some gold jewelry belonging to your friend." He saw my eyes light. "But we can't give them back until we can settle with everyone. The problem is that several people are dead."

"There will be lawyers involved," Captain Mathy added with disgust.

"And the Sûreté will keep your travel papers and passport during your questioning."

I doubted Max and Emma were going to wait around for this.

"But what has us confused is the amount of money you left in the safe. Did the two of you really only bring $101.20 and 442 Pesetas with you to Europe?"

"We were to be met in Brussels, where I have friends, and I have a bank account there."

"Still. That isn't much contingency money. As you now know, many things can go wrong when you travel."

"Lufthansa will certainly reimburse you your airfare and loss of property, but that will take time," added Captain Mathy.

"We've been talking it over and the best we can do for you is to delay your release to the police for a few hours. My tailor, I hope, will be waiting at the docks but the ship will have to file a claim against your account." Then he sat back in his chair. "But with only $100, what will that leave you for day to day expenses."

My Spanish money apparently didn't count.

"You will have hotel expenses paid for a few days, until the police release you, but how will you get to Brussels?"

Captain Mathy frowned and looked a bit embarrassed. "Lufthansa will probably pay for train tickets, but our airships are booked months in advance, and it will take time for them to arrange that as well. I'll have to telegraph Berlin as soon as we arrive."

This was all sounding very complicated.

"She said she has an account in Brussels."

"She did."

Turning to me, "I hope it's more substantial than your travel money."

"It is."

"Good. Then the best solution would be to open an account in France. That will speed the transfer. We generally don't write checks here. I suggest Banque de France."

"She'll need to change her money," Captain Mathy added.

"We can't put her in the hands of the dock money changers!"

And on and on they went, just so I could get a new dress! I talked to Aleta about it when I got back, but Emma was there too so there wasn't much I could say. One thing was clear. We weren't running for the Belgium border. Not for a while.

Brest is a lot like Lisbon. It's a city on the side of a large lagoon. But, unlike Lisbon, instead of warm sunshine we came in through a light rain and cold winter wind. The lagoon has an easy entrance with wide deep mouth marked by a central lighthouse. Brest harbor itself is behind a breakwater, but we weren't going there. We were heading for the Penfield, the river mouth next to it. We edged in under wheeling sea gulls and gray blue-flecked sky, pulled by two tugs. The entrance was flanked by fleets of fishing boats anchored in the shallow water. The Penfield is where the naval base is, strung out along the river's edge, beneath a huge medieval fortress that guards the entrance.

I got a good look at it all while we here holding station, waiting for the tugs. High straight walls of smooth gray stone that end in pointed roofs and those square zig zag things that castles have on top, like a storybook. It was the perfect place for an evil prince. They were using an old semaphore tower at the harbor mouth for communications too. Practically Napoleonic! The dock facilities were modern, but oddly configured with floating wharves that held the ships back from the old quays, in deeper water. The original stone quays were built long ago, back when ships had shallower drafts.

The shore was full of cheering people too. I was so busy watching that I didn't think. It turned out people were taking my picture. I didn't see the cameras until it was too late. I turned and went inside, but the damage was done. It was the image they showed the world. Me leaning casually on the railing in my blood stained dress. It would be the first image of me my family saw, but I didn't know it then.

I was no longer being led around. I was free to roam. I think Captain Mathy put in a good word for me. So I went down to the crew mess for some coffee. It was practically empty, but there's always coffee on Navy ships.

I was taking it back to my bunk when I remembered that the captain's tailor would want to see me, so I turned and climbed up toward officer country, balancing my mug, only to be met by a running seaman.

"Miss Carmichael, I'm to take you to the captain."

"I was already going," I replied with a grin. He was blushing, his new haircut looking nice.

We were walking when he asked me timidly, "Ma'am." He stammered. "We are all wondering, did you really seduce a prince?"

I thought for a second and decided not to be angry. A lot of people were going to ask.

"No. But he tried to seduce me. He kept my family prisoner. The German invasion saved us all."

He nodded, and then we walked, the ward room hatch already open. He muttered to himself, "I didn't think so." Then he brightened. "They've set up in here ma'am."

"Thank you."

Inside they had dropped the deadlights down over the portholes and turned on the lights.

The captains were there along with their translator and another man, the tailor. He brought a stack of boxes and had a satchel sitting on a table. He was surprisingly young, in his early twenties.

"Miss Carmichael," Captain Duval said, as a greeting.

"*Guten Tag*," Captain Mathy added with a smile. "Please sit." I sat down at the only clear table corner. They laid out papers and a pen.

"We have your money and we've even managed to change it."

"At reasonable rates," Captain Mathy added, clearly proud.

"We'll need you to sign here," he said as he pushed forward a piece of paper.

I took the pen and signed, then Captain Duval put an envelope down and slid it across to me. Inside was a stack of bills.

"Seven hundred and six Francs," he said proudly. "And we're going to take those who wish to go, to the bank later this morning."

"Thank you," I replied.

I'm not one for tears, but I almost teared up. They were trying so hard and I was so glad for the help.

"Now we'll leave you with Paul, my tailor. One of the few who makes shipboard calls and does so at rates a poor navy man can afford." Paul frowned at that last bit.

Then he introduced us. "Paul Poiret, Calista Carmichael."

"Aleta will be here shortly to chaperone," Captain Mathy added.

Then Captain Duval said to Captain Mathy with a tired look, "Now to deal with the Sûreté."

"Yes, the murder. They will want to question both of them."

"But not now. Now we leave you with Paul." And they got up to leave, only to bump into Aleta at the door.

"In you go," Captain Mathy said, shooing her in before they left.

She stopped and stared. "Cali, is this the tailor?" She sounded doubtful.

"I am," Paul replied with authority in heavily accented English. Aleta squinted at him, but Paul continued. "Paul Poiret, custom clothier.

"Aren't you a bit young?" she stated flatly.

"You are definitely American," he replied, as if it were an accusation.

"I'm English," she replied.

He looked away, crossing his arms. "I can leave if my services are not acceptable."

We needed him. "M. Poiret, please stay," I said. I gave him a smile and said, "I think you will do fine."

"Do fine?"

Switching to French, "You'll do. Do very well I think." He relaxed.

"Your height," he said in French, giving me the eye. "It's all wrong. But I knew he wouldn't get it right so I brought several sizes. All manufactured of course. There's no time to make anything. You're not wearing a corset."

"No. I'm not."

"If this is all going to be in French," Aleta said. "Then I'm going to get coffee."

"That's why your dress bags so." Then he added in English, "I want mine with milk." Then he continued in French, clearly a snub aimed at Aleta. "I have heard about you."

"How rude of me to want to be included." Aleta rolled her eyes. "Cali, do you want one?"

I groaned. "You got to speak nothing but German all through the flight." Then I turned to Paul and said in English. "You've heard nothing true."

"Too bad. Fame is precious," he said, continuing in English too.

"I don't want it."

He shrugged. "It's brought me here," he replied. "It will get you a dress."

"You wouldn't have come?"

"Of course not," he sighed. "I'm going to make nothing off this."

"You came because I'm famous?"

"Not directly," he replied with a little smile. "I came because I want to be famous."

"Maybe I don't want to know." Aleta exclaimed. "Go ahead and speak French."

"You have no idea what's been going on the other side of that dock," he said, looking back and forth between us.

What was going on was why I needed him. "I don't want to wear a corset."

He pursed his lips. "Setting fashion already? It's dangerous. I like it."

Then he stared at me quite frankly, looking me up and down. I felt my cheeks flush.

"You'll look thin and girlish."

"I'm a girl."

"So you are," his voice trailed away and stepped over to his pile of boxes. He pulled out a box, but tisked and put it aside mumbling to himself, "I had so little go on." Then he picked another, shaking his head. "Maybe this," he said as he opened a box.

He held it up, looking over the edge at me. "He told me your hair was red, but it's really almost blond."

"Someone told me I had seen too much sun," I replied.

"Who?"

"A dressmaker."

"Who?"

"A woman named Omama."

"Omama? You know her?"

I frowned. "Yes."

"And you're just a girl from Boston," he trailed away half to himself again. He held up the dress, letting the box drop to the floor. "We'll try this."

Chapter 16 – Infamy

Paul's price for that dress was to walk down the gangway behind me, but I bargained. A second dress and alterations for Aleta so she could dump her corset as well. I had no choice. I had to have a change of clothing and I just had time to change. It was pale seafoam green with ridiculously large blousing shoulders. His hands flew as he took it in, the stitches less than perfect but still acceptable. He definitely had skill. I changed in the next room, Aleta helping. He topped it off with a hat from a box. It had a huge bow. I wasn't pleased, but tried not to show it. I think he knew anyway and was amused. Aleta ran down to our cabin for me to bring up petticoats, stockings, and shoes. In the end, it had to do. I think we all had to shrug our shoulders.

Outside, the crowd roared as we emerged blinking in the sunlight, blitzlicht popping in balls of blinding smoke all around us as we walked by. It left spots in my eyes that made it hard to see where I was going. This was all just for us as the others had all gone on hours before. They had the way clear for us, lining the way with gendarmes in their capes and képis.

Really, it all happened very quickly. Everyone was yelling and calling things out. I couldn't tell what anyone was saying. At the end of our walk we were hustled into a waiting police van that ground its gears before chugging away.

We were driven along the river, past quays crowded with cheering and yelling people. Behind towered huge iron monsters, warships sitting like grand castles of iron and pennants, some with no masts at all. We drove up the side of the river's bluff, then over the top of a crazy train trestle thing that stretched all the way across, high over the water. Before we drove over it, I thought it a crane. Like maybe they could pick cargo off of boats without having them dock, which is a crazy good idea, but it was a giant swinging bridge. I never got to see it turn.

Brest's streets were just as narrow and crowded as Le Havre but they had fewer trollies to dodge. Fewer wagons and cars as well. Instead they had people. The sidewalks were so narrow that most walked in the street. Men in suits and hats, dames with parasols and hats like sails, begrudgingly giving way despite the police and our horns.

We bumped and rolled down the *Rue de Siam*, then right on to *Rue de la Rampe* to a large paved squared, the *Champ-de-Bataille*, the field of battle. As it turned out, it was an appropriate name for what was coming. We stopped in front of a wide gold domed building, the Grand Hôtel. Apparently, where we were to spend the night.

In front were more gendarmes, reporters, and gawkers. It wasn't as bad as the docks, but bad enough to make our entrance up the stone steps and through the polished brass and glass doors hurried and unpleasant. Inside, it was thankfully quiet, the insanity outside muffled by thick Persian carpet and dark carved wood. I was fairly positive I couldn't afford it.

We met the others in a side parlor. It was then, as we gathered, that I noticed that Max wasn't with us. Neither was Philip or Belle.

Our spies had somehow jumped ship.

"Emma," I asked her. "Where's Max?"

"Oh. He doesn't like his picture being taken." Then she whispered to me with mock conspiracy, "Then again, perhaps he doesn't want to be questioned by the Sûreté."

"What about you?"

"Oh, I'll be helping. You forget. I work for France."

"What about their passports?"

"They'll get new ones from their embassies," she sang. "Assuming they don't have three or four sewn into their clothing somewhere already."

"Oh."

"You need a lot of them. You're always handing them over to hotel clerks and police officers."

But then we were interrupted by a prim man, judging by his suit, the hotel manager. He too had one of those awful thin mustaches. It was definitely a fashion!

"Madams and Monsieurs, I would like to welcome you to the Grand Hôtel. We have rooms prepared for all of you, complements of Lufthansa," they said, in both French and German.

Not having to pay! Then I worried that it might not include food.

The hotel had elevators, my first. They're big iron cages, raised and lowered by cable. A part of the cage slides together to allow entry and exit. Our operator pulled ours open to let us in and then shut before he started it up. He was a young man, perhaps my age, who kept giving me sidelong glances as he pulled the lever back, then forward to lift us to our floor. I supposed he read the papers and was curious. We rode up with the Jefferies so it was a bit crowded. You don't think about the floor beneath you when you're in a tall building, but when they go by one after another, you begin to realize how thin they are and that the roof of your room is the floor of the room above.

Lufthansa booked the entire third floor for us. We were paired for our rooms based on our airship booking, so Aleta and I were together. Our room, when we finally found it was amazing! Two bedrooms and our own bathroom. It looked like a cake. Pastel green painted walls, carved white wood trim, and brocade covered carved wood furniture. Our windows looked down on the square. Most of the benches nearby were occupied by what I was fairly sure were reporters. It was the cameras. But out in the middle of the square, sitting on the steps of the fountain was a man feeding pigeons. He looked a bit like Max.

We had an hour before lunch so I arm wrestled Aleta for the tub, which was big shiny white, with silver spigots. I let her win because I figured I'd have more time after lunch. Sadly, I couldn't have been more wrong. It turned out most of the passengers had already been interviewed by the police. Our turns would come after lunch.

While I was waiting, I had time to think. I was sure the Dewars had said nothing to the police or they would have been taken away, or at least separated from us. Surely the local police wouldn't know how to handle this. They would surely have to defer to those who did and it would take time for them to get here. But Emma knew too. She was a French spy, wasn't she? She should have told them, or taken charge. Nothing made sense. I had to find a way to talk to Vic and her da.

So I wandered the corridor. We were, at that time, not confined to our room so the gendarmes watching our corridor didn't stop me. I walked down the hallway listening, hoping to hear their voices, but that didn't work. Then I asked a gendarme who pointed out their door.

"Vic?" I asked as I knocked.

"Cali?"

"Let me in."

The doctor was lying in bed, his feet up.

"Oh, you're here," he said. "Awful experience."

"Yes," I agreed. "Vic. I need to know what you said to the police."

"We didn't say anything," she replied. "They didn't ask."

"That's strange. Was Emma there?"

"No."

"That makes no sense."

"Now that you mention it, I suppose it doesn't." She frowned. "Maybe her kind don't get along with local police."

We both chewed on that for a second.

"Well, we'll find out for sure eventually," Vic added.

"She's a Frenchie," Dr. Dewar added from the bed. "There's no telling with them."

"I suppose," my voice trailing away in doubt, ignoring the fact that she was Spanish, not French. Then I asked Vic, "Should I say anything to them when they interview me?"

She grimaced. "I don't know."

"I don't know either."

"We'll leave it up to you."

I rolled my eyes, "Thanks."

So, I thought about it, and thought about it some more. Then someone knocked on our door to warn us about lunch. We were ready, but poor Aleta's hair still wet and not put up. I vowed to find someone to cut it straight. We'd chickened out on the ship. Now her crazy hair was in all the newspapers.

We took the elevator down alone with me still thinking about what to tell the police, most of the others being already downstairs. The elevator boy pointed us in the right direction. As we walked, I figured we had to take a chance or we wouldn't make it.

"Aleta," I whispered.

"What?" she whispered back.

"Say nothing about the Dewars. We know nothing about what the spies were fighting over."

"You're crazy."

"If they know about them, they'll lock them up."

"Lie to the police?"

"We have to."

Then we were in the dining room, and a man with a table cloth over this arm was leading us to our table, handing us cards with a hand written list of choices on it. Aleta frowned at me as they held our chairs for us.

The dining room was large and airy, with tall windows that filled the room with wan light. It started to rain.

Eight passengers and five crew died, seven were in hospital. Poor Herr Hochberg, one of our airsickness patients, should have been as well but he'd been seated with us. Four of our living spies had vanished, but we still had Emma. The Dryers and the Harmons were missing. We found out later that they'd gone down with our tow ship. We were much a much diminished crew. Out of the original thirty one passengers, only twelve of us were left to be seated. Three tables. Sadly, despite making shore, it wasn't to be the end of it. So many more were still to leave us. Even after we made shore we kept on dying.

It was a quiet meal. Most, I think, were very tired. I know I felt a terrible melancholy. The Péans were sitting across from us. Both Émile and Olivie looked worried, but there were police with us to keep away the curious, leaving us no privacy to talk.

They fed us some sort of seafood soup, which looking back was probably a bisque, peas, and a stew over bread, which poor terribly starved Herr Hochberg had to avoid because it was pork. They brought him chicken instead, which was very nice of them I thought. It must be hard to have to avoid so many common foods. I was going to try the wine, but Émile shook his head no, which started me worrying. We finished with lemon mousse and coffee. The meal was great after our filling, but bland, navy porridge.

After the meal the Péans stopped me on the way out.

"You should know, the police are very interested in you," Émile said. He looked worried.

"They weren't interested in anything but you," Olivie added.

"It's those newspapers!" Aleta spat.

"Newspapers?" Émile asked.

"The English are blaming me for the Congo," I said, the shine from the meal gone.

"How odd. Have they questioned you yet?

"No."

"They will, and you will need your wits!" Émile added. "I saw them in the lobby as we went to lunch. The one you have to watch out for is this Inspector Roux."

"He was awful, wasn't he?" Olivie added.

"A hopeless bureaucrat." Émile shook his head.

Then we were interrupted by a gendarme, standing behind them chuckling. He said in French, "Yes. That's Inspector Roux. He can seem course." Then he continued in English, "Mlle. Carmichael, Mlle. Rucker." I saw Aleta wince. "Come with me please. The inspector would like to speak with you."

Émile reached out and squeezed my arm. "We'll be waiting for you." And we were led away.

"You speak French?" the gendarme asked, brightening, as we walked.

"Aleta speaks German and Spanish," I replied, in French.

He frowned. "Then we will continue in English. If you will follow me." He motioned toward a hallway off the lobby. We followed.

The hallway wasn't long. Two doorways deep, ending in a table and a vase full of very pretty flowers. Three of the doors were open. Inside I could see men, both gendarmes and men in suits.

"Mlle. Carmichael, please go in that room." He pointed to a door. "Mlle. Rucker, please follow me." I paused, standing there in the corridor, very frightened.

"Mlle. Carmichael," a man in a suit called from inside.

"Yes, of course." I blinked and walked in.

A gendarme shut the door behind me, cutting me off from the hallway. Three men stood there staring. The gendarme and two men in suits.

"Mlle. Carmichael," one of them said, and they tipped their heads. "Please sit." He motioned toward a couch. I sat and the men in suits sat down on chairs, the gendarme moving to the edge of the room.

"I'm Chief Inspector Roux. This is Inspector Bellamy. You have no idea how glad I am that you speak French. These interviews are tiring enough without translators. Is your French good enough to follow me? Do you understand?"

"Yes."

"Good. Then we'll start with the delay. I want to hear your explanation as to why this couldn't have been done on the ship."

I explained about the newspapers and my dress. They asked for details about the Congo, which took some time, the assistant inspector writing furiously, filling his notebook and starting another.

"Which explains the note at the desk requesting that M. Poiret be allowed access. We will be interviewing him soon. Please, tell us about your flight. Start at the beginning."

The poor assistant inspector was into his third notebook by the time I finished that. Inspector Roux, was quite pointed in his questioning about details and, to be frank, I hadn't had time to put it all in order in my mind. But these were familiar subjects and I'd grown comfortable as we talked about them. That quickly ended.

"And can you explain why you were on top of the gondola during departure."

How did he find out about that? "We wanted to wave to my

174

parents. They couldn't see us in the window."

"You have no fear of heights. Neither of you do."

"No. You can't when you work on a ship."

"Of course not," he said, half to himself. "You seem comfortable working inside a zeppelin."

"Aleta. . ."

"Mlle. Rucker," he corrected. Her passport of course.

"Yes. She's ex-crew. I tried to help, but unless someone was there to tell me what to do, mostly I wasn't much use."

"Which brings us to the central question. Why was it sabotaged? Why was it full of spies? What were you all fighting about?"

"I'm not a spy. I wasn't fighting anyone." I'm also a terrible liar. Just ask Vic. So I decided on half the truth, but he struck first.

"You behave like one. You were clearly defending the Dewars. If it barks like a dog, then it must be a dog."

Max would agree, I thought.

"You're friends with the Dewars."

"Yes."

"Why was their bodyguard killed?"

"He was killed?" I asked.

"What else?" Roux snapped back.

"He might have fallen out a window," I said.

"Then why did Petrov attack you?"

"I don't know."

"You are either very good or a fool."

"Perhaps," I mumbled.

"A young fool."

"Ask Mme. Calve."

"We, unfortunately, no longer have access to her." I wanted to know more about that. She was with us at lunch. "How do you know her?"

"I met her on the flight."

"Yes. You performed together."

"We did."

"You seemed to know them all."

"Only Max."

"The German?"

"Yes. We met in the Congo."

"Before the invasion."

"Yes. He saved my family."

"As you said." He sounded annoyed. "And you were on that flight because . . ?"

"I was given a ticket."

"By . . ?"

"The Duke of Tervuren."

"The Belgian duke." It was almost a sneer.

He seemed to know Lucien too. Who was this Roux?

"To go to music school," I added.

"Music school," he said flatly. He sat back, slapping his hand down on the table. "This is nonsense. You're lying." He was tapping his foot. Perhaps a nervous tic?

I sat there for a moment in shock. "I'm not!" But in a way he was right. I'd said nothing about the Dewars.

"You know nothing of the source of this conflict, the Dewars?"

"Why don't you ask them?"

"They're off limits. But you aren't, and you know."

"I don't know, and I didn't want to know. Max said that if I valued my life, I wouldn't ask."

His eyes narrowed as he stared at me.

"Enough!" he spat. "This is foolishness. How can you not know? We're posting a guard at your door. Do not leave your room without permission and escort." Then he waved his hand, shooing me away. "We will continue this later."

His assistant woke from his scribbling with a start, the interview over.

"Leave," Bellamy said, reaching for my arm to help me up. I'd been there for two hours. Two gendarmes led me back to our room.

Aleta was already back, laying on one of the couches, fuming.

"I can't believe these people!" she snapped. "They searched our trunks."

"I'm so tired," I said.

"That damn policeman kept asking me over and over about fuel doping. Like I could have done that! Like I would commit suicide."

"What time is it?" I asked.

Aleta squinted at the clock. And yes, the room had its own clock and a fireplace. They wound it for us too!

"Four thirty. You should try the bath. It's really nice."

I moaned, "A bath." I started undoing buttons as I staggered toward the bathroom, leaving my clothes on the floor.

"With hot water," she called smugly.

"Hot water," I sighed, closing the bathroom door. And if you're waiting for something to interrupt what was probably the best bath I'd ever had, perhaps police or spies, you are wrong. It was glorious. I spent an hour in the tub and came out all wrinkled. They had pink powder in little tins that smelled of roses. You pour it into the tub as you fill it. I figured this out after first trying to rub it on my skin. The tin got wet so I dumped it in the water to wash it out and realized that was the point of it. I was warm and clean in my hotel bathrobe and slippers, thinking seriously about a nap, when I remembered about Aleta's hair.

"We need to do something about your hair," I said.

"It can wait," she said. I think she knew I was tired.

"They're going to take more pictures."

"True," she replied, glancing at the mirror.

"Let's talk to the front desk."

"You'll have to put your dress on."

"I'll have to for dinner anyway."

"Also true."

So I staggered through dressing, Aleta helping. I was that tired. I couldn't do the buttons! At least not quickly. Then we met the guards at our door. There were two!

"Yes?" one asked, probably in charge.

"We need to go down to the front desk."

"Out of the question. You're confined to your room."

Great, I thought. I dressed for nothing.

"Can you send someone?"

"We are to guard your door," he replied curtly.

"Look at her hair," I said, pointing at Aleta. "We need a hair dresser."

"Yes you do, but we cannot leave."

"What if I set fire to the room?"

"You would go to jail," he squinted.

"Would one of you go for help?"

"Yes, of course. But I still wouldn't let you leave."

He was so stubborn!

"I don't need to leave if you send someone. Aleta's hair got burned and they're going to take our picture."

"I can see the need." He stared at Aleta, who stared back with frank need.

"Go knock on the Dewar's door? Vic will go for us," I replied.

The sagacity of my argument won through. I bet you didn't think I knew that word. I've had an excellent education. I've even read Socrates and Dracula. He finally gave up, his friend going downstairs for us. When he got back, they told us the desk would send someone in an hour.

She arrived with her bags and some folded sheets. When she saw Aleta she took a step back.

It was that bad.

She walked around Aleta surveying the situation and her first words were, "It must have been worse even than the papers said." Then she put down her bags. "You're lucky I'm here. I come by in the afternoon to help before everyone goes out for the evening."

Then she looked at us both.

"My name is Agathe. You are?"

"Cali," I said.

"Aleta."

"It's an honor to help two of the survivors recover," she replied.

"I don't need to recover," I said.

"But your hair," she replied, in clear distress. "The deprivations of your experience have clearly taken their toll."

I had to block a laugh.

"But I'm here now and all will be made better," and she began opening her bags.

When they knocked on our door at seven thirty to warn us about dinner, we were thoroughly coiffed. Aleta's beautiful long hair had been trimmed way back. It would take years to make it back down her back again and we still had nothing to wear. This left me thinking that we were going to need better, something formal as well. Not just travelling. I needed to talk to Paul and I needed money to pay him. Our hairdresser was charged to our room, which I desperately hoped would be paid for by Lufthansa along with everything else.

So it was two rather nicely coiffed but shabbily dressed girls who showed up that evening with our police escort, drawing glances and even some frank stares. Obviously they were envious of our hair, and that we'd thought to have it done.

We had two new gendarmes dressed in their blue capes and kepis. I guessed it was the second shift. They actually looked quite handsome as we walked together. And my dress wasn't blood stained either.

We were early so we got to pick our seats. We chose ones next to Vic and her Da. We got bigger tables this time, so we had M. Marmontel and Frau Abbink as well. With the loss of Emma, who'd finally disappeared with the rest of her kind, our group was down to eleven, one table with an empty seat. Poor Aleta had to speak to poor Frau Abbink, who knew no French or English.

"I heard that someone from Lufthansa will be here tomorrow," Vic said.

"You'll be moving on," I whispered back.

"We don't know what to do."

"I don't either. They won't let me leave. They think we blew up the airship."

"That's rubbish."

I couldn't have agreed more, but I only sighed.

"Can you visit?" I asked. "We're locked in our room."

"I can try," she replied.

"Bring your cards."

She grinned.

After dinner, some sort of fish in sauce, we were escorted back to our rooms. They lit our fireplace while we were gone and our room was warm, and there was a note from Paul asking to see us in the morning. Vic visited and I lost again, but it took her time and a lot less lecturing. I was getting better at lying.

Chapter 17 – Fame

Our lack of clothing had become a big problem, so I presented our problem to our guards. If we were staying, I needed to open an account at a bank to transfer money, and we needed clean clothing, and more of it.

"I'll tell them Mademoiselle," he frowned, then conferred with his friend.

Really, it was all I could do.

They lit another fire that morning, sneaking in before we woke. The staff were quite good at that. We never caught them.

Vic came to visit and walked down to breakfast with us. We had orange juice! It was my first time eating grapes too. We had raisins onboard Red, but grapes don't travel well. Grapes are not as sweet. Vic couldn't believe I'd never had them, but they don't grow in the tropics. Vic had never had a mango.

After breakfast, it was back to our interrogation. We missed our meeting with Paul. They didn't even let me send him a note!

"Tell about the first time you climbed up on top of the zeppelin."

"I told you about that."

"Tell us again. Did your friend Max go with you?"

"No. I never saw Max go up top," I explained.

"Did he tell you to go?"

And on we went. I told them everything again and again.

"Your friend Comeau . . ."

"He was not my friend," I corrected.

"Just Comeau then. He had breakfast with you?"

"Yes. With Mrs. Jefferies."

"He told you about the newspapers."

"Yes."

"What did you do?" he asked.

"I didn't do anything." What could I do?

"You didn't try to defend yourself?"

"No," I answered.

"You surely could have said something."

"I said nothing."

"Why not?"

"What could I say?"

"That they were wrong."

I rolled my eyes. "I didn't like him."

"Does that matter?"

"Yes. I didn't care what he thought," I snapped back. Oh the frustration!

"Is that why he attacked your friend?"

On and on it went, until I was in tears. Until finally at the end, out of the blue, "You know. You know everything!"

"No!"

"How?"

"I did my best not to know."

That one ended in a frustrated sigh and another wave of his hand. "Out!" he snapped. He turned away and said nothing more.

Aleta had gotten out earlier and met Paul, who was waiting for us in the lobby. He brought a box for me, which the police had opened and searched of course. Aleta and Paul, along with Vic, were waiting for me in our room. It was clear I'd been crying and Aleta gave me a hug, which got me crying again, so I hugged her back. I stood there for a moment, until she let go. Then I flopped down on a couch vowing never to move again. I wanted to hide.

Paul crouched down and stared into my eyes, apparently thinking.

"What?" I asked, still crying just a bit

"Try on the dress."

"Not now," Aleta snapped.

But he kept staring, eyebrows up, eyes bright, clearly saying, "Well?"

I growled and got up. "Give me the dress."

"We're lucky my models are a close fit. I actually had to take it in." A benefit I guess of being on the small side. He opened the box. Inside was a glowing stretch of creamy white fabric. It certainly wouldn't last. Folded I couldn't tell what it looked like, so I took the box in my room and shut the door. I didn't have shoes for it, which was clearly daft.

As I put it on, I could feel the quality of the workmanship, and it fit! First a simple blouse. I had to take off my bloomers to pull on the socks. They were so thin. I was afraid they'd tear as I hitched them up and clipped them. The skirt fell in perfect even folds, practically to the floor. How did he do that? It was all so light, flowing around me as I turned. I had no problem moving. The jacket was long, over my hips, all of it with modest shoulders and a wide collars that could be buttoned close in the cold. It was entirely unfashionable. I loved it immediately. Shoes or not, I was going to wear this.

When I stepped out, both Aleta and Vic stared back, two clouds of doubt, but Paul merely smiled like a cat who had eaten a mouse.

"There's a hat, purse, and shoes, which I really hope fit because changing them will be difficult. The police still have them. I'll try to get them."

"It will never stay clean," Aleta stated flatly.

"I love it," I replied.

"You look like a crème puff," Vic said. "And I can tell you aren't wearing a corset. People will talk."

"Oh, like they aren't already."

"They won't serve you in restaurants."

"As if I would eat in those. It's perfect Paul!"

Really. Don't hate me. I'd lived my life up to that point in school uniforms and rags from the sloppes. To wear something so beautiful was like a fairytale, even if it was going to get ruined at my next meal.

He looked back, smug. "Let's see about the police." And he left.

"I suppose it does have something," Aleta said. "Maybe with the shoes."

"I can't wait for lunch," I smiled at Aleta. "I won't be a charity case."

Aleta frowned, "What about me? He said he was going to alter my dresses."

"They're probably still being cleaned."

Aleta sighed.

"Cali, there's something you need to see," Vic said, sounding a bit worried.

"What now?'

She handed over a folded newspaper from the end table.

As I opened it, all my newly acquired happiness drained out of me. The headline read, "The Rabbit Returns!" Someone had taken a picture of me as we were docking. I was standing at the railing in my blood stained dress.

"This is awful. I've got to write Ma and Pa."

"They interviewed your Paul," she added.

"Did they? Where?"

"Page three."

"The Rabbit's Personal Dressmaker." A laugh burst out of nowhere. And why not?

"Let me see," Aleta reached for the paper, which I handed over, but she immediately handed it back.

"It's in French," she said.

"They'll speak German in Belgium," I said with sympathy. I read the important details out loud.

"Her wardrobe was damaged or destroyed."

Aleta shrugged. It was true.

"The blood was from helping the wounded and fighting to save the airship."

"What about me?" Aleta growled.

"Newspapers," I sighed. "They say here that, as far Paul knows, she has no idea who attacked the ship. She has many enemies, but he thinks it was either the British or the Belgians." I frowned. "I'm going to kill him."

"They were attacking Da and me." Now Vic sounded hurt.

"Oh, Lucien. Where are you?" I moaned to myself. Then I realized that there was no way for him to get into the hotel. We were surrounded by police.

"Aleta." She looked up. "If they question you again, you mustn't mention Vic. Let them think it's me. It's the only chance they have of getting out of this hotel."

"That's not fair," Vic said.

"No, it is. Emma knew about you, so they know already. It's the police here in Brest who don't. But someone somewhere in the French government knows it wasn't me. I'll get through this. If you can get out today or tomorrow, then you have a chance."

There was a knock on the door and the guard let Paul in.

"We're in luck," he said, glancing at the boxes in his arms. "The police didn't cut anything apart."

"Paul. We need to talk about the newspapers."

He looked at me and blinked.

"Is there a problem?"

He had three women taking turns, but he had an answer for everything.

They'll never let her alone! "All the better."

She has enemies? "Who doesn't," he said with a shrug.

You've heard me play? "Well . . . I've heard of your playing."

I'm friends with Annie Oakley? "That will play well in Paris."

The Belgians? He laughed. He clearly didn't take this seriously.

"Honestly Cali, we ought to go to Paris," he continued. "Brussels is so stuffy."

He clearly wanted me famous and through me, himself. His price for the dresses. And at that moment, I realized this was to my advantage. I *wanted* the police looking at me, not Vic. So I demanded a third dress and two for Aleta. Paul practically swooned, "Naturally!"

The shoes fit after a fashion. He promised the next would be better. My new hat was fascinating. Not a boater or a bonnet, the brim turned down rather than up as fashion dictated, and the dome was – a low dome. No massive bow or sprays of feathers. And it had a beautiful pale blue ribbon that hung down the back. And the best part was that, unlike Omama's work, I would get to keep this one.

I drew stares at lunch. It was fun until I saw the look on Émile's face. It was as if he couldn't match me to the woman he knew. That doubt, that hurt me. I almost turned around. I should have. I wanted to hold his hand and tell him that it was me, that I wasn't a spy, but there was no room at his table.

And so I walked on and very carefully ate lunch in my new dress.

There was no interrogation that afternoon. No one came for us. We were confused and relieved. I dearly hoped they were satisfied. We played cards instead until that afternoon, when they called us all downstairs to the dining room. They had two men waiting to speak to us. A barrister who was supposedly representing us and a representative from Lufthansa.

We had to fill out claim forms for lost property, which took some thought. They explained we would be compensated six hundred goldmarks per day and all medical expenses, plus an additional three hundred francs and first class train fare to our destinations. Not everyone was happy. Mr. Kappel was crying quietly to himself, thinking of his wife as they thoughtlessly handed him two tickets. Mme. Yount had her arm around his shoulder.

Frau Abbink, on the other hand, was bubbling with joy.

"My most exciting trip yet, and I got paid for it!" she laughed.

"Honestly, I hope they don't get more exciting than this," I replied.

I had no idea how much a goldmark was and was going to ask, but the Lufthansa man had turned and was heading toward poor Mr. Kappel. He told Mr. Kappel that none of this applied to him.

We filled out our forms, signed papers, and received envelopes filled with marks, which they firmly suggested that we put in the hotel safe. They would be visiting us that afternoon and evening to discuss schedules.

Altogether, I felt pretty hopeful that the Dewars would be on their way very soon, but afternoon turned to evening, then dinner, without them coming to see us. Vic sat with us in our room while we moped about, worrying what would come next.

At dinner, the four of us sat with the Hochbergs. Again, there hadn't been room at Émile's table. I was going to have to find a way to visit.

"I suppose this is our goodbye dinner," Frau Hochberg said as we sat down.

"They haven't visited us yet," Dr. Dewar said.

"How strange. We're on the train tomorrow morning," Herr Hochberg said. "But I'm sure they will see you soon. Be thankful to be on solid land," he added as he worked his way around the edges of his steak. He didn't like rare meat, but wouldn't send it back.

"Damn French would have fit if I asked them to cook it properly," he said.

His wife chuckled.

"They would probably start chewing on the cows in the middle of the field if it weren't for the getting dirt on their shoes," he continued, which got Frau Hochberg laughing.

They were not the best company. I was glad he'd been sick and unable to speak during the trip.

"You're going to be down for the picture aren't you?" Frau Hochberg asked.

"Picture?" I replied.

"Yes. You and that interesting dress." She sounded doubtful. "They want a picture of us all together for the newspapers."

"They hadn't told us." I looked at Dr. Dewar. He looked back confused.

"Well," she continued. "They'll probably get around to you after dinner."

Émile and Olivie were leaving, having gotten there earlier. So I excused myself and followed.

"Dr. Péan?" I called.

They turned, then smiled.

"Cali," he said.

"I want to talk to you before you go."

"Of course. We would have stopped by before we left."

"When are you leaving?"

"We have an afternoon train to Paris."

"Not as good as an airship," Olivie added. "But I'm a bit tired of airships at the moment."

I smiled.

"You aren't leaving tonight are you?" Émile asked.

"We don't know yet. They haven't talked to us."

That got a flash of worry from him.

"They will, dear," Olivie added.

We sat down at an empty table and a waiter trotted right over.

"May I bring you anything?" he asked.

That stumped Dr. Péan for a moment.

"I'll have another glass of that lovely wine you brought us at dinner," Olivie replied, taking Émile's hand.

Then he added, "Yes, me too."

"Mademoiselle?"

I didn't want wine. "May I have orange juice?"

He blinked for a moment and Émile broke out in a real smile, the waiter following with, "Yes. Right away."

I tried my best to reassure Émile that nothing in the papers was true and that I was dressing this way to help friends. I don't think he understood, but I still felt that trust.

That evening went by and they still didn't come to talk with us about travel plans. Neither us, nor the Dewars. I did, however, have another glorious bath.

Chapter 18 – Kidnapped

They knocked on our door to warn us about the picture that we hadn't been notified of. It was very rude. Despite that, we dressed and primped as best we could and were ready on time.

As we were heading downstairs with our police escort, with the Jefferies walking ahead of us. Mr. Jefferies kept glancing back at me until Mrs. Jeffries yanked on his arm. Perhaps it was our escorts, I thought.

There was a crowd waiting for us in the lobby.

The first thing I noticed was that Captain Mathy was there in dress uniform. I gave him a big smile, which melted when I saw Mme. Calvé standing next to him. If she was back, then trouble was coming just behind her. She gave me an odd look. Was it concern? Sympathy? But she turned away and continued her conversation.

We had time while the others came down and I had a chance to look over our audience. There were at least ten cameras with far too many helpers, all held at bay by gendarmes. Undoubtedly they were all reporters. Half the hotel and even some of the staff were there. I saw Paul and his eyes brightened and he held up an armload of boxes. Then I saw that awful woman that I thought we had left at the aerodrome in Boston. Her eyes narrowed as she caught my gaze. I felt Aleta's hand tighten on my arm. I think she had seen her too.

But then again maybe she hadn't because she left and walked through the crowd, her gendarme scrambling to catch up, ignoring everyone's shock and stares. She walked right up to Paul.

"And where is my dress?" she snapped.

Really. She didn't look that bad. She hardly worn her dresses on the flight and she was wearing her corset so it fit.

He chuckled and nodded, saying something I couldn't hear, and then they walked away together leaving me to trade stares with the nob-woman friend of Max's. Max, by the way, was nowhere to be seen. To give him credit, I suppose he couldn't show himself. Not here. Nor were any of our other spies, except Emma. Not for a picture.

So I was at ends until I had an idea. My dress showed a lot of, I'm sure, very controversial neck that begged for jewelry. It would be perfect for a locket, but all I had were my pearls, so I went to the front desk, my escorts perking up and following. I had to sign a paper to get them back. They were there, still in their box.

I had to get one of my escorts to do the clasp. When I looked back at him, he was beet red. Looking down, I thought they looked very nice, but everyone was acting so strangely that I became a bit self-conscious about the dress. It showed a lot less than the sloppes I wore on ship and it's not like I wore a corset anyway. Three weeks ago I'd been just another girl in a school uniform and nobody cared then!

We were left in the lobby with nothing to do but compare destinations. If they had return flights, Lufthansa let them reschedule, but everyone's itineraries were in shambles and Lufthansa was trying it's best to help, paying the costs of letters and telegrams. So far, I had sent three letters, all airmail paid for by Lufthansa, but Lufthansa let me send a cable to the States too! A very short cable mind you. They charge by the letter and they encourage the use of contractions without punctuation.

MA PA IM OK (STOP) DONT WORRY

I knew they would anyway, but then, as they were at sea they wouldn't hear about any of this for weeks, perhaps months. The cable was really for Grandpa and it was free.

I finally said goodbye to Captain Mathy. It was difficult because we couldn't really talk. His eyes though said a lot and I gave him a hug. Emma kept herself turned away until I tapped her on the shoulder.

"Emma, you've been gone," I said.

"Yes," she replied, turning back with her sunny smile. She was probably very good at poker, I thought. "I've been attending to business."

"Does it have something to do with us?"

"Of course," she chided. But when she saw my frown, she smiled and said, "Don't worry. Everything will work out for the best for everyone."

"Emma, the best thing you could do is to leave us alone."

"Don't worry," she with finality and turned to talk the Lufthansa representative. It was all a bit abrupt and I was sure there was every reason to worry.

We were all waiting for our truly wounded to arrive from the hospital, M. Yount with his shoulder wound and M. Laurent who lost part of his foot. Sadly, Éléonore with her broken hip, couldn't come, but her husband Eugéne was there.

Then Aleta came back. Can you see me smiling?

Paul had somehow managed to make her a dress. He couldn't be doing this by himself, I thought. It was something I needed to ask him.

She was walking through the crowd, almost like a sprite drifting through the woods. She practically glowed. Men and even women were turning to stare. Paul walked behind with his smug smile, arms still full of boxes. Someone's camera went off as she joined us. It was very much like mine in cut, but her jacket was lavender with matching flowers sewn into the dress. It set off her green eyes, I thought.

"Now I'll draw attention from you," she said with a grin as she rejoined us.

"You're helping, right?" I replied, grinning back.

"Maybe I can get a dress from him too," Vic said.

"We're both drawing attention away from you," I replied, which got us laughing and someone else's camera went off and I realized that we were doing the opposite. We were drawing attention to Vic. It seemed to me, I thought with frustration, that I could do no good.

Our patients finally arrived in an ambulance with police escort. M. Laurent was on crutches and M. Yount in a loose coat that was clearly not his. We stood together in the lobby while they removed their camera lens caps and the *blitzlicht* burned and flashed. Then all semblance of order broke down and the photographer's helpers rushed forward followed by onlookers to ask questions, mostly aimed at me.

In my defense, I was taken by surprise. This was my first time facing the press. So many questions I couldn't make out what most of them were saying. I didn't have time to think except to take business cards as they were thrust at me.

"Why were you on that flight?"

"To get to Brussels," I replied.

"Is it true you helped the crew?"

I nodded.

"Who did it? Who tried to kill you?"

"Tried to kill me? That wasn't it at all."

"Do you know why?" someone asked, but I was still reeling from what I had just said. Sometimes I can be so stupid. I looked up at the voice, suddenly afraid, and his eyes went wide. He must have misunderstood completely, thought I was afraid of some enemy. His hand scribbled in his notebook.

What did I do? I thought. I would relive that moment over and over. That was the moment I truly became "The Rabbit." They never let me escape from it.

"No, no more," I said, trying to turn away.

"Are you going to be performing?"

That caught me by surprise and I paused, but then I continued on, walking away, my escort catching up as I headed to the elevator.

Back in our room, I finally surprised two maids who were packing our things, and really, doing a better job of it than I could.

"What are you doing?" I asked.

"Packing," said the older one. "You've checked out."

"We didn't."

"Then you should tell the desk," the other replied with sympathy.

I was definitely not going back in that lobby. So I asked the guards, but they knew nothing. I could do nothing but sit and wait until Aleta came back.

I looked at the cards in my hand. They were an even mix of reporters and photographers, probably wanting interviews and pictures. I left them on a side table.

"What are they doing?" she asked as she came in half an hour later, seeing the maids. The reporters turned on her after I left, but she told them nothing.

"We've checked out," I replied

She growled, "Now what?"

I sighed and flopped back in the chair, knocking my precious hat forward into my lap. Then Paul entered with his boxes.

"What's going on here?" he asked. Next it will be Vic, I thought.

"We're checking out," Aleta replied.

"Where are you going?"

"Who knows?" I tried to add in French, which didn't translate well, stupid idioms, and he stood there looking confused.

"We don't know," Aleta explained. Then she looked at the maids and sighed, "I guess I won't have time to take another bath."

"Paul," I asked. "How did you make these dresses so quickly?"

He brightened. "I have a studio, which I'm moving to Paris by the way."

I blinked at him.

"I employ three seamstresses. They worked very late on these, and were very excited about it too. You're doing very well. Soon, every girl in Paris will want to be you," he paused. "And I will make dresses for all of them." He looked so happy. "You wouldn't believe all the cards I've been given!"

I didn't know how to reply. Even in hindsight I'm not sure what I could have said, both to Paul and the reporters that could have stopped this. But in saying nothing, I left great blanks in the story which they gleefully filled in with speculation. I was becoming the center of everyone's expectations. Both the good and the bad. Please forgive me. I was still very young.

We were down to one maid, who eyed Paul's boxes. "Do we need to pack anything else Mademoiselles?"

"My old dress," Aleta replied. "But it's dirty," she added, looking worried.

"We can wrap it," she replied, with a little dip of a curtsey.

"Did you bring me anything?" I asked.

Paul brightened again and stepped forward, "Oh yes!" And began sorting through his boxes.

It was better than the first and would be just as impossible to keep clean. No one could possibly have missed me when I finally made my exit from the hotel, which happened quite abruptly. There was a knock at our door, followed by two moustached men in suits and bowler hats.

They eyed the crowd in our room with clear suspicion.

"Who is this man?" one said, eying Paul. "Who said you could have visitors?"

"Who are you?" Aleta asked.

"She doesn't speak French?" he asked his friend.

"According to Bellamy, no."

The first one grunted in disgust. "What did she say?"

"I have no idea Chief Inspector."

"She asked who you are," Paul said.

"You are French?"

"I am," Paul replied.

"Take him to room 301," the chief inspector called to the gendarmes.

"Wait. What are you doing?" I asked, but the gendarmes were already reaching for him. He hurriedly handed his pile of boxes to me, which I took, my eyes wide with surprise as they led him out the door.

The last thing I heard from him was, "What are you doing?" I wouldn't see him again until after Christmas.

I was stunned. I turned and handed the boxes to the maid.

"Search those, and the luggage," the inspector said.

"We've already been searched," I said.

"She speaks French. Good. All the more reason to search it again. Roux is an idiot."

"Why are you doing this?"

"Why?"

I said nothing. I already asked.

"Because I'm François-Marie Goron of the Sûreté. That is reason enough. Welcome, mademoiselle to the *Deuxième Bureau*."

"François, it's time to go," Emma called from the hallway.

"I'll need to search them," he said.

"They've been searched and searched. I've told you. They're

foolish girls."

The inspector frowned. It clearly went against his grain.

"Then get them to the cars," he said, with a wave of his hand.

"Where are we going? What about our luggage," Aleta asked.

"Damned English," the inspector snapped.

"It will follow," Emma called, in English. Then in French, "We must go François. We can't keep him waiting."

"Him?" I asked, but we were being led out by two more gendarmes. I just had time to grab my violin. The inspector scowled at it, but let me keep it.

"Cali, what is going on," Aleta asked.

"I don't know," I replied as we were led down the hallway.

"You will be detained," Emma said. "Consider it a rap on the knuckles for playing in games you shouldn't."

We were taken down the elevator to the lobby where the Dewars were waiting, also in custody.

"François, this is bad," Emma said, when she saw the Dewars. "I told you to take them out earlier."

"It's the crowds. The damn mob out front is hard to clear. Doing it once will save time."

"Cali?" Vic called.

"Miss Carmichael?" Dr. Dewar added.

"You're a fool," Emma said to the inspector.

"Are you all right?" I called as we approached.

"We're being arrested," Dr. Dewar said, somewhat incredulous.

"Damn English," the inspector added. The language seemed to irritate him. Perhaps he felt left out, I thought. At least, for once, it wasn't poor Aleta who couldn't understand.

"You are not being arrested," Emma chided Dr. Dewar. "We only need to talk to you."

Vic crossed her arms and pointedly looked back and forth at their gendarmes.

"Madam, I must protest," Dr. Dewar added.

Inspector Goron, having understood none of this, only frowned, whistled, and pointed toward the door. His men scrambled. Opening the front doors, they began to push a corridor for us down the steps.

"Goron, if you spoil this, I'll have your head," Emma muttered.

"You're all damn spies," the inspector spat. "Calvé, be thankful I don't arrest you too."

Of course the hotel staff and at least a dozen reporters heard all this and it ended up in the papers. Emma's career as a spy ended that day, but her career in opera was greatly enhanced.

We made our way down the hotel steps, blitzlicht popping, reporters shouting, all the way down to the sidewalk. I stood there blinking at the rare fall sun when I saw a face in the crowd. He was dressed in a simple suit, but it was Lucien! I was about to say something, but he put his finger to his lips.

Then Vic piped up.

"Why are there two cars? I want to ride with Cali."

"Nonsense," Emma replied. "And actually there are four. Please, you and your father go in the first."

But she was having none of it. "I want to ride with Cali."

Emma looked up at Goron with a frown. "I told you!"

But the inspector would tolerate no dissent. "Get them in their cars!"

"No!" Emma snapped back. "You will not create a scene."

The gendarmes stood there, at a loss as to whose orders to follow. Emma and the inspector glared at each other.

Then Aleta said, "Cali, go with Vic. Dr. Dewar, won't you join me?"

Dr. Dewar added, "Come on lass. Vic, go with Cali." And he and Aleta headed for the second car.

The inspector growled. "Go!" he barked and waved his hand to say he was through with us.

Emma's only contribution after that was to say, "Cali in the back. Vic, you take the front."

With the top up, the car blocked out the noise from the street. I slid easily across the leather seat.

"That went poorly," Emma said, as the car door closed on us.

"You were trying to separate us," I said, leaning my violin case on the seat next to me.

"I was trying to get you out of a bad situation," she replied.

"By turning me over to M. Goron?"

"Chief Inspecter is perhaps a bit generous of a title for him I agree," Emma said. "But he wouldn't be able to hold you. Not for long. I would have made sure you had a proper barrister." Then she muttered to herself, "Calling Roux an idiot. The fool."

"So where are you taking us?" Vic asked.

Emma glanced at the gendarme driving and said, "On a train ride." Then she looked out the window at the cloud spotted blue sky. "It's a lovely day for it."

We drove though narrow crowded French streets, passing people, wagons, and the occasional car, around the square I never got to walk in, uphill towards the train station. It was small but very pretty, with beautifully painted geometric designs, not that I had much experience with them then. It was my first train station. Our line of cars pulled up in front, sticking half out in the street as there wasn't much room with the baggage carts, carriages, and people. We'd taken the newsmen by surprise so we had no spectators besides lounging sailors, but that didn't last long as a tram load of reporters topped the hill. But we were already inside by then, practically running between the benches. I looked at it all with interest as we rushed through. The room was high and airy with a big signboard at the far end. Men with long poles where reaching up to change train names and times while another yelled out impending departures.

I slowed to look behind. To be frank, I was far more wary of reporters at that point than whatever fate awaited us. Paul's dresses are lovely, but they stand out and I doubted we could have escaped unaccosted on our own. Behind us, gendarmes from the other two cars had set up a delaying action as we ran for our train.

How was Lucien going to follow if reporters couldn't? How would he know which train? I could see at least ten waiting beyond the doors, out on the platforms. Mme. Calvé stopped for a moment and scanned the boards before she led us on.

I should tell you about trains. Those were my first. I'd been on trollies and seen freight cars parked on docks, but this was my first close encounter with the real thing. They are very big. Bigger than a house. Mountains of black iron with steam and noise popping out all over. So many pipes and levers. I could feel the heat from their boilers as we dodged baggage carts and crowds of people. Someone pulled the whistle cord on one before they began to pull out with much bell ringing. It was very loud. The step up to our car was quite a climb. We left our remaining gendarmes at the steps.

Lest you think we could have run at that point, we still had two very formidable and equally silent men in suits with us.

"Oh," Emma said, out of breath. "I hope no one saw which train we boarded." None of us wanted to talk to reporters.

The car was empty, so I supposed we were early. Emma ducked into the first empty cabin and closed the curtains.

"No, not this one," she said to us as we followed. "We'll sit in the middle one."

Aleta looked at her questioningly.

"It's so they can't look for the compartment with the curtains closed," she replied. "We need to close some of them," and she went to work on the corridor curtains. After that we split up and closed curtains. As I was closing some in a compartment, I peeked out and there at the top of the platform was Phillip, the American agent!

"Leave some open," she called from behind me. "We don't want to be the car with all the curtains closed either."

She was clearly a professional. I wondered if two men would be enough to keep everyone out?

The men in suits positioned themselves at the ends of the car. It wasn't clear if their job was to keep us in or others out.

"Where's Goron?" I asked as we flopped down in our cabin seats.

"He's off beating his underlings, I'm sure," she laughed. "He was supposed to get a high profile arrest and now he's caught in Brest, a place he has no business being." Then she looked squarely at me. "And don't think of running."

I scowled back.

"Now if we can just get out of the station without drawing the attention of the mob."

"Oh, you mean like Max?"

"Oh yes. Absolutely Max."

I was thinking that maybe I should start opening the curtains.

"I saw that English woman," I said. "Max's friend."

"Where?" she said, suddenly worried.

"In the lobby."

"That would be Stroud. She's the worst of them all. Stay away from her if you can. Just run."

"She's that dangerous?" Vic asked.

"Yes and no. She and Max are true professionals. They're working at a different level."

"You aren't a professional?" Dr. Dewar asked.

"Oh heavens no," Emma smiled. "I really am an opera singer.

197

Spying is simply a hobby."

"But you're paid?" the doctor asked.

"Oh yes, by the French."

"Ah," he replied, and settled back into his seat. Dr. Dewar and his "affairs of honor." I almost rolled my eyes.

Passengers boarded, but strangely, not in our car. We could hear them on the platform. We could hear reporters as well, but we were left alone until the train began to roll. There was a knock on our door. Emma fished through her bag for our tickets, but instead of a conductor, in walked Lucien!

Emma looked up at him, stunned. Dr. Dewar brightened.

"Oh there you are!" the doctor said.

"Sorry I'm late," he replied, and he gave me a smile.

Even dressed in a common suit, he looked better than I remembered. It was almost frightening the jump I felt inside.

"Lucien?" Emma said.

"Emma," he replied, shutting the door.

"How?"

"I got on and listened."

"I had men posted."

"You did?" A moment of concern crossed his face.

"You didn't see them?"

"No."

The train lurched, Lucien grabbed the luggage racks, and we began to roll forward.

"We need to get off," Emma said. She looked stricken.

"I don't see how," Lucien replied. "Not with them. I doubt Dr. Dewar would survive the jump uninjured." He turned and checked that the corridor curtains were drawn. Then turning back he looked around the cabin.

"May I sit?" he asked. "Next to the window if you please. I'll be able to watch both the corridor and the side of the train."

"It's that Stroud woman isn't it?" I asked.

He didn't ask who at first. He was too preoccupied sitting down as Emma made room for him. Emma said to run from her, but how do you run on a train?

Finally it clicked. Lucien frowned and looked at me.

"Cali, how do you know her?"

No "hello." No "I'm sorry I got you into all of this." I was about to say something, most likely impolite, when Dr. Dewar spoke instead.

"Who are you talking about?"

"A British agent," Lucien replied.

"The Institution?" Dr. Dewar asked, almost climbing up the back of his seat.

Emma gave Lucien a worried glance and said, for our benefit, "Emilia Stroud. One of their best."

Then Lucien's eyes darted about.

"This isn't the express to Paris."

Emma replied, "Lucien, you have such a suspicious mind."

He gave her a wry smile, "The Deuxième Bureau has made me that way."

"Lucien," I said. "Hello."

Then he looked at me and almost winced. "I've been rude," he said. "Cali. I'm sorry I got you into this. I had no idea things would spin so out of control." He was looking me over, glancing up and down. "You weren't hurt. I was worried when I saw your picture in the paper."

"And what about me," Aleta barged in.

"I'm glad everyone made it to shore."

"Not everyone," I said quietly.

He gave me a strange look, but rallied.

"That's an interesting dress."

Suddenly I felt self-conscious about it all over again. Maybe I had been foolish. Maybe I should have worn my old one.

"All her dresses were ruined," Aleta snapped.

"She got blood all over everything," Vic added with a shiver. Lucien winced again.

"I am truly sorry Cali," he added.

"Practically the whole crew died," Aleta added bleakly.

"And a lot of passengers," I said.

"It was unpleasant," Emma added. "I think you owe her more than an apology." She had a wicked look in her eyes.

"I'll replace everything she lost."

Emma groaned. "Lucien. You are the worst kind of man. Well meaning, but dense."

There was a knock at the door and everyone's heads snapped up to look.

The formerly locked door latch clicked, then opened, and Max poked his head in.

"Is there room for me?" he asked.

"Max," Emma said flatly. "I suppose I'm glad you're here. Things have gotten out of hand."

"It's a bit crowded," Lucien quipped.

"So many beautiful women," Max replied with his friendly grin. "You can't keep them all for yourself." And he stepped in, closing and locking the door.

"Max, you followed us," I said.

"I followed your luggage," Max said brightly.

"You know him?" Lucien asked, looking at me with worry.

"He was at the prince's party. He warned us about the invasion."

Max looked a bit embarrassed. "It was a small mercy. We had already won at that point." Then he looked down at Aleta. "May I sit next to you?" and it was our turn to make room. "I can watch the corridor."

Then he looked at Aleta again, more closely. "I don't believe we've been introduced," he said, as she arranged her dress. "You were part of the airship crew."

"I was helping."

"She's retired crew," I answered.

"You must have grown," Max replied with sympathy.

"Yes," she sighed.

"Well, we were all glad of your help. If it's any consolation, our new lines of airships are larger and use the new diesel engine. Crew weight won't be such a problem.

Lucien growled with impatience. He wasn't to be deflected. "Emma. Why the slow train. All the stops will bring nothing but trouble."

"It was the best I could manage," she replied.

Max snorted.

Emma gave him a hurt look.

"For a thief, you've always been a sloppy liar," Max said. "There was an express on the next track." Then he pulled out a paper bag from his coat pocket. "I bought some toffee in the terminal. Would anyone like some?"

He took one from the bag and began to pull apart the wrapper.

"I would," Vic said.

"Lass, this is hardly the time for candy," Dr. Dewar said, looking very distraught.

"You might as well," Max said, offering her the bag, which we passed around.

"We're being kidnapped!" Dr. Dewar snapped.

Max looked at Emma and said with mock disapproval, "Really, Emma." Then looking back at Dr. Dewar. "It seems to me that, except for being stuck on a very slow train to Paris, you're no longer kidnapped."

"We can get off?" Dr. Dewar looked surprised.

"You might want to stay on until Rennes at least," Emma said with dull resignation. "Then, at least, you can catch an express. Or, you might stay on to find out where we were going. You might find it interesting."

"That is unless you want to go back to Brest with me," Max added. "I can fix everything. Berlin isn't far by air." Which got them started again. Berlin this, Paris that, Brussels whatever.

"Enough!" Dr. Dewar finished the argument. "We're going to Belgium!"

Lucien sat back, looking smug, and an awkward silence stretched. The sound of the wheels on the track clicking away. We left the railyard and the city behind. We could open the curtains to let in light. The sky turned heavy gray as we passed stone farm houses and green, tree lined fields. I saw a cow. Eyeing the sky, I thought it looked like rain.

Max glanced at the window and muttered cryptically, "I hope she isn't on the roof."

She was close, I was sure.

Then something occurred to me. "You followed our luggage? Emma, you took our luggage! It should be with the police."

"I couldn't let them paw through it. Who knows what would have disappeared."

I stared at her.

"I would have sent it to you," she said firmly.

I sighed and flopped back in my seat. At least we had it now and I still had hold of my violin and my pearls.

"My money!" Aleta moaned.

"We left it back at the hotel!" I wailed. "We're penniless."

"It's our fate," Aleta sighed in bitter distress.

It was also a problem if we were going to run. We would have to rely on Lucien.

"How are we going to get it back?" I asked.

"When we get back, I'll cable my accountant," Lucien replied.

"Please," Aleta said.

"It's Emma's fault," I growled.

"I'd cable my accountant," Emma replied. "But the hotel won't listen to me. They'll want your signature."

Then silence ensued. Everyone was tired and inclined to sit. We were back to listening to the car wheels, punctuated by the occasional thump from the corridor that no one wanted to investigate. Lucien looked away from his guard duties to look at me. He seemed happy, and then worried.

He was twenty-six last summer. I wondered when his birthday was. He looked just like I remembered, his dark hair and hazel eyes. I thought, perhaps, that he may have lost a little weight, but then again his clothes were ill fitting. I remembered our kiss on the dock at Cabinda, then blushed. His glance back at me still had that worried look. He should be, I thought. I was a bit angry with him. He didn't even say hello when he came in.

"Emma," Max asked finally. "I'm curious. Where were you taking them?"

"Dinard," she said as she stared out the window.

"Dinard?" both Max and Lucien said together, their eyes locked on her.

"What's Dinard?" Aleta asked.

"A beach resort," Lucien replied.

"You aren't working for the French are you Emma?" Max asked.

"Not directly."

"This is a problem," Lucien said half to himself. His face seemed to have lost some of its color.

"It does change things," Max added.

"It's a bad choice of season," Lucien mused, looking out the window.

"What's *in* Dinard?" I asked.

"If it were summer, I'd say Gustave de Rothschild," Max answered. He looked amused, opening another toffee.

"He's opened his villa just to meet you Dr. Dewar," Emma said, looking bleakly at him. "He came all the way from Chantilly. He has a car waiting for us at St. Brieuc."

And then out of nowhere Lucien said, "I think you should go."

"What?" Dr. Dewar snapped.

"Lucien?" Emma added, confused.

"Lucien?" I asked.

"Pa!" Vic moaned.

Max was laughing.

"What is this, Lucien?" Dr. Dewar at last asked with alarm.

But it was Max who answered with a laugh. "It all comes down to money."

Lucien took a breath, thought a moment, and then looked at Dr. Dewar. "We'll need investment capital." He waited for a reaction, but seeing none he continued, "New factories and retooling old will not be cheap. He's our largest banker. We'll have to talk to him sooner or later."

"Either him or his brother. They're everyone's bankers," Max added.

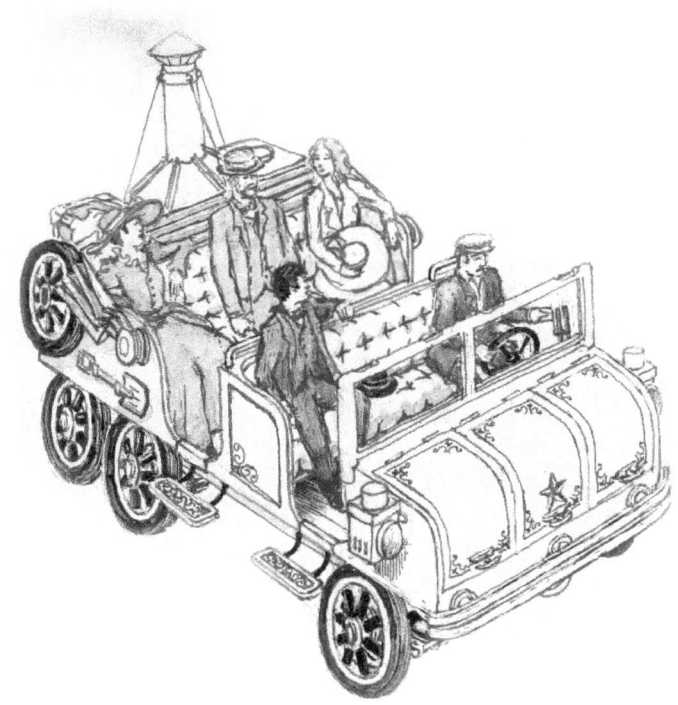

Chapter 19 – A New Game

We cowered in our compartment. I thought it strange that one woman could inspire such fear. From what I'd seen at Eagleston's, I could think of a lot of very unflattering words to describe her, but frightening wasn't among them. It was hard though to ignore the opinions of Max, Lucien, and Emma, so we sat in our airless compartment through Morlaix Station, until need drove me to exit.

I rose to leave.

"Where are you going?" Lucien asked sharply.

Emma tisked. "Lucien, there are things a man shouldn't ask a woman."

"Lucien, I have to go."

"I'll go with you," he replied.

"Lucien," Emma scolded. "Cali, I'll go with you."

"Thank you," I said, and opened the door.

"Not that I could do much against Stroud," she added as she stepped over everyone's legs.

We walked down the hallway, the damp French countryside flying past rain streaked windows on our left and compartments, most, with curtains drawn, on our right. Anyone or anything could be hiding in them. The corridor itself was beautiful polished wood, red patterned carpet, with a pale green, tin ceiling arching over us. I could feel the wheels banging beneath my feet but the air was still and dry inside despite our speed and the rain on the windows. At the end, the corridor jogged to the right and ended in a door. I could see the next train car bobbing around through the door window, full of passengers. It looked like a good place to run if we ran into trouble.

"You first," Emma said, offering to open the lovely carved wood door.

"Thank you," I replied with an actual smile. Really, trains are amazing!

The head was very nice. It put ours on Red to shame. It was all polished brass and a sink with faucets and soap. I stepped out and let Emma in.

As she closed the door I heard a door in the corridor, but thought nothing of it until a deep voice spoke next to my ear.

"Miss Carmichael," he hissed. It was Philip, the U.S. agent.

I turned, but he was altogether too close and I had very little room to back up.

"Yes," I replied firmly.

"Why are you heading toward Belgium? Need I remind you of your duty to your country?"

"Philip, back up."

"Our men are dying and you can help them," he replied, and moved closer.

"Philip." I said quite firmly and brought my heel down on his instep. "Back up!"

He hooted, his foot probably broken, staggering off balance, trying to reach for me. So I pushed him just as the head door opened against my back. Mr. Henson fell backward and banged his head against the window glass, which cracked.

"What's going on?" Emma asked, having rushed, still adjusting her dress.

I let her out and replied, "Philip was rude."

"Oh." She looked down at Mr. Henson with a confused frown.

He was sitting on the floor holding his head as we carefully stepped over him. We said nothing as we returned, meeting Max and Lucien at the door.

"We heard a noise," Max said. Lucien looked wild with worry.

"It was nothing," Emma replied, waving them back.

"Ooo . . . now I have to go," Vic said.

"Maybe you should go with Cali," Emma said tartly. "She seems perfectly capable of taking care of herself."

"I'll go," Dr. Dewar said.

"Oh no you won't," Lucien and Max said together.

"They'll jump you for sure," Max continued. "Emma?" Max looked up at her.

"Very well," she said, and they were off.

"What happened?" Lucien asked me.

"Philip was rude," I couldn't think of any other way to put it. Then I complained, "I would have listened to him if he'd been polite."

What he said though, stung. It was true. Our men were dying, but then so were the southern men. I thought of Captain Cavanaugh of the Saint John's in Le Havre. They had all been good men, some with families. If Dr. Dewar's discovery was as bad as they said, I couldn't see how slaughtering them could be any kind of solution. The United States would have to wait.

"The further this goes, the less polite everyone will become," Max muttered.

Then Vic came running back to our door.

Dr. Dewar stood up.

She was so flustered it took her three tries to open the door as Emma walked up behind.

"Da!" She cried as she stumbled past our feet and into his arms.

"What is it?" he asked her.

"There was a body," Emma sighed. "Philip was a foolish man." Then she added as if it couldn't get worse, "No sign of the conductor either!"

"He's dead?" I asked.

Emma nodded. "I suspect so."

"We can't leave Philip there," I said.

Emma stared at me.

"You want to move him?" Aleta looked at me with skepticism. "Cali, we're in enough trouble already."

"I'm not going back in there with a body," Vic said.

Emma looked at Max. "A garrote." Then she sighed, "At least it wasn't wire. No blood."

I had no idea what a garrote was. I was too embarrassed to ask.

"She's thinning the competition," Max muttered.

"I wonder where she's putting the bodies," Emma added, half to herself.

"How can she do this?" Aleta asked. "Aren't there other people? It can't be just us."

"I'm afraid I booked the whole car," Emma replied.

"Da!"

"Quiet lass," Dr. Dewar replied. "So you think we should go with Emma?" he asked Lucien.

Emma replied instead with a satisfied smile. "It's the next stop."

Lucien looked up at Emma, who was still standing with her back to the door. "We'll either need to get rid of the body, or abandon our luggage," he said.

"They'll be discovered before the train leaves the station," Max added.

"I'm not leaving my violin," I said, firmly.

"Or my flute," Aleta added.

Lucien sighed and looked up at Emma and Max. "Feel up to some dirty work?"

Max sighed as well and started to stand. "This is hardly worth it to me. I've already failed the mission."

"It's worth your time to avoid the police," Lucien replied.

"Yes," he said. "You're right, of course."

They filed out, Lucien saying as they left, "Keep the door locked."

Then I could hear them moving down the corridor, opening doors, until Emma exclaimed, "Oh, here's Sr. Henriques!"

We were sitting there, waiting, when the formerly locked door clicked and in stepped a woman.

She was as pretty as I remembered her. Her hair perfect, despite having probably crawled across the outside of the train, with flowers worked into the side even! She wore a smallish hat, her lips lightly rouged. Her dress was spare, flowing freely around her with little noise.

As I said, she stepped in. We sat there stunned as she closed the door.

"Who are you? Dr. Dewar stammered.

She replied with a voice as smooth as a bell. "You must be Dr. Dewar. I'm Mrs. Emilia Stroud. It's a pleasure to finally meet you."

She seemed to take in the entire cabin with a glance. "It seems everyone is here."

Then she looked at me. "You must be Miss Carmichael. I've been so wanting to meet you as well."

"We've met before," I replied.

"Did we?" she said, with a tinge of doubt.

"In Boston."

Her eyes dimmed for a moment, lost in thought. "Ah yes, we did. In that store. Both of you," and she gave Aleta a charming little smile. She had perfect teeth.

"Do you mind if I sit down? At least until the next stop."

There was silence. I don't think anyone wanted sit next to her, but she didn't expect an answer and made for Lucien's spot.

Once settled, she eyed Aleta and me. "What interesting dresses," she said, with conviction. "Entirely unfashionable. Scandalous even, and yet intriguing. I must know your designer." Apparently we were talking clothes. Actually, mostly she talked, as I know very little about fashion. It seemed so normal though. Dr. Dewar just stared at her in alarm.

Lucien finally popped his head in the door, "I told you to keep this locked."

Behind him I could hear Max telling Emma, ". . . they always end up under the wheels."

Then Lucien stopped just inside the door and stared at Emilia.

Max came up behind him and said cheerfully, "Oh, hello Emilia."

So everyone was either dead or together. We could finally open the window and door a bit as the cabin was even more crowded and stuffy. The best part of this was that Lucien got to sit next to me! His leg was so warm. I must have been blushing as Emma gave me a knowing look.

Both Max and Emilia were apparently, in a strange way, old friends and they chatted away, discussing the mission. His making her miss the flight sent them both laughing. And I gathered from their conversation that she intended to join us in Dinard.

"I hope my dear," Max asked her. "That we are done with the deaths. I'm quite tired of bodies."

"Max. How can you ask me that?" she smiled. "How can I know?" she replied airily. "Dr. Dewar though, is coming with me. Just as soon as we're done with the baron. Just from his dossier, I can't see how he could possibly agree to any offer the baron will make."

"Perhaps," Max replied, then paused. "I do agree that it's best to give them a chance. It would be unwise to offend the brothers. I'm sure we can all agree with that." Then he leaned forward a little and said to her, "Let me guess. You spared Emma just for the introduction in Dinard. You're curious aren't you? You want to meet him don't you?"

"Oh good," Emma said. "I'm done after Dinard. You can ignore me," she said, half to Emilia and half to herself. She looked relieved.

Emilia just smiled.

Max smiled back. "But how did you know our destination?"

Emilia's looked disappointed. "Max, the guard."

"There were two."

"Philip took care of the other."

"And the conductor?"

She frowned. "I don't know. I never saw him."

"You've spared the Duke because he's in the royal line."

"Unrecognized," Lucien added.

"No one believes that but you. So let's see . . . you've spared me because you need to catch me alone."

"Max, it would take a direct order for me to kill you." Then she added as almost an afterthought, "Although I might push you off the train."

"But I don't understand why you spared Cali in the corridor?" Max continued.

"As you said, I was curious. You actually like them. It's piqued my interest." She thought for a second, and then continued. "Then she dealt with Philip, which surprised me. But I'm being rude," she said, looking at me. "I'm talking about you and you're right here."

I looked back at her. That was a lot to take in all at once.

"So you have no orders for her yet?" Max asked.

"No, but then I wouldn't would I? I'm not an assassin. And of course," she added. "I had to find out about her dress. You're wearing no corset?"

"No," I replied, brightening. It was finally something I could respond to. "I hate them and Paul doesn't mind."

"Really," Emma answered, thoughtfully. "You have heard about the new health corsets?"

"There's no such thing," Aleta replied defiantly.

"Mine are specially designed to allow me to move," Emilia added.

And we were off, lost to the men, the wheels clacking onward to Dinan station, the closest station to Dinard. Shoes and corsets. Did you know she's absolutely in love with Japanese fashion? I vowed to ask Paul about it, or at least find a library. I wondered if this was what it's like to be the mouse in the lion's den.

It turned out to be a lovely station with a great domed ceiling topped with a big clock that loomed over the benches. The station had a young man there to help us down from the car who gave me a strange look. I later learned that he recognized me from the papers and that our presence would eventually be reported. Frankly, I think it was the dress. The government's efforts to hush up the bodies found on the tracks only made things worse. Yet another mystery for The Rabbit.

The baron had sent only one car. Mind you, a large one, but we were a large group. Max called it a limousine. But when I asked him what made it one, Emilia looked at me strangely and asked cryptically, "They don't train you?"

I blinked at her, completely confused. Max backed me up saying, "She really doesn't know." Which only confused us both more. I suppose if I had been a real spy, I would have known about them.

Watching Emilia, as we walked to the street to look for a second car, was amazing. She seemed to float, but I couldn't see her feet to see how she did it. Thinking about it now, I suspect that she had had ballet training.

We found one parked in front, driven by a local and hardly as nice. It was waiting on the street, apparently for people like us who needed a ride. And then there was the negotiation. Everyone wanted to ride with Dr. Dewar, the uniformed driver enduring it stoically. It was finally resolved by Dr. Dewar himself, "I'll go nowhere without Miss Carmichael." So I rode in the second car with him, and Lucien and Emma, as a sort of insurance. I really didn't mind. It was my first ride in a car, hugging my violin in my lap. I was unwilling to let them put it in the cargo compartment.

The things were big, with wheels that rattled on the cobbles, the driver pulling long levers to make it go. The boiler behind us was warm, which was nice, and the chugging rhythm after the excitement wore off, almost put me to sleep. Lucien sat in the front with the driver, but I could still see the back of his head.

I suppose I was growing used to French cities. Dinan was as beautiful as all French cities are, with its age flattened, narrow, cobbled streets, and looming buildings. Its skies were relatively free of coal smoke and the streets were clear of cars, with most of the traffic being people on foot. An airship passed by overhead so I suppose they had an aerodrome somewhere, but no trollies. The town still had its walls and we drove through a great stone gate with towers as we left.

Outside, it was back into beautiful French countryside. The sun came out and I saw flowers glowing, their colors dancing as we bounced over the rutted road. Light dappled the dirt and grass, the trees overhead making it dance with the wind. Our driver stopped to put down the top. I laughed and Lucien turned to look. Emma looked happy too.

"All we need is a picnic basket," Emma sighed.

"And a bottle of wine," Lucien added with a wistful grin.

"What's a picnic basket?" I asked.

"I'll show you when this is over," he replied.

Emma said nothing, but looked at us both with a little smile, which made my heart jump for some reason.

We passed through villages, past farms and wagons pulled by horses who were not pleased with our smoke and noise.

It took us an hour to reach Dinard, which was hardly so much a town as a great sprawl of mansions around a large-round bay spanned by a low-wide beach. I could smell the sea, the English Channel spread out before us, the breeze wet with salt and sea birds.

The blessed sun lit the wind-driven white caps that rolled across the water under tumbling clouds. We were making for what turned out to be a point ending in sharp cliffs. On top loomed great houses.

These were manned by liveried guards who were confused enough by the arrival of two cars to make us wait while someone, having taken down our names, went to the house for instructions. I didn't mind. I could have soaked in that sun and breeze all day. Emma was slumped down in her seat too, her hat over her eyes.

At last, they said we could go and the driver pulled back on his big lever, and with a venting of steam we chugged forward up a smooth packed earth driveway. We could see sheep grazing on the lawn, and then a little temple sitting above a stone pond. Unlike the prince, the baron had few statues, nor was there a grand entrance. His house had a restrained marble stairway in front leading to an entrance out of sight, hidden among shrubbery, but we didn't go there. Instead we went to the side under an arch that led to a covered gas lit alley that was designed to deal with trains of arriving cars and poor weather. It had long stone steps on the left leading up to warm windowed rooms with many doors and welcoming lights.

Uniformed men helped us out and took our trunks from the car lockers. We were led up the steps and through wide glass doors into a long wood room filled with art and books. The carpet was thick, its colors bright. The air was scented. It took a moment, but I realized it was onions and rosemary. And they were baking bread!

Oh, my stomach growled.

Aside from candy, we had yet to eat that day and it was already afternoon. Things had been so strange and gone by so fast that I hadn't noticed.

"That smells so good," Aleta said next to me.

"Food would be wonderful," I replied. Really, it was almost a whine, but I said nothing more. Pa would be proud.

Instead of lunch, I was confronted by an older woman with dark hair wearing a maid's uniform.

"If you will follow me miss?" she asked with a curtsy.

"Where?"

"Surely you've had a long drive." I could hear someone explaining to Aleta in English. "I'll help you. . ," and then something I didn't understand. She saw my confusion and pointed at her head. "Your hair? Wash?"

"Oh! Thank you." I didn't want to tell her that my hair was always like this. I had two styles, ponytail and down, my earlier makeover long gone.

We were led to a lovely room just off the hall. The gauzy curtains shimmered with light reflected from a green pool in a small courtyard. It held vanities, screens, and an unlit fireplace. Through an open door I could see a bathroom.

"Me first!" Vic piped up and ran for the bathroom.

"Your coat and hat?" my maid asked.

She took them to a stand to hang them. I eyed the pictures covering the walls. The room was dominated by two large paintings of nonsense countryside with Indians lounging around it. What was the artist thinking? Around them were photographs, many of which interested me. Quite few were of men riding horses with long hammers, clearly a game. Then there were the people. I recognized none of them of course, that is until I saw a young woman in a western dress and hat, holding a rifle.

"The papers say you're friends." I almost jumped. It was Emilia. She needed a bell.

"The papers lie," I replied, somewhat bitterly to be frank.

"Sometimes a lie is more useful than the truth," she replied, somewhat cryptically. She saw my confusion and added, "It's what people want to believe."

"Who takes these?" So many personal photographs, someone in the family had to like photography.

"I've never worked with the family, so I've no briefing."

Which I took to mean she was in the dark as much as I.

"It's their son, André," Emma said, from one of the vanity seats. "The polo player would be Robert."

"Very good Mademoiselle," the maid fixing her hair said.

"If you're ready," my maid said to me.

"What do I do?"

Emilia's eyes twitched.

"Just sit over here and let me do the rest," she said gently.

We moved to the second vanity and she set to work on my hair with a brush.

"What did I miss?" Vic asked, as she came out.

"Nothing," Aleta sighed. "We were discussing photography."

She was looking out the window into the courtyard.

"Oh," Vic answered flatly. She sounded as disappointed as Aleta. She walked over to the window as well. "That's nice."

"The tilework reminds me of Spain," Aleta replied.

"It's a Moorish design," Emilia added.

When had she looked out the window? Then my tummy rumbled. Once it gets started . . .

"Fear not Mademoiselle. Lunch is coming," my maid said. She was putting clips in my hair as Vic and Emma chatted and another maid entered.

Hair finished, up in a bun, I was turned over to the new maid. She curtsied with a look of worry and said, "I'm so sorry, but most of your dresses are ruined. You have one dress if you wish to change."

I'd hardly worn the one I had, so I said no.

Then she set to running a brush over the dress I was wearing.

Emilia was sitting at the vanity, waiting patiently while my maid, now hers, reworked her hair. Really, there was very little to do.

Vic's hair, on the other hand, was taking shape. Her maid was teasing it back into sweeping curls to ultimately end in a flowered bun. She worked so quickly. Vic looked beautiful! To be honest, it was the first time I'd seen the back of her neck. Then again, mine felt a bit drafty too, so I dipped down behind Emilia to look in the mirror.

Mine was swept back as well, ending in a smaller bun, leaving several curling strands to dance down my back. For a moment, Emilia's and my face shared the same mirror.

She didn't look pleased.

Chapter 20 – Out of my Depth

"Ah, the women have arrived!" Gustave said. The men all stood from their seats. It was a room with big leather chairs and couches, and a huge fireplace, carved from the stone of the clifftop. The ocean facing wall was glass paned with doors that led to a balcony that looked out across the channel. I so wanted to go look, but courtesy kept my attention focused on our host.

He was a small man with curling white hair and mutton chops that dropped to the tops of his collar. He looked like a hound. A hound in a suit. All the men had changed into suits.

"And I don't think this house has ever been so blessed. Not at least since I brought my dear Cécile home." He continued. A woman who had to be his wife, Cécile, gave him a knowing, patient smile. It was clear she'd heard this before.

We'd been measured in the dressing room. Apparently our clothing wouldn't do for dinner. Most had changed for lunch except Aleta and me, who, sadly, had nothing to change into. I expected that we were excused this once and that more appropriate clothing

215

would be supplied. Vic complained about formal dining throughout our preparation. I had little experience at that point in my life with such things and so had nothing to say.

The men had been drinking brown rum or whiskey from round glasses. Lucien smiled at me, which was reassuring.

"Come. Come sit," Gustave said. "We're trying a brandy."

"It's a bit early for brandy," Emilia replied.

"It's just a taste. We've cracked a keg of the '78 for tonight and I had to have a taste. I couldn't wait."

"Oooo," Emma said. "I'd like some." And she walked forward.

"'78 you say." Emilia looked thoughtful. "Just a taste."

"Me too," chimed in Vic.

"You're too young," Her father scolded.

Gustave laughed.

"If she's too young then I am too," I added.

Aleta shook her head slightly no.

We all sat down while Gustave brought glasses.

"On the way in I saw a yacht flying a Rothschild pennant," I said.

"That was the Octave. I named her after our first."

"She's beautiful. You had to have been making sixteen, maybe seventeen knots?"

He looked pleased. "We were racing. Do you really like boats?"

"She was raised at sea," Lucien said.

"I like ships," I added.

"And this is your friend, Aleta? Just Aleta?"

She looked annoyed, but answered, "Yes." At least he didn't call her Rosemary.

"And you sail together?"

He knew a lot about us.

"Yes," Aleta answered.

"You're English. I can hear it."

"Yes," Aleta replied.

"And not happy about it." He paused for a moment in thought. "Women sailors are far rarer than women spies." He took a sip of brandy while everyone waited. "I think the papers have missed the real story. Perhaps we'll go sailing and I'll give you a turn at her helm."

He must have seen a flash of true hunger in my eyes because his smile warmed.

"Yes. I think we will," Gustave continued.

What we had was called luncheon. I have no idea why.

Gustave fended off all questions. It wasn't right to talk business on an empty stomach, he said, and so we ate. We had a buffet. That's similar to what I had at the ball in the Congo. You walk around putting bits of this and that on your plate from trays and pots, and it let me sit next to Lucien. I had the impression he wanted to help me navigate the array of silverware we had to choose from, but was held back by our audience. The food was, of course, all yummy and it took an effort to remember the advice of the Duchess Baudouin to not overeat in difficult social situations. We had wine as well. Something else to watch.

No business while dining is a laudable ideal, but with our strange mix of people, all of us competing, it was impossible to avoid.

"Mme. Stroud, I've heard a great deal about you," Gustave started.

Emilia gave Max a sideways glance. "Have you?"

"Your victory over the Japanese in the Pacific made for very interesting reading."

"One shouldn't believe everything one reads," Emilia replied. "There were others who deserve more credit."

"There are always others, of course. Hawaii, I'm told, is very beautiful."

"I was there to work. I had very little free time."

"I can attest to its beauty," Max added. "The water is clear blue to the bottom."

"Blue?" Gustave exclaimed.

"You can see down perhaps a hundred feet." Max continued. "It's impossible to tell. I took a boat around the harbor and went fishing and never lost the bottom."

"I can attest to Max having been there," Emilia added off handedly.

"Blue. I'll have to see that sometime."

"It's blue in the Caribbean too," I added.

"Ah, now that's a place I can go on my own."

"After the war," I said somberly.

"Yes," he cleared his throat. "After the war."

"I hear pirates are common in the islands," Lucien said.

"Pirates?" Emma asked me.

"You do have to be careful," I replied. "Africa too. We share information as best as we can."

"Rebels, pirates. Mademoiselle I did want to ask you about Africa."

"I would rather not talk about it."

"I don't blame you," Max said. "What with that Prince and half the colony betting on you."

"Betting?" Gustave said, looking at me, eyebrows up.

"They had odd ways of passing the time," I responded bitterly.

"Max, she doesn't want to talk about it," Emma added in my defense.

"I was only trying to show sympathy."

"I believe you were there too," Gustave said to Aleta.

"Yes, but I caught dengue fever. I don't remember much. I woke up in a German mission hospital."

"I think Aleta was the lucky one," Lucien added with sympathy.

"I don't know," I said. "She was at the last stand at the docks."

"They almost overran us twice," she said quietly. I could see the start of tears. There had been a wide stretch of bodies leading right up to Red.

"You're right Miss Carmichael," Gustave said, clearing his throat. "We should avoid Africa."

All through this Emilia's eyes had been darting back and forth. I had the impression she was confused. Max on the other hand kept glancing at her with a smug smile. Vic frowned at me.

"You're both musicians," Baroness Rothschild, Cécile, asked.

I knew what was coming. It's hard to deny when your violin is sitting next to your feet.

"We were wondering if you both could play something for us sometime."

"Now?" Aleta asked, hardly recovered.

"Oh no! Perhaps after dinner."

Playing for my supper again.

I looked at Aleta and she frowned back. She was still upset about Africa. It was an odd request if we were prisoners so I decided we had to be guests and it would be best to stay on their good side while we were there. And as always, we could use the practice as well.

"Yes. We'd love to."

The conversation, such as it was, turned to nicer subjects. We talked about sailing, opera, and the Baron's children, one of whom, André, would be arriving that night from Cannes.

Luncheon over, we retired to his balcony where I discovered, thankfully, that Lucien didn't smoke. Cigars are nasty things. The smell gets into everything. The sun was out for a bit and the waves were blue. We could see the surf against the cliffs below and the point itself sloping gradually down into the sea on our right. After the rocks, the water was deep green down to a sandy bottom spotted with sea grass. In the distance other points reached out into the channel, purple and gray under the clouds.

"The harbor is around the point," Gustave said, pointing. "We generally take the horses down."

One more thing I couldn't do.

"I didn't see your stables when we entered," Emma said.

"They're on the other side of the house," he replied, obviously proud of his horses too. And then to me, "I can show them to you if you wish."

"I'm afraid I know very little about horses," I said, a little uncomfortable.

"I can show them to you anyway."

"I'm afraid my Gustave seems to like you my dear," Mme. Rothschild said. "You best go or he'll be terribly disappointed."

"I wouldn't mind seeing them," Lucien said, turning away from his conversation.

"Ah, you like horses?"

"I have my own stable."

"Excellent. Then we can talk bloodlines."

"Why? Are you keeping a stallion?" Lucien was eying him with anticipation.

"I am," Gustave replied, with a bit of Vic's shark-like glint in his eye. "Sadly though, not here."

"That's too bad."

The other side of the house, as it turned out, was quite a walk. It involved going down a hallway, then downstairs, and along another hallway, through a study with a large cluttered desk, and out through glass doors. I was assisted down the hallway at every turn by Lucien, who always seemed to be putting his hand on my shoulder or leading by my hand. I think he was worried by Gustave, which made no sense to me. Gustave was married and way older. We emerged in a very lovely garden with roses. I could smell them. I wanted to stop to look, but the men, now entranced in their horse talk, walked on. I was no longer noticed.

Gustave's stables were at the edge of a fenced grass field which, judging by what I assumed were the neighbor's stables on the other end, was shared. I supposed land was tight on the peninsula. Most of the villa seemed to be carved out of the rock itself. The stable had ten stalls under a high gabled, wall-less roof that ended in a loft. We entered into an open end with freestanding racks for saddles and hooks and shelves for tack. A small house abutted the stable and out its door skipped an older man.

"*Bonjour Monsieur*," he said. "Are we wishing to ride?"

"No, not today," Gustave answered. "But we will tomorrow after breakfast, early."

I hoped that didn't include me. "Going sailing?" I asked.

"Yes."

It did.

"Do you know how many?" The stableman asked.

"I think nine, but I'll send word"

"Margot still has that bruise."

"Then we'll see."

Perhaps I could go by cart, I thought.

"*Oui Monsieur.*"

"Now let's show our guests our children."

We stood there while his groom walked horses about and they discussed lines, spring, and lineage. I could tell he and the groom were saving something. It was the next to the last. The moment the groom led it down the aisle I could sense Lucien's surprise.

"What, is that?"

It was half brown, half white, with gray spots.

Gustave was smug. "An appaloosa, American. I purchased her from the Nez Perce."

"A quarter horse."

"Ah, but what a quarter horse. Want to give her a try?"

"Of course!"

"She's trained to rein."

"Naturally. They're split."

"Naturally."

Then it was the saddle.

"It's huge," Lucien exclaimed, running his hands across the leather.

"They stay in their saddles for days on end. This spreads out the weight."

"Days on end. Amazing."

I, on the other hand, was wandering amongst the tack. The workmanship was interesting. Some of it had designs and bits of polished metal. And then there were the sparrows and finches nesting in the eves.

I'd about given myself completely over to boredom when I noticed they were heading for the field. The appaloosa was saddled and being led by the groom. I could see rain coming, a dark blue bruise rolling in from land's end, but still a ways off.

Lucien practically leapt on the poor thing's back and he was off before he'd hardly sat. They took off at a gallop that was across the field before it had hardly started. Then he spun in place and bounded back, the horse's hooves rattling across the dirt, pulling up in a shower of turf.

"My god!" Lucien exclaimed. "It almost makes me wish I had my saber."

"You should see her on the polo field," Gustave laughed.

The groom was standing next to me. He said quietly, "Don't worry, mademoiselle. The Madame doesn't care for them either."

"It's not that I don't like them. I don't know how to ride. I don't know anything. Except for school, I've rarely touched the shore."

"Not at all?" Gustave had heard.

"No sir."

"We'll have to do something about that, but you're hardly dressed for it today. Lucien, why haven't you taught her riding?"

"The world hasn't given us a moment to breathe."

That was true, but I wasn't sure Lucien and I were that familiar, and how did Gustave know?

Lucien took the horse around the field a few more times, weaving about, then flying off scattering dust and dirt. When he came back, he was out of breath and happy.

Then it was past the roses, back to the house. The rest were downstairs in a game room. Emilia and Dr. Dewar were playing a game, poking balls with sticks on a large green table. Vic was playing some sort of card game by herself. Aleta was sitting, watching the balls bounce around the table.

I sat next to her. "What is it?"

"They say it's called billiards."

"It looks easy."

"It's not. Keep watching."

I did. Emilia seemed to have the ability to bend the flight of the ball beyond all logic. The Doctor was no better. And their ability to send the white ball in exact directions was almost magical. I realized I might, someday, be passable at cards, but this was, like my violin, the work of a lifetime. The balls bounced and careened. Apparently it's important how many times they strike. The last ball was finally sunk, which seemed to signify victory. I began to applaud as I would for a musician, only to realize that it was completely the wrong thing to do.

Really though, it was deserved.

The Doctor smiled, but that Stroud woman sent a look my way and began tossing balls into the triangle.

"Make yourselves at home," Gustave said, as he entered followed by Lucien. "This is a fallow moment. They're picking up André and some friends at the station. I think you'll be pleased."

Someone, a servant, sat at a piano and began to play. He wasn't bad, although a bit mechanical. There's a big leap between the technical and emotional expression of music.

He instead made me think of Aleta and how little time we'd had to play. I looked her way. She was still concentrating on billiards but I could see her flute case, at the foot of the couch.

"Let's find somewhere to practice," I said.

She frowned. "I suppose I should. It's been ages."

I stood and held out my hand. I thought of the garden, but the rain was starting to hit shore, the drops spotting the balcony, the clouds almost ready to block the sun.

She took my hand and stood. "Where?"

I shrugged. "It's a big house."

"We should ask."

She was right, of course, but our host wasn't present.

"Let's ask him," I said, nodding toward our piano player.

He suggested one of the parlors and led us down another corridor, I think toward the front steps. Being dug out of a clifftop made for a very strange floorplan.

"I'll send someone to light the fire," he said as he closed the doors.

Our room was somewhat dim with a lovely fireplace. We had two high, rain-spotted windows that looked up into gray sky. It seemed that every room in the villa had bookshelves and electricity. We had several lamps as well as the tables and chairs. He left two turned on.

There was a low table between our sofa and the fireplace and we opened our cases there. The smell of smoothed wood worked to the near perfection drifted out of the case. Oh I do love her.

Rosin.

Tighten the bow.

Aleta's glance was a physical thing.

My first note as I tuned, adjusting the tailpiece, dragged across the room breaking its lines.

Then her first thick, rasping note pulling it back.

She blew a slow tentative D. I replied in like, then E, and she replied. I replied in D, then A, with me thinking *Toss the Feathers*, but then she lit into *Wild Maid*. Sometimes this can sound strange because she has to pull it down an octave because she's not playing an Irish flute, but that doesn't make it less fun.

A maid entered, unnoticed, lighting the fireplace.

"Again, first chord," Aleta said.

That's the chord game. We pick a song, but only the first bar. Those notes become the chords of a new song. You play them forward and then backwards, sometimes doubling notes or sliding, trying to keep some sort of counterpoint under your fingers.

We danced as we wound away the time, her breath dished out like coins as we sat in our twilight room, lit by sound and the fire. We played I don't know what, for I don't know how long until I realized that others had come to listen.

"Cali. I want to hear Bach," Aleta said.

"No."

"Please, for me. I never got to hear it."

That was a hard thing to ask, but she knew I couldn't say no. I'm being serious, really. This was hard. There are a lot of bad things attached to that song.

I picked a note, and then another, and then once committed I had to pick another. They jabbed along until I forgot where I was, it flowing far too smoothly for my peace, rolling through that hated adagio despite my twists and turns and attempts to derail it. But it was too much. I couldn't help it. I just couldn't play it, so I tore it, slicing down on the draw without warning, dashing it, then hating myself, dragging it over its hard center. I couldn't stop.

The fugue began without a breadth or any indication. I was completely scattered at this point, hammering it. The thin outlines of soldiers and men in rough clothes holding dark rifles began to form in the corners of the room. Bach must have been tumbling and spinning in his coffin all the way up to the drippy Siciliana. I'm surprised he didn't appear too. I was in no mood for his thoughtful melancholy. A cold breeze crossed the room despite the fire. Emma crossed her arms, hugging herself. They had all come to the room to listen.

I will now admit it. I'll come clean. I cut most of the Sicilana out. I dumped it. I stood, waiting until the right moment and then jumped into the presto. Gone. And good riddance. I'm so sorry Mrs. Hartnoll.

I was far more rested than I was in the Congo and I gave it what I had, presto and all. Altogether it wasn't my on purpose worst, but there comes a point one realizes that one has a certain responsibility to the music and at that moment I felt, for the first time, shame for what I'd done. It wasn't the music's fault. Perhaps though, perhaps it was mine.

The darkness in the room didn't clear after I finished, but they didn't notice or couldn't see my face, what I was seeing in the dim light. They were all happy. But I think Aleta understood.

It was from that moment on that I finally began to take the music itself seriously.

Come late afternoon Aleta and I were called away to a . . . let's be frank. I've run out of words for rooms. He had so many. Study, parlor, library? It was private and it had a lot of paintings, so perhaps it was a gallery, but it had a screen to change behind as well. Somehow, in those few hours dresses had materialized. They tugged and pulled, measured and debated. We had three men and two women working on us, taking the dresses off and putting them back on, one after the other

They glistened of silk and brushed wool in the pale blue evening light – of course with corsets. I politely asked if they could leave them out, they looked at me askance and said they would see.

We swayed like bells on Sunday.

And, thankfully, sent them back to the tailors for final alterations with little doubt that we would be uncomfortable come evening.

Dinner would be at nine.

I had a bath in a glorious tub. Can you hear me, sitting in that water, swooning? It was bigger and warmer than The Grand. I could practically swim. Aleta and I met in our common room to be laced and buttoned – without corsets! Our hair took twice as long. We finally emerged at their command, met in the hallway by the other women.

We were trussed up at eight thirty, my dress squeezing the limits of respectability. And here I will give you an example of the power of our host. It was our dresses and his efforts at editorial design. We were clearly meant to play roles. Mrs. Stroud and Emma had brought their own dresses, but Vic was dressed as a girl, virginal and not yet marriageable. Aleta looked like some sort of distant Spanish countess, quite respectable draped in lace. I, on the other hand, practically had my breasts squeezing out my top, in thin pink silk! You could see everything. It was not what I'd tried on.

Aleta stared at me open mouthed.

"This is unacceptable," she said. Really it was a rant, bless her.

"What are we going to do?" I asked. "I need to eat."

"Tell them you're ill."

"I'll starve."

"They'll send food."

I did.

They sent a different dress instead, which made us late. How many had he made? It was deep sea blue, like the water between storms, its cut far more modest. And they built the bodice in! I'm sorry, but I loved it. I took it with me. I have it to this day.

We, the women, met and walked down the hall, having been called forth. They greeted us with campagne in tall crystal. Oh the glory of champagne, which I do love.

We were meant to mingle before dinner. I saw many new faces. They had already been drinking by the time we arrived. Gustave talked about rigging and wind, for my benefit I think. There was a young man, André I believe, and a mix of six older men, some quite old. One wore a military uniform, his hair oiled back, his moustache thin and pointed. Dr. Dewar tried to avoid them, sticking instead to me until Max and Emilia approached, then he fled to Emma, still quite frightened of Emilia.

Gustave kept wanting to talk, but I needed to catch Vic. It seemed like we were being kept apart. She had André's attention instead and it wasn't long before it was time to sit.

I sat to the side of Cécile, across from Gustave. Across and next to Gustave was an older man with a gray beard named Camille. I had André on my left. Lucien was on the other side, across from André, out of reach. Before me was an array of spoons and forks, and plates. I had three glasses, all empty. I was clearly out of my depth. Simply put, I'd run aground! How was I supposed to eat with these?

They brought soup. I watched Emilia as she skimmed it, but it made no sense to me as you just get the liquid. So I ate with my spoon, the same kind she was using, but I ate the hard parts and all until I saw Lucien shake his head no slightly. It was very unnerving. Then came a salad with cheese which, taking Lucien's warning to heart, I picked at. But then they brought a delightful fish. I which ate more than I should. Then they brought chicken, which I barely touched because I was too full. And then beef and peas! Then chocolate, which I couldn't resist, but hurt afterwards, and coffee. And! And I mean this, really I'm grimacing, they brought little cakes, lemon sorbet, and ice crème.

Insane.

Utterly insane.

During all of this, we were expected to talk.

Camille and André wanted to talk music. But that crossed between Gustave and me, Gustave wanting to talk about the Bremen. It was very confusing. André wanted to know how long I had been playing, who were my teachers, and where I studied. Camille talked about concerts. He played the piano! He made his living at it. All Cécile wanted to talk about was Gustave. Gustave this, Gustave that. She obviously cared for him, but perhaps she seemed worried. I wondered if he was ill. But Gustave brought it all to a standstill.

"Did they tell you who sabotaged it?"

It took me a moment. *Sabotaged what?* I sat there blinking until it hit me. "No. They said nothing," I replied, genuinely curious. Who had done this to us? Everyone turned to listen. I looked about, surprised at the silence.

"Well. To be fair, they probably don't know." Then he made us wait while he chewed his beef. "It was Edison."

Max laughed, "I knew it!"

"He's not far behind the doctor. Killing him would give Menlo Park time to bring his product to market."

"Murder an airship full people?" one of the men exclaimed.

"And why not," Gustave replied with a wave of his hand. "The profit from this will be enormous with customers extending around the world." He looked at Vic. "We can help you. Think of your child Doctor. She could buy her own country."

"I don't want one," Vic replied, bitterly.

Dr. Dewar put his hand on hers. "Be polite, lass," he chided.

Gustave sighed, then turned the conversation toward boating, I think mostly because I was there in front of him.

We ended in the games room. Gustave and I talked about racing keels. Lucien kept by my side. He even put his hand on my back! And Lucien knows quite a bit about sailing. He said it was from the navy. I was really looking forward to tomorrow, despite the horses. To again have water under my feet and to get my hands on that yacht!

Yachts aside, I really needed to talk to Vic. Dr. Dewar was talking to some of the men who had arrived that day, who I hadn't been introduced to by the way, which even I knew was rude. He seemed cornered. Clearly we weren't kidnapped and dragged here for fun.

Then it came. Despite our having played earlier we were asked to play again. A servant appeared as Gustav mentioned it, my violin case in hand. I had to adjust the frog on my bow again. It was playing too close and I was thinking it still hadn't been rehaired since we bought it in the Canaries and how was I going to find somebody and the time to get it done? But play we did and we had fun until Camille asked if we knew classical pieces, which Aleta didn't.

"We really haven't had the time to work on any," I apologized.

"I want to though," Aleta added defensively.

"I'm afraid it's all I know," Camille replied, firmly. Then looked at Aleta and said with a not towards me, "Do you mind if we play?"

When she sighed, it hurt. We needed to hurry up and get to music school so we could fix this, but it seemed like things kept getting in the way, again and again.

Camille looked at me, eyebrows up.

I stared back, then suggested, "Vitali's Chaconne?" It had been awhile. I hadn't played it since the Congo.

A slow smile spread. "Yes. I think that will do," he replied.

Quiet spread through the room as he sat at the piano.

"Let me start," he said needlessly.

I waited.

The piece is a dark moody moan laced with pointless bitter triumph, which is not how I usually play it believe me, but I doubted he was going to go anywhere I liked. I don't know why I even mentioned it!

He started it at its darkest. Deathly slow, his fingers sure on the keys, the notes carefully placed like stones on a grave. It was obvious he did more than play the piano. He was seriously good. When I joined, it came as a low cry in the night, alone and afraid. He let that stand for a while, growing until his counterpoint was crushing, my response a desperate clawing upward for air. I think he was testing me, so I added edge to the notes and then extra notes adding harmonics.

He gave me a frowning smile and chided, "Stay with the music please."

I frowned back at him, but settled down and cried with it, choosing instead to pull the notes out of shape, allowing it the frantic hopelessness that I genuinely felt.

He seemed satisfied and said nothing.

I'd last performed it at Leopoldville, with Aleta's life in the balance, the jungle pressing down on us. I realized it was no different now. The walls began to dissolve into dim shadows, no different than that pitch black of the jungle.

Mrs. Hartnoll had given me the piece when I was, I think, eight. But it wasn't the piece, but the context, their eyes, practically all strangers. I realized my cheeks were wet, tears running down, and there was an uncomfortable shift in the room. I think it was the smell of the smoke from the fires. They didn't know what to do or how to react.

Lucien was already up, confused, but Camille shook his head no.

My bow raked across the strings drawing out harmonics and overtones, three maybe four notes, leaving thin trails of blood in the air in wasted bitter triumph, grasping at illusive stability. But that's what the piece is about isn't it? It's about futility. I finished on the up stroke, having remembered at the last second not to cut the end off, which I don't like. That need to adjust had given me a needed moment to remember where I was.

In a room filled with men who were all staring at me.

My cheek itched and I scratched without thinking and my hand came back wet.

That's when I panicked. I wasn't thinking. Instead I ran. I was down a hallway, into a dark moonlit room, bent over a chair trying to breathe.

"Cali?"

It was Lucien, followed by Aleta.

"Cali," she said, kneeling down next to me.

"It's nothing," I said, but it came out a sob. "Give me a minute."

"It's the Congo isn't it?" Lucien asked. "We made you play it."

"I'll be fine," I replied. I didn't want to talk about it. I could see the silhouettes of others in the doorway.

"Is she all right?" I think it was Cécile.

"She needs a good stiff drink," Gustave said.

"No," I replied. "Well, yes. I'd like some water, please."

"Maybe I need a good stiff drink," Gustave added and turned to find a servant.

I stood, a bit unsteady, Lucien helping. "I'm fine. I can go back."

"Are you sure?" he asked, worried.

"Yes." And I began to walk back, just to prevent being asked if I was sure again.

Back in the game room, Camille was still sitting at the piano. He seemed lost in thought.

Walking up to him, I apologized, "I'm sorry. I haven't played that piece in a while. It has bad memories."

"Do you really think that's what happened?" It almost sounded like an accusation. "No. It was something else." He seemed almost angry.

Then he saw the look on my face and started. "I'm sorry," he said quickly. "It's just that I hate it when I don't understand."

André was there with us. "Camille?" André asked.

"A strange moment. It's nothing," and he waved him away. Clearly though, something was bothering him. Then he looked at me, "Let's start again."

"I can't. Not tonight."

"You must."

"No."

"Camille," André said to his friend.

"Tell her she must."

"It's late," André replied, trying to soothe him.

He looked down at the piano keys, upset. "Tomorrow then."

"Yes, tomorrow," I replied.

He shut the lid on the keyboard. "Then goodnight," he said curtly and stood.

"Camille, it's early," Gustave said, sounding hurt.

"I must admit that bed does sound nice," Emma added. "It's been a long day."

"We've had a long train trip," one of the newcomers said.

Gustave sighed. "Very well. I'll call the staff."

But before bed, there was something I had to do. In our common room, I played Bach again for Aleta, this time properly.

Chapter 21 – A Promise of Air

Someone was in my room.

In the dim moonlight I could see a figure sitting in one of my chairs watching me. It seemed Gustave lodged ghosts with poor manners.

"I should kill you," she said quietly. It was Emilia. I might have been scared. I should have, but I was too tired.

"Then why am I still here?" I sighed, head back on my pillow.

"Our game is suspended while those that rule decide. At this point, it would be simple murder."

"Surely that's not a problem for you."

"I don't murder," she hissed. Then she paused, clearly

considering. Let her, I thought.

There was only her voice. I could see nothing but her outline in the dark and quiet. "But I have to admit," she continued. "I'm surprised I haven't. I think I'm beginning to understand Max's fascination."

"Max isn't fascinated. He's a friend."

Again, the quiet. She moved slowly, templing her fingers. "The world is littered with the bodies of Max's friends."

An interesting statement. They clearly were friends; were they so different? Then we heard the doorknob. It clicked, then turned, opening a tentative inch, and then another.

A head peeked in, the outline of a short man. It was Gustave in his pajamas.

"If you don't mind my dear Baron, . . ." Emilia said.

He jumped. "I must have the wrong room!" He almost squeaked.

"You have the right room, but we're having a talk."

"Oh, pardon me," he stammered and backed out, leaving the door open. We heard the doorway to the hallway shut.

Then I heard a blurry, "Cali." Aleta moaned from inside our common room as she came up to my door. "What's going on?" she said.

"Fear not," Emilia chimed. "We're just talking."

"Cali?"

"It's okay," I said.

She groaned and turned to walk back.

"It should have been my room he was sneaking into," Emilia almost whispered.

"Believe me, I wouldn't welcome his attentions."

She blocked a sudden laugh. I think I had surprised her.

"To be honest, I wouldn't either." Then she added as an afterthought, "Not unless I had orders. Now that André on the other hand . . ."

"Yes. He does seem nice."

"Or your lovely Lucien."

She couldn't see my face, but I think she heard me shift under the covers. I was giving her the eye and she knew it. She was teasing.

"Growling," she chided, her voice almost a laugh. "Is so unladylike."

I realized that I'd lost track of her in the dark. Then I heard the door close as she drifted silently out.

They woke us at seven. A maid came in quietly, laying out our clothes and starting our fire. I wanted to say good morning but she was gone so quickly. The dresses looked very much like my school uniforms only the dresses weren't actually dresses. They were pants! They were split dresses. I mean they draped like dresses when we were standing, but they were really two dresses, one for each leg. I think this was so we could ride without a side saddle or hitching them up. It was very unladylike, but the upper crust can do as they please. And, no corsets! Gustave, I suppose in this respect wasn't a bad sort – as long as you can keep him out of your room.

He was waiting for us downstairs at buffet, which isn't any different than serving yourself from the stove except they put the food in nice dishes.

"Miss Carmichael, may I have a word with you," he said as we entered.

Aleta grabbed my arm. "I'll be right here," she whispered.

He led me over to the window, away from the food.

"I wanted to apologize for last night," he said.

I thought he was talking about my room, but he continued.

"Saint-Saëns is a man of passion. He thinks of little else other than music."

"Will he be sailing with us?" Camille Saint-Saëns? The same as Mrs. Hartnoll's sheet music?

"No. He hates sea travel. The only thing that got him to travel off the continent was the arrival of the zeppelin. But I expect he'll be after you to play. He can be very single minded."

"I think . . ." I paused for a moment. "I think I was taken by surprise. I'll be better prepared next time."

"That's good," he sighed. "I would hate to have anything spoil the day."

"Oh there you are." It was Emma. She wearing a light day dress with sensible shoes.

She looked me over critically.

"You've been at it again," she said to Gustave. "Be careful," she said to me. "He must like you."

Gustave laughed. "They all have them," and Vic chose that moment to come in wearing a sailor suit as well.

"Gustave. An all-girl crew?"

"It will make a great photograph."

"And you left me out?" Emma feigned hurt.

"My tailors have their limits," he sighed. "Emma, don't think that I didn't ask. I wanted six, just for the symmetry," he said with emphasis.

"Who was the sixth?"

"Bertha. She came in this morning."

"His daughter," she said to me. "This is turning into quite a party."

Gustave looked smug.

I glanced at Vic who was selecting her food. She looked unhappy. Somehow I needed to talk to her alone. The doctor was met again by two of the men from last night and looked little better than Vic. My new cynical mind said we were being kept apart, but if they were going to be rude, then I could be too.

"Pardon me," I said and turned away without a by-your-leave. Walking toward Vic, I realized they'd made a mistake. With buffet, we could sit where we liked. The room was all windows and I could see a balcony with tables outside through a pair of glass paned doors.

Vic looked up as I approached.

"I haven't had a chance to talk to you since we got here," I said. "I really want to go through odds again and you owe me."

She gave me a blank stare, then blinked. "I guess I do." Then smiling her grin, "Besides. I've decided. Next time it's for money."

"You wouldn't! I'm not ready."

"Perhaps. But if you aren't, it will only be fair pay for my lessons."

I was spooning out some eggs.

"You're going to eat that?" she said.

"I bet it's good."

"They put things in it," she replied as she stared at it with misgiving.

And we carried on. Only to be joined by Aleta, Lucien, and then Gustave as I made for the balcony door. Behind Gustave I saw Emma give me a smirk. Gustave clearly wasn't going to let go.

I was about to open the door when I heard a voice behind me.

"Miss Carmichael!" It was Camille. "I need to talk to you."

I sighed and gave Gustave the eye. He looked relieved. The breeze from the door had been cold anyway. So I dusted off third year etiquette and turned to Camille with a smile.

"M. Saint-Saëns."

He was standing at the head of the table, the buffet behind him. Sitting nearby were Max and Emilia, who both seemed be quietly observing.

"Let her eat her breakfast first," Lucien said.

"I'm not going to ask her to play." Camille looked annoyed. "It's far too early. But there are things I want to understand."

Then Max spoke to Emilia. "She was like this in the Congo," he said. "I could make off with half his artwork and the contents of his safe and no one would notice."

Everyone turned to look.

"It is an interesting talent," Emilia replied, enjoying the sudden quiet as she took a sip of tea.

"I tried to recruit her," Max continued.

"Did you."

Gustave blew air from between his lips like someone had squeezed him. "I think," he interrupted. "We should all sit down."

And we did, but somehow Gustave ended up across from me, Lucien on my left, Camille on my right, and poor Vic several places away.

We sailor girls were issued lovely, thick, waterproofed wool coats. This was supposed to be our foul weather gear, but they didn't prevent the breeze from blowing under our skirts.

They didn't have enough horses for all of us. I would have gladly ridden in the car with Vic, but Gustave felt certain that he had to explain riding to me. We were joined by André and Bertha, who apparently had their meals in their rooms. Bertha kissed Gustave a good morning on his cheek. "Hello Papa," she said.

She was older, in her early twenties, dark auburn hair, and a round face with calm, steady eyes. She gained her horse with simple ease, wearing pants of course, calming his skipping about with a few simple gestures.

I looked up at mine. Horses are simply huge. The groom held it for me and I gained the saddle on the first try. This, I knew from experience, was the easy part.

"Papa," Bertha said, looking upset. "Gunther says that I can't ride Dahlia."

"She took a stone in the hoof. It needs time."

She groaned, then she glanced at me as I sat stock still, afraid to move.

"And who is this and what have you done to her?"

Both Gustave and André laughed.

André pulled his horse close and leaned in. "This is Calista Carmichael, from America."

"The girl in the papers?"

"Calista Carmichael," André continued. "This my sister Bertha." I replied, "*Bonjour.*"

"I apologize for my father," she said. "Since André took up the camera, he's been mad about photographs. You would not believe the things he's made us do just to have something new to hang in his study."

"If you mean the dress, it's better deck wear than what I usually have," I replied. Although I wondered why I was defending Gustave.

She looked skeptical, but said nothing. Lucien edged his horse up beside me.

"Papa. You gave her Brillant too."

"She's American," Gustave replied. "He's a quarterhorse."

"She doesn't ride," Lucien said. "Not the best choice."

"She can have my horse," Max said.

But Bertha frowned. "Best if you give me the reins," and she moved closer, arm outstretched. "Just relax. He only knows rein."

"I can lead her," Lucien said, also reaching out.

"I'll take them," Bertha replied. "It's no trouble," and she snagged them at the horse's neck and drew them over. I let go. "We should go, Papa."

"Yes, it's getting late," Gustave replied.

Then my horse lurched forward as she drew me along, leaving Lucien behind.

The trail took us around the top of the cliff and then down the side, surf crashing below. Beyond, the water looked sweet and clear.

I don't mind heights, but it's a different thing when you're being carried along, at the mercy of a giant beast. Somehow the height next to the cliff edge seemed dizzying, and I had to duck under the brush and small branches that clung to the rocks above.

We rounded a rocky point and faced a cove filled with mooring buoys, most empty, it being winter. The harbor had been fortified at some point and was lined with old gray stone walls, the cliff tops above crowded with mansions. The trail turned into a worn cobbled road that led past old gates and towers, the tumbled down rocks from the cliff above were mixed in with green grass that rippled with the wind. Ahead was the town, a beach filled with fishing boats, and a stone quay that reached out into the water in the bay. I could see rain rolling our way, out in the channel.

"Let's take the high route," André said.

"It's late," Gustave replied.

"This will hardly give the horses any kind of run."

"I want to have lunch at Bouley Bay."

"It would be wise to point out that it's winter," Bertha said. "It will be dark early, and that Jersey is currently English."

England. The last place I wanted to go.

"We'll make it. Good weather."

"The English aren't happy with our guest at the moment."

"I don't have my passport," I added. What was he trying to do?

"We're not staying the night, and no one ever asks."

"I'm not going to England," I added firmly. I looked back at Emilia, but I could tell nothing of her thoughts. She was probably devastating at cards.

"Granville," Berta suggested.

Gustave growled, clearly upset, "If we must."

"You're spoiling Father's day," André added with a smirk.

"Don't listen to him," Bertha said. "The Cécile has a deep keel and there are few ports where we can dock. With so many of us, we'd be all day shuttling ashore by dingy in Bouley Bay." She paused for a moment in thought, then added, "He's been to them all so many times that I think he's become a bit daring in his search for novelty." Did I detect a touch of doubt in her voice?

Gustave growled again in response, then muttered to himself, "The track will be closed."

Somehow he'd managed to have servants waiting to take our horses at the quay. The harbor lifeboat, as they often do to raise money for upkeep, doubled as a shuttle. She had locks for eight oars, but only two men to row and a third at the tiller. The extra seats for rowers were there for hard weather. We piled in with no lack of places to sit.

The Cécile was anchored out in the center. She was a hundred feet with two masts and a narrow white hull. With all that length and only two masts, her yards were very long and I figured her sheets were hell to crank up. Her ladder was beautifully varnished. It was all wood too, angled to be practically steps. What a crazy thing to waste paint on. Then again, she had brass railings too. They'd tarnish if you put your hand on them. It was all so clean. What if they spilled a bucket of paint – or tar!

Her stern and bow were both steeply sloped, but her hull was wide below water to make room for cabins below. The single deck cabin, masts, and the wheel were varnished wood, every piece of metal, even her winch, was polished. And mid-deck she had a skylight instead of hold doors to let sun in below! Clearly she never carried cargo. She was a boat meant for nothing more than the pure joy of sailing.

To keep her trim, she had a permanent crew of five, all with matching uniforms. They were waiting for us in their dress whites, standing at attention in a line, one of them piping us aboard. Gustave, who had a bag passed to him by the car driver before boarding the boat, pulled out a captain's hat before climbing the ladder.

"Captain on deck," the piper called, and the crew clicked their heels.

It was a ridiculous show and knocked Gustave down a few pegs in my eyes.

"All hands, prepare to make way," Gustave replied.

"Man the booms," the piper, probably the chief mate called, but they all had so much braid it was hard to tell.

"Engineer to the engines," he continued.

Engines? I didn't see any stacks.

"Aye," the rest barked, and ran for their stations.

I sincerely hoped it wasn't going to be like this the whole trip.

"I'll show you around," Gustave said, as we crowded the deck at the top of the ladder. He led us toward the deck cabin.

"She's custom designed by Fife," he said proudly, as if that meant anything to me.

We stepped down into the galley area, the central table bright under the skylight. To the side was a deck hatch leading down. He had steel sinks, of which there were two, like our zeppelin. Naturally, the walls were decorated with photographs of previous passengers, which I wanted to look at, but Gustave didn't stop.

"All areas forward are for crew only. All areas astern are for passengers only."

He led us astern, down a small corridor lined with doors.

"These are all cabins. If you need to lie down, feel free to pick one. The end of the corridor is our family apartment. We have a small library and a bar, which you're welcome to. Try not to get drunk or we'll lock you in a cabin. Pitching decks don't mix well with unsteady feet."

It doesn't help seasickness either, I thought.

Then I heard a deep thrum.

"What's that?" I asked.

"The engines," he replied, with a twinkle in his eye.

"Can I see them?"

"In a bit. Let the crew make way first."

Their apartments took up the last thirty feet of the hull. The bar was really a small counter with a sink and a liquor cabinet, the library, two shelves of books. They had their own table in a side nook and several more cabins, probably for children.

Initial tour finished, we were left to ourselves while Gustave retired to his cabin to change. Up top, the morning calm had been broken by a sea breeze, raising a bit of chop. Sea gulls wheeled overhead. We were making way under power, but I could still see no smoke other than a stream of thin blue-gray blowing out the starboard hull amidships. I made it five knots toward the breakwater entrance. The crew were releasing the booms, making ready to raise sail.

I made my way forward. It was pleasant feeling her move under my feet, and I stood there with my eyes closed riding with it. The cool breeze washing away my troubles.

"What do you think those are?" Lucien asked, referring to the thrum of the engines. He'd come up behind me.

"I have no idea," I replied.

"It's a diesel." It was Max, who had followed Lucien.

"Impossible," Lucien replied.

"No. We've started producing them in small numbers for experimentation and product development. They're terribly expensive though."

"You mentioned them on the Bremen," I said.

"They're a new type of engine," Lucien replied.

"Like on the zeppelin?"

"No," Max said, clearly proud. "More powerful and far less dangerous. I'm looking forward to seeing them."

We cleared the breakwater and the deck began to pitch with the open sea. I took a deep breath. The feeling was glorious, but then I heard, "There you are." It was Gustave. It seemed I wasn't to be allowed to enjoy the moment. "Ready for the rest of the tour?"

"Yes," I said, resigned.

"None of that," he chided. "I think you'll like this."

He'd changed into a passenger liner captain suit in creased, dark blue. At the very least, I didn't feel ridiculous standing next to him in my dress anymore.

The tour picked up again below. This time we went forward. He had a navigation room with a desk and its own compass! We were heading north, hopefully clear of the point. His library of charts, almanacs, and notebooks, filled the wall. I so wanted to get my hands on them, but we were moving on. On to a generator propelled by a belt that disappeared below the deck. To sail hoist cables that ran down through the mast steps. His sail winches it turned out were electric, hidden below. His crew would not be doing any turns on the winch to make way. But what did they do if the generator failed, I wondered?

The same was true of his anchor winch. Only I could see that they could be hand cranked, but with room for only two and the small size of capstan, it had to be fiercely difficult.

I opened one of the lockers and found it full of rope, neatly coiled and stowed. They all looked as well cared for as the boat itself.

Then it was down through the bow hatch into the hold itself, which smelled awful. Machinery can be like that. The hold was bisected by the keel, a big deep one, and the mast steps. Batteries lined the bulkheads and hull, and then, finally, Max's favorite, the diesel engine itself. It was as tall as me, oily, and smoked. Its roaring and clanking was deafening. Our engineer sat next to it reading a book. He'd changed clothes into a more practical oil stained jumpsuit. At first sight of Gustave he stood and saluted.

"*Nein, nein,*" Gustave yelled over the engine. "*Gunter, fahren Sie bitte.*"

The mechanic took a breath and sat down again with his book. It was spotted with diagrams.

Aleta talked to him for a bit and told me later that he came with the engine, and that he only spoke German.

Gustave, on the other hand, told us that he'd purchased it only a year ago, the Cécile having just come back from the dockyard. All of this was new.

Next to the engine was the gearbox, which sat on top of the propeller shaft. Apparently she had three gears and could vary the speed of the engine as well using a throttle that changed fuel flow instead of steam pressure. I looked at the controls with interest, thinking about the Nellie Thomson back home. They mostly made sense, at least the gearbox.

Tour over, I was back up top. I could see Bertha at the wheel and made my way back. Behind me, the sails were running up the masts all by themselves!

"Amazing isn't it?" she said, as I approached. "It's the first time I've gotten to see her since the refit."

"I'd be afraid it would break."

"Yes. I don't trust it either." Then she laughed, "But it's working now. You have no idea how often we had to run those sails up as kids."

"Maybe," I replied.

We were clearing the breakwater, heading into the wave tossed English Channel, hitting five to six foot wind chopped swells. Enough to toss the bow.

"So I hear you were a sailor," she grinned.

"Was?" I think she had seen my longing looks at the boat.

"Want to take the wheel?"

Then it was my turn to grin. "Sure!"

So we switched places, but let's be clear. I leapt for it.

"I figure if we stay at the wheel, Papa won't pull any tricks."

"Like giving me to the British?"

"He's up to something," she said, the grin gone.

"He wants Dr. Dewar."

She sighed. "As if we aren't rich enough."

The sails had snapped taut, but she hardly heeled.

"What do you have down in that keel?" I asked.

"Lead."

"I wondered how long it would take you," Aleta said, as she made her way back. I gave her a gleeful smile.

"When I tell you, we'll bring her around NNE. We'll take her wide around the point."

We held steady as we passed the fort on the point.

"Almost there," Bertha said. "Now."

"All hands," I yelled. "Ready about NNE!"

Everyone jumped.

"Hard a lee!" I called, and I swung the wheel.

It wasn't my best turn. She was new to me. We struck a wave on the edge and she tried to roll with it, but that keel kept us straight. Instead, it drenched everyone on the bow, their exclamations drifting back against the wind. But the crew was good and the booms came about, the sails snapping taut, the ship taking the next wave right where it should.

"That was sloppy," I muttered.

Aleta stared forward with a skeptical eye. Emma, Max, Emilia, and Lucien were all upset. It serves them all right, I thought.

But Bertha laughed. "Nonsense," she smiled. "Papa's probably laughing on the deck."

Then I saw André leaning against the starboard mast, his camera in hand. He looked happy.

Bertha blinked at him, then said, "He never stops. He's turned his cabin into a lab. No one goes in without permission. Not even Papa."

"I wouldn't think anyone could keep your father out."

"Papa loves his photos too much to chance spoiling them."

"Hmmm . . ," Aleta said thoughtfully. "I'd like to see that."

"Oh he'll show you," Bertha chuckled. "As long as he's not using it. You should ask."

"I think I will," and she headed below.

I think Aleta was angling for André. We knew so little back then.

It was impossible for either of us to marry into the Rothschilds. They were not only Jewish, but aristocrats, and had very strict rules about matches. But fear not – later – she would marry into the DuPonts. But I am, again, ahead of myself again.

We kept on our heading for a few minutes until she asked the inevitable question, "Did you really seduce a prince?" And I had to explain, again. It was getting old. Maybe I should have cards printed. The subject though, kept us going for a bit.

"Oh," she exclaimed. "We should have turned. Take us fifteen points leeward."

"Aye, aye," I replied, turning the wheel with an eye on the binnacle. I'd barely looked up before the crew were at the sails, and they really didn't need adjustment.

But she was making great headway in clean deep, gray green. The spray from the bow glinted like pale stars in the wan early winter sunlight. I could have stood there all day feeling that deck beneath my feet, the cold wet at my back. We were passing the point, heading across the bay before Berta spoke again.

"Cali," she said quietly. "Perhaps you should stay in Granville."

I said nothing.

"I can divert him sometimes, like today. But I can't stop him. He'll get his way eventually." She paused, then looked at me. "I don't want you to get hurt."

"I can't," I replied reluctantly.

"Then take your friends and run. Don't get back onboard."

"I don't have my passport or money. I bet they don't either." I patted the sides of my dress. "No pockets. We can't even stay in a hotel."

It was her turn to say nothing.

A shadow passed as we sailed under a cloud and then it hit me. Would our passports be in our rooms when we got back? I was finally at sea and now all I wanted was to get back!

Chapter 22 – Escape

We crossed the bay and found Granville perched on rocky bluffs spotted with manor houses, forts, and churches. The harbor itself was improved, with a sturdy stone breakwater, but Bertha gave it a wide berth, passing the entrance. Behind the breakwater I could see why. That side of the harbor was shallow. The tide was out leaving boats high and dry on a mudflat, all exposed to the sun. She instead steered us around a second breakwater to deep water docks filled with fishing boats, facing a wide sweep of easy lapping beach.

Granville is a fishing port and as such, it has little cargo moving on her wharfs, no harbor pilots, and no traffic. Mostly fifes and yawls, yards and sails down for one reason or another, the main fleet out to sea leaving the docks mostly empty. Nothing but stacks of empty catch crates and the smell of fish. At the end of the wharf was a cannery, the shallow side of the sea wall next to it fetid with discarded detritus waiting for the tide to wash it away. The air around it was thick with seagulls. Canneries are nasty but they mean work and this one was busy.

"Oh, this is awful!" Emma moaned as the wind shifted our way. "Why did we come here?"

Gustave grunted, glancing at me as if I had chosen the port! I could see back of the wharves, up on the bluffs, it looked a lot nicer and Gustave clearly knew the place so I expected it probably wasn't terrible. But I didn't pick it!

"It's a nice town really," André replied. "At least once you get past the cannery. Of course it's off season."

"Papa likes the racetrack," Bertha added.

Someone must have seen us dock because there was a carriage waiting near the office. They hadn't reckoned meeting a crowd though. It was too small for all of us.

"We'll need a second carriage," Gustave said, stating the obvious. "I'll go have to have someone call one at the harbor office. I have to check in anyway," he said. Then he looked at me, "Would you care to join me?"

"I've seen enough harbor offices," I replied.

"Still, I'd like your company."

I felt a wash of dread, but what choice did I have? "Of course."

"Do you want company?" Aleta asked.

"No. It's okay," I replied. I was kind of curious to see what he was up to.

The rest waited with the carriage as we walked to the office. I think they were all a little curious too. At least the carriage was parked upwind of the cannery.

Unlike the shipping ports my family frequents, Granville, had no warehouses lining the docks. Instead, it immediately gave way to ship fitters, sail lofts, and rope alleys, all right on the water. And, naturally, the odd saloon as well. These were all fitted out to cater to the local fishermen, festooned with nets and floats, with the crippled and retired sitting in chairs in front playing checkers or cards, watching us as we passed by.

He said nothing at first as we walked. Deciding on strategy I guessed.

"Miss Carmichael," he said.

"Yes?" I waited for the first volley.

"I've decided that it's time for us to part ways."

Very direct. I could be direct too.

"Then the four of us will stay here. Please send our things."

"I'm afraid it would be just you," he replied

"I fear as well, but that will be impossible."

Then I turned around and started walking back

"Miss Carmichael!" he called, but I kept walking.

He trotted a bit to catch up.

"I will pay you."

"That's insulting. I'm not a mercenary."

"Clearly not. But you must work for someone."

"That is doubly insulting."

"You're American, at least."

"It gets worse," I muttered.

He started to say something but stopped, clearly at a loss. He'd stopped walking so I stopped too and looked back at him. He was definitely confused.

"You're not working for anyone?" he asked.

"No. I want them to get to a place where they'll be safe and happy. And so far as I can tell, they'll get neither from you."

Then I turned and kept walking, calling back, "I'll be waiting at the boat. Enjoy the day."

He didn't follow.

When I walked by our group and continued on toward the boat, Aleta and Lucien leapt up to follow.

"Cali, wait," Lucien called.

"What did he say to you?" Aleta spat.

"Nothing." I was fuming and kept walking.

"Tell me," Aleta said.

"He wanted to buy me off."

Aleta growled, but Lucien chucked as he fell into step.

"What?" I snapped.

"It's that you tend to confound people," he replied.

"He has no conception," Aleta ranted.

The Dewars started to follow us too.

"I'm so tired of this." Which was almost a whine, so I stopped. "Lucien. Why did you put me on that airship?"

He stopped too and frankly looked embarrassed.

"I had no intention that you would get any more involved than telling the Dewars to stay on board. I had lawyers and men waiting to protect them." Then he sighed, "But things spun out of control."

Then he looked down at me with those hazel eyes. "I'm glad you're alive."

I decided then that it was the eyes. That I would always have to be wary of them, no matter how I felt about him. They could melt stone.

"Cali." Aleta broke the spell. "Are we going back to the boat?"

The Dewars caught up, and I could see the others following.

"I am." I picked up walking again, ignoring the cannery. "Who knows what he'll do next."

"Cali!" It was Vic calling, so I had to wait for them as well. Then we had to discuss the situation while we walked. All pretense of civility had broken down. Max had to put in his pitch for Berlin. André and Bertha apologized endlessly as we boarded, the crew looking a bit surprised we were back.

When Gustave finally showed up, all he did was mutter about having to pay docking fees. We set sail with no lunch. The crew made us sandwiches instead. I ate mine out on deck, sitting with Bertha, Aleta, and Vic.

"Da is waiting for you to tell him what to do," Vic said.

"I have no idea what to do," I replied. "If we leave the villa, Emilia will be free to do what she wants. Perhaps even Max too. And who knows who else will follow. Even your Papa," I nodded toward Bertha.

"Yes," she agreed. "He can be like a cat on a stalk. He's definitely focused on this. Your da must have something very valuable," she said to Vic.

"I guess so," she said.

"Are you going to get in trouble for talking to us?" I asked Bertha.

"Oh, maybe. He might send me away," but she shrugged. "The last time was terrible fun. He sent me to a convent on Malta. It was a dormitory full of bad rich girls with nothing but nuns to avoid." Then she laughed, "The best part is that I'm Jewish!"

"He might make you get married."

"He will eventually anyway. Probably to some awful cousin. It's the Rothschild way."

"You should run with us."

She laughed again. "Oh, you can't run," she said. "We might be the richest family on Earth. Certainly the richest in France.

247

Practically everyone in the country owes us money and literally everybody will be looking for you."

It all really did seem hopeless, but that was the moment it came to me. My plan. The idea just popped into my head, and it was brilliant. If we couldn't go through France, we would go around it! And to that end I turned the conversation to our lodgings, most notably which rooms Vic and her Da were in.

Since we were back early, the horses hadn't been brought down for us yet and we got to take the cars up instead, which didn't sit well with Gustave. All together Gustave was having a well-deserved bad day.

These had been my first rides in a car and I must to tell you that they're amazing contraptions. Big and smoky, the big boiler in back radiating welcome heat. We all piled in together on long, padded, leather bench seats, the sea breeze carrying away the soot and smoke. Our driver pulled a big lever and we chugged forward, just like a trolley, only he could steer using a big wheel. With all the gauges, it looked very complicated and modern. It had rubber tires and springs too. Something I wished they'd put them on wagons. They took out a lot of the clatter and rattle from the cobbles.

But there was enough bad day to go around. My big helping, Camille, was waiting in the front hallway ready to wreak ruin. He asked me to play even before we had taken off our hats.

"Camille, we're famished," Gustave said. "Let it wait until after dinner."

"But I've been thinking about it all day," he replied.

"Then two hours won't make much difference will it?"

Camille threw up his hands and turned away in frustration.

Aleta and I retired to our room for glorious baths. Gustave had neglected to take our passports. I suppose he hadn't thought I would survive the day and it would make for easier packing. I debated with myself about letting Aleta in on the plan, but then thought better of it. Who knows who was listening in this place? No, it would have to wait and she would be spared the need to lie. But I so wanted to. What good is it thinking of something clever when you can't share it with others?

Dinner went as if nothing had happened. Camille sat across from me again. This time I was ready for the courses, but we'd barely begun before he started in.

"You played again last night," he said. "I heard you."

"Yes. It was for Aleta." Then I paused for a moment. "And for myself."

His eyebrows twitched. A momentary frown of annoyance.

"It was to make up for something," I added.

"It really doesn't matter why," Bertha said. "It was lovely. Something nice before bed."

Emma and André were down and across the table from me, trying to teach Aleta French. I think André liked her, even with her burnt hair.

"And I haven't been practicing enough too," I replied. Really, I can be hard on myself about that. Since people had been noticing my work, it had gotten worse. I told Camille about learning one of his pieces, which pleased him.

For my plan to work I needed muscle. I needed Lucien, but I had no idea where his room was and I hadn't been able to get him into a situation where I could ask. I swear, Gustave was doing his best to keep me separate from everyone. After dinner, both Camille and my violin were waiting in the play room. Lucien was asked to the billiards table.

Camille naturally wanted Vitali's Chaconne again. I was ready for him, but it was the last thing I wanted to play.

"Can we do something else? You play it so darkly."

"Is there any other way?" He looked smug.

Really, it's easy. Raise the pitch and tempo on the parts you don't like, then add flourish as needed. Maybe cut some parts out. I put my violin under my chin, waiting for Camille to approve, but he just stared. So I launched into it anyway. As I played his stare turned to surprise, then shock.

"No! No! Stop," he sputtered. "That is a travesty!" He said each word. "You will certainly not play my works that way. I forbid it!"

He leaned his elbows on the piano music stand and rubbed his temples.

"No. You will not rewrite other's works. You will learn to do it right. Start again."

"Really Saint-Saëns," Lucien said, standing there with his queue. "It's not done!"

"Cali?" Lucien asked.

"Let him," I replied wearily.

I don't like the way it's written. It's the disingenuousness of the piece. It's so hollow. Like the funeral of some terrible man. Worst of all, to me it was the Congo. The docks in Leopoldville. Aleta's fever. The walk in the night.

But begin he did, without another word, and I followed, drawing notes down out of air for him. They fell like dead sparrows. Slower and darker than before, pulling the Congo slowly out of its shell.

This time though, I was braced for it. Its darkness tried to crowd out my vision, but I sneered back, flattening the notes to coffin lid rasps, bleeding anger. But rather than object, it seemed to drive Camille on. He dove deeper. We fought. At least I was fighting. I swear I heard gunfire and felt the heat of the flames, the burning wagons, the wounded screaming as they fought while burning alive. Sometimes I can't help it. It has a will of its own. We had yet to finish when I dropped my violin, letting it dangle in my hand.

"I will not play this," I said, not recognizing my voice.

I realized I'd been crying.

He stopped playing, looking up at me blinking.

"Cali," Aleta said, worried. She had her hands on my shoulders, trying to see my eyes.

"That's enough Saëns," Lucien snapped.

"But . . ."

Then Lucien looked at Gustave with barely disguised fury. "I've had enough of this."

Gustave glared back.

Lucien took my hand and said, "May I escort you to your room?"

I nodded.

"I'll get your case," Aleta added, reaching to bring it. I was still holding my violin and bow loose in my hands.

At the top of the stairs Lucien spoke quietly.

"This can't continue. He'll be rid of us all sooner than later."

"He's already tried twice," Aleta muttered.

"Lucien," I whispered. "I need to know where your room is."

"Why?" He looked at me alarmed.

"Not here," I pleaded.

Then as we walked down the hallway, he reached down and squeezed my hand tipping his head toward a door. It was the last piece I needed.

The crew won't let us, Aleta finished in her hasty scrawl.
I took the paper and the book and wrote back, *They'll be on shore. Why would they be?*
Because it's their home port. Wives and kids.
They'll arrest us.
Maybe. Lucien can help.
We were sitting on Aleta's bed passing a piece of notepaper back and forth, arguing about my plan. We had to stay up to make it work anyway. I figured to wait until at least 1:00 AM, but not too much later. It was going to take time to get everyone packed and down the hill. I figured cooks and servants probably got up early. The hard part was going to be getting the Dewars out of the house.
He'll be in jail too, she wrote.
Do you want to face Stroud on the train?
She frowned at that.
Are we leaving our things? she asked.
We pack what we want in bedsheets. They'll be quiet.
Carry our shoes, she added.
I nodded.
We snuck out at one thirty, carrying our meagre possessions on our backs. The hallway was empty and amazingly, Lucien's door unlocked!
His room was pitch black. I could hear him move as we came in.
"Cali," he whispered, as Aleta closed the door.
"Yes," I whispered back.
"Wait." Then he turned on the bathroom light.
He was already dressed!
He put his finger to his lips and I motioned with my hands like I was writing. He looked at the desk before sitting back down on the bed and taking off his boots.
I wrote, *We're going to the boat.*
He wrote back, *I know.*
Which sent a bolt of fear through me. If he knew, then others

probably did too, but he was staring at my sailor dress of course.

I scribbled quickly. *If you knew we were coming then Stroud knows!*

Probably Max too. Then he shrugged.

How could he not care?

Then he wrote, *It can't be helped.*

He was quickly packed, taking practically nothing. My bundle felt so big, but I couldn't let go of my new dresses. I kept losing them and I had so few.

We crept back out into the corridor only to encounter Max, standing patiently in front of the Dewar's door. I practically went into a panic, but Lucien put his hands on our shoulders and shook his head no. Max smiled, opened the Dewar's door, and bowed hand out to usher me through.

"Cali?"

I tried to shush.

"What is it lass? Who's that?"

I tried to shush. Aleta tried to shush.

"Who are you?"

"It's Cali," Vic said.

And I was still trying to shush them.

"Da. She wants you be quiet."

"Oh." He paused, and then, "Then why is she here?"

He simply had to talk.

Lucien turned on the bathroom light and I stood in front of him and said, "Shuosh!"

He stared at me for a moment and blinked. "What's that on you back?"

"Her clothes," Aleta said.

"We're leaving," I added.

"Good," he snapped. "It's about time."

"We're never going to get him out of the house like this," Max said, sitting his small valise on the floor and finding a seat.

Since when was Max part of *we*, I thought.

I went to his desk and grabbed a sheet of paper and a pencil, which strangely wasn't that sharp. He must have been writing. And wrote *please be quiet* and *write here instead of talking*, while Vic and her Da discussed trivialities, thankfully, quietly.

He stared at the page for a second then looked up at me. I held out the pencil.

Pursing his lips, he grabbed a book from his bed stand to write on and wrote, *How are we getting to the train station?*

I wrote back, *We're going by boat. Pack what you want in a sheet.*

"Boat?" he said.

I rolled my eyes and clenched my fists.

"Sorry," he replied, then wrote, *What boat?*

I wrote back, *His.*

At that his eyes went wide and he looked up at me.

I smiled with a touch of glee and nodded.

Somehow, we made it out. It helped that the house was so large. The servants probably slept in the basement. Wherever it was, we didn't see them, nor did we see Emilia.

It was cold and windy outside, but thankfully not raining. And we had a bit of moon as we trudged down the horse trail.

"Lass," the doctor said to me. "Why couldn't we have waited for summer?"

We had our ship coats, thanks to our host, but it didn't cover my legs.

"I'm afraid it's tonight or never," Lucien answered. "Max, where's your friend?"

"Fear not," Max said, sounding tired. "She's here somewhere."

"When do you think she'll move?"

"Before the docks. She can't let us leave. Once we're at sea, she'll have no way of knowing where we'll make shore."

This was the last thing I needed to hear.

Dr. Dewar chose that moment to stumble on the uneven trail. We stopped to let him pull himself together. His knees hurt and there was a problem with his shoes. We were sitting there waiting, listening to the surf below, me thinking about the British, when I heard several rocks tumble down on the trail ahead. Max sighed. Then suddenly he ducked and something dark flew between us. Then another, this time hitting Max's suitcase. He was holding it up in front of himself as a shield.

"Emilia!" he called. "Enough."

More rocks fell. She was moving, her voice drifting down from over the lip of the bluff.

"Give me the doctor."

"We need to talk," Max called back.

"No."

"There's a better way."

"No!" and something hit Max's suitcase.

"Emily, we can both win."

And then it was quiet. We sat there, holding our breaths, but there was nothing.

"At least it was only rocks," Max mumbled.

"She would shoot us?" Aleta asked.

"No. She hates guns." And then half to himself, "She prefers knives."

Chapter 23 – A Bad End

She stood in the center of the trail, waiting, oblivious to the cold. I saw a glint of moonlight from something in her hand, she was standing in front of us. We all stood still.

"What are you proposing?" she asked.

"Let them go," Max replied.

"Max. Not this again," she said, with exasperation.

"Emily, where are they going?"

"I won't."

"It's the only way to keep balance."

It was quiet, except for the surf and the wind through the grass.

"It's Belgium," he continued. "Everyone will have it within a week."

"I take umbrage at that," Lucien snapped.

"Yourself aside," Max said with a smug smile. "Your country's security is terrible."

Then it was Lucien's turn to be silent.

"What are they saying?" the doctor asked me.

If he knew, he'd quit. He couldn't quit, not now. "Max is trying to convince her that your plan is best for everyone." I was getting so much better at lying.

"Well, that's what I've said all along," he replied, shaking his head.

"Da . . ," Vic started before I put a hand on her shoulder.

"Don't," I said.

She gave me a hard look, but I shook my head ever so slightly no. "We'll talk about it at the docks." The doctor looked back and forth at the two of us, but said nothing, clearly confused.

"Let this one go," Max called to Emilia.

She sighed, then gestured, waving the back of her hand at us, clearly disgusted.

She found a spot on a rock to sit on as we walked by. The knife had vanished.

As Max neared, she said, "Max."

"Of course," he replied with a smile, and then to me, "This is where we part."

"You're leaving?"

"The game's over," he said with a shrug. "Go ahead, make the last play."

"Thank you, Max," I said, hopping over a wet trail rut to give him a big hug. He was clearly surprised.

"It becomes clear now," Emilia said dryly.

Max could only mumble, "You're welcome."

"Let's get down the hill. We're late," Lucien said.

"Hurry," Max added.

And it was goodbye. We stumbled on, pushing the doctor as best we could, the trail turning to road and then harbor.

The harbor boat was tied up in its spot, no locks or anything. I couldn't pick out the Cécile in the darkness, but we knew where she tied up.

"What would you have done if there hadn't been a boat?" Lucien asked.

"She had to be here."

"What if she had been locked?"

"I figured you'd know what to do. But if that didn't work, there have to be fishing boats on the beach. Help row?" I nodded toward a seat. "Vic, can you steer? Aleta, cast off."

"I don't know how," Vic said.

"It's not hard and I'll tell you what to do. Just try not to hit any boats. We don't want to wake anyone up."

We wended our way between the moored boats, me dividing my attention between managing Vic and enjoying watching Lucien row.

The Cécile was right where we left her, a silhouette in the moon flecked water.

"And your plan here?" he replied.

"We board. He'll have to put us all in jail if he sends the police, and he'll never get Dr. Dewar that way. Besides, we won't hurt her. She'll just be in Antwerp."

We shipped oars and bumped her side as I leapt up and climbed her rail. "Toss me the line."

But a figure walked up the steps to the deck and called out, "*Wer ist hier?*" It was the engineer. He was sleeping on the boat!

Aleta rattled back in German.

"*Ja, komm,*" he replied and waved for us to come onboard.

"What did you say to him?" I said.

"I told him we left things on the ship and that we were leaving."

I was thinking we should run, but he waved again and said, "*Komm,*" and everyone was climbing.

"*Kommen Sie an Bord,*" he added cheerily and showed us a big revolver he'd been hiding, pulling back the hammer. The sound was singular.

I heard Lucien curse and he stepped back down into the boat.

"Are you going to shoot us in our boat?" I asked.

"No," Aleta translated. "I'll hole you and watch you sink. Come aboard. You might as well be comfortable."

We had no choice so we climbed up on deck. He sat back by the wheel waving us below with the point of his gun.

"This is kidnapping," Aleta snapped.

"This is piracy," he snapped back.

Below, it was dark until the light clicked on. He was halfway down the steps, one hand on the light switch, barefoot in shirt and pants. Apparently this was how he slept.

With his gun still pointing at us, he said, "I'm going to get a big bonus for this." He stepped down, but as his foot hit the deck at the bottom he slipped, the gun going off. The noise in the small space of the cabin was stunning.

I stopped, trying to make sense of it.

A flash of light, then Lucien decked the engineer, the gun kicked to the side.

Vic was screaming and crying.

Somehow, I was sitting on the floor crawling backwards toward the corner. Away from the blood that slowly inched toward me across the floor.

Aleta was kneeling over someone, cursing.

"We've got to get to shore," someone, I think Lucien, said. Then he was pulling at me. "Cali, you've got to get up. We've got to hurry."

Vic was still sobbing.

"Cali, help damn it!" It was Aleta. They were trying to lift someone. And I was up, only it wasn't me. It was someone else and I was looking through her eyes.

Someone had been shot and there was blood all over, the deck slippery with it.

We were carrying the body, hauling it by its clothing up the steps, up top. It wasn't moving. Just dead weight. We almost flipped the boat getting it in, Lucien, standing legs spread, trying to balance as we edged the body over the side, trying to hold on. It was so heavy and Vic kept crying. Aleta and I trying to keep a grip.

Down in the boat I let go of everything and crawled back into the stern.

"Steer Cali, damn it!" Lucien said.

I blinked and put my hand on the tiller.

We were making for the dock. As we closed with it I turned to bring us in on the port beam. Then Aleta was up over the side, on the dock running, yelling for help.

We were in the police station when I started to cry.

I'd killed him. Dr. Dewar was dead.

I tried to help, but killed him instead. Aleta was right. I hurt everyone around me. I was a curse.

Bertha was sitting with her arm around me telling me I don't know what and all I could do was cry. That beautiful man was dead.

The police were asking me questions which I couldn't answer, but they stopped when Gustave arrived. He mustered the decency not to have us taken back to his villa. We were given rooms at an inn on the waterfront.

The main room was empty when we entered, with only the proprietor's wife holding a lantern. The hearth cracked with unburnt coals left over from that night, our rooms up creaking stairs.

"Lay down Cali," Aleta said as she sat me on a bed and began undoing my shoes.

"I killed him," I said.

"You didn't. It was Gustave."

But she was wrong. I lay down anyway, though I didn't deserve to. And to my shame, I slept.

It was afternoon and the sky was heavy and gray. A cold wind blew through our windows from across the bay. For a harbor, it was strangely fresh, the fish market having long closed. I could see a crack in the ceiling in the dim light from the window. Everyone that died because of me was in the room. It was so crowded. Mme. Verbeeck looked down at me and slowly shook her head.

"You need to take a bath," Aleta said. I hadn't realized she was there for the crowd. The inn had a bath, down the hall next to the WC. The inn keeper had shown us when we came in. "It will help. Come, let me help you." And she pulled at my covers, but I didn't move. The weight of the air above held me down, that and guilt. I stared at the ceiling, the tears having started again. "Oh, Cali," she said. Then she gave me hug. "This is foolish."

She got up. "I'll be back." And she left.

Time passed. I was so tired of death, so tired of people dying around me, so tired of my mistakes, but I would not die despite my efforts to will my heart to stop.

Lucien came, his beautiful eyes looked down at me. He sat. He looked worried.

"Cali," he said. "You can't leave us. We need you." He paused, clearly in pain. "I need you."

I didn't deserve him. This world and I were both too fragile to be together. It was a bad match.

My hand was sitting on the bed where Aleta left it. He lifted it gently and kissed it. It was sad. Must I live just to break him too?

He was sitting there holding my hand when we were joined by Vic.

Vic's eyes and nose were red and she looked bad.

"Cali," she said. "You have to stay with me. You still have to get me to Belgium."

I began to sob. It was the worst thing I could have heard.

"You have to help me finish what Da started."

"You'll die too," I croaked.

"I will if you don't help. I can't do it alone."

My sobbing got worse. I didn't know what to do, until a stray thought crossed my mind and my eyes darted up, looking up at Vic.

She looked back and gave me a little nod, then blew her nose on her wet handkerchief.

It hit me with a jolt. She knew the secret. It wasn't over. We were still in danger!

"Oh dear God," I moaned.

Lucien's look of worry turned to a frown of confusion.

I reached for him. "Help me up."

He gently lifted me, his hands warm, and I put my feet on the floor. Someone had put my slippers out.

"I need a bath," I said. I could see Aleta sitting on her bed. I think she was smiling.

The rest of our things had been delivered from the villa, nicely searched then neatly packed, along with a note offering a boat ride to England for Vic, which was insulting. I hadn't noticed their arrival, sitting stacked in the center of our room.

Vic was in little better shape than me, lying in her bed as I dressed.

We had to leave. We had no time for grieving. We finally pulled her out of bed and down to dinner.

"He's almost certainly watching us," Aleta said as we sat.

"You know I can't go to England," I reminded Vic.

"I don't want to," Vic replied. "It was never my home. Da needs to go back to Edinburgh though. But I'd rather swim than accept anything from that man."

"We have to move soon," Lucien said. "He may be off balance now, but the more time he has to think, the more he'll prepare. Saint-Malo is a rail hub."

"Cross the bay and find a ride?" I asked.

"Yes. By train and then what we can find. Mail coach or riverboat."

"He'll know we've gone and he'll be searching," I said. "It will take forever that way. He'll have so much time to chase us."

"What else? Steal one of the boats out there?"

"We can't do that. That really would be stealing. Those are people's livelihoods."

"Then an airship. We need to get to an aerodrome."

"And pay them with what?" I asked.

"Pay them on delivery," Lucien replied.

"They don't know who we are," I said. I suppose, as a noble, Lucien always had good credit.

"They'll know you," Vic said, looking at me.

"Maybe, but that's no reason to trust me," I replied.

"We'll have to try," Lucien said.

"And do you know where there's an aerodrome?" I asked. "One with loose airships waiting to fly to another country? They'll want our passports when we land and they'll know who we are."

"I admit, it's risky."

"It's unlikely."

Meanwhile, the owner's wife was standing behind us with plates of food, watching us argue.

"Why don't you steal his boat?" she said. "You seemed to think you could before."

"We tried that," I moaned.

"But no one's on it now," she replied. "Take the bastard down a peg." Then she plunked down our plates.

Chapter 24 – On the Run

We had to leave Vic's father behind with just a note that we would telegraph instructions when we arrived in Belgium and that the coffin should be simple, but solid. The doctor had a bit of travelling to do still.

The row back was harder this time. I felt so many mixed feelings, fear, depression, exhaustion, and anger. It made it twice as hard to do anything. I was exhausted when we finally bumped the side of the Cécile and we still had to haul our trunks up on deck and down below.

I turned on the galley light expecting it to be awash in blood, but it had been cleaned. We found no sign of the violence except a ragged bullet hole in the base of the paneling next to the sink.

Vic let out a little wail halfway down the ladder and dropped her suitcase. I held out my arms and she fell into them, both of us crying.

The memory of that night was too fresh and we were too exhausted for control.

"Aleta," Lucien said. "Help me with the engine."

"Yes," she sighed and then they headed below.

I helped Vic down off the ladder and onto a sofa where we cried for a bit, until the engine started and Lucien came back up.

"Cali, I need your help."

"What?"

"I started it, but I can't make it go."

"You need to engage the prop, set the gear," I replied, remembering the Nellie Thomson.

"The gear," Lucien replied flatly.

"We aren't going anywhere," I replied. "Until we weigh anchor and someone's at the wheel."

"Weigh anchor," Lucien mumbled. "I can do that, I think. Cali, this is nothing like any ship I've seen."

"I've never seen one with a diesel motor," I said, trying to smile.

"They're easy. I pushed the start button," he replied with a shrug.

"Well then, push the weigh anchor button."

That got a twitch of a smile, "That might work." And he trotted forward.

"Aleta," I said. "The helm?"

"Me, really?" First a zeppelin, and now a ship.

"Yup."

"Aye aye!" and she was up the ladder.

Then it was my turn.

Down in the hold, Lucien had left the light on. The engine was there, plain in the bulb light, making smells and noise. I could hear the anchor, its electric winch clanking away, which meant it was my turn.

The gearbox was still where I'd last seen it, the big lever sticking up abaft of the rear mast step. But when I pulled it, it only ground the gears, which was wrong. Down next to it was a steel pedal, clearly meant to be pressed with your foot. It had to be the clutch so I applied pressure and pushed the lever to one, which I hoped was the biggest slowest gear.

The gears meshed with a thunk and when I lifted off the pedal, it stayed. I could hear the propeller shaft turning in its channel.

Then it was back up top, to the helm. Aleta was doing well avoiding boats and we were making reasonable headway through the harbor, but it would be different when we made open water and had to put out sail. Since Aleta was doing so well, I ran back below decks to find the controls for the sail winches. I hoped they were as simple as the others. They were, up and down. Really, given enough fuel anyone could run this boat. A sobering thought for a sailor.

How much fuel did we have? It was back down to the engines, running into Lucien in the galley.

"Did you see where they keep the fuel?" I asked him.

"No," he replied.

"Let's find it."

It was in a big tank attached to the engine, next to the big spinning metal wheel, and judging by the glass tube we had a quarter of a tank. That probably wasn't much.

"They must have more fuel," I said, but just then I felt the deck shift. We were hitting swells. I groaned, "But I have to go up top."

"I'll look," Lucien said.

"No, I'll need you to help with the sails." The deck rolled under our feet, despite our keel. "We need to hurry."

It was Lucien's turn to groan. "She's hitting the troughs."

Up on deck, judging the wind, waves and Granville lighthouse, I set a new course and then Lucien and I tore at the sail lashings, but it took forever. There were only the two of us and her booms were huge.

"Aleta!" I yelled over the wind. "Tie off the wheel."

Once we'd raised them, we were going to have to swing them. Vic was no use, so the three of us were going to have to swing them by ourselves. They had no electric motors for that.

Down below I cursed that I hadn't watched the crew when they raised them. She was bermuda rigged and simple so I picked the fore gaff to start. That part was easy. I just pushed to top button on the mast control box and up she went. I held the button until the ratchet on the winch started to clank.

Up top she caught the wind, but was hardly trim, flapping loose in the wind, so we let go the preventer and eased the boom across until she caught properly and snapped taut. We were already out racing the engine! She was that amazing. So it was back down to disengage the gearbox, then over to the aft gaff to do the same. Then

I raced back up only to find Lucien at the wheel making course corrections. We were underway.

We decided to raise two jibs before shutting down the motor, leaving only the galley light on to drain the batteries. None of us were sure how long they would last, nor did we have any idea how to start the engine without them. We'd save what fuel we had to charge the batteries each day, at least for a bit.

I was sitting with Vic. She started sobbing into my shoulder, which of course got me going again, while Lucien sat in the chartroom working on our course. There were obstacles all the way up the coast with no clear water until we rounded Cape de Hague, which we made at dawn. After that it was straight up the channel, two days to Ostend.

We were all so tired. Lucien offered to take the first watch if I made coffee, which wasn't hard. Then we found beds and slept.

"Cali?"

We were underway, but this wasn't my cabin, and sunlight? Where was I?

"Cali?" It was Lucien.

Then I remembered, my feet hitting the deck before my mind had caught up. Lucien was standing at the cabin door with an amused smile.

"It's dawn," he said. "We're near the cape. We'll need all hands for the course change."

"I'll get Aleta." We were nearing the channel. There had to be traffic, and he needed to be up top.

I debated waking Vic as I woke Aleta. We really could use the help. But then again, she really needed time.

I finally did wake her. She made breakfast.

We sailed up the channel, Lucien, Aleta, and I taking turns at watch, making sure one of us was awake when Aleta had the helm. That didn't leave Lucien and me much time to be together. It always seemed to be like that with us. The world never seemed to let us alone. But I made a point of waking early on our second day, the air cold in morning darkness, and climbed up on deck.

It had rained and he was in his coat, with everything wet. The sky was cloudy, threatening more.

"You should be asleep," he said.

"I can't," I lied. It was cold and pitch black. We kept the lights off to conserve battery. Just a bow lantern. I could just see his outline from the binnacle light, standing at the wheel. The light from a lighthouse danced in the water to our starboard.

"Which one is that?" I asked.

"*Boulongne-sur-Mer*," he replied.

"Almost to the border." I felt awkward. I didn't know what to say! I was glad he couldn't see me roll my eyes. I'm so stupid sometimes.

I sat down on the starboard bench, the sea surging at my back. In the dim light I could see him shift. I think he was shy too.

"What do we do when we make port?" I asked.

"Catch a train home. We'll help Vic with the funeral, but I'll need to find a patent lawyer for her first. She won't be safe on the islands until they're secure."

"Can you take me dancing? We never got to waltz."

I could hear a smile in his voice. "No. We didn't. It would be . . ." and then he was at a loss for words for a moment. "I was a fool not to have pulled you off the train in Lamballe. All of this be damned. We could have headed south and had a holiday."

Now he was being silly. "It's too dark and wet for a holiday."

"Not for dancing, but we won't have time when we hit port. I'll need to cable for assistance, and we may have to answer for the boat."

"We can't dance here," I sighed.

I could see him tie off the wheel before he sat down next to me. I could feel his warmth despite our coats.

"We could wake Aleta. She could take the wheel."

I was going to say that that would be selfish, but he was kissing me. His lips and breath warm in the cold wind.

And if you think I'm going to tell you any more, you are sadly mistaken, but can you see my smile?

Cali's Songs

Most of Cali`s music and any other songs mentioned in these pages are available on YouTube. Below is a list of suggested search terms and a few specific examples, although many more exist.

Violin Sonata No. 1 – Camille Saint-Saëns

Blind Tom – Brilliant Quartet

Sonata for Piano and Violin – Joseph Haydn

Nocturne for Piano and Violin – Frédéric Chopin

Six Etudes de Concert, Op.16 - Henri Vieuxtemps

Toss the Feathers – I suggest perhaps The Corrs

The Wild Maid

Bach Sonata for Solo Violin No. 1 – Johann Sebastian Bach

Chaconne for Violin and Orchestra – Tomaso Antonio Vitali, I suggest the version by Zino Francescatti

Turn the page for a preview
of Mark Bondurant's next
Calista Antoine adventure . . .

Paris!

Available June 2018 from
Bongo Books

(Sorry for the delay, but I
moved to Alaska)

Chapter 1 – Brussels

"Absolutely not!"

We sat with our instrument cases in a paneled, well carpeted office, in front of a large wood desk, behind which sat an elderly man with spectacles. Behind him stood a tall thin man, looking down his long nose at us. The man at the desk's accented English was terrible. He rarely looked at us, but when he did he squinted. He clearly felt our presence was unpleasant.

"We a telegram sent to you. Told you not come. Told you!"

"Clearly you sent it after we left," Aleta replied. "We received no telegrams."

"This is not important. You will not attend," he finished at the end of his breath. Breathing in, clearly wanting to reach for his cigarette, he finished, "The scandal. The endowment. Our reputation is not worth this. Or our standing." Then he hammered in the last nail in the coffin lid. "Accepting street musicians," he hissed. "Against it I was. And now the news. Your female," and he trailed away.

He looked up at his friend and they jabbered until they came to an agreement.

"Proclivities!" he huffed. "Your immoral behavior of the royal family. How could you coming here think?"

I was sitting there in shock, but Aleta lit into him, "You have no idea what happened! What we've gone through for the sake of Belgium," she yelled. "What you did to us!"

But he didn't care. "It is best. You leave now must. Go to Germany back."

But Aleta was on her feet, hands on his desk.

"We have no connection to Germany."

"I care not your plans. It will not happen here."

"We gave you the patents for cordite!"

"Leave."

I leapt up and grabbed her, pulling her back. I think she was about to go for his throat.

"Be thankful. We could the airfare repayment ask," he continued. Of course they didn't offer to pay our return fare!

"You have no idea what you're doing," Aleta yelled. That ended in a sob. I pulled her back towards the door. This was Aleta's one big chance in life vanishing in a puff of smoke.

"No!" she sobbed.

They looked smug.

We'd been offered a scholarship to the Royal Conservatory of Brussels to study music and had spent a harrowing three weeks crossing the Atlantic in a sabotaged zeppelin full of spies. We'd barely made it across only to be kidnapped by Gustav Rothschild, possibly the richest man in the world. Everyone had been after Dr. Dewar's discovery, cordite. A revolutionary artillery propellant.

He died during the crossing, but his daughter Vic had his notes and understood them too. Lucien, the Duke of Tervuren, my beau, helped us escape and led her to lawyers. They helped her file pending patents, contracts, and found her an apartment in Brussels three blocks from the palace. She had a new dual British and Belgian citizenship, or she would when her new passport arrived. The crown was very pleased with her, but apparently not with Aleta and me.

I expected it. The Prince would have to admit he been wrong. The British made up stories about us to cover their failure and Belgium was going along with it, something they exceled at. But I hadn't expect it to extend to our school. Coming from America, I didn't yet understand just how much the aristocracy controlled every level of society. At least they hadn't arrested me. The English would love to get their hands on me. A quick show trial was what they wanted.

We were staying with Vic, who was only two blocks away from the conservatory which, naturally, was close to the palace. We just moved in – and I had my own room! The apartment came furnished and we had barely begun to explore. There were cupboards with linins, clocks to be wound, candles, and paintings to eye. There was no place to cook. We didn't know how to turn on the gas anyway and we had no wood, so it was dark and cold and Lucien couldn't help. He had been called away.

Oh! But he took me dancing! We waltzed. He bought me a new dress just for to go dancing in. And we polkaed too. It was so fun! But I'm digressing again. I suppose it's because I don't want to talk about this part.

The day started with such optimism. We were going to report to school and start our new lives. We had breakfast downstairs, outside at a café in the Grand Sablon, which is halfway between a street and a square. We were wearing nice dresses, with corsets, coats, bustles, and horrible hats. We were definitely not wearing our spy dresses. Then Vic had the doorman find her a carriage and left for the lawyers. Brussels doesn't have steam or cable trollies, but the streets are cobbled. The sweeps are very diligent, practically walking behind the horses, so everything is very clean. We were left to walk to the conservatory, which was around the corner past the cathedral.

And as you know, it didn't end well.

Paris!

Poor Aleta cried all the way back, and it was raining too! We had no umbrellas. People stared, but we ignored them. I was so worried about her that I didn't think about it myself until later. We climbed the stairs, the doorman asking if we needed help. At least I think that's what he said. Everyone in Brussels speaks Dutch or in a pinch, French. Aleta's German and Spanish were still useless, except at court of course where they all speak German. But it was highly unlikely we would be allowed near there.

Upstairs we flopped down on couches in abject misery. We were alone. This was what Pa had meant by getting me to transfer money for contingencies. At least we weren't poor. I had over seven thousand francs in cash – goldmarks, Belgian francs, French francs, and pesetas in my new purse. Aleta too. Most if it came from Lufthansa as payment for our hurts and trouble. And I had my bank account I transferred from home. I meant to go to the bank once we were settled.

I looked over at Aleta. She was laying on the couch across from me. They'd put a table between them, which seemed silly. You had to lean forward, practically getting up to reach it. She started crying again.

"We'll find another school," I said.

"How will I pay for it?"

"I don't know. We don't know how much they cost."

"I don't have any schooling. I can't read music. I don't know any classical music."

"We'll work on that."

Then she took up sobbing again. I felt so bad.

Eventually I got up and took off my wet dress and moved to my bed, laying there in the gray afternoon light. It was all too much. It seemed that the Congo would follow me for the rest of my life.

When Vic came in we had to go through it all again. It was her turn to be outraged. She came back with someone to turn on the gas. I had to hide because I was in my night dress, but we would have light and hot water that night. It would be a complicated evening as we had only one tub, but we really had nothing else to do. At least we didn't have to heat the water on the stove. When we finally adjourned downstairs for dinner and she told us all the news.

Paris!

We were going to have servants. She was going to an agency tomorrow. They wanted to teach her Dutch as well, but she insisted on French. Dutch is useless outside of Flanders and she still wanted to move someplace warm. Aleta wanted to learn too, which wouldn't be a problem since her tutor was coming to the apartment. I think Aleta wanted to go someplace warm as well. I couldn't blame her. I just wanted to see Lucien, but he was gone and I had no idea when he would be coming back.

Lastly, Vic was going to see the king. She insisted she was going to plead my case even though I told her not too. I couldn't see any way for them to back down. It would only cause trouble and embarrassment. It might even prod them into arresting me.

No, your poor Cali was completely at a loss. She went to bed early not knowing what to do, which isn't hard when you're deeply depressed.

Our new help arrived on our fourth day, the morning after Vic went to the agency. Aleta and I shared a maid, my first. It came as a complete surprise. Her name was Sarah and she barely spoke English, but she did speak French. She was a nice girl with blond hair and pale round face, about my age, but I couldn't get her to be friends, which was vexing. She kept calling me ma'am even though I wasn't older.

"I'm keeping my bodices in that drawer."

"Yes ma'am."

"No don't put that there. I'll never find them," I said. As if I was supposed to! She was in charge of all of this. I had no idea.

"Please don't call me ma'am," I added looking at her with concern.

"Malady?"

"Cali."

"Yes Cali."

"Oh. That doesn't sound right."

I caught a ghost of a smile.

Looking back I realize that she was very patient with me. I had no understanding. She lit the fire and put out my clothes, helped me with my corset, and shoes. She wanted me to buy more dresses, but that could wait for Lucien. Trying on dresses in front of Lucien is fun.

Apparently the downstairs part of the building was where the servants lived. They moved in. That's where the kitchens were too. We had no idea. And we weren't supposed to go there! The doorman works for Vic as well. He came with the building. We didn't know. Even Vic! She had a staff of eight. Apparently she was now very rich.

I got a letter from Lucien. He was reviewing the work on the king's palace at Laeken. Apparently it burned up. He missed me! Unfortunately, I had no way to write him back as he was living in temporary housing of some sort and he wasn't expecting to be there long. I think he was living in a tent. I did write Grandpa, airmail, to tell him our address and received a letter back a week later, again airmail, telling me Ma and Pa were still at sea. He was amused once he knew I was alright and wanted to know everything.

Brussels is boring. I now understand what M. Marmontel meant about it being "stuffy." We visited the cathedral, which seemed kind of small and plain, thus said Cali the critic of cathedrals. But really, it was. We went to the parks, but they were just trees and benches. And then the art museum, which wasn't nearly as interesting as the one I saw in France. We looked at the palace, but as you might guess, it was much like the rest. There was nothing to do when it wasn't raining but walk and try to explore. Walk in my corset and awful shoes. Eight weeks ago I'd been able to skip down the street in my school uniform. Life was pretty bleak until I found the music store on High Street. Don't look at me like that. It was Hoogstraat. I'm not completely ignorant. I was picking up Dutch.

Aleta and I were working on her reading music, which was why the music store was a godsend. The owner had instruments too. I finally got my bow rehaired. All he had for violin and flute was Vivaldi which, except for having to adapt it a bit, wasn't terribly challenging. It took some thumbing through the pages to find something fun.

So life was pretty boring with us just sitting about listening to tutors or practicing. That is until Vic went on her visit to the palace.

She had a new dress made just for the occasion and they came for her in a gold carriage with men in livery and horses with feathers.

Oh, and I received another letter from Lucien. He was in Ghent negotiating with the Bishop. It's always been like this. They never leave him any time. This time though I had an address and I wrote him. And how do you mail a letter in Belgium? I have no idea. You give it to a servant and it just disappears. I've always found not knowing to be very uncomfortable.

Two hours later Vic stomped in through the front door. She had walked home. I told her not to try. The queen had actually yelled at her.

Two days later I received an anonymous letter, although I was pretty sure who sent it. It contained ten thousand francs and two zeppelin tickets to Boston leaving in two weeks. The hand written note in French said:

This is for expenses. I'm deeply sorry for all of this.
    L.

Vic shocked, asked, "From Lucien!?"
"No," I replied with a laugh. "It's from Leopold."
"The king?"
"No, his son. The one I told you about."
"I don't want to go back to Boston," Aleta moaned.
"I don't want to accept anything from him," I replied, but I wasn't sure what to do.
"What a cretin," Vic observed.
I laughed again because it was the truth.
Vic looked at me and then added, "I could think of a lot worse." Which got us all laughing.

But I really didn't know what to do. As my smile died away, I just stared at the tickets. I couldn't leave Lucien, but I think that's what they wanted me to do. They were trying to buy me off.

"Cali," Aleta said, carefully. "Maybe we should try for Paris. You have so many offers there." I think Aleta was worried that I would leave her or perhaps drag her to Boston. Would she leave if I went back?

"Maybe," I said. "But it's so far from Lucien."

"You could write M. Marmontel. Maybe he has advice."

"That's a good idea, but what's wrong with Boston?"

"The war. I'd never make any money. There's too much competition and too little pocket change."

"True, but you like Chinese food."

"True too, but I bet they have it in Paris. And more."

"Brussels –is- a bit boring," I said wistfully. Then I added, "We could go to Paris anyway." Which got a smile out of her.

"Now I want to go to," Vic whined.

So I wrote M. Marmontel. Then I fretted about it. I didn't want to be that far from Lucien, not that he wasn't far away already. At least in Brussels he had a chance of visiting.

I was sitting on my bed with my violin case on my lap, thinking about working on Saint-Saëns when Sarah timidly asked me a question.

"Pardon miss."

I looked up at her, "Yes?"

"If you don't mind, when are we going to Paris?"

"Going to Paris?"

"Yes miss. I need to make plans. We'll have packing and travel arrangements. The cook needs to plan for meals."

"We haven't decided yet," I replied. I hadn't thought of what would happen to the servants if we left. Clearly, I had to talk to Vic about it. And how did they know?

I caught Vic in her room.

"I have no idea," she replied. "I don't know what happens if I go away. I'll ask M. Deprez."

"M. Deprez?"

"My lawyer. I'm seeing him tomorrow."

M. Deprez requested that Vic not take any vacations until at least the start of March. He would be needing signatures as he crafted business contracts and set up accounts. Vic had new business interests all over the world.

If she left, the servants would stay behind with the house, except for her maid, and await her return, that is unless she wanted to close the house and take them with her. Some people did that when they went to Italy or Southern France in the winter. But then they rented entire villas, or even owned them! The alternative was to dismiss them, which could be a hardship. It was that European class thing! It had Vic trapped, and might even trap us too. Another reason to leave. It didn't occur to me that if I married Lucien, I'd be caught in it even tighter than poor Vic.

So we decided that rather than sitting around Brussels we would try to find a school in Paris. We would come back if we failed or Vic could follow when she could. We would trade our Lufthansa tickets in for tickets to Paris. And then, naturally, there was an explosion.

Vic had just left for the lawyer's and we had just gotten our instruments from our rooms to work on Vivaldi. We hadn't even taken the out yet when the windows burst in and the building jumped. I was on the floor under a painting that had come off the wall. There was screaming, but I think it was from outside.

Those pictures are a lot heavier than you might think, especially if a table and vase follows it down. I had to crawl out from under it. The room was a mess.

"Aleta?"

"Cali," she moaned. "What happened?"

I didn't know. I stood up. Aleta's chair had been knocked over backward with her still sitting in it. She had to roll to the side to get her dress clear of it.

"Vic," she said.

"No!" I ran to a window. Below, the street was a mess. They were pulling people out of the café. The screaming was coming from one of the carriage horses, the other dead. The carriage itself was spread about the street. Aleta stood beside me cursing. We ran for the stairs.

Most of the house staff were already there, some kneeling next to a figure laying on the front steps. It was Vic.

"Vic!" I wailed and ran to her. Part of head was crushed in. She had hit a wall. I could see blood darkening her dress, but none flowing.

"She's dead ma'am," someone said.

"No." I was sobbing. "Damn them, damn them," I repeated, as I sat curled up on my knees next to her. This was their revenge. The

Paris!

British had to have the last word. I should have thought. I could have known. They'd waited until her patents were public record but not yet granted. She had no heirs and no will. It was now free knowledge for the world to use as it saw fit.

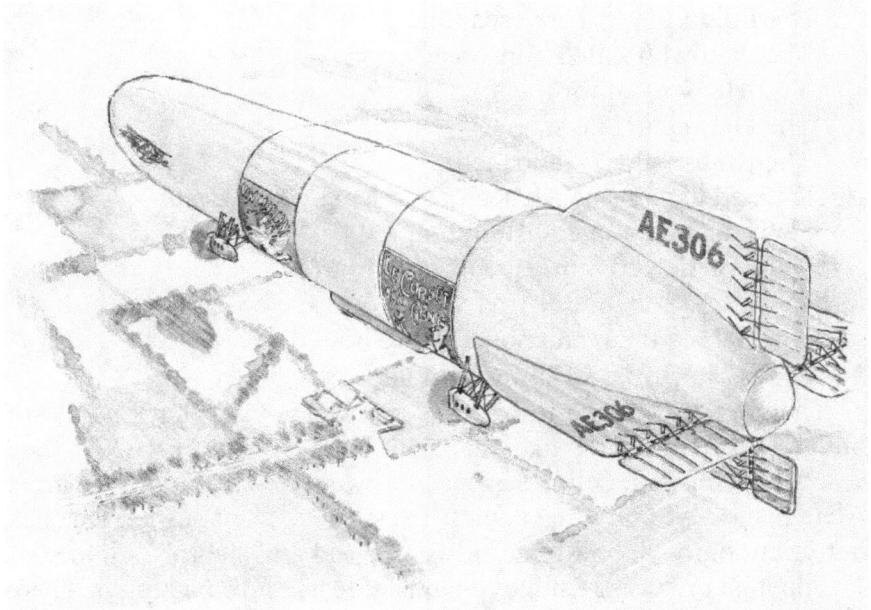

Chapter 2 – A Punctuation Point

The police, naturally, arrested me. After all, I'm the infamous Rabbit. I'm the cause for all the world's woes, especially the ones caused by the British. They picked me up off the ground, still crying and literally tossed me in the back of a van. I was handcuffed and pushed into a corner by two rough men. Thankfully they left Aleta behind.

"And why are you in Belgium?"

"To go to school," I replied. I'd already told them at least six times.

"I thought you were here to take care the Dewars."

"They wanted to get to Belgium."

"Victoria died."

"They killed her."

"Her father died as well."

"It was an accident." I was so tired. They'd been at me all day with no meals and little water."

"You told him to go on that boat."

"No. I didn't. We were escaping."

"The man who killed him was German."

"Yes. He worked for them."

"The Germans?" he snapped.

"The Rothschilds," I moaned.

He hated that answer. It seemed to leave a bad taste.

"He wanted to come to Belgium."

"And you helped him. He and Victoria."

"Yes."

"You helped them and now they're both dead."

"It was the British. The Institution."

That answer seemed to leave even a worse taste, but I wouldn't budge. We carried on like this until long after dark, when they "escorted" me to a cell. I suppose he wanted to go home. At least Aleta had my violin. They couldn't destroy it. They pushed me back onto a cot onto which I gratefully collapsed and slept. No dinner.

I opened my eyes past the remains of tears and a bad night. There crouching in front of me with a look of concern was Lucien.

"I always seem to find you in trouble," he said, attempting to smile.

"I don't ask for it," I mumbled. My mouth was so dry.

He could see my predicament and stood to get the cup and pitcher they left on the shelf above the chamber pot. He looked at it and frowned, then sniffed the water.

"Get her fresh water," he said to the guard.

"Sir."

He returned with a fresh cup and pitcher. I drank it greedily, then rubbed some on my eyes.

"They killed Vic," I said, my voice dead.

"I should have set guards at the door."

"I think they kept you away," I replied.

"Perhaps." He sounded tired too. "It's an unpleasant thought."

"We have to leave. We're going to Paris."

He said nothing for a moment. "Can you stand?"

I felt terrible, but that got a snort out of me, and I got up with a groan.

He was thinking. "It will be harder for me to help you there."

"They're not in the pocket of the British."

"Cali. I'm sorry I started this."

That surprised me, mostly because it was so wrong.

"You didn't start it. I did. I sent us to the Congo. It was my bright idea."

"I put you on that zeppelin." He put me there to help Vic.

"We were only trying to help," I said, half to myself.

Max had warned me. The British Foreign Office wanted this all cleaned up. This was just another correction. I was destined to be another. Somewhere soon there would be an anarchist or an accident waiting for me.

We were walking through the jail hallways. No gendarmes to be seen. Looking down at my dress I could see that it was hopeless.

"Another one gone," I said. "I can't seem to keep clothes." Spooky, tall tales, bloody, now prison Cali, I thought.

"Were they difficult?"

"I'm getting used to it," I replied. He winced.

We walked past the desk. I didn't have to sign anything. Outside I blinked at the sunlight, a rare occurrence in winter Belgium. He had a carriage waiting, which I fell into. Then we clopped back to Vic's.

Of the original thirty eight passengers and crew that left with the Bremen on October 14th, only fourteen lived to see the Christmas of 1892. I need to add Éléonore to the list. She died on the operating table as they tried to fix her hip. So many of us died on that voyage. We kept on dying long after it was over.

We stopped on the way to Vic's and had a late breakfast, but I'm afraid I wasn't the best of company despite my having not seen Lucien in almost a month. It wasn't just grief. I felt a deep unresolvable anger. Vic had done Britain no harm. She held no malice towards anyone. It had been pure spite on their part. An example. Examples are the last resort of the small minded.

The servants had left except for Sarah. Gone. Back to the agency. The front of the house was scarred by broken windows and loose and scattered brick. The front door lay on the floor in the hallway, the house open to the street. The gendarme guarding the house saluted. I ignored the blood as we stepped through.

We found Aleta pacing upstairs.

"Finally," she said when I walked in. "They let you go."

"Yes," I sighed.

"Aleta. It's good to see you alive," Lucien said.

"Lucien," she sighed. "I'm better off than Cali."

"Yes," he agreed. "She needs a bath and some rest. Do you still have hot water?"

Aleta nodded.

"I've had Jacobse removed from the case and the case itself closed." Then he looked at Sarah, "Who is this?"

She curtsied and replied eyes down, "Sarah, milord."

"I think she's my maid," I replied.

Lucien seemed to shrug and moved on to asking about the state of the house and our place in it. It struck me that he seemed to take Sarah for granted, but really we knew nothing about her. It was a big blind spot. Were all the upper class like this?

In my room, Sarah helped me out of my dress and into the tub, which was gloriously hot. I soaked the jail out of my bones. I even washed my hair. Sarah laid out a dress for me. She'd been packing.

"Sarah," I said, when I came in from the tub. "You work for Vic, not me."

"Not any more miss. I could use work." She gave me another of those infuriating curtsies that I'd yet to manage properly. Then I realized that she was asking me for a job. Me!

"Sarah, you don't know who I am."

"Oh but I do. We all did. You're the Rabbit."

"Then you know you could get killed." I shuttered as I thought of the bomb. I didn't even know the doorman's name.

"Oh, I know, ma'am."

I squinted at her. She seemed to relish the thought. I walked to the door and called, "Lucien. I need some help."

He stared at me for a second in a daze. It was my night robe. I guess he liked it. He helped me buy it.

"Is there a problem?"

"Sarah wants to be my maid."

He looked at Sarah, I think for the first time.

She looked back with angst.

Then he looked at me. "Cali. You want me to make this decision for you?"

14

Oh! Lucien, you are worse than Pa.

"Honestly, miss," she pleaded. "I want the position."

"What do maids earn?" I asked Lucien. Perhaps I couldn't afford her. But apparently they earn very little. About two thousand dollars a year, fourteen thousand francs. I had that much in my purse. Of course it's far more than that because I would have to clothe, house, and feed her. She'd need airfare to Paris. And I had no income, although people did seem to be constantly thrusting money into my hands. But that was to make up for their trying to kill me!

"I can't Sarah. I have no income and we want to go to music school and we're going to have to pay for it. And they may call me the Rabbit, but I'm not really a spy. If I was, I'd have money and protection. I've just made some bad enemies."

"I'll work for free," she replied.

She was desperate. She was crazy. We all looked at her.

"Please," she begged.

Lucien rolled his eyes. "I'll hire her."

"Lucien?" I asked.

"Really?" Aleta added, a little incredulous. I think she liked having a maid.

"Then you'll have to stay in touch," he said with a smile.

We had a chance to bargain. My inner merchant leapt up. "Then you should pay her more. She'll be in danger." I knew this was pocket change for him.

"And she'll have more to deal with than a normal maid," Aleta added.

He was halfway between a frown and a laugh.

We settled on twenty four thousand francs and I realized that I might not have to pay for airfare either. I could cash in the prince's Lufthansa tickets. They had to cover three tickets to Paris. For once it was all going to work out.

"Lucien? How do I find Lufthansa?"

He frowned. He was wondering what I was up to. I think he caught on to that fairly quickly. It's strange, but I think that was one of the things he liked about me.

The next morning, at breakfast, we saw the papers. They said the explosion was the work of anarchists. It had been covered up.

Paris!

We spent the next two weeks at the Hotel Metropole. It wasn't far and it was brand new. It even had electricity. Lucien booked two adjoining double suites, picked a room, walked in and fell asleep. He'd been up for two days.

I wasn't much better. I picked the next. It was so romantic. When I woke, I remembered and cried. It was late afternoon. It took supreme effort of will to make myself get up. I was becoming so familiar with these things. Familiar with police interrogations, the sight of blood, the sound of guns and explosions, and the worst of all, the death of friends. Heavy in melancholy I stumbled back from our bathroom towards bed. Aleta followed along trying to entice me into eating food. Halfway back I realized she was right. I'd had as many meals in the last two days, but I didn't feel it. Just a dead numbness.

"I'll eat," I said.

It helped, but I still went back to bed. I won't kid you. There were times back then when I thought seriously of suicide. But fear not. Paris is coming soon and for a time, all will be right. Just wait.

I woke again at six in tears. Vic had been there trying to console me. Her arms had been warm. She made sure if it. She had put that extra effort in for me even though it hurt her.

Lucien was up when I woke and we had dinner downstairs.

Sarah couldn't come with us! Apparently she shouldn't even be sleeping in the room with us, which is crazy. The hotel had a special section for servants with their own place to eat. Sarah claimed not to mind. In fact, she seemed strangely eager to get down there.

Our hotel restaurant was lovely, the ceiling all painted and hung with chandeliers. I was down to one dress again. That is unless I wanted to go formal or wear my spy dresses. The spy dresses would announce the presence of the Rabbit to the press, which was something we wanted to avoid. It might even get us thrown out of the hotel. Not that we hadn't already been identified. If we had looked, we would have seen that the Rabbit was again in the papers.

Lucien took time off. I think he was as bitter as me and I'm not really sure if he actually asked for it. We both suspected that the Belgian Sûreté and perhaps even the crown had been involved.

We picked a day that promised sunshine and took a car out of town for a picnic. I would like to say that the outskirts of Brussels were an adventure, but it was mostly tenements and factories. I supposed we were living in the much nicer center of town. Eventually, it gave way to sweet fields of hay nestled between woods and fences. Hay is soft when it's under a blanket and the sun warm, even in fall, when you're nestled within. Rain though, drove us back to the car and its leather top where we snuggled in our wet clothes under our blanket. We sipped wine and ate sandwiches packed for us by the hotel. These were the moments that kept me alive back then.

Lucien does nothing without reason. He and Sarah seemed to have an understanding. She was bent on teaching me how to behave around servants. It's very hard to let go when you've been raised to do when you see things that need doing. The only time she relented and joined us was when we included her in our self-defense practice. We moved the furniture back to make room, Sarah making sure the hotel staff didn't put it back.

Those two weeks until our zeppelin flight were two of the most beautiful of my life. Lucien worked to bring me back to life. He took me to salons, stores, and dance halls. I deposited my Goldmarks and transferred half my money to the Bank of France.

We visited Duchess Baudouin! She huffed when she got up to move about even without her corset and finery. It was good to see her again and to know she had escaped. So many others didn't.

"My dear, how can you have lost weight?" She asked as I sat.

"I guess I've been a bit busy." Looking down, I asked, "Do I look bad?"

"No," she smiled. "It's raw jealously. I hope you don't mind while I look you over."

I must have looked surprised because she added, "I'm looking for scars."

I grinned. "It really is amazing isn't it? I'm surprised myself."

She laughed. A deep gurgling thing. "It's your youth. I'm sure I wouldn't have made it out of the palace grounds."

"I had help."

She glanced at Lucien. "I'd need a wheel barrel and two strong men."

"You could have shot while they pushed."

She laughed again. "That would have been a sight." Then she

looked up. "Oh good. Here's the tea."

They put the trays down on the table.

"Try the orange ones. My doctor has forbidden me from eating these things, so naturally I stocked up in case they cut me off."

I do love her. We carried on like that for an hour. I think she was a surrogate mother to Lucien. I caught her eying me curiously occasionally, taking inventory I think. Or perhaps she was assessing the damage I would cause. She told me Omama has escaped as well, along with her evil assistants. They were in Brussels too. Before we left I had to promise to visit again but it would be a long time before I came back.

The day before we left for Paris, I received a letter from M. Marmontel telling us he would be delighted to have a visit, which was a huge relief. I had little hope of friendly advice in Paris without him.

Did you know that Zeppelins are life's punctuation marks? They represent endings and beginnings, leaving one place and moving on to another. The world that you knew is left behind and shortly an entirely new one unfolds before you. They are not to be treated casually. Our world ended two weeks later at the Brussels Aerodrome. The next would be a new, different place.

I couldn't hold back the tears as they were calling for us to board. It's like we had grown roots that tore and hurt as we pulled apart. I could see tears in Lucien's eyes, damn the British for making us go. He promised to follow soon.

With Lucien at my back, we boarded. We looked around as we climbed in through the side door. There were spartan wood seats in long rows, windows, and nothing else. Huh?

"It's what you get when you fly small-hub carriers," Aleta shrugged. "We're lucky to not have to sit next to livestock."

We were flying Aero Europa, an Italian firm. The best we could find on short notice. Apparently they went for maximum profit and that meant maximum bodies packed under the minimum envelope. We sat in our thinly padded seats elbow to elbow. Aleta got the window, Sarah and I the aisle. The whole cabin turned breezy each time the crew opened the hatch to go up top or someone opened the head door.

We flew much lower and much slower, individual details such as cows and wagons were clearly visible below us. I had an elderly French woman next to me.

"You play the violin?" she asked. I was holding my case, having refused to check it.

"Yes."

"My son is learning, but he's very head strong and doesn't practice."

"I can understand that. It can be hard to practice sometimes."

"I tell him you must practice to learn, but he says he doesn't want to learn." She looked about. "I don't think you could practice in here."

"I don't think I could open my case, let alone draw my bow."

Which got a guffaw.

That was what it was like. It wasn't just the hard seat that kept me squirming. But all flights end – eventually. Ours took four long hours and when the breeze wasn't blowing through the cabin, I was too warm in my coat, but couldn't find room to take it off.

Paris Aerodrome is amazing. We came in under gray skies, threading our way through a maze of airships. Looking past my seatmate, I got a glimpse of the Eifel Tower through the window as she told me all about her little dog Philippe. It was the first time I'd actually landed successfully in an airship. It's a lot like the Liberté, the ship that rescued us. You get winched down by a big steam winch, pulled down until you're close enough to the ground for them to lash you down to huge buried concrete blocks. But instead of a swaying ladder and a pitching deck, you get pleasant level steps.

In Paris they take you in big steam cars that carry twenty passengers each to and from the carrier terminals, and then cable trolleys that take you to the aerodrome train station.

Porters helped us with our baggage onto the trolley. Sarah watched them carefully to make sure we had no mistakes. It's something you should remember when flying second class carriers. They can be quite careless. The floor of the Aero Europa terminal itself was littered with cigarette butts and candy wrapping. Soot gathered under the seats. Their windows were covered with hand and nose prints. This was definitely not Lufthansa. But our cable trolley was clean, though open to the cold wind. It had a roof though and we sat enclosed without fear for our dresses, as it was raining.

We rolled through endless meadow grazed low by wandering sheep. Above us, mixed with the clouds was a forest of cables and airships, painted in bewildering mix of colors, sporting flags and advertisements.

Perhaps it's because of the rain that women wear such big hats in Paris. It can't be because of the wind which constantly threatens to sweep them off. We rolled in to the trolley wing of the train station as the rain really started rattling down, battering the glass and iron roof above us. It was fascinating. It made me think of Gustav's skylight in the kitchen on the Octave. That had to be crazy fun during storms. The station ironwork was beautiful, cast to look like plants and trees.

Sarah had our luggage checked, keeping the chit. The trolley wing led in to a main gallery with buildings actually inside under the station roof! It was past lunch and we were hungry, so we picked a café, its tables spread out across the marble floor under seemingly unnecessary umbrellas. As we sat though, I noticed pigeons begging despite our being indoors, perhaps explaining why they had them. We were surrounded by sound. The roar of a thousand conversations and thousands of shuffling feet. Our eyes darted this way and that, trying to see it all.

Aleta laughed, "I never got to come in here."

"Never?"

"We were always busy with maintenance. And catching up on sleep."

I was looking at the card. "What are you going to get?"

"I was thinking croque-monsieur. It's all I recognize," she replied

"Hmmm, miss," Sarah voice tinged with disapproval. "I suggest the sole."

"Really?" Aleta asked.

"Yes. croque-monsieur is for the lower classes. I'm surprised it's on the menu. I suppose they must cater to all sorts. I suggest white wine as well."

We smiled. This had become a running joke with us. It was her lessons in upper class etiquette. The sole was good though. We finished with coffee.

Sarah purchased tickets. She now controlled the money although I had no idea where it was coming from. She dealt with the luggage too, then she pulled us along to the platforms, which were in a separate building. We got to them by going up sweeping marble steps and through revolving doors, which are a hoot. You could just keep on going around and around. Honestly though – I didn't. But I might have if Sarah weren't there.

The train platform building had a great arching ceiling open at both ends, with the trains sliding in beneath. We stood on a bridge that let you walk between platforms over the tops of the trains, their steam flaring around you from beneath as they passed. But I should warn you that before you go anywhere in these sorts of terminals, you must first opened your umbrella. Sooty water drips down from the roof. It's best not to linger on the platforms if you value your clothing as well. Luckily, trains left for Paris every few minutes. We had no reason to linger. Ours was a very nice one too. They built a blue and gold shell over the engine so it fit with the rest of the cars and to make it look less forbidding. Inside we sat in a parlor car with pleasant seats and a man offered us tea and milk.

Outside Paris grew until, fields gone, we were engulfed by it. A sea of black smoke rising like seaweed merging with the gray sky. Our train cut between endless gray tenements and rude dirt streets flashing suddenly though the brown stone of the outer city wall tunnel into the paved streets and better homes inside, pulling in to North Station. The trip had taken thirty minutes. A porter appeared with our baggage on a pull truck to escort us to the street and one of the waiting carriages.

Review
ME!

If you liked the story,
and want to help the
author, then please
rate it, or even better
- review it - on
Amazon.com

THE
ROSE OF THE WEST

PURE AMERICAN STEAMPUNK
ON SALE NOW AT AMAZON.COM

MAX AND Mrs Stroud on AMAZON.COM

From Mark Bondurant and Bongo Books

Dig It!

www.ingramcontent.com/pod-product-compliance
Lightning Source LLC
Chambersburg PA
CBHW070554260626
47161CB00002B/600